FIRE AND ICE

Margaret couldn't remember ever being more excited or nervous, not even on a first teenage prom date. She set the bowl of fresh vegetables on the table and turned to the stove. Perhaps she was more distracted than she realized, for she grabbed the hot lid with her bare fingers. She jerked her hand away and shook her fingers as pain stabbed through her skin.

In one step, Jonathan was beside her. He took her hand in his and turned it over, examining the smooth red area on the tips of her fingers. Then, pulling her with him, he stepped to the refrigerator and opened the freezer compartment. He took an ice cube and rubbed it on the ends of her fingers, then tossed the ice cube into the sink and slowly, very slowly, pulled her hand toward his lips. She held her breath as his mouth touched the tip of her finger and kissed it. When his lips moved around her finger, sucking it gently, her eyes closed and she felt herself begin to tremble.

She wasn't sure how it happened, but she was in his arms. She felt his quiet groan as he released her burned hand and freed his arms to gather her closer to him.

She loved the way he held her. So tightly, as if she were a precious something he couldn't let go. Nothing had ever, ever felt so good as the feel of his body against hers.

"Maggie . . ." His eyes warned her as she hugged him more tightly and lifted her face for him to kiss. But his warning went unheeded, and their mouths melded together . . .

TOMORROW'S PROMISE

CLARA WIMBERLY

ZEBRA BOOKS
KENSINGTON PUBLISHING CORP.

ZEBRA BOOKS

are published by

Kensington Publishing Corp.
475 Park Avenue South
New York, NY 10016

First printing: August, 1992

Printed in the United States of America

Part One

Yesterday

In our happiness we should form very sweet bonds, full of confidence and attachment, in order that the sundering of them may cause us that priceless rending of the heart which is called unhappiness.

— *Proust*

One

Margaret Avery was just going out the door when the phone rang. It was Sunday afternoon, her bridge day at the club and she hesitated, not wanting to be late. She ran her fingers nervously through her already tousled dark hair and turned back to pick up the phone.

Her first thought on hearing the deep, masculine voice was that it was pleasant, even sexy. And she did not recognize the soft drawl as belonging to any of her husband's friends. But almost immediately those thoughts vanished as a certain tone made her heart stand still.

"Yes, this is Margaret Avery." She knew her voice had become shaky but she couldn't help it. Something was wrong; she knew it.

Her first concern was for her three girls. Where were they? Within seconds her mind was running back to her last conversation with her daughters Claire and Cyndi. They had been at Cyndi's apartment and planned on having dinner there with Cyndi's husband Steven.

Gincy . . . her youngest daughter. Had something happened to her? They hadn't heard from her in months.

Quick spurts of adrenaline seemed to rush through Margaret's body, causing her legs to tremble and her heart to accelerate rapidly.

"My name is Jonathan Bradford. I'm your father's neighbor in Ocala."

"Dad? What's wrong?"

Margaret sank slowly onto the white brocade sofa. She had to be mistaken, there was nothing wrong. She had spoken to her father this morning as she did every Sunday. He had been on his way to church.

"I'm afraid I have some bad news about your father, Mrs. Avery."

"Is he ill? I know he's been feeling tired lately, but I spoke to him earlier today and he . . ." Her voice grew weaker and she realized she was rambling on and making no sense at all. "Oh please," she whispered. "What's wrong?"

"Mrs. Avery, is there someone there with you? I'm so sorry to have to give you such news on the phone. I came over to visit your dad as I usually do on Sunday afternoons and I . . . I found him."

"He's not . . . he's not . . ."

"I'm sorry. Is there anything I can do? Anyone else you'd like for me to call?"

The word seemed to hang in midair. *Dead.* She could make no sense of it for she simply could not believe what this man was telling her. "No . . . no, I'm his only child. Where is he? Are you still at his house? Perhaps you're mistaken . . ." Why couldn't she stop, and why wouldn't her mind seem to work properly?

His voice continued, slowly and calmly as if he were trying very hard to be patient. "I'm at the hospital in Ocala and the doctor just came out and told me. He thinks it was a massive heart attack, a very sudden one. Your father probably did not suffer."

The words finally hit home. He was dead; her dear, sweet father was gone, so suddenly and without warning.

Maggie was not sure later what she said to Jonathan Bradford. She had managed to pull herself together long enough to make a few arrangements and to get his phone number. There were no relatives in Ocala. Her father was the last of the family, then herself.

That thought alone was unbelievable and it made her realize more than ever her own mortality. At the age of fifty-two she was no longer a young woman. And yet when she thought of her dad and his dying, she felt like a very young child.

9

She managed somehow to call the girls and tell them the news.

"We'll be right over Mom," Claire said, her voice sounding breathless. "Where's Dad? Does he know yet?"

"No . . . I . . . I suppose he's still on the greens. His golf . . ."

"Oh yes, his *precious* golf."

Margaret winced at the disapproval in Claire's voice. Her oldest daughter often urged her to put her foot down with Charles, to insist that he spend more time at home with her.

Margaret hung up the phone as visions of her father raced through her mind. She tried to remember every word he'd said that morning.

He'd talked about the early days and what a good life he'd had. And he spoke as he often had lately about how much he loved her mother and how he missed her. And when they said goodbye, she remembered how sweet he had been.

"I love you Maggie," he said. "Give the girls a kiss for me."

Had he known or feared what was about to happen? Guilt ate at her, making her remember all the times she meant to call and didn't, all the things they planned to do together but never got around to doing.

"Oh Daddy." She wept then, long and hard, the way she had when she was a little girl. And somewhere in the back of her mind she knew she wanted to get the grief out and over with before her daughters arrived.

She didn't know why, but Margaret always felt she had to be strong for her daughters. In her mind that included being calm and unemotional during the hard times.

She finally found Charles at the club. When he answered the phone, he sounded annoyed.

"Yes, Margaret, what is it?"

She took a deep breath, trying not to cry. Charles was an impatient man, she knew that. Besides, there was no way he could know what she was about to tell him.

"Charles, I just received a phone call from a man in Ocala. He says he's Daddy's neighbor." She began to cry.

"What is it darling? Is he sick?"

"He's dead, Charles. Daddy is dead."

"Oh baby, I'm sorry. Jesus, I should be there with you right now. Look honey, you just hang on. I'll be right there." But his words sounded uncertain, as if it would be almost impossible to do.

"It's all right Charles; there's no need to hurry. If you have something there that . . ."

"Well, actually, I was just having a drink with Randolph Simmons . . . but that's not important now. I'll come home right away. I know you need someone there with you. Where are Claire and Cyndi?"

"They're on their way here."

"Good . . . that's good. Well, look sweetheart, this Simmons account is very important, a big one, you know? But I promise I'll finish up here just as soon as possible."

Margaret's lips tightened and she could feel her insides becoming hard and rigid as she bit back the words she wanted to fling at him. It was always the same. Charles said one thing, usually the expected word or phrase, but he always ended up doing whatever suited him.

"Margaret? Hon, you're not upset, are you? Because if it's going to upset you, I'll be home right away. It's just . . . I thought since the girls are on their way. They should be there any minute now . . ."

"It's all right, Charles," she said again with a deep sigh. "I'm fine; just come home as soon as you can."

She hung up the phone, not bothering to wait for his reply. If she knew him, he was already breathing a sigh of relief and heading back to the bar and Randolph Simmons.

Later that night Charles was still not home. Margaret and her daughter Cyndi decided to go on to the airport to catch their flight to Florida. And Margaret called Jonathan Bradford who graciously insisted on meeting them in Ocala.

Claire had already agreed to stay home and look after the house and her father. But her

12

offer had made Margaret wince.

When Charles had called from the club to say he would not be home soon, she could see Claire's disapproval and anger. Margaret worried that she intended to give her father a good lecture. Usually Margaret would be the mediator, the one to step between them and try to smooth things over. But not this time; she simply didn't have the strength or the heart for it today.

Margaret and Cyndi hurried onto the plane, and quickly found their seats.

"I wish your father could have made it home before we left; I wish he could have come with us."

Cyndi sank back against the upholstery and pulled her seat belt snug around her slim hips. She turned to her mother, and her dark eyes held a quiet warning.

"Don't start, Mother. You know how busy Daddy is with the new clients. Besides, he said he'd fly down for the funeral, didn't he?"

"I know, and I'm not being critical. It's just that this is going to be so hard." Her voice caught as it seemed to do every time she thought of her father and of having to tell him good-bye.

Cyndi's pretty face changed and her eyes softened. They glittered now with tears of sympathy.

"I know, Mom, but it's going to be all right. I'm here. And you know Granddad is happy now; he's with Grandmother."

Margaret's lips trembled. It seemed so odd, being soothed and comforted by one's own child.

"I know that. I guess I'm only being selfish. I wasn't ready to let him go."

Cyndi reached for her mother's hand and held it tightly as the plane taxied out onto the runway. Its jets roared and the huge plane shook as it gathered speed and lifted into the night sky.

The airport in Florida was small and practically empty at this hour of night. Margaret and Cyndi exited the plane ramp and stood looking about.

Margaret recognized Jonathan Bradford immediately, although she had never seen him. She thought his deep masculine voice matched his physical appearance perfectly.

He had said he was tall and had gray hair, but she thought she would describe it as silver as she watched him walking toward them.

She guessed he was near her own age, but his long jean-encased thighs and youthful stride made him appear younger. His look was kind and sympathetic as his intense blue eyes gazed down at Margaret with real sincerity. And she wondered, one of those crazy thoughts that come so inappropriately at times, if he was married and what his wife was like? Was he kind and gentle to her, too?

She shook her head, wondering how she could allow herself to have such thoughts under the circumstances.

Margaret watched as Jonathan Bradford placed their luggage in the back of a dark green Bronco, then helped Cyndi into the back seat and Margaret up front beside him.

Cyndi had said very little since their arrival in Florida and Margaret guessed that the plane ride had made her nervous. Cyndi hated to fly. And although she hadn't said as much, Margaret knew she hated to leave Steven. They'd been married less than a year and this was the first time they'd been apart.

Margaret turned her head and looked into the backseat. Cyndi's eyes were closed and her head was leaning back against the seat.

The night seemed very dark and quiet as they made their way from the airport and onto the long straight roads into the country.

"Will your husband be joining you later?"

Margaret thought Mr. Bradford's question was more an attempt at polite conversation than anything. "He hopes to make it to the funeral. But he's a lawyer and right now he's working on several important cases."

He flashed her a quick look, his eyes dark and questioning in the glow of the dashlights. But he said nothing.

The look made her wonder about him. There

was something familiar, something about him she could not quite place.

"Mr. Bradford, I want to thank you for helping my father . . ." Her voice cracked. She had deliberately waited until she was more composed to thank him and still she couldn't seem to control her emotions.

"Call me Jonathan," he said, gazing over at her. "And I was happy to do what I could; I only wish it could have been more."

"You said on the phone that you visited him sometimes on Sunday afternoons."

"Yeah, we usually played checkers or dominoes. Sometimes we just talked. He liked to talk about old times and about his days in the army."

"Oh yes," she said, smiling into the darkness. "Mother always complained about those stories. They got a bit raw sometimes as I recall." She laughed. "Oh, I'd forgotten all about that."

They drove through the night, past dense stands of palmetto and pine trees, past ponds where croaking frogs made loud choruses across the swampy ground. And when finally they turned into the driveway of her father's house, Margaret was surprised to see the lights on.

"I left the lights on," he said, seeing her look of surprise. "I didn't want it to be dark when you got here."

He seemed to think of everything; how unusual to find a man so solicitous of someone else's comfort. She watched him as he opened the car door and stepped out.

A part of her dreaded entering the house, as if she might somehow see evidence of her father's death. But everything was in place; there were no reminders of what had happened only a few hours ago. And looking at Jonathan Bradford, she thought she probably had him to thank for that as well.

Inside the house as they stood in the small living room, Margaret thought that Jonathan seemed to occupy the entire space. She had forgotten how tiny the house was, and how small her father was compared to this athletic-looking man.

"Are you sure you two will be all right here alone? I'd be more than happy to drive you to a motel if you'd prefer."

"No. I want to be here. I just need to be here for awhile. But thank you very much Mr. Brad . . . Jonathan, for all that you've done."

"Yes," Cyndi echoed as she moved to put an arm about her mother's waist. "We appreciate your help."

He said good night and reminded her that he lived just down the road. "You still have my phone number?"

"Yes . . . yes I'm sure I have it somewhere." She felt distracted and tired.

He turned to go, then stopped at the door and

turned back toward her. She had sensed earlier that there was something more he wanted to say.

Slowly he walked back to her. "I don't mean to intrude, but I know how hard tomorrow is going to be, when you make the arrangements. If you'd like, I can go with you."

She had thought of that often on the plane; the moment when she would choose the coffin and later when she would have to actually see her father lying in it. And she was surprised that Jonathan seemed to know exactly how she felt. Tears sprang again to her eyes.

"Yes," she whispered. "If it's not too much trouble for you, I think I would like that very much." She was surprised at her feeling of relief knowing he would be with her.

After he had gone, Margaret and Cyndi stood for a few moments as if uncertain what to do.

"It seems so strange being here alone, without Granddad."

"You know that's exactly what he said when Mother died," Margaret turned and looked about the room. "And now I wonder if he ever really got over losing her."

Cyndi patted her mother's arm. "I think I'll make some coffee. Will you be all right, Mom?"

"I'm fine, honey, really I am. I just wish your dad was here and Claire."

"And Gincy?" Cyndi's brown eyes focused on her with a glint of accusation.

"Yes, of course . . . Gincy, too. You know I tried to call her but . . ." Her voice trailed away. She didn't want to think about Gincy now, or about all the things that worried her about her youngest daughter.

"We'll be fine," Cyndi said. "We're lucky, I guess, to have met that nice Mr. Bradford. He seems like a real 'take charge' kind of man, without being overbearing in the process. Just the kind of man you always liked, Mom."

Margaret knew Cyndi's last sentence was meant to cheer her. She recognized the teasing quality in her voice as she went through the wide doorway toward the kitchen.

But somehow the words made Margaret think of Charles and she felt anything but comforted.

"Yes," Margaret sighed, pushing her hair back from her eyes. "Just the kind of man I always liked."

Two

Later that night, long after Cyndi had gone to bed, Margaret moved quietly about the small house. She didn't know yet what she would do with the place. Perhaps fix it up a bit, keep it for a winter home.

Of course she preferred it the way it was, rustic and cozy, just as it had been when she was a girl. But Charles . . . Margaret stopped and frowned at the turn of her thoughts.

There always seemed to be Charles's disapproval floating in her mind, waiting and intruding when she began to make plans. He'd never liked the house, or Ocala, or any part of Florida for that matter. Sometimes she wondered if there was anything about her or her early life that he had liked.

During the thirty-three years of their marriage, she had tried to mold herself into something that would please him. But nothing ever seemed to work, at least not for long.

Margaret smiled, recalling her daughter Claire's words. "Don't worry about Daddy, or what he wants. Just be yourself Mother! Do whatever pleases you."

"Ah, the younger generation," she mumbled with a wistful smile. "If only it were as easy as that."

How simple it was for young women now to say such things and to demand what they wanted from their husbands. But Margaret and Charles had married in a different time; the entire world had been different back then.

Finally, knowing she'd never be able to sleep, Margaret propped up on the end of the worn sofa. She read until her mind grew dull and her eyes gritty with weariness.

She woke early before the sun was up. The thoughts that she'd tried to banish were immediately back. She groaned as she sat up and reached back to rub the stiffness from her neck.

She was glad it was early so she'd have time to shower and dress before Jonathan Bradford showed up at the door. She had the feeling he was terribly self-sufficient. He probably never went to sleep on a sofa or woke up looking tired and rumpled.

She and Cyndi were having coffee when he knocked at the door. Margaret went to let him in and looked up at him for a moment in the morning light. In the shadows of the front porch, his eyes looked darker. His hair still looked slightly damp and he looked fresh, with a just shaved smoothness about his face and the tantalizing aroma of some spicy aftershave that drifted around him.

He seemed very tall and rugged, potently masculine with the light of the sun behind him. Perhaps it was the casual way he dressed; after all she rarely saw Charles in anything except an expensive custom-made suit and handpicked tie. She liked the look of Jonathan's soft faded jeans and the blue striped oxford shirt that emphasized the color of his eyes.

Margaret had to shake herself mentally. She had been staring at him like a fool. And she had to hold her hands practically behind her back to keep from brushing her hair back in that oldest of feminine gestures, that primitive ritual of preening before a handsome male.

God, what on earth was wrong with her? Her father's death had left her muddleheaded and confused.

She stepped back, letting him walk past and giving her a chance to breathe in a huge gulp of the fresh, fragrant morning air.

As she glanced again at Jonathan's easy, casual look, her black silk pants and expensive plaid blazer seemed suddenly out of place and overdone. She wished now she had worn something more relaxed and feminine.

Quickly she chastened herself, reminding herself of the seriousness of the occasion. How selfish, how immature she was to be thinking of such trivial things now.

Margaret glanced at Cyndi and saw her watching her mother with an odd look. Margaret frowned, feeling the flush on her cheeks and the way her hands fluttered nervously as she poured Jonathan a cup of coffee.

And when another knock sounded at the door, Margaret practically jumped a step backward.

She went to the door, then smiled broadly when she greeted her visitor. She stepped forward to embrace the woman, reaching across a dish she held in her hands.

"Lettie! Oh, it's so good to see you. Come in, have some breakfast."

"Margaret, honey, I was so sorry to hear about your dad. But I can't stay; I have to get to work. I just wanted to drop off this casserole before I go. All you have to do is pop it in the oven and bake it about thirty-five minutes. I would have baked it myself and let you reheat it, but I was sure your dad wouldn't have a microwave in his house."

Margaret smiled down at the shorter woman as she took the dish from her hands. She and

Lettie had gone to school together, and had terrorized the countryside, as her father often teased. Lettie's shining red hair styled in the latest cropped fashion, and her long, long red nails attested to her occupation. She owned her own beauty salon, or at least she had the last time Margaret heard.

Margaret stood aside and motioned toward the wide doorway that looked directly into the kitchen. "Please can't you stay for a cup of coffee at least?"

Lettie looked around Margaret into the house. Her eyes widened as she saw the man sitting at the kitchen table.

"Why, Jonathan, I thought that was your Bronco outside. How you doing?" Lettie walked into the house with a certain provocative swagger that had always been part of her outrageous style.

Margaret put the casserole in the refrigerator and turned with a curious look toward Lettie. How well did she know Jonathan Bradford?

"You and Margaret renewing old acquaintances?" Lettie asked.

Jonathan chuckled but didn't reply, then took another sip of coffee. Margaret stared at him, feeling oddly confused. Old acquaintances? Was she supposed to know him? That would explain why she'd thought there was something familiar about him. But she didn't remember anyone like him from school, and she would have remembered.

"I . . . I don't know what you mean." Margaret stopped and stared at him. "I'm sorry. Do we know each other? Did we go to school together . . . or . . ." Her hands went to her cheeks as she felt the flush of embarrassment warming her skin. How could she possibly forget such a man?

"I could hardly expect you to remember me." His voice was deep and smooth, his blue eyes so steady and clear. "I was only here one summer when I was fourteen. You, on the other hand, were a very mature and beautiful fifteen year old who hardly had the time of day for a long-legged, skinny kid like me."

Margaret frowned and shook her head. She was acutely aware of Cyndi's wide-eyed look and of Lettie's obvious enjoyment at her friend's discomfort.

"Lettie . . ." She looked to her for identification, for she simply did not recall Jonathan Bradford at all.

"Don't look at me," Lettie said with a shrug and a twinkle in her dark eyes. "But I'll give you a hint. You used to call him 'Johnny be square.' "

Margaret's mouth flew open and she turned to look at him again. His lashes lifted, revealing those incredible blue eyes that held just the hint of a smile.

"Oh my . . . Jonathan Bradford . . . but you were . . ." Her eyes moved, taking in every inch of his lean muscular frame.

"Skinny."

"And your eyes were . . . you wore . . ."

"Glasses."

"You had come to spend the summer with your grandfather. Why, he owned the farm just next door." Margaret's gray eyes were wide with wonder as she remembered that summer. "You were such a serious boy and so very . . ."

"Square."

Margaret's hand went to her forehead and she frowned, feeling awkward and embarrassed.

Jonathan seemed to be enjoying himself tremendously. His eyes never left her face and Margaret could see he wasn't about to let her forget anything about that summer, or about any cruelty she had inflicted on him.

At that moment she wished she could disappear.

Cyndi began to giggle. "Oh Mom, if you could only see your face!"

Soon Lettie joined in, until they were all laughing and the little house rang with the sound.

"I'm sorry," he said, even though amusement still sparkled in his eyes. "We shouldn't tease you."

"No," Margaret mumbled. "You should. I'm

26

very embarrassed."

Lettie hugged her and turned to go. "You should be," she said in her feisty way. "Jonathan's been back for a couple of years and I, thank God, have already made my peace with him. Now it's your turn." With a soft giggle, the red-haired woman went toward the door, waving blithely back toward the kitchen. "I'll call you later, sweetie."

"All right, Lettie. Thanks . . . thanks for the casserole." But Margaret's mind was still in a muddle as all the silly, pretentious, little things she had done as a fifteen year old began to revolve in her mind.

She turned back to find Jonathan standing at the sink, his blue eyes steady and watchful.

"Don't worry about it," he said.

"Oh," she said with a shake of her head. "I just feel very stupid."

"Don't be silly," he said. "We'll talk about it later. I hadn't meant to bring up that summer in exactly this way." His eyes were kind, and he was looking at her as if he could not understand her embarrassment.

Cyndi was watching the two of them with unabashed curiosity. She even went into the bedroom with her mother to retrieve her purse. She stood very close when she spoke.

"What's this all about, Mother?"

"Oh, Cyndi . . . nothing. Just silly childhood

things." She gathered her things and turned to her daughter, shaking her finger toward Cyndi, without really looking into her eyes. "Just let this be a lesson to you, dear. Always be nice to people; you never know when they might come back to haunt you."

"Well, I must admit I'm very curious to find out exactly what kind of silly childhood things you mean." She wiggled her eyebrows in a theatrical way.

"Oh . . . hush." Margaret pulled Cyndi with her back toward the main part of the house.

The morning talk and laughter had distracted Margaret, for a few moments at least, and she was grateful. Knowing Lettie, she had probably planned it exactly that way.

But now that they were on their way into town, she remembered with a sharp pain what the real purpose was. She felt a twinge of guilt that they'd all been laughing and having such a good time. But then, she smiled wistfully to herself, knowing exactly what her dad would say to that. "Don't grieve for me." She'd heard him say it often. "I've had a good life, and I don't want anybody mopin' around when I'm gone."

Margaret didn't know how she would have gotten through the day without Jonathan Bradford. Thankfully there was no problem with expenses and she could afford to buy her father the very best.

But as she stood with her hand on the shining cherry wood coffin that cost in excess of ten thousand dollars, she turned and saw the look of skepticism on Jonathan's face.

"Is this too much?" she whispered. "I feel as if I should get the best for him." She tried to keep her lips from trembling.

"It's beautiful," he said with a nod, his eyes moving over the smooth shining surface. "But your father was a simple man, Margaret."

She knew he was right, that this was not what her dad would want. But again, she was being selfish; she was soothing her own pain and her own conscience.

"You're right," she said. "But I do think the wood is beautiful. Perhaps a less expensive one . . ."

He nodded and smiled. "I think so, too."

Cyndi had not wanted to go in and she was waiting outside for them when they finished.

"Cyndi, are you all right? You look a little pale. Are you sick?"

"No, Mother." But her answer seemed too quick and too pert.

Margaret gazed at her daughter from time to time, studying her delicate face and the curve of her slender throat. She had mentioned feeling tired lately. Margaret made a mental note to make sure Cyndi went to the doctor for a checkup when they got back to Atlanta. Perhaps it was just the strain of being away from Steven and the death of her grandfather. Cyndi was such a sentimental, tenderhearted girl.

"Are we ready to go?"

"Yes," Margaret said, feeling the warmth of Jonathan's hand beneath her elbow as they left the building and walked toward the parking lot.

"Mornin' Mr. Bradford," someone called as they moved toward his Bronco.

"Morning," came his deep reply.

Margaret had noticed in the funeral home just how solicitous everyone was to him. He was obviously well-known in town and she wondered exactly what he did for a living.

"It's lucky for me you were able to get away from your work."

He opened the car door, first for Cyndi, then for her. "I'm my own boss, sort of."

He was a mystery and he seemed to want to keep it that way.

"So, you work on the farm . . . your grandfather's?"

"I have some cattle and a few horses for pleasure riding." Smoothly he backed out of the parking space and turned the vehicle toward the main street.

"So, you're a farmer."

He shrugged and wrinkled his brow. "Hmmm,

I enjoy farming, yeah. Is there anywhere else you need to go? Grocery store, maybe?"

"We do need a few things, Mom," Cyndi said from the backseat.

"Well, then I suppose if it's not too much trouble, we do need to stop at a grocery store."

"Not at all. I suppose I could stock up while we're there myself."

Stock up? Sounded like a bachelor's term. Was he married? Somehow after the morning's embarrassing fiasco, she didn't have the nerve to ask any more personal questions.

They were all quiet on the drive home from the store. Margaret seemed unable to lose the image of her father's face, of his sweet, easy smile. She wanted nothing more than to hold on for a few more minutes, a few more miles, until she could get home to the privacy of the small bedroom.

Jonathan seemed to sense what was on her mind, even without her saying anything. He insisted on carrying the groceries in. "I'll pick you up tonight if you wish and—"

"No," she said. Then she hesitated, feeling that she needed to give him some sort of excuse. "That won't be necessary; I'll call Lettie. It will give us a chance to talk. But thank you for everything you've done."

Sensing her distress, Jonathan said goodbye politely and walked away.

31

After he left, Margaret turned to find Cyndi's dark eyes on her.

"What? What's wrong?" Margaret questioned her daughter.

"Nothing." But she thought Cyndi's answer came too quickly.

"He's a very nice man isn't he? Handsome, too." Cyndi began taking groceries out of the brown paper bags without looking at her mother.

"Yes, he is." Margaret turned and placed her jacket across a chair. "I wonder if your father called. I hope he won't forget his flight; you know how distracted he can be sometimes. Perhaps I should call and remind him."

"He'll be here, Mom," Cyndi said with a quiet smile.

"Yes . . . yes, I'm sure he will. But I am going to call Claire and see if she ever got in touch with Ginger."

Margaret was surprised when Claire answered the phone on the first ring. "Well, that was quick. You must be sitting on the phone."

"Actually I am. I just finished talking to Gincy and—"

"Oh, you did?" Margaret couldn't help the sigh of relief that escaped her lips. "Is she all right? Is Catherine Jane all right? Where are they for heaven's sake?"

"They're fine Mother and they're still in Las

32

Vegas. Evidently her phone had been disconnected, but I finally tracked her down where she works."

"At one of the casinos." Margaret tried not to let the disapproval in her voice show.

"She has a daughter to support Mom, and evidently being a cocktail waitress pays very well."

"Then why was her phone disconnected?"

There was a pause, then a sigh at the other end of the line. Margaret knew she could usually depend on Claire for support, no matter what, except on this one subject. Ginger was a subject Margaret couldn't seem to agree with anyone about.

"I didn't ask; I didn't want to embarrass her. But in case you're interested, she was very upset about Granddad. She was crying."

"I'm sure she is upset, Claire. You make it sound as if I don't believe anything Ginger says."

"Mother, let's not get into this, not today."

"You're right," Margaret said.

"Are you doing okay? Have you made the arrangements yet?"

"Yes, we did that this morning. The funeral is scheduled for tomorrow at ten o'clock."

"I wish I could be there with you, Mom."

"I wish you could, too, sweetheart. But it's all right. We all decided it would be best if you stayed home with your dad. Where is he by the way?"

There was a long pause on Claire's end.

"Well, I'm not really sure. He's been busy and—"

"Has he been home at all?"

"Yes, of course, he's been here."

"There's something you're not telling me, Claire."

"I'm telling you everything I know. I don't feel that I should pass on anything I'd just be guessing at."

"All right. But he is coming down for the funeral, isn't he?"

"I don't know that either."

Neither of them spoke for a long moment.

"Mother, why do you do this to yourself? You know Dad better than any of us and yet you act surprised each time he does something like this. You know you can't depend on him; he's going to do exactly what pleases him and to hell with anyone else."

"Please Claire," Margaret sighed. "Don't start analyzing me again. I don't know what on earth you expect me to do . . . leave him? Is that what you want? Should I throw away all our years of marriage and divorce him?"

"Frankly, I think we'd all have been better off if you had done that years ago. And now you'd have a life of your own instead of—"

"Instead of what? Instead of hanging onto your father's coattails as you so often remind me? You're not married, Claire, and you have no idea what you're talking about. Marriage is about compromise and . . ." Her voice cracked with emotion. She felt so tired.

"Mom, I'm sorry. I don't want to argue with you about him, not now. I just get so mad when he treats you this way. Really, I'm sorry."

Margaret sighed.

"I'm sorry too, sweetheart. Listen, I have to go now. Just tell your father to let me know if he's coming. Tell him he'll have to rent a car at the airport. Do you want to speak to your sister?"

"Yeah, let me talk to the squirt. I guess I should make sure she's taking care of you well enough."

Margaret smiled and handed the phone to Cyndi who was watching with an expectant grin.

Soon the two girls were laughing and chattering as Margaret finished unloading the groceries. And all the while she tried not to think of the niggling doubts that had crept into her mind.

Charles was not coming; she'd sensed it all along. How could he let her face one of the most dreadful times of her life alone? But looking back it seemed that every major event in her life could be marked by her husband's absence and by his complete lack of interest in her needs.

Three

Visitation at the funeral home that evening seemed to pass in a quiet, jumbled blur for Margaret. It was a long, torturous evening and she wondered several times why grieving families put themselves through such an ordeal.

She saw Jonathan come in, saw his tall form and the play of the dim lights on his silvery hair. She hoped he would not stay and she had no idea why she would wish such an uncharitable thing for a man who had been so kind to her.

But he didn't leave; he stayed all evening. Several times she caught the steady gaze of his blue eyes on her. There was sympathy in those looks and questions.

She knew she was avoiding him and she told herself it was only because of her discovery about who he was. But something about him disturbed her and made her feel as if she had done something wrong. And Cyndi's speculative looks whenever he was near did nothing to dispel that feeling.

She had to face him sooner or later, if only to discuss the past and to apologize for treating him so shabbily. But not now — she just couldn't face him now.

Margaret had never been so tired in her life. But when Lettie urged her to go home, she refused. How could she bear leaving her father here in this cold, impersonal place? The mere thought of it made her tremble, made tears spring hotly to her eyes.

It was well past visiting hours and there was no one left. Lettie and Cyndi sat on one of the brocade couches, watching Margaret sadly as she stood gazing down at the still form in the casket.

Margaret didn't see Jonathan enter the room behind her, nor was she aware of Lettie standing and speaking to him. She only knew he was there when she felt his touch on her arm and heard his deep voice beside her.

"Maggie?" Funny how his tender use of that childhood name affected her.

She turned to stare at him and her lips moved ineffectually as tears overflowed and ran down her cheeks.

37

Her movements were entirely instinctive, born of a need that she didn't stop to wonder about. And she couldn't be sure which of them reached out first. She only knew that she was in his arms. And that the feel of him, of his hands at her waist and her head upon his chest, felt right and gave her solace. She felt comforted for the first time since her father's death.

The embrace lasted only a few moments before Margaret pulled away. What must he think of her?

When she looked up into his face, she saw only kindness and infinite compassion.

"Let me take you and Cyndi home," he murmured.

"No, Lettie will take us. But thank you, Jonathan. Thank you for being here. It means so much to me."

He stood very still for a moment, looking down at her.

"All right then. I'll see you tomorrow."

"Yes . . . tomorrow."

Margaret watched him leave the room. He looked different in a suit and tie, yet his long-legged grace was still the same. He was the kind of man who seemed to adapt to any occasion and to any life-style.

She walked to Lettie and Cyndi and they positioned her between them with their arms supporting her. It was a sweet, protective gesture, and it threatened to make her cry again. There was no accusation in her daughter's brown eyes concerning her behavior with Jonathan, only love and understanding.

Oddly, what Margaret felt toward Jonathan now was resentment. Jonathan Bradford shouldn't be here offering her such sweet comfort, making her aware of the strength of his arms and the leanness of his body. Her traitorous emotions seemed horribly inappropriate, and made her shake her head wearily at her inability to understand her own reactions and feelings.

She didn't know how she made it through the funeral. Or through the hours of polite conversation with her father's neighbors and her own childhood acquaintances. She was not even aware, after a while, of waiting for Charles. She had stopped watching the doorway hours before. And she wasn't sure where the pain of saying goodbye to her father ended and the pain of Charles's indifference began.

She supposed that the old rural custom of coming to the bereaved's home afterward was a blessing. It gave her little time to reflect on what was happening. There was only time for polite, endless chatter and offers of food and comfort. And it was true; it did stave off the grief, for a little while at least.

Later, after everyone had gone, Cyndi insisted on cleaning up the kitchen alone.

"Mom, go rest. Go out and sit on the porch where it's quiet."

Margaret didn't argue but kicked off her shoes and took a glass of iced tea out to the front porch. She brushed at the seat of the old porch swing and sat down, pushing her bare feet lightly against the floor until the swing began to move.

At home in Atlanta, the autumn leaves were changing, but here it was still very warm. Besides there were so many pines surrounding the house that fall would be hard to recognize here. The sun was just setting over the top of the trees into a horizon that seemed far, far away.

The sky was almost dark when Margaret saw Jonathan's Bronco slow down on the highway and turn into the driveway. Her heart began to beat faster and she considered for a moment running into the house and asking Cyndi to tell him she was already in bed. But she knew he'd seen her sitting in the swing; the lights from the truck dipped and scattered across her. Besides he had been very kind to her; she owed him the courtesy of saying goodbye at least.

She watched as he emerged from the truck and turned toward the porch. She felt the tension in her legs and realized she was sitting forward in the swing, like some small, senseless animal, prepared to run. She forced herself to relax as he stepped up onto the porch and stood quietly, leaning his shoulders against one of the porch supports.

"How are you?"

"I'm fine," she said with a quick nod. "I'll be all right." She paused then, feeling awkward and wondering why he had come. "Would you like a glass of iced tea?"

"No, nothing thanks. May I sit down?"

"Of course." She moved to one end of the long swing and felt the weight of his body pulling at the heavy chain support as he sat at the other end.

"Lettie tells me you're leaving tomorrow."

"Yes, tomorrow night actually. We're going to pack up a few things, pictures mostly, then we'll take a late flight back to Atlanta."

"Is there anything I can do? Do you need me to look after the house or—"

"No . . . I . . . I can't even think about the house yet. I suppose sooner or later I'll have to sell it, but right now I just can't bear it. In a month or two, perhaps after Christmas, I can decide what's best."

She took a sip of tea, forcing her eyes away from his steady blue gaze.

They sat for a long while staring out at the darkening sky.

"I had forgotten how beautiful it is here," she said. "And how peaceful."

"Yes, it is. I suppose that's why I came back after all those years. I was never quite able to put this place out of my mind. No matter where I was or what I was doing, this old farm was always kind of like a haven for me, waiting quietly in the background until I was ready to see and appreciate its unique beauty." He turned to smile crookedly at her in the dim light. "It took awhile, but I finally do appreciate it."

"You have a lovely way of putting things," she said. "Poetic almost."

"Why, thank you Maggie. That's probably the nicest thing you could say to me."

She ducked her head and looked away.

"Jonathan I'm really sorry about that summer. I mean, I know I was probably a senseless brat but—"

"Hey, you don't have to apologize for that," he said with a laugh. "That was a long time ago. We were kids. Besides, one doesn't die from a broken heart."

She turned to stare at him, wondering if he

was teasing her again.

He laughed, the sound soft and warm in the darkness. "Don't tell me you didn't guess? I had a terrible crush on you that summer as I recall. Haven't you heard that young boys always fall in love with older women?"

She laughed then; she couldn't help it. The idea of herself as an older woman at fifteen was ludicrous. She had been as innocent as he was, and probably just as afraid.

"It's a shame children don't know how to really talk to each other, isn't it?" She gazed out across the yard and into the sky. "We do things and say things when we're young and sometimes they haunt us for the rest of our lives. All because we don't know how to communicate."

"I'm not so sure that's only a problem with the young."

She thought of Charles and even her relationship with her own daughters.

"You're right; it isn't." She turned to look at him. He, too, was lost in thought, perhaps some vague memory of yesterday. And she wondered what or who it was about.

He stood up to go and she stood, too, placing her tea on a small table beside the swing.

"Goodbye Maggie. And if there's anything I can do, anything that needs to be done here, all you have to do is call. I hope you know that."

They walked to the steps and she was leaning against one of the wooden posts.

"I do. And thank you Jonathan. I don't know what I would have done without you. I'm awfully glad that my dad had a friend like you in his life."

She blinked back the tears and thrust her hand forward in a gesture of friendship. She knew it was a mistake as soon as his warm fingers curled slowly over her own.

But by then it was too late.

He pulled her forward, bending his head quickly before she could move, before she even realized what was happening.

His lips touched hers only briefly, and she wondered if he meant the kiss as a comfort or a gesture of friendship.

It was anything but that.

The scent of his cologne and the wild, sweet taste of his mouth sent her head reeling with surprise and she stepped back, pulling her hand from his and staring up into his shadowed eyes.

"You take care of yourself, Maggie," he whispered in the darkness.

She stood staring at his shadowy figure as he retreated across the yard. He stopped at the door of his car and looked back at her for a moment before stepping inside. Only when the vehicle had backed from the drive and turned to go toward the west did her breathing begin to return to normal.

She turned and went back to the swing, watching as the red taillights of the car glimmered through the trees and then out of sight.

She doubted Jonathan could possibly know what that kiss had done to her, or how long it had been since she'd been kissed that way.

Hundreds of thoughts and questions whirled through her mind as she tried to sort through her feelings. She was still sitting quietly in the swing minutes later when Cyndi stepped onto the porch.

"Mom? Are you all right?"

"Yes, sweetie, I'm fine. Would you like to come out and sit for awhile?"

"No, I don't think so. I think I'll take a bath and call Steven. Then I'm going to bed. Did I hear someone drive up a little while ago?"

"Yes, it was Jonathan. He came to say good-bye and to ask if there was anything else he could do."

"He seems very nice. And I can tell he liked Granddad a lot."

"Yes, I'm glad your grandfather had someone like him . . ."

"Mom, Granddad was happy. We all loved him and he knew that. He had a wonderful life. He told you that a lot of times, didn't he?

He wouldn't want you feeling guilty about anything."

"I know that."

"Mom, if you feel you need to stay here a few days longer, I can go back to Atlanta by myself."

"No, Cyndi. There's no need for that. I can come back down to Ocala soon. I know how you hate to fly; the least I can do is give you moral support." Margaret smiled at her daughter who stood leaning against the doorframe.

"I dread it."

Margaret noticed the tightness around Cyndi's mouth.

"You're not feeling ill again, are you?"

"No. I'm just tired, that's all. Well, good night. I'm going to call Steven."

"I'll be in soon."

Margaret hated to admit it, but she felt relieved to be alone for awhile longer. She needed to think.

Jonathan's kiss had shaken her and she had to get her feelings back into perspective. She was vulnerable right now, that was all.

She frowned, thinking of Charles and wondering again why he had not come. Why hadn't he even bothered to call and give an excuse? But he would have an alibi; she could be sure of that.

She had never admitted to anyone how desperately unhappy her life had become the past few years. No one would believe it. Outwardly she looked like a woman who had it all.

She had a beautiful home in one of Atlanta's most fashionable areas. She could afford clothes from any designer. And yet there were many times when she would have given all of that for a quiet, romantic evening with her husband.

She thought she was still relatively attractive, her face smooth and unlined. Her body was rounder and fuller than when she and Charles had married, but she kept herself active with tennis and swimming. God knew she had little else to do, now that the girls were all gone.

Her friend and bridge partner, Dina, often chided her for her romantic nature. "How many fifty-year-old women still have a romantic relationship with their husband, for God's sake? You need to start living in the real world, Margaret. If it's just sex you want, there are plenty of muscular young studs right here at the club who would be more than willing to accommodate a woman like you. I can even recommend one or two myself," she'd added with a twinkle in her eye.

Margaret laughed softly in the darkness. She

had been so shocked by Dina's blunt confession.

But that kind of thing would never work for her. Oh, there had been times when she was angry with Charles, when she'd been stung by his coldness. She'd wished she could be like a man, and take sex just for the pleasure of it. She wished that the *when* and *where* and *who* did not matter.

But she couldn't be that way; it was simply not in her nature.

It was her daughters that were important now. They had become the most important thing in her life. She even thought sometimes that they alone kept her alive. They shared so much with her, had been so generous with their time and their lives. Margaret wondered if her girls had any idea how sad and lonely her life would have been without them.

Margaret thought again of what Dina had said. And she thought of the flirtations at the club among their friends. She'd indulged in a Saturday night fantasy or two. Nothing could compare to the attention of a man. It made a woman's heart beat faster, made her complexion glow with excitement and pleasure. But with Margaret, that was as far as it ever went.

Margaret had never made love to any other man except her husband.

She laughed again at herself.

"Margaret Avery," she whispered into the darkness of the soft Florida night. "You are sorely out of touch with the times."

Four

Margaret was very quiet and thoughtful on the plane trip home. Cyndi had taken a Dramamine before they left and was now sound asleep beside her mother.

Margaret had asked Lettie to drive them to the airport, then she'd tried to push away the unreasonable wish that Jonathan might come anyway. She had even foolishly glanced about the airport, hoping to see his tall form and the searching glance of those blue eyes.

Another flirtation, she thought dryly. She'd promised herself she would not indulge in another meaningless flirtation that left her empty and dissatisfied.

Her gray eyes darkened as she gazed unseeingly out the window, thinking of her husband. He had finally called. The phone had wakened her near midnight with its shrill, persistent ringing.

She had jumped out of bed and stumbled into the kitchen, her heart pounding and her eyes still blurry from sleep.

"Margaret? Sweetheart, were you asleep?"

"Yes, I was," she mumbled. She glanced at the clock on the stove. "It's late . . . is anything wrong?"

"Wrong?" His forced laughter was uneasy. "No, of course not. I just wanted to talk to you and tell you how sorry I am that I couldn't make it down to your dad's funeral. I hope you understand."

There had been a long silent pause while he waited for her response. What did he expect her to say? She didn't understand!

"Margaret, honey, please. We'll discuss it when you get home. You are coming home tomorrow, aren't you? There's a party at the club this weekend and I really need you to be there with me. I think I almost have this Simmons contract wrapped up, but this weekend should ice the deal. You always make such a good impression on the clients. The old gent is a family man and I know he's going to love you."

He had chattered on about Mr. Simmons

and the party as if nothing had happened. As if she were not standing in her father's kitchen, still shaken and hurt by her grief. He had not even asked how she was.

Charles had managed to throw in a comment or two about how busy he'd been and how completely impossible it was for him to get away right now. But she understood, didn't she?

Of course she understood. She always understood. It was her job as a dutiful wife to understand, wasn't it? And to wear the right clothes and make just exactly the correct flattering remark to one of Charles's clients.

The plane jolted Margaret back to reality as it forced its way through a section of turbulence. Margaret glanced at Cyndi, but she was still sleeping.

Margaret moved restlessly in the seat, leaning her head wearily back against the headrest. God, but she was sick of it. Sick to death of pretending that her life was perfect when she was so miserable.

As they approached the Atlanta airport Margaret reached across to make sure Cyndi's seat belt was still fastened.

The girl woke and frowned toward her mother. Then she closed her eyes and her hand reached shakily up toward her head.

"Oh no," she muttered. "I think I'm going to be sick. I have to get to the restroom." Her eyes darted around frantically.

"Do you need me to go with you?" Margaret looked at her daughter worriedly. She seemed very ill indeed and her face glistened with a light covering of perspiration.

"No." Cyndi bolted from her seat and past the stewardess.

"Miss," the woman cautioned. "We'll be landing soon; the seat belt sign will be coming on any minute now."

"I'm sick," Cyndi managed as she dashed out of sight toward the back of the plane.

The stewardess came to where Margaret sat turned in her seat, staring down the corridor.

"Is she all right?"

"I hope so," Margaret said, but she was fearful for her delicate daughter.

Cyndi came back just as they were being advised to fasten the seat belts. She had a damp paper towel clutched in her hand and she looked very ill.

"Darling, what on earth is wrong?" Margaret watched Cyndi fall weakly back into her seat. "You've not felt well since before we left. As soon as we get home I think you should make an appointment to see Dr. Bowman."

Cyndi's only response was to roll her head over and stare into her mother's eyes. Her look was baleful and humorous.

Seeing that look, Margaret gasped and clutched Cyndi's arm. "Oh sweetheart, you're not . . . are you pregnant?"

Cyndi frowned and the laughter that followed had a hollow sound.

"Oh dear God, I should have known that was what you'd think. No, I'm not pregnant." Cyndi lowered her voice a tone. "Just the opposite, as a matter of fact."

Margaret couldn't help the twinge of disappointment she felt. It would have been so wonderful and exciting. The vision of Catherine Jane when she was born ten years ago flashed through her mind. Margaret had been sick with disappointment that her youngest daughter was having a child at sixteen and without the benefit of marriage. But that baby . . . how sweet and perfect she had been.

"What do you mean just the opposite? How can you be just the opposite of pregnant?"

"Maybe opposite is not a good word to use. I mean, I'm on the pill, my darling Mother. The doctor said some women get sick the first few days they begin. And unfortunately I seem to be one of those women." Her lips twisted wryly and she turned to gaze out the window.

"The pill? Birth control pills?" Margaret knew how witless she sounded. But she was simply not taking it all in.

"Yes Mother, birth control pills." Cyndi glanced about at the other passengers.

"But I thought you wanted to have a child right away. I thought you and Steven—"

"I wanted to have a child. Steven doesn't."

"Never?"

Cyndi shrugged. "Oh, he's willing to have children later. After he's been made a partner in the law firm."

"But, honey, that might take years."

"I know." Cyndi turned and fastened her eyes on the approaching ground.

"I'm sorry." Margaret didn't know what to say. She could see the disappointment in Cyndi's brown eyes.

"It's all right. I can wait. Steven is very ambitious and I feel lucky to have a husband who wants to provide for me."

Margaret's groan was not soft enough to remain unheard.

"What does that mean?" Cyndi challenged.

"It means, my darling daughter, that Steven

has a lot to learn. And so do you. Children and a family are the most fulfilling things in life and I just hate for you to miss out on that."

"I won't miss out," she insisted, her look closed now and stubborn. "Are you sure that's all that's bothering you?"

"I just hate for you to end up like me."

"End up like you? Good grief Mother, you sound as if you're ninety years old and in the poor house. What is so terrible about living the way you do? And please, if you're going to complain about Dad, I don't think I want to hear it."

Margaret sighed and pushed her hair back. She shook her head and gazed into her daughter's lovely dark eyes. Cyndi adored her father and always had. Margaret was beginning to see more and more every day that Cyndi had found in Steven a man molded perfectly in Charles's image.

"I'm sorry," she finally said. "This is between you and Steven. It's none of my business."

"You're right. It isn't."

They had nothing else to say to one another, even after leaving the plane and making their way with their luggage through the long maze of airport corridors.

Margaret drove the shining black Mercedes along the freeway and to the quiet neighborhood to Cyndi and Steven's condominium.

Cyndi opened the car door, but instead of getting out she turned to her mother.

"Mom, I'm sorry. I shouldn't be so hateful, not now with all that you have on your mind. I didn't mean to hurt you."

There were actually tears in Cyndi's eyes. Without thinking, Margaret switched off the ignition and turned to take Cyndi in her arms.

"It's all right sweetheart," she murmured, soothing the girl's soft blond hair with one hand. "I know you didn't mean to be spiteful. And I don't mean to be an interfering mother. We all do and say things at times that hurt one another. But I'm fine."

She kissed Cyndi's cheek and pulled away to wipe the tears from her own eyes. Margaret had become so emotional lately.

"Now, you scoot in the house and give your handsome husband a big kiss from his mother-in-law, you hear?"

Cyndi smiled. And as her daddy often told her, she had a smile that would light up half of Atlanta.

"I will," she whispered. As she slid across

the seat she blew her mother a kiss. "I'll call you. 'Night. Drive carefully."

Margaret waited until she was back on the main street and away from Cyndi's house. Then she pulled the car over to the curb and shifted the gears into park.

She put her face into her hands and leaned against the steering wheel as the tears came once again. She just couldn't seem to stop crying. The grief and pain seemed to build up and then it would take only one word or one look to start her off again.

Her sobs were deep and cleansing, free of any self-conscious need for control. She wondered if anyone ever died from feeling such overwhelming sadness.

Finally, she lifted her head and blew her nose. She wiped her eyes and took a long, deep breath.

"There," she said, moving the car back out onto the street.

She was surprised that Charles's car was in the garage when she got home. With a quiet humorless laugh, she thought that he must be desperate to get her to agree to the upcoming party.

"Shame on me," she whispered as she closed the car door and let herself into the house.

Claire met her in the kitchen and threw her long, slender arms around her.

"Oh, I'm glad you're home. Are you tired?"

Claire stepped back to gaze down at her mother. Margaret didn't know where her eldest daughter received her height, or her slender, willowy figure. Certainly not from her side of the family.

She smiled into Claire's green eyes. "A little, but I'm okay. Where's your dad?"

"In the den. He's pretending he didn't hear you drive in, so you can catch him reading the paper, with his feet propped up. I haven't seen this dutiful husband routine in quite awhile. Why's he trying to impress you this time?"

"Claire," Margaret's dark look held a warning.

With a mischievous grin, Claire shrugged her shoulders and lifted her eyebrows in a look of innocence.

"Go into the den and see for yourself," she said. "I'll take your bags up to your room. Then I have to go."

"It's early yet, only ten thirty. Do you have to go so soon?" Margaret turned to her daughter. "Do you have a late date?"

"Are you kidding?" Claire scoffed. "Heavens, no! Now that I don't have to babysit Dad, I intend to take a long, leisurely bath, wash my hair and do my nails."

"Well, I guess you can't beat that," Margaret said with a teasing grin. "I hope your father wasn't too demanding while I was gone."

"Actually I hardly saw him. Most of the time I'd be in bed when he got home. I just left his supper in the oven."

Margaret frowned. "Oh? I hate that you had to stay here in this big old house alone. But you know how preoccupied your dad can be when he's in the middle of a case."

"Yeah, I know. Besides, I'm a big girl now. And I wanted to stay here in case you called." She draped a long arm around her mother's shoulder. "Are you really all right? Was it terrible for you?"

"It was pretty awful," she admitted with a nod. "I just can't believe he's gone, that I'll never see him again, or talk to him . . ."

"I know."

Claire put both arms around her mother and hugged her. "But I'm here Mom . . . and Cyndi. We'll make it a point to get together often and talk about everything. And if you want me to go back to Ocala with you soon,

I'll see if I can get a few days off."

"Thank you, darling. I don't know what I'd do without you and Cyndi. Now go on, go home and pamper yourself. Would you like to come over for dinner tomorrow night?"

"Sure. We'll talk; I'm sure Daddy will be tired of his husbandly routine by then and you'll be here alone."

With a shake of her head, Margaret watched her beautiful daughter leave the room. Claire made her comments about her father sound teasing, but Margaret knew that she meant every word deep down inside. She had always been protective of her mother and she resented Charles's neglect.

With a sharp pang of regret, Margaret remembered how Claire had been the one to find Charles with one of his lovers at his office. Claire had been only thirteen and it was a traumatic experience she had never forgotten . . . or forgiven.

And it was the first time Margaret had real proof of her husband's suspected infidelities.

"Oh God," Margaret groaned, not wanting to remember any more. She thought she could not bear one more shred of pain in her already bruised and battered heart.

Five

Margaret shook off her uneasy thoughts about the past. She discarded her white Dior jacket and walked through the house toward the den.

She stood at the door for a moment, smiling at the sight. Claire was right about Charles being so transparent sometimes.

He did seem to be waiting for Margaret to discover him. A fire flickered in the fireplace and lit the dark paneled walls with a warm amber glow. The music on the stereo was a selection of Bach, one of her favorites, and Charles was seated in the dark blue wingback chair with his feet propped on a hassock.

He had even gone to the trouble of putting on the maroon and blue paisley silk robe she had given him for his birthday.

With a rattle of the newspaper, he turned toward the doorway.

"Margaret . . . darling." Quickly he lowered the paper and got up from the chair.

He was a handsome man still, she thought. His face had grown a bit fuller with age and his mustache and thinning hair were graying, but he was just as handsome and charming as he'd been the day they married. She saw the evidence of that in other women's glances whenever she and Charles were out together.

He came to her and put his arms around her. His body felt warm and he smelled slightly of pipe tobacco. For a moment she let herself be drawn into his arms and held. She tried not to think about how disappointed she had been that he did not come to Florida.

"I'm really sorry about your dad, sweetheart. And sorry I disappointed you by not being there."

"It's all right," she said, her voice husky with emotion. She wasn't used to such sympathy from him. "I'll have to go back down there after Christmas; perhaps you can come with me then."

She could have kicked herself. Charles

pulled away from her and took her hand, leading her to the sofa near the fireplace.

When would she ever learn? Charles did not like to make plans and he hated making commitments to anyone. There were simply too many distractions in his life, and it was as if he feared that something better might come along. Of course, he made commitments for business and friends, but rarely would he let her pin him down about anything, not even vacations.

"We'll see," he said. She sensed he did not want their conversation to lead to another argument. And she had to agree that there had been too many of those lately.

"I'm surprised you're home so early," she said.

He turned and looked at her with a pained expression. "Why, darling, of course I'd be home when you arrived. Where else would I be?"

She stood up quickly, clamping her lips together to keep from saying what had come automatically to mind. *Where indeed?*

Even before she went to Ocala, she had seen the telltale signs: Charles's absences, his late night business meetings, his avoidance of her and the girls.

She had pushed those thoughts out of her mind, as she'd done so often. It simply hurt too much to know the truth.

"Would you like a drink?" she asked.

Charles stood up and came across the room to the gleaming mahogany bar. He stood behind Margaret and gazed into the mirror at their reflections. His hands caressed her shoulders, then moved to brush her hair back as his head bent to kiss the side of her neck.

Margaret could not help the shiver that ran down her neck.

Her hands clumsily set the heavy crystal decanter back into its footed silver container. Almost instinctively she leaned back against him, giving in to the rush of pleasure she felt, and knowing she should not.

"Darling," he whispered against her ear. "What's wrong? You seem tense." His lips nuzzled and moved back again to her neck. "Hmmm, you always smell so good. I've missed you."

"Nothing's wrong," she murmured, turning in his arms so she could see his dark eyes. "I'm just tired, that's all."

Could she be wrong about Charles this time? Should she just keep pretending that everything was all right between them? She wanted to. God, how she wanted to believe he really wanted her this time.

She was surprised by his kisses. He rarely kissed her. Their lovemaking the last few years had been sporadic, even clinical at times, as if Charles simply wanted to have his pleasure quickly and then be gone. She missed the love play between them and most of all she missed being kissed.

She closed her eyes and leaned toward Charles. And suddenly a vision flashed through her mind and she almost gasped aloud. She saw Jonathan Bradford's blue eyes so clearly; saw the image of him as he lowered his head to kiss her.

Her eyes flew open and she looked almost frantically into Charles's face.

"Darling," he said with a frown. "What on earth is wrong with you? You're acting very strange."

"I . . . I don't know. I just felt a little disoriented for a moment. Perhaps I'll feel better if I take a warm bath and change into something more comfortable." As Margaret spoke, she felt her heart pounding. She actually felt as if she had done something illicit.

"Will you come back down?" he asked in a sly whisper, trailing kisses across her cheek. "I like it here in the den, with the fireplace. We'll have a drink and . . . relax."

There was a certain look in his eye as he emphasized the word relax. Margaret knew she should be pleased. Isn't this what she wanted? Was it possible that her father's death had made Charles realize how important she was to him? It had certainly made her stop and think about such things. And yet, there was something in his manner that seemed contrived and rehearsed. As much as she still wanted to believe him, she was afraid.

Upstairs in their large bedroom suite, she walked through the dressing rooms and into the bathroom. She turned on the gold plated faucet and sprinkled a handful of french bath crystals into the steaming water. She undressed slowly and draped her clothes across a chair. Tying a robe around her, she went to the gilded mirror at the sink and gazed at her reflection.

She pushed her dark hair back, seeing the coarser strands of gray that had begun appearing last year. Her fingers pushed at the skin across her cheekbones, noting the fine lines at the corners of her gray eyes. Then, with a frown, her eyes moved over the reflection and down to her lips.

What had Jonathan Bradford seen when he looked at her? Had he seen an aging woman, a mother and wife whose past was reflected in her eyes, whose hurts were clearly visible? Did he still see the girl she was that summer so long ago? A silly teenager who infatuated and intrigued him?

Or did he simply see a woman? A mature woman who loved being kissed and held . . . a woman whose nature was more passionate now than when she was first married. Could he possibly know those things about her? Was that why he had kissed her?

She could hardly imagine a man like Jonathan Bradford feeling desire for a woman her age.

She closed her eyes and turned from the mirror, shaking her head. Why on earth had Jonathan's face flashed before her when Charles kissed her? It troubled her and puzzled her, too.

It wasn't like her. She had always prided herself on her loyalty to Charles, no matter what, no matter how he conducted himself. She had decided long ago that she would not lower herself to retaliate for Charles's indiscretions.

And now, thinking of Jonathan, she felt herself in danger of forgetting those vows. She felt lucky that he was in Florida and she was in Atlanta. She could not allow even these visions of him to happen again.

She began humming a distracting tune as she marched resolutely to the bathtub and stepped out of her robe and into the warm, foaming water. It was stress that made her so confused; she was certain of it. All she had to do was forget about Jonathan, forget about everything except being home and being with her husband.

After her bath, Margaret decided against something warm and comfortable. Instead she chose a black negligee of silky material that was shot with silver threads and trimmed in expensive black lace. Charles had given it to her for their anniversary last spring.

It had been a very long time since she'd dressed this way for Charles.

He was waiting for her in the den and when she entered the room his eyes glittered in the firelight as he handed her a glass of wine.

"You're still a very beautiful woman, Margaret."

She took the wine, drinking it quickly and hoping its effects would erase the guilt and confusion she was feeling. She hoped it would banish Jonathan's face from her mind for good.

When Charles took the empty glass from her hand and pulled her into his arms, she gave in to the pleasure and warmth that was beginning to move over her.

His lips became insistent and she felt his hunger feeding her own desire. She felt pleasantly weak, and she could almost feel the warmth of the wine moving through her veins. It caused her to respond more freely than she had in months.

Charles drew her down to the carpet before the fireplace. The fire had almost burned itself out and there was only a warm glow left that cast a shimmering light along the curves of their bodies as they undressed.

"I still love you," he whispered as he moved over her and positioned himself between her thighs. "Only you baby . . . only you."

Their lovemaking was familiar and easy, the way it had been in the beginning. And

Charles's surprising new intensity excited and pleased Margaret.

This was real, she told herself; this was not something that either of them had to fake. And Margaret found herself wishing it could last forever.

When Charles arched his back and shuddered against her, he laughed aloud.

Margaret understood that laugh; she'd heard it before. It was Charles's laugh of pleasure, embodying man's ultimate triumph. She tried not to be disappointed that his reaction was not more intimate and romantic, more in line with her own mood.

She wanted to lie there before the fire, wanted him to hold her and kiss her, tell her that she was his life and his only love. She supposed that was the one thing she felt Charles had never given her—his need.

"Baby, you're good," he chuckled as he rose and sauntered naked to the bar. "Hotter than ever. I thought women your age were supposed to cool off a bit."

Ice jangled into a glass and he poured a splash of bourbon over the top. Still looking at her, he brought the glass to his lips and tilted his head back, downing the liquid in one quick gulp.

Margaret sat up and pulled the crumpled black silk negligee toward her, thrusting her arms into the sleeves.

"I suppose I never thought of myself that way," she said.

"Never thought of yourself as hot? That's one of the things I always liked about you. You know the old saying, 'a man likes his woman to be a lady to the world, but a whore in his bedroom.' "

"Oh yes," she muttered. "That old saying."

He laughed again, then poured himself another drink and filled her wine glass. He padded across the carpet and handed it to her.

"Don't be so sensitive," he said. "You know what I mean."

"Yes, I know what you mean." She sipped the wine. It tasted flat and bitter.

"Tomorrow I want you to go out and buy yourself the most expensive gown in Atlanta. I want you to knock 'em dead at the club Saturday night."

"Don't you think I'm getting a little old for that game, Charles?"

He had pulled the paisley robe back on and was beginning to tie the belt. His hands became still as he turned to gaze at her. She could see the impatience beginning in his dark eyes.

"What the hell does that mean?"

She sighed and shook her head. She took one last drink of the wine, then set the glass down on the bar.

"I'm sorry," she muttered. "I guess I'm just tired. I'll buy a dress and I'll do my best to impress Mr. Simmons."

He walked to her and took her in his arms, letting his hands slide down past her waist and over her hips. Then he pulled her against him and patted her behind.

"Good girl," he said, placing a quick kiss against her hair. "That's my girl."

That night in bed, she lay very still beside Charles and listened to his steady breathing. She stared into the darkness until her eyes began to burn.

"Rewarded," she whispered to herself.

That's how Charles made her feel. *Rewarded*. As if she were a trained puppy who had obeyed its master and received a pat on the head, but Margaret's reward was her husband's sexual favors. This time he had managed to put a little warmth into it, even made it seem real. And his intensity, feigned or not, had fooled her into believing once again . . . if only for a few desperate moments.

She continued to stare into the darkness for what seemed like hours. Tears ran from the corners of her eyes, dampening her hair and falling finally onto the expensive designer pillow cases beneath her head.

Six

She was awake next morning when Charles slipped quietly from bed. She heard him in the shower and then in the dressing room. He was humming softly as he dressed.

Even when he came to the bed and stood looking down at her, she pretended to be asleep. Only when he bent to brush a quick kiss against her cheek did she open her eyes.

"I didn't want to wake you, sweetheart. You get some rest; I'll eat breakfast downtown."

She muttered something and watched through narrowed eyes as he glanced at himself in the mirror over the dresser and ran a hand over his hair. He seemed very cheerful and very eager to leave.

Margaret could not explain the lethargy that seemed to have control over her entire body. She wasn't sleepy, but neither could she force herself from bed.

And even in the light of morning, her thoughts were still troubled, a whirl of confusing doubts. They alternated between what had happened last night with Charles and what she wished for in her most private, intimate thoughts. Then there was her father and the anguish she felt every time she envisioned his face.

She'd never see him again. She supposed she was trying to make herself feel something more by thinking of his death, but the more she thought about it, the more deadened her senses became.

And there was Jonathan. This morning, alone in her bed, she allowed herself to think about him and about her response to Charles last night when she had seen Jonathan's face instead of her husband's.

It was only a fantasy, she told herself.

Millions of women have fantasies, some even resort to fantasies when making love to their husbands. Margaret had admired handsome movie stars, celebrities whose faces were pasted across every magazine cover. She had never been able to fantasize about them, though.

Besides, Jonathan was not some distant celebrity on a magazine cover, though she had to admit, he was handsome enough to be. He was real; he was someone she knew. If he lived nearer, her fantasies about him could be downright dangerous.

Her friend Dina had suggested once that Margaret see a therapist, someone who could help her understand why she still clung to Charles, even when she was so miserably unhappy. Now with her dad's death, perhaps it was something she would consider doing for herself.

Finally she pushed herself from bed and made her way to the bathroom.

The next few days were busy ones and she was thankful for the distraction. She went almost mindlessly into town and shopped for an expensive new gown to wear Saturday night. She had Claire over to dinner, and pretended indifference when Charles called to say he wouldn't be home.

Each day she told herself that her life was not so bad. She should be ashamed for feeling the way she did, most women would be thrilled to be in her shoes.

Saturday evening, Charles dressed first and

told her he'd be waiting for her in the den. Margaret had indulged herself that afternoon with a facial and makeup session at one of Atlanta's most exclusive salons. As a result, her dark hair was full and shining, brushed back away from her face to expose the glitter of diamond earrings.

Finally she slipped on the black taffeta gown, pleased that it zipped so easily over her hips. Then she turned to stare at herself in the mirror. She forced herself to smile and lift her chin, telling herself she looked younger if she smiled.

The wide neckline of the dress dipped into a low vee between her full breasts. The sprinkle of sequins that ran from one shoulder down her breast and waist ended up at her opposite hip. The light cast bright little dots of glitter up onto her face and bare shoulders.

"Not bad," she whispered, turning to look at her exposed back.

When she walked into the den, she could see the pleasure in Charles's eyes. He had a look of smug satisfaction on his face.

"Darling, you look spectacular. Whatever that dress cost me, it's definitely worth it."

The evening at the club passed pleasantly

enough. Mr. Simmons, who sat beside Margaret, was a quiet, elderly little man who seemed out of place among the talkative lawyer crowd that Charles always favored. Mr. Simmons told Margaret that he had lived a modest life until about twenty years ago when an invention made him extremely wealthy.

"More money than I'll ever spend," he said with a sad, little smile. "I lost my wife last year. And I found out just how meaningless money is when it comes to illness and death."

"Yes," she said, feeling immediate empathy toward him. "I just lost my father, and I know exactly what you mean. It's such a helpless feeling."

"I'm sorry," he said. "Losing a parent is hard, makes death seem very real and very near, doesn't it?" His frown held a wealth of sympathy. "But at least you have children. My wife and I never had children."

"Yes, we do have," Margaret said, smiling. "Three daughters."

"I believe I saw one of them with your husband just last week. A small girl, petite, with dark hair, much like your own," He gazed at Margaret's face and hair with a smile. "They were having lunch at The Abbey, and I thought what a nice thing that was—a father and his daughter spending time together. Very nice . . ."

He turned back to his meal, his thoughts seeming to drift away to something else.

Margaret's stomach had lurched at his words. A petite girl with dark hair? Claire and Cyndi were both blondes. Gincy was the only one of the girls who had inherited Margaret's dark hair and she was hundreds of miles away.

The old familiar dread crept over her, threatening to suffocate her. Suddenly the delicious food, the wine, everything seemed bland and tasteless. She looked across the table at her husband who was laughing and talking with a woman seated next to him.

Margaret stared at him, studying his face, the way he held his fork and gestured over his plate as he spoke. She wondered sometimes if anything ever really got through to him. Did he never feel remorse or guilt for what he had put her through?

Margaret sat stiffly beside Charles as they drove home from the club. She listened to his effusive chatter about Mr. Simmons and how she had impressed the old man.

"You put the icing on the cake, baby." His hand reached across to stroke her knee.

All the while, as Charles talked, she could think of only one thing. Who was the young dark-haired woman Mr. Simmons had seen him with? She found herself hoping Charles would not touch her tonight, would not try to reward her again with his lovemaking as he had done that first night home from Ocala.

She was afraid that if he touched her she would lose control completely and smash his face with her fists. And she didn't want to lose control.

She needn't have worried. Now that Charles had the Simmons account, he no longer seemed interested. Almost immediately they went back to their old routine.

After that weekend Charles immersed himself again in his work and all the trappings of his status. Margaret went her own way, almost as if she were a widow.

She found that she was relieved.

It was the week before Christmas. The weather was mild, although the sky that morning looked gray and threatening. Margaret was just going through the kitchen, on her way to pick up Dina for a last minute shopping trip.

Charles had come down early and was standing in the kitchen at the small island with its blue hand-painted tiles. He gazed at her over the rim of his coffee cup.

"Going shopping?" he asked with a disinterested smile.

"Yes. Dina and I are going to drive out to Kennesaw to the new shopping mall."

"Great. Have a good time, darling." He stepped forward and kissed her, his lips sliding across her face to land somewhere near her ear.

"Aren't you going to work today?" she asked as she gathered her purse and coat. She glanced at the casual slacks and knit shirt he wore.

"Sure. But I'm going to meet Stan at the club first. I'll shower and change into my suit there."

"All right. See you later." She left with a wave of her hand, distracted by thoughts of picking up Dina and wondering which road would be best to take in the holiday traffic.

In the garage the car started quickly and smoothly. Margaret sat for a moment and pulled on a pair of driving gloves, then turned to check her purse for cash and credit cards.

"Oh," she whispered with a frown. "Forgot my list." She rummaged through the contents of her purse.

She had made a list that included sizes and color preferences for Claire and Cyndi. They teased her often about her list making. She must have left it on the kitchen cabinet where she would see it as she went out the door.

She left the car running and let herself quickly back into the house. The kitchen was empty; Charles had probably gone upstairs to get his suit.

She found the list and glanced at the clock. She was late and Dina was a stickler for promptness.

"Better call her," she mumbled, sticking the piece of paper into her jacket pocket and moving toward the phone on the wall.

The phone was in her hand and her fingers were poised over the buttons. Margaret turned her head to one side, listening. She'd heard a quiet hissing noise and now she realized there were voices on the phone.

She smiled, glad she had not dialed in Charles's ear. He would not be pleased if she had interrupted his conversation with one of his important clients.

Almost without thinking she lifted the

phone to her ear before hanging up. When she heard the soft tone of Charles's words, her gray eyes widened and her lips moved silently.

". . . she's going shopping . . . in Kennesaw. She'll be gone all day."

"Lucky for me." The feminine giggle that followed was not one Margaret recognized, but she sounded very young.

Margaret held her breath as her heart began to thud against her chest. She could feel her arms and legs tremble from the rush of adrenaline.

"You better believe it, baby," Charles murmured.

The tone of his voice sickened Margaret. It was blatantly suggestive and held the thick languid rasp of desire.

"I have something new to wear today. You're going to love it." The girl's throaty voice purred, reminding Margaret of some silly, mindless television commercial.

"Hmmm, baby, I can't wait. Give old Charles a little hint, why don't you? You know how I love to hear it."

"Well, I can tell you this, it won't be anything like that gaudy rag you bought your wife last spring. You remember? The first time we met?"

The black negligee Charles had given her for their anniversary. Margaret's stomach tightened with revulsion as she realized what the girl meant.

Charles laughed. "Coming to that expensive little shop of yours was the best thing that's happened to me in a long time, Shell."

Shell? Margaret couldn't think of any of their acquaintances called Shell. Was it short for Michelle or Shelley?

"Does she look good in it?" the girl purred. Her voice sounded petulant and silly.

Again Charles laughed. Margaret's hands were shaking so badly now she was afraid Charles could hear the phone tapping against her gold earrings.

"Yeah," he said, his voice boastful. "She looks damned good in it."

"Good enough to screw?"

Charles groaned. "Oh hell, baby, you know better than that. I've already told you. It's over between Margaret and me, has been for years. We live in the same house simply for convenience. But we haven't slept together in . . . God, I can't even remember the last time."

I can, Margaret wanted to shout. The last

time you needed something from me. His words hurt, even if it was the typical lie told by a married man to pacify his mistress.

"Yeah, that's what you told me." The girl's voice persisted in its petulance and Margaret thought she must be very young and very silly.

"It's the truth, Shell. It's you I want, baby . . . only you."

His words, so familiar, went like a knife to Margaret's heart. How many times had he told her that? She winced and for a moment she was afraid she might actually be sick.

Softly she hung up the phone. She couldn't bear to hear another word.

She ran out to the car and jumped in, quickly backing out of the garage. Tears blurred her vision and she felt her throat tightening until she could hardly breathe.

What was she going to do? She didn't want to face Dina, didn't want her friend to see her completely losing herself in the pain of her discovery.

Her thoughts turned immediately to Claire and Cyndi. Besides being her daughters, they were also her closest friends. As she pulled out onto the street, she knew this was not something she could discuss with them.

Claire would be furious and Cyndi would only defend her father. She couldn't let this cause a division between her girls.

She glanced back at the large house with its immaculate lawn and landscaped gardens. She wiped the tears from her eyes, thinking for a moment of following Charles, of finding out once and for all who his latest girlfriend was. But her pride would not let her do that.

She had no idea what to do or where to go. After more than thirty minutes of driving up and down different streets, she found herself within a few blocks of Dina's house. Almost automatically she drove to her friend's house, put the car in park and got out.

Dina was standing in the open doorway frowning toward the drive as Margaret walked toward her. Her platinum blond hair was perfect as usual and she looked elegantly casual in maroon slacks and a matching cardigan.

"Margaret, where on earth have you been? I was worried to death about you." She stopped as Margaret walked closer and stared at her through teary eyes. "My God, what's happened? Are you sick? Is it the girls?"

"No, the girls are fine. May I come in, Dina? Could we stay here instead of going shopping? I . . . I need to talk to someone."

Dina's dark eyes were worried as she watched her friend walk silently through the door and into the house. Knowing Charles Avery as she did, Dina thought she had a good idea what Margaret needed to talk about.

Seven

Dina Clark and Margaret had been friends for years. They were often bridge partners at the club, although they were entirely different kinds of players. Likewise, they were also very different kinds of women.

Dina was often blunt and outspoken. She was also the model of sophistication, preferring only the most stylish of clothes and wearing her silver hair cropped short in the latest fashion. She was the kind of woman who dieted rigorously, cautious lest an extra pound creep onto her one hundred and ten pound frame.

Dina was never quiet and could be counted on to enliven any party she attended.

But today as she sat across from Margaret, she was quiet as she leaned forward to offer unspoken sympathy. Today she meant only to listen and lend her support.

Margaret explained how she had left the house, then gone back in to look for her gift list.

"Charles was on the phone . . . he was talking to a woman . . ." She looked into Dina's eyes as if for help.

Dina didn't bother trying to pretend Charles's phone call was something else or that Margaret had misunderstood. That would be an insult to Margaret. She listened quietly as Margaret detailed the conversation she'd overheard.

"He told her we never slept together!" Margaret's eyes blazed with anger and disbelief. "My God, he said we hadn't slept together in years. Can you believe that?"

"Typical," Dina said with a soft grunt. "You'd think women would figure it out after awhile. I mean, give me a break, it's the same tired old line that's been used for hundreds of years."

"She sounded young," Margaret said. "Very young."

"Did you say anything to confront them?"

"No," Margaret said with a quick shake of her head. "I couldn't; I felt so confused and hurt. I just wanted to get out of there."

"I know how you must have felt. Believe

90

me, when it happens, the pain a woman feels is universal. It hurts enough to die. That's why, after my last divorce, I decided never to put myself in that position again. Honey, I don't get involved with anyone. From now on, any relationship I have is strictly for pleasure, no strings attached."

Margaret looked into Dina's dark eyes. Even now, years after her divorce, there were still shadows of pain in their depths when she spoke about it.

"How did you ever get through it?"

Dina sighed and lifted her eyes toward the ceiling. "I don't know. Anger I suppose. I was mad as hell." She laughed softly and looked back at Margaret. "Don't take this the wrong way, but I've often wondered why you didn't get mad. It's not the first time this has happened with Charles, is it?"

"No." Margaret stood up and walked to the long windows that faced the street and pushed back the heavy drapes. "Oh, I've been angry. Believe me, I've been angry enough to kill him. But Charles is clever; he knows exactly when to stop his philandering and come home and begin his 'husbandly act' as Claire calls it. There were so many times when I suspected he was seeing someone but could never prove it."

"You never tried." Dina's words were not accusatory, but rather a soft-spoken reminder.

"Not very hard, no." Margaret turned. Her smile was weak and did not reach her troubled gray eyes.

"Honey, you look pale. Let me get you some coffee or a cup of hot tea."

Margaret took a deep breath. "I would like some tea." She sank back into the soft comfortable chair while Dina got up and went toward the back of the house.

Margaret supposed she had become an expert at keeping her anger hidden from the world, but now it would not be contained so easily. It boiled within her, knotting her stomach and making her head throb with pain.

Damn him! He had made a mistake this time. She intended to use that mistake to rid herself of a miserable existence . . . once and for all.

Did he really think that she would sit by and let him humiliate her at this stage of her life? Did he expect her to pretend that everything was fine between them, even while their friends laughed at her behind her back and shook their heads in sympathy?

"No!" she shouted, hitting her fist against her thigh.

"That's the way, sweetie . . . get angry." Dina's eyes watched her, bright with speculation as she carried a tray toward the two chairs.

"I am angry, Dina. I don't think I've ever been so damned mad about anything in my life. He's not going to do this to me again."

Dina placed the tray on a small Queen Anne table and silently poured two cups of tea.

She handed Margaret a cup and motioned toward the creamer and sugar bowl.

"Do you still love him?" she asked.

"I think at this moment I hate him. I hate what he's done to my family, to my daughters. And I hate what he's done to me." Her gray eyes over the cup searched Dina's for a little understanding. "We could have had such a wonderful life, you know? We had everything, and Charles just tossed it aside, threw our lives in the mud as if it were nothing."

"What are you going to do?"

"I'm getting out." She looked at Dina with a firm nod, her eyes bright and determined. "This time, I'm really getting out."

93

"It won't be easy in this town, you know. Charles is a prominent lawyer and a member of Atlanta's legal aristocracy."

"I know. I've thought of that, but it doesn't matter. I'm not going to let that stop me from doing what I should have done years ago. Even if I have to hire a lawyer from up east."

"At least you'll have the house—"

"I don't want the house. It's Charles's house, not mine. His architect designed and built it . . . placed it in just the right neighborhood. It's not me, never has been." She looked up and her eyes were thoughtful. "I still have my dad's place in Florida."

Dina placed her cup on the tray and leaned toward Margaret. "I understand your feelings, but don't make any hasty decisions right now. You're angry as you should be, but promise me you'll give this some thought. Don't run away to Florida and don't just go barging into the house tonight and demand a divorce. Wait until you have all the facts and you know exactly what you intend to do. Will you promise me that?"

"Oh, I have no intention of doing anything right now. In fact I don't plan to mention it to Charles at all. I have Christmas to get through . . . and I need to explain to the girls . . ." For the first time since coming to Dina, Margaret's eyes filled with tears. The thought of telling her daughters, of ending a marriage and dissolving a family was too real and too painful.

Dina reached forward and patted Margaret's shoulder.

"Are you sure you'll be able to handle the silent masquerade?" she asked.

Margaret shook the tears away and lifted her chin.

"Oh, yes. I'm very good at it by now. Charles has taught me well, you see. I've learned to be the silent, long-suffering wife . . . for the children's sake." Her gray eyes glittered and there was a spark there that Dina had never seen before. "But not for much longer. The girls are grown; they have lives of their own now. I don't intend to let him hold family and tradition over my head one moment longer. I'm past fifty, Dina. Do you know how few of those years were happy ones? When my dad died I think I realized that if I intended to do anything about my life, it was time I got started."

"Good," Dina said, amazed at her friend's strength and determination. "And I'll be here to help if you need me. Whenever and whatever you need."

Margaret stood up and reached for her jacket.

"Where are you going? Are you going home to . . ."

"We're going shopping," Margaret said with a haughty lift of her brows and a determined shake of her head. "And I'm going to buy my daughters something beautiful and expensive for Christmas. I've let Charles spoil so many Christmases for my family. I don't intend to let him spoil this last one."

But for all her bravado, that day was one of the hardest Margaret had ever endured. Everything reminded her of the conversation she had overheard. And everywhere she looked she was bombarded with the joy of family traditions at Christmas.

And for some reason it was Ginger who was on her mind, even more than her other two daughters. After Claire had spoken with Ginger, she evidently moved to another job. Margaret hadn't been able to contact her since, and she wondered if Ginger had done it deliberately.

She'd have to tell her about this, too. Although at this point, Margaret was not sure it would make any difference to her youngest daughter. She had made it clear for the past five years that she wanted nothing to do with her parents or Atlanta, but Margaret had to find her.

Now, if she could just get through the holidays.

Those words became a mantra for Margaret; an incentive that once uttered strengthened her resolve and gave her a goal to work toward. She found out, as Dina had warned, that divorcing Charles Avery was not going to be easy.

She drove next day to the small town of Marietta where she'd deliberately chosen a law firm with attorneys that Charles probably would not know.

"Oh, I know Charles Avery all right," the man behind the desk said. "Every lawyer within a hundred miles of Atlanta knows Charles Avery, but I wouldn't let that stand in the way of representing you. But let me give you a little free advice."

Margaret stared at the man sitting across from her. He was an older balding, man. His very pale blue eyes that drooped slightly at the corners were gazing at her with a roguish twinkle.

"If you think this divorce might get messy, you'll want to get yourself a woman lawyer, Mrs. Avery. Someone who doesn't have to worry about the established order of male ascendency in greater metropolitan Atlanta."

She smiled wanly. He certainly sounded like a lawyer.

"What are you saying? I should choose a woman because she wouldn't want to move up in the world the way a man does. And therefore, Charles's retaliation would be meaningless against such a person?"

"Oh no, I'm not saying that exactly. The women lawyers I know are every bit as ambitious as their male counterparts. But it's less likely that your husband and his lawyer will hold any personal grudges against a woman, you see? Call it the chivalry of the Old South if you like, or just say that men like Charles Avery are not threatened by female opposition."

Margaret nodded. He did seem to know Charles very well at that.

"In any case, I think you'll be better represented by a woman."

"Is there anyone you would recommend?"

"Matter of fact, there is. Jane Ann Tilton. Has an office just down the street. Here, I'll look it up for you." He pulled a book out of his desk and began to riffle through the pages. "In fact I'll give her a call if you'd like, make an appointment for you."

"Yes," Margaret said, fighting her weariness. "Please."

The lawyer stopped, holding the phone in midair. He lowered his head to gaze meaningfully at Margaret.

"Another thing. Tell Miss Tilton to get you a good private detective. Get some pictures . . . have all the goods on your husband before you go into court."

Margaret winced. She hated the very idea of spying on Charles. Hated the thought of gathering the sordid details that would prove facts she'd rather not know.

But she knew the man was right. Slowly she nodded and saw his smile of satisfaction as he began to dial the number.

Margaret felt better after she left the office of Jane Ann Tilton. The woman was mature, probably near Margaret's own age, and she had an air of purpose about her. Margaret had the feeling the woman was tough as leather and would put up with little nonsense, either in court or in her own private life.

She had not batted an eyelash when Margaret mentioned a good private detective. She'd only nodded and made a note on the pad before her.

And when Margaret told her that she wanted to wait until after Christmas to tell Charles, Miss Tilton had smiled sympathetically and nodded her understanding.

"I agree," she said. "If you can hold it together through the holidays for your family, I think that will be to your benefit and certainly to your daughters' benefit. But I'll get the detective work going right away. Why don't you come back to see me the week after Christmas, say January fifth? We'll see what we know and then we can proceed with the filing and the notification."

Margaret drove almost unseeing through the busy interstate traffic back toward Atlanta. She felt calm and resolved. For the first time in years she felt as if a huge burden had been lifted from her shoulders. Her decision to divorce Charles and begin a new life gave her a heady feeling of power and freedom. She was in charge of her destiny now, not Charles, and she found that she liked that feeling.

Over the next few days she threw herself wholly into preparations for Christmas. She hired a janitorial service to do most of the cleaning so she would be free to bake and decorate the house.

"Wow, Mom, you're certainly going all out this year," Cyndi observed one night while visiting. "Any special reason?"

"No," Margaret said. "I just feel like it. And you know how I've always loved Christmas."

"Me, too," Cyndi said, accepting her mother's explanation. "Move over, let me sprinkle the colored sugar on the cookies."

Claire, on the other hand, had been a bit more probing.

"What's wrong, Mother?" she asked one night after dinner. "You've been awfully quiet lately."

"Nothing's wrong. I'm just tired."

"You look exhausted. Maybe you should forget all this cooking. Get a caterer to do it. Besides, we don't really need this much food, do we?"

"Well, you know me. I like to have plenty

on hand. People will be dropping by. And your father always has friends he likes to invite in at Christmas."

"Then let him do the cooking," Claire mumbled. There was always that edge to Claire's voice when she spoke about her father.

"Claire . . ." Margaret scolded.

"Well, I think that after Christmas you should try to get away for a few days. Take Dina with you, lie on the beach, maybe even spend a few days in Ocala. You always say how peaceful it makes you feel to go back home to Ocala."

"Yes," Margaret said. "It does."

If only Claire knew the truth. It was something Margaret thought about constantly. The idea of going home to Ocala and her father's little house was like a bright beacon, destroying the darkness for her. The thought of being there, of going home, had become an almost tangible longing like a physical ache. It was something she did not fully understand herself.

Soon, she could decide what she wanted.

And then she would be able to begin a new life . . . wherever that might be.

For the first time in years, Margaret held

a secret, positive thought within herself, the promise of a tomorrow that would be filled with freshness, excitement, and hope. She was more certain than ever that she was making the right decision.

Eight

Charles was home for Christmas Eve, but Margaret noted his restlessness. She wondered if he had promised his mistress he would be with her that night, too.

She had seen little of him the past week, but that was actually a relief. She was afraid if she was alone with him very long she would just blurt out her pent-up frustrations.

She didn't want anything to warn him, or to interfere with the detective's investigation. She knew Charles Avery better than anyone and she knew what a devious man he could be. To him, living the good life was always winning. She didn't intend this time for him to have the advantage; she didn't intend for him to win.

Margaret and her two daughters chatted

and laughed as they carried food from the kitchen into the dining room. They could hear the murmur of male voices in the den as Steven and Charles discussed their work.

Later Margaret glanced up when Steven came into the dining room. He is cute, she thought with a quiet smile. His little boy face and crooked grin made him look much younger than thirty. She always suspected he wore the heavy tortoise rimmed glasses to make him appear older and more sophisticated.

She watched as he put an arm around Cyndi's waist and pulled her against him. He was only a couple of inches taller than his wife and Margaret thought they made a very attractive couple.

The meal was festive enough. Margaret forced her eyes away from Charles. She was so afraid he would be able to second-guess what she was thinking. She felt such anger toward him that she was sure he could see and feel her animosity.

But after awhile she almost laughed at herself. When had Charles ever looked at her and wondered what emotions were hidden inside? Never, she answered silently. He was usually too busy thinking of himself, just as he was tonight.

He glanced at his watch often until finally Claire noticed it, too.

"What's wrong, Dad? Surely you don't have an appointment on Christmas Eve?"

"What?" he gazed at her as if he had been deep in thought.

"You keep looking at your watch. Can't you relax for once . . . even on Christmas Eve?"

"Oh, I'm sorry, honey." He grinned rather sheepishly at his oldest daughter. "Just force of habit, I guess. Say, where's your fellow tonight? I thought you would bring him for dinner."

"Who? Brian? I'm not seeing him any more, didn't Mother tell you?"

Charles turned to stare blankly at Margaret. She glanced down at her plate.

"Yes, I told him."

Charles laughed, a bit too heartily, as he often did when he was trying to hide something. "I guess I just forgot."

"Well, you didn't tell me," Cyndi said with a frown at her sister. "Why aren't you seeing him? I thought he was very nice. Sexy, too."

Claire shrugged and made a slight grimace. Margaret watched her oldest daughter, wishing she could understand her better. Her tall, willowy figure and green eyes turned heads wherever she went, yet her relationships with men were often short and troubled.

Tonight in a black sequined sweater and glittering earrings that dangled down past her short blond hair, she was stunning.

"He was too serious."

"As in marriage minded?" Steven's question was said with a teasing grin.

"Yes, dear brother-in-law. He wanted to tie me down, just the way you did my little sis." She laughed as she spoke and shook her head in a silly girlish way.

"That's the way it's supposed to be." Steven reached for his wife and pulled her toward him, nudging her gently with his chin. "Hogtie 'em and brand 'em."

Everyone laughed, except Claire. Her green eyes glittered seriously in the light of the crystal chandelier than hung over the table.

"Well, I guess I just wasn't ready to be hog-tied and branded, Steven." Her words were clipped and cool.

"You would be if you found the right man," he declared, determined to have the last word.

"Like you?"

"Hey, don't pick on my husband," Cyndi

said, smiling at Claire good-naturedly.

"I'll probably end up marrying a gas station attendant," Claire muttered, turning her attention back to her food. "At least he wouldn't be so career minded that I'd never see him."

"There's nothing wrong with a man providing well for his family, Claire." Charles's face had turned serious. His head was lowered as he stared at her.

"I didn't say there was. Maybe it's all the other qualities that go with it that bother me." Her eyes glinted and her pink lips tightened as she looked at her father.

Margaret could see the resentment in her daughter's eyes, and she felt her insides tighten immediately. Dear Lord, she didn't want their last Christmas together as a family to end with an argument.

"I want a man who puts me first and my children, if we ever have any—" Claire explained heatedly.

"Better get started," Steven interjected with a laugh. "You're not getting any younger."

Claire glared at him, then continued as if he had not even spoken. "I won't marry a professional man who is constantly jockeying for position, one who plays politics at every occasion, even at the expense of his family.

I'd rather marry a mechanic."

Charles's dark eyes did not leave Claire's face. He knew what she meant; she had brought this subject up enough times in the past.

"You always had everything you needed Claire, even if it was necessary for me to miss a birthday party now and then."

Margaret closed her eyes. Please, not this again, she inwardly begged.

"Now and then? You never came to one, Daddy. Not a single, solitary one." Claire's green eyes were shining now and had darkened to an emerald color.

"What difference does it make now, for heaven's sake?" It was Cyndi who spoke. Cyndi who always sided with her father.

"It matters Cyndi," Claire said in a soft voice. "And if you'd ever admit it, his negligence mattered to you, too."

"Negligence! Now wait just a minute young lady. This is still my home and I'll not have you sit here at my table and accuse me. . . . I never neglected my family and I certainly never . . ." Charles began to rise from his chair. He seemed barely in control of his anger.

"Charles, please sit down. Can't we just

have a quiet, peaceful Christmas Eve dinner without — "

The ringing of the phone halted Margaret's words and shattered the awkward silence that had fallen over the table.

Margaret took a long deep breath as she rose from the table and went toward the kitchen. She felt that same old lethargy moving over her, felt as if her body was so heavy she could barely move across the floor. Her hand went to rub the back of her neck where an ache had begun and was rapidly turning into a headache.

She picked up the phone listlessly, her eyes turned toward the people in the other room who sat silently around the festively decorated table.

"Hello?" Margaret intoned.

"Mom?"

Margaret's breath caught in her throat and she swallowed before being able to breathe again.

"Ginger? Honey, I can hardly believe it's you."

"Merry Christmas, Mom." Her voice was soft, only a muffled whisper, as if she had her lips right against the phone.

"Merry Christmas, sweetheart. Where are

you? I've been trying to find you since I came back from Florida."

"I know. I'm sorry about Granddad, Mom."

Margaret frowned, concerned by the tone of Ginger's voice. She was always so cool, tough as nails, but now there was a hint of tears and a certain sadness.

"It's been hard," Margaret said. "Harder than I ever imagined. Ginger . . . are you all right? You don't sound like yourself."

"Sure, I'm all right," she said, her voice lifting to a brighter level. "I've got a new job and C.J. is going to a new school. It's really nice and it's kind of away from the city. You'd like it Mom and—"

"How is Catherine Jane?"

"She's fine." Ginger's voice was beginning to return now to normal. "She's right here. Would you like to speak to her?"

"Yes, I would." There was a pause and Margaret felt a moment's panic, afraid that they might lose the connection and she would still have no idea where Ginger was. "Wait . . . Ginger."

"Hello." It was Catherine Jane's voice now on the other end of the phone.

"Catherine, sweetheart, how are you? Oh, it's so good to hear your voice."

Margaret could feel her throat tightening. This situation with Ginger and her daughter always made her feel misty-eyed and helpless. She had to keep the thought of her two lost lambs pushed far away into the deepest recesses of her mind. It was the only way she could survive being apart from them. But now, with only one phone call, she felt all the pain of their separation. She knew she would continue to feel it for days.

"I'm fine," Catherine Jane said unemotionally.

C.J.'s words sounded cool and uncaring, so unlike a child's. She had never talked like a little girl, and even now she sounded fifteen rather than ten.

"Do you like your new school? Your mom says it's very nice and—"

"I hate it. The people there are snotty."

Margaret could hear Ginger's voice in the background. She was laughing and there was also the clink of glass against glass.

"Oh, I'm sorry. But give it a little time, honey. Perhaps after you're there awhile it will get better. What's your mom doing now?" Margaret frowned, wondering if the girl would answer the question.

"Making herself a drink, I guess." The

child's voice sounded distant as if she had turned her head away from the phone.

"Catherine, listen to me. I have some Christmas presents here for you. I'm sorry you won't have them to open tomorrow morning. I promise now that I know where you are, I'll put them in the mail the day after Christmas. Will that be okay?"

"Yeah." The girl's voice sounded flat.

"And will you write to me? I'd love to get a letter from my only granddaughter."

"Yeah, I guess."

"All right, I'll be waiting. Goodbye sweetheart and I hope you have a wonderful Christmas. I wish you could be here with us."

"Bye . . . here's Ginger."

"Hey." Ginger's voice sounded bright now and full of fun.

"Darling, are you really all right? Where are you living . . . still with that young man?"

"Tim? Heavens, no! He kicked us out a long time ago."

Margaret's heart dropped as she envisioned Catherine Jane's small face. The connotation of the words "kicked us out" almost broke her heart.

"Then where are you living? I told

Catherine I'd send her Christmas gifts and I—"

"With a friend, Mom. I'm living with a friend, but I won't be here long. I'm getting us a nice new apartment real soon, so don't bother sending anything here. Just send it to general delivery. I'll pick it up there. As soon as I have my new address I'll let you know."

"Do you know where the apartment is? How soon will you be moving? You said Catherine is in a new school. I hope she won't have to move again—"

"Hey, cool it, Mom. I can handle it, okay? I've been living on my own for several years now and we haven't starved or anything. All right?" The testiness and the anger were still in her words, just like always.

"I'm sorry. It's just that I worry about you so much."

"Hey, is Dad there? Let me wish dear old Dad a Merry Christmas."

"Yes, he's here. So is Claire, Cyndi, and Steven."

"Oh well. Great times at the Avery household, huh? The family gathered around the table, sipping nog and singing Christmas carols. How quaint and so very traditional. Gee, I wish I was there." There was a muffled giggle on the other end of the phone.

"Ginger, are you drinking?"

"Oh Mom," she drawled. "Lighten up, will you? It's just one little drink to celebrate Christmas Eve."

"I'd hardly call that an appropriate way to celebrate—"

"Well, you never called anything I did appropriate, huh Mom? Guess that's why I'm out here and you're down there. Can I talk to Dad now?"

Margaret took a deep breath of air and blinked her eyes hard to keep the tears back.

"All right. Merry Christmas Ginger. I love you."

"I love you, too, Mom. And sorry I didn't send any gifts but with no job and everything, it's kind of hard, you know—"

"It doesn't matter . . . I understand. If you need me to help I can—"

"No," Ginger said quickly. "I don't need any help."

"Well . . . here's your dad."

Charles had risen from the table. Everyone by now had figured out who was on the phone. Charles walked toward her and took the phone from her hand. Margaret walked back into the dining room.

Claire stood up and put an arm around her mother's shoulders while Cyndi looked up from the table, her brown eyes wide with sympathy.

"That was Gincy, I take it," Claire said.

"Yes." Margaret nodded, swallowing hard to keep from crying. She didn't know what was wrong with her; she could hardly seem to control herself lately.

Claire wrapped her long arms around her mother and pulled her close, rocking her back and forth like a child. And for the first time in her life, Margaret Avery cried in the arms of one of her children.

Hearing her mother's quiet sobs, Cyndi immediately jumped up from the table and ran to them. She put her arms around her mother and sister.

"She'll be all right, Mom," Cyndi said. "She'll get her life straightened out one of these days."

By now Charles had come back into the room. He stood quietly and with an odd expression, watched his wife and daughters. Margaret turned to stare at him, surprised at the look on his face. It was the nearest thing to understanding she'd ever seen registered in his dark eyes.

"Here now," he said. "What's this? Gincy's fine; there's no need for the female population to have a crying party."

"Your father's right," Margaret said, wiping the tears from her eyes and straightening her shoulders. She had one arm around Claire's waist and one about Cyndi's. She patted each of them on the back. "I'm just glad she called and that I got to wish her and Catherine Jane a Merry Christmas." The words made tears come again and Margaret shook her head, almost angry at herself. "Now, let's finish our meal, so we can open gifts."

Nine

Claire and Cyndi stood outside in front of their parents' house. Most of the beautiful houses on the block were lit with expensive, understated elegance.

"You know, I'd love to put a big old gaudy plastic Santa out here on the lawn," Claire said with a dry laugh.

"Yeah, or a Rudolph with a giant red light bulb for a nose." Cyndi bent over with laughter at the thought. "At least we'd find out if anyone actually lives in any of these houses."

Claire looked up at the clear night sky, noting the bright stars and the thin shape of a crescent moon.

"I wish, just once, it would snow for Christmas."

"I guess we'd have to move farther north for that."

"Cyndi, have you noticed anything peculiar about Mom? Doesn't she seem tense to you, or kind of melancholy?"

"Well, yes, but I suppose that's natural; she was awfully close to Granddad."

Claire frowned and shook her head as she stared out toward the street. "No, I think it's more than that. Like tonight, after she talked to Gincy. I can't remember ever seeing Mom cry like that, can you? You know she never lets anyone see her cry."

"Maybe it's her age."

"Maybe. But maybe she's depressed. I think I should say something to her about it."

"Oh, I wouldn't if I were you. You know how she is, how she hates anyone to think she needs help."

"Hmmm, well. I'm going to talk to her anyway. I'm worried about her. What if she were so depressed she . . . did something to herself?"

"Mom?" Cyndi stared up at her sister with a look of surprise. "Mom would never do anything like that. Why would you even think such a thing?"

"I don't know. I can't really explain it. Except that lately I get this feeling she's trying to . . ." She shrugged, searching for the right phrase.

". . . say goodbye or something."

"Claire," Cyndi cautioned. "Now stop this! You're scaring me."

Claire's face changed and there was a little frown of chagrin across her features. She stepped forward and put her arms around Cyndi.

"I didn't mean to scare you Cyndi-belle. Look, I'll make it a point to talk to Mom tomorrow after Christmas dinner. Maybe, like you said, it's only grief that's making her act different. She does tend to bottle everything up inside herself."

From the street came a low beep as Steven tapped the car horn.

"I'm coming," Cyndi shouted. "Look, I have to go. I'll see you tomorrow. We'll both talk to Mom."

"All right. Good night Cyndi-belle." Claire's voice was light and teasing as she pulled a strand of her sister's blond hair.

Margaret was already in bed when Charles walked out of the dressing room. She glanced at him briefly, noting the new silk pajamas he wore. Did his lover's lingerie shop carry menswear? She practically flinched when he slid into bed beside her.

Charles sighed and nudged his head down into the pillow. He was lying on his back with his hands across his chest.

"Bed feels good," he muttered. "I'm tired." He turned his head to look at Margaret. "You must be tired too; you worked hard today."

"I enjoyed it." She didn't look away from the book in her hands.

"What's that you're reading?"

"A romance novel."

"Aren't you a little old to be reading that silly stuff?"

There was a note of teasing in his voice and Margaret knew he was only trying to be funny. She also sensed he was trying to pull her out of her shell and make her laugh. She wondered why he bothered. She turned to stare at him coldly.

"A woman is never too old for romance."

She could feel his eyes upon her as she went back to reading. She had depended so much upon his inability to read her thoughts or even to care. She had expected his usual blithe behavior. She found herself hoping he wasn't about to change now, not before January fifth anyway.

"Tonight was nice," he said with a sigh of satisfaction. "Steven is a fine young man; I couldn't ask for a better son-in-law. He and

Cyndi seem very happy together, don't you think?"

Margaret frowned, thinking of what Cyndi had told her on the plane. Despite that confession, Cyndi did seem happy. Margaret hoped that didn't mean her daughter had learned to hide her feelings, too. God, I don't want her relationship with Steven to be like mine and Charles's.

"Yes," she answered noncommittally.

"And I know Claire resents me. She's based this illusion about career men on all my shortcomings. But that's okay. I admire her spunk, her independence. She's a very beautiful young woman, any man in Atlanta would be lucky to get her."

Margaret smiled. Beneath Charles's observations she sensed him patting himself on the back, as if everything good about Cyndi and Claire was attributed somehow to him.

"You're not very talkative tonight," he said, turning to look at her again. "Are you worried about Gincy?"

Margaret felt the pain stab at her chest again, and she wondered if Ginger would ever come home. Would she ever be her little girl again?

"Yes, I am worried. I think she was drinking tonight."

"Hell, Margaret, it's Christmas Eve. Everyone has a drink on Christmas Eve."

She turned and stared at him with a cold glint in her gray eyes.

"Everyone except the saintly Margaret Avery, that is," he snorted humorously, still staring at his wife. "Gincy's all right; she's just different, that's all. A lot of people our age have children who live in a different part of the country. It's normal, darling."

"How can you say that? You know very well that Ginger's leaving was not normal. She was bitter and hurt. I think she still is. She thinks we let her down."

"For God's sake, are you going to bring that up again? The girl has been gone for five years. Just leave it alone, Margaret. Let her live the way she wants. If Las Vegas and nightclubs is what she wants, then why can't you be happy for her?"

"Because *she's* not happy, Charles." Margaret could feel the heat rush to her face as she turned to confront him. "And if you could ever see past the surface of anything, you'd know that."

He closed his eyes wearily. She could see the displeased stretch of his lips beneath his mustache. Then he sighed and turned over, his back to her.

123

"Margaret, you're tired. You need to get some sleep; we have a big day tomorrow."

She wanted to scream at him. Her hands actually ached to strike him, to beat and scream at him until she made him feel something . . . anything. And she wanted to confront him about his mistress. Instead she threw the covers back and stepped out of bed, reaching for a white silk robe that lay nearby.

"Where are you going?" he asked, turning to look over his shoulder with an impatient frown.

"Downstairs. To fix myself a cup of tea."

As she left the room she heard him mumble and thump the pillow. Then there was the click of a light switch and the room grew dark.

Later when Margaret came back upstairs to bed, she went into the guest room. She didn't know why she had continued to sleep in the same bed with Charles except that she hadn't wanted him to suspect she knew anything.

But lying in bed alone, she knew that wasn't the real reason. Had she been hoping subconsciously that he would reach for her one night and confess and beg her forgiveness? That somehow, after all these years, he would miraculously come to his senses and realize what a wonderful wife she was?

"And they lived happily ever after," she whispered.

Silently in the darkness, she shook her head against the pillow as tears burned her eyes.

"Dream on," she sighed. "Maybe I *have* been reading too many romances."

On Christmas day both Cyndi and Claire were early. Margaret smiled, thinking how they turned the kitchen into a warm place, filled with humor as well as the mouth watering scents of cooking.

The three of them looked up when Charles and Steven came through, each of them pulling on a jacket.

"Where are you going?" Margaret asked. "Dinner is almost ready."

"We won't be gone long. There's a house for sale just a couple of streets over. I want to take Steven by to see it."

Margaret saw the look on Cyndi's face as she stared at Steven. Worse yet, he seemed blatantly unaware that his actions disturbed his wife.

After they left, Cyndi turned immediately back to buttering the rolls, just as if nothing had happened.

"Why don't you speak up for yourself, Cyndi?" Claire asked, wagging a spoon in her sister's direction.

Cyndi shrugged. She looked so small and

vulnerable in her red angora sweater and skirt. Like a little girl, Margaret thought, at a party with no one to talk to.

"Steven's the boss," she muttered, still not looking up.

"Oh my God!" Claire tossed the spoon on the counter. "Has the man brainwashed you? Don't you know that women have rights now? This is not the Dark Ages, Cyndi; women don't have to be chattels to their husbands any more."

"Claire, it's Christmas. Please don't be profane." Margaret eyed her daughter cautiously.

"I don't even know what chattel means," Cyndi muttered.

"Oh gee," Claire began sarcastically. "It means slave, ninny. It means that Steven is not the boss; no one is the boss for heaven's sake. You have as much right to express yourself as he does. And if you wanted to go look at the house, why didn't you just say so?"

"We can't afford a house, especially one in this neighborhood."

"Then, why didn't you say that? You know how Daddy is . . . he'll have the agent out here on Christmas day. And you'll be the owner of a house you don't want and can't afford."

"Steven wouldn't do that . . . without consulting me."

"Oh sure."

"Girls, please," Margaret said. "Let's put the food on the table. No one is going to buy a house. And this is something Cyndi and Steven should decide between them, Claire."

With a slight quirk of her lips, Claire glared at her mother. Her green eyes were wide and accusing.

"You should say something to Dad. All he's doing is causing trouble between them, Mom."

"I'll speak to him Claire. After dinner."

Claire gave her a look that said she didn't believe her, but she turned silently and began to gather the dishes of food to take into the dining room.

The two men came back, stamping their feet against the cold. Steven was grinning and turned boyishly toward Cyndi. He moved behind her and put his arms around her small waist.

"You should see that house, Cyndi. It's out of this world."

"Steven, you know we can't afford a house like that." Her voice was quiet, as if she didn't want anyone else to hear.

"I know . . . I know." His eyes behind the dark rimmed glasses were bright with excitement. "But your dad says I should be thinking about it . . . you know, planning for the future.

And this is the kind of neighborhood that could really help someone like me."

"You mean a young, upwardly mobile, and totally ambitious Atlanta lawyer?" Claire's voice rang sarcastically through the kitchen.

Steven frowned at her, then turned his attention once again to his wife.

"What's wrong, honey?"

"Nothing," Cyndi said with a smile at her husband. Her brown eyes glittered brightly and she reached up to stroke his cheek. "Everything's fine."

Their meal was quiet. No matter what conversation Margaret tried to initiate, it fell flat. She wondered, as she had so many times before, what was wrong with her family. Why couldn't they seem to be happy together?

After dinner, Margaret and the girls began to load the dishes into the dishwasher. They were all very quiet until Claire stepped toward her sister and put an arm about her waist.

"I'm sorry Cyndi-belle. I didn't mean to hurt your feelings earlier. I just want you to be happy, that's all."

"I am happy," Cyndi said with a sad, little smile.

Margaret could see Claire's effort to keep quiet. She seemed to grit her teeth to keep from replying.

They all worked silently for a few more moments before Claire spoke again.

"Mom, Cyndi and I were talking last night. You seemed awfully sad. Is everything all right with you? You don't seem like yourself lately."

Margaret was speechless. She couldn't think of one word of denial that would make any sense, or that Claire would believe.

"I don't? Well, I . . . I guess . . ."

She stopped and stared at her daughters. They were both very still and waiting as they gazed at her. She could see the concern on their faces, and Margaret knew she could not bear to deceive them for one moment longer.

"Sit down girls," she said, moving to a small table in the corner of the kitchen.

Claire and Cyndi looked at one another, as if their worst fears had been confirmed. Then they sat quietly at the table, staring across at their mother who distractedly twisted a dishtowel in her hands.

"I should have told you this before. Maybe I was hoping it would never come to pass, that somehow your father would . . ." She looked up at them and saw the worry in their eyes. "I'm filing for a divorce. I haven't told you before because your father doesn't know yet."

"Mom," Cyndi whispered, her eyes dark with denial.

Claire reached across the table and took her mother's hands, staring hard as she did into Margaret's face.

"What's happened, Mom?"

Margaret sighed and closed her eyes briefly. "Nothing that hasn't happened many times in the past. But it's different this time; I'm different. Perhaps it's because Granddad died and I see how short life really is. I'm just not willing to live this way any longer." She shrugged and gazed into her daughter's incredulous eyes.

"But Mom," Cyndi said, her voice low. "You love Daddy, don't you? How can you divorce him if you love him?"

"Oh Cyndi," Margaret said. "Honey, I'm not even sure I know what love is anymore."

"It's him, isn't it?" Claire's voice was cool as she sat back in the chair and crossed her arms across her dark green sweater. "It's Daddy. Who's the woman this time, Mother? Anyone we know?"

Margaret frowned, pain in her gray eyes. She hated seeing Claire become so bitter. Perhaps she should have suggested counseling for her years ago, after the experience with her father.

She swallowed hard, wanting to appear calm and unemotional. She didn't want to turn Claire further against Charles, even after all he had done to her.

"Actually I'm not sure who the woman is. I overheard her and your father talking on the phone one morning. He thought I had already left the house. I hate having to ask you to carry such a secret for awhile, but I must. Until I have the proof I need, I hope you won't mention this to anyone. Not even to Steven, Cyndi."

"What do you mean . . . proof?" Cyndi asked, her brown eyes turning cool and hard.

"My lawyer has hired a private investigator."

"To spy on Daddy? For God's sake, Mother, don't tell me you have some goon following him around, taking pictures, and . . ." She shook her short blond hair and frowned at her mother. "I can't believe this."

"Yes, Cyndi, that's exactly what I've done. I'm sorry if you don't approve, but I've had enough finally. I don't intend to let your father squirm his way out of it this time." Margaret's struggle to be calm vanished and her voice became hard with determination.

Cyndi only shook her head, as if she could not quite believe what she was hearing.

"You're doing it for the money, aren't you? And the house. You think if you can find someone to spy on Daddy and take pictures of him in a compromising situation, you will get everything."

"Cyndi . . . is that what you think of me? Do you honestly not know me any better than that? Good heavens, I don't want this house . . . this monstrosity your father had built without so much as a question about what I wanted."

"Mom, don't upset yourself," Claire said. "If Cyndi chooses to side with Daddy as usual, don't let it influence your decision. Personally I think it's about time. I admire you for going through with it. He won't make it easy for you, you know."

"No," Margaret said. "I don't expect he will."

"I can't believe the two of you. How can you talk about Daddy that way? He loves you Mom. You know he's always loved you. Why can't you try to understand him instead of always condemning him? So what if he's had little flirtations in the past? That doesn't mean he loves you any less."

"Good grief," Claire groaned. "You sound just like *him*. He must have whispered those words in your ear while you were still in the cradle."

"He's your father, too, Claire," Cyndi snapped. "And if you would stop thinking about yourself long enough, you might see that he loves you, too."

"Yeah, well if he loved me one fourth as

much as he loves himself, I'd be a happy child, wouldn't I?"

"Girls, please," Margaret said, her chin trembling. It seemed that every word lately was cause for an argument. She simply could not stand another minute of it.

"I'm sorry, Mom," Claire said. "I know this is hard for you and I want you to know that I'm here for you. Whatever you decide to do, I'm here."

"Thank you, baby."

Margaret's eyes turned automatically to Cyndi. Her daughter only lifted her chin stubbornly and her full pink lips were flattened into a line of rebellion.

"I think you're wrong, Mom. If you cared anything about our family, you wouldn't do this."

"I'm sorry, Cyndi. Sorry you feel that way. But nothing you say is going to change my mind. I'm divorcing your father and I'm going to live the kind of life I want . . . before it's too late."

Ten

Just after noon on January fifth, Margaret sat in the parking lot outside Jane Ann Tilton's law office. It had begun raining that morning and now tiny pellets of ice mingled with the cold rain. It sprayed down on the windshield in a quiet hiss and scattered in sparkling bits across the shining black hood of Margaret's car.

She paid little attention to the sleet or to anything else around her; she felt too sick to notice. The nausea she felt was reflected in her face, and in the dark circles beneath her eyes. She sat quietly, unmoving. She was afraid she might actually be sick right there in the parking lot.

Margaret leaned her head back against the headrest and closed her eyes, then opened them immediately as the car seemed to spin beneath her. What was happening to her? Was she having a heart attack along with everything else that had happened?

She began to talk silently to herself and to take long, slow breaths of air. As she blew the air from her lungs she murmured to herself, "It's all right . . . it's all right."

Finally the beat of her heart slowed to a near normal pace and she felt herself breathing more easily.

She turned her head to stare at the brown manila envelope that lay on the seat beside her. Suspecting Charles of having an affair and actually seeing the proof herself were two very different things. She had been totally unprepared for this powerful response.

With a wry grimace, she remembered her lawyer's reaction.

"This part is always the hardest. Would you like a drink, Mrs. Avery?"

Margaret had only shaken her head mutely, her eyes glued to the pictures spread on the desk before her.

So now she had them, had the evidence that would silence Charles's attempts to persuade everyone she was imagining it all.

Actually in retrospect, she wondered if it had been necessary. She wasn't asking for the moon after all, only her share of what they had built together over the years. Surely Charles wouldn't begrudge her that; he was not an ungenerous man.

Slowly her hand reached toward the envelope beside her. She picked it up and slid the pictures out onto her lap.

The dark-haired girl in the photos was young, probably no older than Cyndi and Claire. The sight of her with Charles sickened Margaret.

Attorney Tilton had told Margaret that the girl's name was Shelley Bainbridge. Her father was head of the Commerce Bank in Atlanta. Margaret was acquainted with him and his wife; she probably had even seen their daughter at the club at one time or another. She wondered if Mr. and Mrs. Bainbridge had any idea who their daughter was seeing.

She stared hard at the pictures. There were several of Charles at a shopping mall, the location of the lingerie shop, no doubt. He and the small, doll-like brunette were always arm and arm. Once he was bending to kiss her upturned lips; the girl was looking at Charles as if he were some golden idol come to life.

Margaret laughed, the sound hollow in the car. She picked up the next photo. This one was obviously taken through a window, but it was the most revealing. Charles and the girl were locked together in a torrid embrace. She was wearing a white teddy that left little to the imagination, even in the slightly distorted telescopic picture. Charles's hands were cupped around her slender buttocks as he held her tight against him.

Margaret swallowed hard, feeling sick again, then closed her eyes for a moment against the disturbing visions.

There were other pictures, Charles and the girl together in a car, kissing good night, more taken through the window of a house or apartment. Those were the most intimate and they were the ones that made Margaret actually feel like crying.

She gathered up all the pictures and quickly jammed them back into the envelope and tossed it onto the seat. After she showed them to Charles, she never intended to look at them again.

She turned on the ignition, then turned it off again as the tears came. All the pain and anguish she'd held inside these past weeks came pouring out. All the attempts she'd made at keeping a calm appearance seemed so useless and futile now. She laid her head against the leather steering wheel and sobbed until there seemed nothing left inside her.

It was over. Thirty-three years of marriage, of being a family, were simply wiped away. She felt helpless to understand the reasons. Did all men feel the need for younger women as they grew older? Did it make them feel youthful and virile again?

Margaret shook her head, wonderingly. All she knew was that she felt terribly inadequate and old. She felt at that moment as if she were worth nothing, either as a wife or a woman. She ached enough from those feelings to die.

All that was left now was to go home, change into something warm and wait for Charles. Tonight he would know she was divorcing him. She just wanted it to be over.

After arriving home and changing into a warm emerald velour lounging outfit, Margaret called Charles at his office. She knew he would not be home until late if she didn't make a fuss.

"Sure, I can come home early. What's up?"

"I just need to talk to you, that's all."

"Okay." He hesitated for a moment and Margaret could almost hear the wheels turning in his head. "Is there anything wrong? You're not sick or something . . ."

A sad smile trembled on her lips.

"I'm fine," she assured him. "See you around six o'clock?"

"Yeah. How about I stop at Antonio's . . . bring home some lasagna?"

The thought of lasagna made the nausea rise again in Margaret's throat, but she shook it off. "Good . . . that will be fine."

She knew it would be a very long afternoon and she didn't want to make it any worse by sitting and waiting. Instead she went upstairs and began to sort through her closet. She had bought storage boxes and tucked them away. Now she unfolded and assembled them and began to pack the clothes she would take with her. The rest she stuffed into a plastic bag to take to the homeless shelter.

She smiled as she held up a white dress trimmed with bright green and yellow plaid. With a sigh she crammed the Yves Saint-Laurent original into a plastic bag; some homeless lady would be very stylish indeed.

She took another box and filled it with pictures, mementos from her daughters' childhoods. That was the hardest part for her, seeing all the good times in pictures. The times when she and Charles were together with their children. She had actually thought they were the perfect family then and that they would be together forever.

Angrily, she poured the rest of the pictures into the box and quickly clamped the lid on top. There was no need making it any harder than necessary today, facing Charles would be difficult enough.

There would be plenty of time to go through these later. Once she was home. . . .

Home . . . the very sound of the word in her mind brought a kind of peacefulness. She felt she had to be careful not to say it too often; she was afraid somehow it too would become meaningless.

Now, sitting on the floor of her bedroom, Margaret could almost smell the warm scent of pine and feel the Florida wind in her hair. She effortlessly conjured up the small house in Ocala, envisioned the wide expanse of sandy yard and the surrounding palms that stirred and whispered in the breeze.

She wanted to go *home*. It had become like a torch burning inside her, a promise of relief from the pain she felt. She could hardly wait to finish the ordeal with Charles and leave Atlanta for good.

It was not long after six o'clock when Margaret heard Charles arrive. She listened to the low hum of the garage door and the slam of his car door.

She was nervous and her hands were shaking. She could feel the anger in her threatening to rise up and betray her. She wanted to be calm, wanted to be able to say exactly what she needed to say, without tears and without falling apart.

Before Charles came into the kitchen, Margaret whirled and went into the den, forcing herself to sit and wait until he came to her.

He was smiling when he stuck his head around the door, that smile almost broke her heart. It reminded her too much of the old times.

"Hey, you hungry? I brought the lasagna if you want to eat it before it gets cold."

"No, Charles . . . I . . . we need to talk."

He frowned and pulled himself, with a jaunty bounce, around the doorframe and into the room.

"This sounds serious," he said, his smile easy

140

and confident as he stood looking down at her.

She pulled the envelope toward her and handed it to him.

"It is serious, Charles."

His laugh was short and forced. She wondered if he had any idea what she was about to say.

"What's this?" He took the envelope, still looking at her.

When she said nothing, he opened the envelope and pulled the pictures out. Slowly the smile on his face changed to disbelief and anger. He swallowed and shook his head as if he did not understand. When he looked at her, she could see how hard he tried to hide his anger and his surprise. But it didn't quite succeed.

"What the hell is this, Margaret?"

"I'm filing for a divorce, Charles." Her voice was calm, although her entire body was trembling and her teeth threatened to chatter as she spoke.

He grunted as if what she said amused him. Then he whirled and took a step toward the fireplace where a small fire blazed.

"Go ahead," she said calmly. "Burn them. There are more copies at the lawyer's office."

"You've gone that far with this? You've hired a goddamned lawyer and had me followed? Jesus Christ, Margaret! Have you completely lost your mind?"

"On the contrary, Charles. I think I finally found it."

He sighed and slammed the pictures down on the table. His hand went nervously to his mustache as he stalked back and forth in front of her. He had always been intimidating and Margaret felt herself shaking at the task of opposing him.

"You've gotten a bit underhanded with this, haven't you? A bit sneaky? Huh?" He whirled around to stare down at her.

Margaret stood up and stared directly into his blazing eyes, then she lifted her chin defiantly.

"Did you think that was an exclusive trait that belonged only to you?"

He gritted his teeth and breathed deeply through his nose. "This attitude does not become you. If you wanted to confront me with this, why didn't you just ask me? Why did you have to bring a lawyer into it and make me a laughingstock with these ridiculous pictures?"

"I can't believe even you would ask such a question," she said.

"Is this what you've been pouting about these past weeks? Is this why you moved out of our bedroom?"

"Yes!"

How dare he try to make it sound as if nothing had happened? As if his affair was something trivial that they could discuss calmly.

"I moved out because you are having an affair. One of many that you've carried on during our marriage. But *this* time will be the *last*. I don't intend to waste another moment of my life on someone who doesn't give a damn."

"Doesn't give a damn? My God, how can you say that? Look what I've given you . . . the kind of life I've provided for you. I love you Margaret . . . I've always loved you. This girl means nothing to me, less than nothing. Can't you see that? Yes, I had an affair! I'll admit that to you freely. Do you want me to tell you why I can admit it freely?"

If the pain hadn't been so great, Margaret might have laughed aloud. He sounded just like he did in court when he began his summation to the jury.

"Oh, I think I know why. You think you can squirm your way out of it, just the way you always did in the past. But I'm through listening to your lies, Charles. Do you understand?" She stood up and started to walk past him.

Charles grabbed her arm and pulled her around and into his arms. She stood stiffly, unmoving as he kissed her, grinding his mouth against hers in a mock passionate kiss. She deliberately kept her mouth closed and unyielding.

When he pulled away, there was only the tiniest glint of surprise in his eyes before he managed to disguise it.

"I can admit it freely because I love you," he said in an emotional whisper. "I don't want to lose you, baby. I was wrong to become involved with this girl; I know that now. But she meant nothing."

Margaret stared at him blankly.

"When I behave this way . . . when I do these things . . . it's nothing personal. It's nothing against you. Don't you know that by now?"

Her mouth flew open. For the first time, she felt her control leaving her.

"Nothing personal?" she screamed. "Of course it's personal, you stupid bastard. Every woman you've ever flung in my face was personal to me. Every betrayal hurt so badly I was devastated for months . . . years! They diminished me as a wife and woman . . . as your lover. My God! How dare you stand here and tell me it was nothing personal!"

Charles was stunned. He even took a step backward away from her blazing eyes.

"Margaret . . . calm down. Please darling, just calm down. I—"

"I will not calm down! I'm only going to tell you this once. Then I never want to discuss it with you again. You have hurt me." She began to cry, the sobs rising from somewhere so deep inside that she didn't even know where they came from. "You have ripped my heart out and tossed it aside as if it meant nothing! I hate you for that. What love I ever felt for you is gone, Charles, and I hate you for that, too." By now she was crying almost hysterically.

Charles could only stare at her, unable to believe this was the woman he had lived with for thirty-three years. He had never seen her so distraught or so out of control. There was fear in his dark eyes as he watched her unravel before him.

"Margaret . . . honey . . ." He reached forward.

She jerked away from him. "No! Don't be kind to me now, you bastard. You are a sorry excuse for a man, Charles Avery. You have lied and cheated without thought or conscience. You're cold and unloving, worse than that you have humiliated me more times than I care to remember. There is no loyalty in you or you would not allow everyone in Atlanta to see how far down you have placed me in your life. But you reveled in it! Bragged about your exploits. Did you think that made you some kind of hero to your friends? A big man?" Then Margaret began to laugh irrationally.

"You're not a man. You're a pathetic little worm . . . you're a user. The only good thing I can say about you right now is that you taught me well. No man will ever use me like this again!"

Eleven

As Margaret packed for the trip to Florida she told herself to think of it as a vacation, as only an excursion from which she could return any time she wished. That would make it easier to leave Claire and Cyndi. Although with Cyndi, she wondered if anything she did would make a difference.

Cyndi was still barely speaking to her. As much as Margaret tried to tell herself it didn't matter, the ache in her heart told her differently.

It had been a week since Margaret's confrontation with Charles. She had needed the time to get her things together and to take care of transferring some funds into a separate account until the divorce was final.

Charles had ranted and raved that night. He had blustered about how she could not make it without him.

"Do you really think you'll be satisfied living in

the sticks again, Margaret?" he challenged. "You're not a country girl any more. I saw to that. I took you from the sticks and put you in an elegant home, dressed you in the finest clothes money could buy. No . . . you'll never be happy going back to that; you know it and I know it. You'll be back; it's only a matter of time."

"Oh Charles, please," she said. "You make me sound like some rag doll you rescued from the trash heap."

"I don't know what the hell has come over you," he said, staring at her with disbelief.

"Some sense has come over me." She hadn't even bothered to look at him, but simply rose and left the room.

And now, a week later as she packed, she hoped he would not make another scene. Not with the girls downstairs to hear it.

Charles had not gone to the office and Margaret supposed she should be flattered. She could not remember him ever staying home, for any reason. Not even when the girls were born.

She closed the luggage and turned to look about the room. There was hardly anything in the house that she really wanted, except for a few odds and ends, things the girls had given her on Christmas or birthdays. She felt a small twinge of pleasure at the thought of decorating the house in Florida exactly as she pleased. What freedom she would feel, arranging things just for herself, with

147

no thought of what was stylish or who it would impress.

With a little smile, she began taking things from the wall and placing them in a storage box. When she finished she walked through all the other rooms in the house, gathering only those things that had a special and personal meaning.

Downstairs Claire saw what Margaret was doing and began to follow, talking casually as if it were any ordinary day.

"Do you want these candlesticks, Mom? They'd look nice on the cypress mantelpiece in Granddad's house."

"Yes, they would, wouldn't they?"

Claire placed the brass candlesticks in the crook of her arm and continued to follow her mother. Cyndi stood at the doorway, watching her sister and mother with sad, accusing eyes.

"Daddy bought those for you," Cyndi said.

"Yes, I believe he did." Margaret moved on about the room.

"What about your books? You can't possibly get all these in the car. Shall I pack them up and send them down to you later?" Claire was standing in front of the floor to ceiling bookshelves in the den.

"No, leave them. I'm taking a few with me, some of my favorites. I'll buy new ones."

"You'll have plenty of time for reading."

"Oh, I suppose I'll find a job somewhere."

Cyndi made a low noise in her throat.

"Doing what? You've never worked."

Margaret turned and stared at Cyndi. "I'll find something, I'm sure. I worked at a newspaper when your father and I were first married."

"She was the most beautiful reporter on the staff."

Charles's voice from the doorway made her jump. She turned to find him staring at her in an odd way. There appeared to be actual tenderness in his eyes. Margaret only gazed at him suspiciously, he could make even a look seem theatrical.

"That was because I was the only female."

The girls stared back and forth between their parents as if they expected a confrontation. Charles only smiled and turned to walk back toward the kitchen.

"Mom, he was only trying to be nice," Cyndi said.

"Your father never does anything without a reason, Cyndi. I can't afford to accept his compliments at face value any more."

"I don't understand you," Cyndi said, almost wailing. "You have turned into someone I don't even know."

"I'm no different than I ever was. I love you and Claire and Ginger just as much as ever. But your father and I simply cannot live together any more. I don't know what's so hard to understand." Margaret pushed a cushion back into place on the sofa.

"I just want to know one thing. Does this have anything to do with that man you met in Florida?"

The question was loud in the room and seemed to hang in midair as Claire turned to stare at her mother as well.

"What man are you talking about?" Margaret's voice had grown very cold.

Beneath her casual, outward appearance, the thought of Jonathan set her heart racing. Seeing him again was not something she had let herself think about.

"Jonathan Bradford. You know perfectly well who I mean."

"This has to do, Cyndi, with your father having an affair. And it's not the first one, I might add." Margaret kept her voice deliberately slow and cold as she continued to move about the room, glancing at walls and tables.

"What man?" Claire said, staring at her mother. "Who's Jonathan Bradford?"

"Oh, for heaven's sake," Margaret said with a sigh. "Your sister is only being dramatic. Jonathan Bradford was Dad's neighbor and friend. I'm sure you remember me telling you about him. He's the one who called and told me Dad was . . . that he had passed away. He is a very nice man."

"He liked you," Cyndi accused. "He hardly

took his eyes off you that night at the funeral home. And you said yourself, he's someone from your past."

"Someone from . . . ? Cyndi, really. You make it sound so clandestine or something. The 'past,' as you call it, happened when we were children, over thirty-five years ago. Now stop this. The problems between your father and me have absolutely nothing to do with Jonathan Bradford."

Margaret's hands were shaking. Her face felt stiff and unyielding. She knew she was probably blushing.

"Mom?" Claire came and took her mother by the shoulders, turning her around to face her.

"Claire," Margaret said with a disbelieving shake of her head. "I saw this man for three days. He was a dear friend of my father's and he treated both Cyndi and me kindly and with respect. That's all." She turned to Cyndi and frowned at her. "Cyndi is grasping at straws. She can't admit that her father is responsible for all that's happened. Or that it was his choice to have an affair, the same choice he's made through most of our marriage. Certainly neither I nor Jonathan Bradford had anything to do with that."

Claire smiled as she put her arms around Margaret, satisfied with her explanation.

Margaret felt a bit bemused as she looked at Claire and Cyndi. Sometimes she felt as if she had two extra mothers in these blond beauties. That was a very strange and not always pleasant feeling.

Cyndi whirled and walked out of the room. Going to her father, Margaret thought.

"Don't worry about Cyndi-belle. You know how sensitive she is. It takes a while for her to cope sometimes, especially when it has anything to do with Dad."

"I wasn't aware she'd ever reached that point with him . . . coping." Margaret knew she sounded bitter, but she couldn't help it. She simply could not understand why Cyndi always defended Charles. It hurt to see how they both trivialized his affairs.

"Sure she has. She knows he's wrong; she just hates to admit it."

"Well, perhaps it will be easier for her after I'm gone." She turned to look into Claire's sympathetic green eyes. "I never wanted to come between either of you and your father. I expect you to continue a good relationship with him. This problem is between us and should not change anything as far as his being a father to you. I hope you know that."

"In my case, it wasn't that good to start with."

Margaret shook her head wearily as she gazed at Claire. "I'm sorry, honey." She turned to glance at the room once more. "I don't know . . . sometimes I think I'm just losing it. I don't know any more which way is up and which is down."

"I guess that's only natural," Claire said with a

tug at her mother's sleeve. "You try to act so calm and cool all the time. It's all right to admit you're confused and afraid too, you know."

Margaret turned to her with a wry grin. "You mean it's not my age that makes me confused?"

"Absolutely not."

They both laughed together, the sound ringing through the den and out toward the kitchen where Charles and Cyndi stood.

Cyndi shook her short blond hair and brushed the tears from her eyes.

"I can't imagine what they have to laugh about," she said.

"Neither can I." Charles stepped to the sink and dashed the cold coffee from his cup. "Evidently your mother is ecstatic to be ridding herself of me."

"Oh, Dad." Cyndi moved toward him and wrapped her arms around his waist. She rested her head against his chest. "She doesn't mean it. I think she would stay if only you would—"

Charles pulled himself away from his daughter. His face was closed and angry as he stared down into her tearful, brown eyes.

"If I would what? Apologize? Beg her forgiveness? I've already done that over and over again. Hell, what does she want from me? Am I the only man in the world to make a mistake?"

"A mistake?"

"Don't be coy, Cyndi. I'm sure your mother has

already told you about Shelley. It was a mistake, that's all, and I've admitted that. It's something I promised your mother I'd never repeat. But she insists on using those pictures against me in court and—"

"Pictures . . . ? Daddy, what pictures?"

There was a sneer on Charles's face as he looked into his daughter's eyes.

"She hasn't told you, has she? About hiring a detective . . . having me followed? I guess she's too embarrassed to admit to her daughter that her actions are less than saintly."

"Mom does have pictures? Of you and this . . . this woman?" Cyndi knew that her mother had hired a detective, but she couldn't accept that he had collected real evidence.

"You make it sound worse than it really is. This woman is Shelley Bainbridge and she's hardly a tramp. She comes from an excellent family; she has her own business and—"

"Shelley Bainbridge? Mom has pictures of you and Shelley Bainbridge?" The look on Cyndi's face was one of horror. Her skin had grown noticeably pale as she stared up at her father. "Dad, she's my age; we were in junior high together."

Charles knew immediately he had made a mistake. In trying to gain Cyndi's sympathy he had said too much. He had miscalculated Margaret's behavior when he expected she had already divulged to the girls every embarrassing detail of his affair.

"Sweetie, don't look at me that way. It meant nothing. I know I hurt your mother, but it's all over now. All I want is a chance to start over with her. You understand, don't you? You do believe me, don't you, baby?"

Cyndi's face was filled with pain and confusion, but her dad's pleading eyes and the tremor in his voice was more than she could take. She stepped toward him and put her arms about his waist again.

"Of course, Daddy. Of course I believe you."

Part Two

Today

Ah! little at best can all our hopes avail us
To lift this sorrow, or cheer us, when in
   the dark,
    Unwilling, alone we embark,
And the things we have seen and have
   known and have heard of, fail us.

— Robert Bridges

Twelve

The sun was shining as Margaret drove south on Interstate 75 out of Atlanta. Traffic was beginning to pick up, but luckily, since she was going out of town, her lane was relatively clear.

She felt like singing this morning. And that, in itself, was a surprise.

Even though she was packed and ready to go last night, Claire had persuaded her to wait till morning to leave.

"What difference will one more night make? I hate the thought of you on the highway at night, looking for a place to stay after dark. And what if you have car trouble?"

Margaret knew she was right, but she was so anxious to go that she could hardly force herself to remain another night. But finally, for Claire's peace of mind, she agreed.

She had told both her daughters goodbye then.

"There's no reason for either of you to get up and come over here tomorrow morning. I'll probably leave early. I'll call you as soon as I get to the house at Ocala."

"Everything will be fine here, Mom," Claire said with a pointed look at Cyndi. "It will make it easier knowing you're at Granddad's house. Somehow that makes it seem you're not so far away."

For all Claire's outward good cheer, her green eyes sparkled with unshed tears. Margaret held her tight against her and kissed her cheek.

"I'll call you. You let me know when there's a new man in your life. Maybe even Brian?"

They both laughed. Then Margaret turned to Cyndi, whose big brown eyes had always gotten her anything she wanted. She was looking at her mother now with those pleading puppy dog eyes.

"Cyndi . . ." Margaret opened her arms and the girl stepped into her embrace. "Sweetheart, please . . . try to be happy for me."

But Cyndi only nodded. Her chin trembled slightly and Margaret cupped the girl's face in her hands.

"I love you. And I love Steven. I won't be far away, so the both of you must come down real soon and spend a few days with me. You could use a vacation. Tell Steven I'll take him fishing."

That brought a smile to Cyndi's face. The thought of her elegantly clad mother fishing was too funny to be true.

160

"I can fish," Margaret insisted, lifting her head as if offended.

"I love you," Cyndi said. "Call me as soon as you get there."

"I will. I love you both."

She kissed the girls once again and watched as Cyndi turned to Charles.

"I'll call you, Dad."

But Claire had marched out the door, not even bothering to tell Charles goodbye.

Margaret gripped the steering wheel more tightly as a huge eighteen wheeler passed her. She was nearing an interchange and traffic was getting heavy again.

Once she was past the distracting traffic of the small community, she began to think again about her last evening alone with Charles. She couldn't help the tears that came to her eyes.

It had been like an ending to a part of her, as if someone had hacked off a piece of her body. It didn't seem to matter that her leaving was necessary, or that it was something she had begun to long for night and day. Severing the marriage still hurt terribly.

Charles had turned to her in the kitchen. And looking into his face, she felt a spark of the old love she'd had for him so long ago. He *was like* a little boy, and this time she thought he wasn't acting.

"You're not really going through with this, are

you?" His dark, pleading eyes, so much like Cyndi's, reflected genuine hurt and bewilderment.

"Yes, Charles. I am."

"But you'll be so alone in Florida, cut off from all your friends, from your daughters. You never liked being alone."

"But I always *was* alone," she said pointedly.

"All right," he said, raking his hand through his graying hair. "I admit it. I did leave you and the girls alone too much. I was too wrapped up in my work and too ambitious. I can see that now. But it's not too late for me to change. It's not —"

"Yes, Charles, it is too late." She almost felt sorry for him then, fool that she was and her voice showed that pity. "It's too late for me."

"No," he said, pulling her into his arms. "I don't believe that. Let me try to —"

Margaret stepped quickly out of his arms, moving so that the kitchen island was between them.

"Charles, don't do this. I don't know how you expect me to behave when you say such things. So I'll be blunt with you . . . I don't want to try any more. And I don't think I care that you're willing to change. You see, I've become a different person through the years. I had to change to survive. And that person, the one who learned to like being alone, the one who came to depend on herself, she even grew in the process. I find that I like her; I wouldn't change her if I could."

He stared at her, aware of a sparkle in her eyes that he had never noticed before. There was a stiffness in her chin that once had trembled and yielded with his pleading. She *had* changed, and he had been too busy to notice.

She smiled tenderly as if he were a child.

"Charles, this is what you've always wanted . . . your freedom. You won't have to pretend any more; you won't have to lie about where you are or what you're doing. I would think this is a tremendous burden lifted from your shoulders."

"How can you say that?" He shook his head and stared into her unyielding eyes across the island that separated them. "My God, what have I done? I feel as if I'm losing the best thing in my life. I took you for granted, Margaret, thinking you would always be here I guess and—"

"You still have your daughters. And if I were you, I'd really take advantage of that." She had the feeling he still didn't grasp what was happening.

He nodded mutely before lifting his eyes toward her again. "At least keep the house. There's no reason for you to leave Atlanta and your home. I'll gladly concede the house to you if that's what it takes to keep you here."

She laughed. He really didn't understand.

"It's not what I want Charles. This . . ." she waved her arm about the beautiful, state-of-the-art kitchen. ". . . this was never what I wanted. I wanted a husband and a family. I raised the girls practically on my own. Now that they're grown, there's nothing to keep me here. I don't want the house, Charles, and

I don't want to live in Atlanta. I want to go home."

Charles had watched, openmouthed as she turned and walked out of the kitchen.

She smiled as she drove, thinking about it. It had been a moment of bittersweet triumph for her, but she had gone promptly upstairs to the guest room and locked the door before throwing herself on the bed and crying herself to sleep.

She glanced in the rearview mirror, her eyes were still puffy and swollen.

She arrived at her father's house in the afternoon. It was warmer in the marshy countryside that lay outside the city. In fact she had felt the change in temperature when she stopped earlier for coffee somewhere near the Florida state line.

She stepped out of the car and stretched, looking at the house with tenderness. She thought it was like greeting an old friend, and it felt just as good being home as she'd thought it would.

She stood for a moment, taking in the comfortable look of the old place. The small frame house with its cypress siding was weathered to a warm gray, and it looked good to her. The old swing on the railed porch moved in the breeze as if beckoning her to come in.

Then her eyes went to the front of the porch, the place she'd been standing when Jonathan kissed her that night.

She was surprised at the immediate tingle that shot through her and the way her heart seemed to flip-flop in her chest.

Shaking off the image of him, Margaret unlocked the door and stepped into the shadowy interior of the house. The air felt cold and stagnant, but even after all this time, the familiar scent was still there. The pungent smell of her father's tobacco, even the lingering aroma of coffee was there, mingled with the mustiness.

The house had deteriorated after her mother's death. Like many men, the state of his home had not really mattered to her dad. There were so many cozy little touches that he allowed to disappear.

Now the smells reminded her of both her parents, and for a moment the ache of not having them hit her like a knife to her heart.

She stood motionless, reluctant to move inside. She wanted to let herself feel, if only for a few seconds, that they were still here, still alive. Any moment one of them would walk from the kitchen into the small living room. They would smile and open their arms.

"I'm home Mama; I'm here Daddy," she whispered to the empty shadows.

Tears filled her eyes and she stumbled into the living room and dropped onto the old, lumpy couch.

She allowed herself a good, long cry, then shook herself and stood up. Her emotional stability was not good lately, but she recognized that fact. She intended to be good to herself in the process of healing.

She went directly to the phone and dialed Claire's number, getting the answering machine.

"I'm here, darling," she said after the low beep. "I've made it safely. The weather is wonderful. Call Cyndi for me if you will. Tell her I'll call later and I'll call you again, too. Bye."

She went through the house, opening the windows and turning on lights. She had not bothered having the electricity or the phone disconnected when she left in the fall. Now she was glad she hadn't; that was one less chore she would have to attend to today.

Margaret spent the remainder of the afternoon carrying in luggage and storage boxes. Soon the little house was cluttered with her belongings.

She was more tired than she'd been in months. She wished she'd had the foresight to stop at a grocery store. Now, if she wanted supper, she'd have to make a trip into town.

She rummaged through the cabinets and found some canned goods. She took a can of soup and checked the expiration date before washing a small pan and dumping the soup into it.

She glanced into the empty refrigerator and turned on the power. The interior smelled musty and stale. She would give it a good cleaning before going grocery shopping. Now that she'd found some soup, that could wait until tomorrow.

When the soup was hot she took a cup of it with her out to the porch swing. There she watched the sway of the pines and palm trees that sheltered the house from the highway and beyond that to the dusky sky.

She couldn't help remembering the last time she'd sat here. The memory of Jonathan's kiss that she'd tried so hard to push away was back.

Her eyes went to the edge of the porch and she took a long, deep breath at the sudden rush of memory: Jonathan's eyes and the sweet, forbidden touch of his lips. She felt a tingle run through her chest and down into the pit of her stomach.

That feeling was exhilarating. There was excitement and desire in it, something she had not felt in years, something she'd thought was gone from her life forever.

Alone in Florida, she admitted just how many times she had pushed the thought of Jonathan Bradford out of her mind these past weeks. She had been a faithful wife, stubbornly loyal to Charles, even when he had not deserved it. Even now, she felt somehow that her thoughts of Jonathan were wrong, forbidden to her still.

Yet, the thought of him would not leave her, nor the vision of intense blue eyes that seemed to look right into her heart. Her eyes glanced to the west, toward his farm. The idea of being so near, of actually seeing him again made her tremble with fear . . . and with anticipation.

Thirteen

After her light supper Margaret felt better. Well enough in fact to drive down the road to the small church and cemetery where her parents were buried. She had only a few moments before dark, but it was enough.

She dropped to her knees beside the graves, brushing away the pine needles and leaves.

"I'm home," she whispered.

Margaret didn't sleep well that first night. She didn't know if it was being in Florida, or worrying about the bizarre chain of events that had brought her there.

Finally she got out of bed and dug through one of the boxes until she found a book. She took it and a lightweight, musty smelling blanket and went to the old couch in the living room. As she snuggled down into the familiar sofa and pulled the blanket up to her chin, she felt safe.

The faint light from the lamp on a nearby table spread a warm, cozy glow over the objects in the room. The sound of the wind blowing in the trees outside was soothing. In the distance she could hear the quiet, lonesome wail of a train and the faint clickity clack of its great iron wheels on the track.

Margaret smiled and laid the book on her stomach. The sound of the train was so familiar and dear. How many nights in her childhood had she lain in this very house and listened to the distant, mournful sounds of the trains? How many evenings had she spent listening to the whisper of the pines and the croaking of tree frogs from the nearby marshes?

There was nothing to hear in her elegant, suburban Atlanta home. The house was too perfectly closed off, too hermetically sealed away from the world.

She closed her eyes and listened to the wind, letting her tired and weary body take in the sweet familiar sounds of home. This was what she had longed for . . . this peacefulness and security.

She woke next morning feeling much better, although her back was a bit stiff from lying so still on the narrow couch. Outside the sun was up, songbirds were singing and flitting from tree to tree.

Margaret went to the door and looked through its glass panes. There were birds everywhere. She'd have to remember to get new bird feeders, the old ones stood empty now. Margaret wondered if the birds still came here expecting to find food.

With a smile of pleasure she turned back to the living room. She folded the blanket and took it to the linen closet in the hallway. Seeing the stacks of quilts and blankets there, she thought twice, then spread the blanket onto the wood floor.

"Probably needs washing," she muttered to herself as she drew several out and placed them on the blanket.

Several quilts fell out onto the pile. Margaret's eyes took in the varied colors, some of them faded now with age. There were two that caught her attention immediately. She had completely forgotten about these quilts, couldn't even remember where they'd come from. She guessed that her mother and grandmother had made them years ago, maybe even before Margaret was born.

With a nostalgic sigh she pulled one of the quilts into the living room and spread it out across the floor. The white background was stained and aged to a pale cream color, but the patterned design, a circle star, was just as bright and colorful as ever. The calicos and old prints were all in delft blue and dark patriot red and the same material had been used to make a scalloped border.

Suddenly Margaret's eyes began to shine as an idea formed in her mind. She turned to look about the small house, thinking how run-down and shabby it had become over the years. The cypress

170

floors were still beautiful and she'd always loved the huge flagstone fireplace in the living room. It certainly had potential.

"I'll remodel and redecorate. Oh, this will be such fun." She was practically dancing as she carefully refolded the quilt and placed it on the sofa.

She would take the quilts to the cleaners on her way to the grocery store. When she got home, she would clean and scrub until the old place was aglow. Only then would she begin to decide how she wanted everything to look.

"Antiques," she whispered, whirling about with her hands on her hips to survey the room again. "I can have antiques and braided rugs . . . lace curtains." She laughed aloud as she danced about the living room, reveling in her freedom to do as she pleased.

Charles hated antiques. He had hated anything homey, or anything that smacked of simple country living. Margaret often assured him that some of the most beautiful homes were decorated in pioneer style, but Charles didn't want anything that would remind him of where they came from. Margaret had always clung to the roots of her upbringing, but Charles had shunned it. He tried most of the time to pretend neither of them came from a poor or simple background.

Now, she could do as she pleased. A small consolation, perhaps, to most women in the middle of a divorce, but it was a small shining ray of hope to

Margaret.

Later she dropped the quilts off at the dry cleaners, stopping to speak with the owner of the store.

"Do you think these can be cleaned without damaging them?"

"Oh yes ma'am," the small slender man replied. His voice was softly accented with the South. "We do quilts all the time. They're coming back in style you know."

She smiled and nodded. "Yes, I know. These are very special to me; they belonged to my mother and perhaps her mother before her."

"Then that makes them all the more unique and precious. We'll take very good care of them."

"Thank you."

Later at the grocery store, Margaret took her time. She enjoyed strolling casually through the section of fresh fruit and vegetables, trying to caution herself not to buy too much. It was going to take awhile to learn to shop for one.

"Margaret?" she heard a voice behind her. "Margaret . . . is that you?"

She turned to see Lettie rushing toward her. Her red hair was lighter now. It had a more golden color, almost a strawberry tint beneath the store's fluorescent lights. The bright pink sweater she wore emphasized the abundance of her curves.

Margaret smiled as she watched the woman totter on high heels that seemed dangerously high and slender. Then with a little shriek Lettie threw her arms around Margaret's neck, hugging and jostling her like a small puppy.

"Oh, you! Why didn't you tell me you were home? How long have you been here?"

"Actually I just got here yesterday afternoon. After I called the girls, I ate a bowl of soup and passed out for the night."

"Well, how long are you going to be here? We'll have to get together. Are you here about your dad's estate? Oh gee, I hope you're not going to sell the old place. There are so many land developers buying up property out there. I hope you're not going to let them get their money grubbin' hands on it."

Margaret smiled indulgently as Lettie continued to ramble and think out loud. It was still amazing to her that they could have been best friends as teenagers. They were like opposite sides of a coin. Even more amazing was that no matter how many years they were apart, one meeting seemed to put them right back on the same "best friend" level as before.

"Oh hell, I'm rambling on again, aren't I? A bad habit of mine. I guess it comes from working at the beauty salon. All I do is talk, talk, talk . . . all day long."

She stopped and grinned sheepishly at Margaret. Then both of them bent over with laughter.

"Oh Lettie, you never change. And I hope you never will. You have more energy than anyone I've ever met."

"Yeah, yeah. Well, are you going to tell me how long you'll be here?"

Margaret's face grew more serious and she reached to push her hair back from her eyes.

"I'm going to stay, Lettie. Charles and I are getting a divorce."

Lettie's dark eyes grew wide and she didn't bother to hide her surprise.

"Divorce? You and Charles? I don't believe it. My word, you two have been married forever. What on earth happened?"

Margaret glanced about, noting the various glances of curious shoppers.

Lettie saw her look and quirked one elegantly plucked eyebrow. "Guess this is not the best place to discuss divorce, is it?"

"No, not really."

Margaret wanted to talk to Lettie. She felt a need to tell someone who knew her about everything. There were things she could never tell the girls, and even Dina did not understand her the way Lettie did. She supposed that was because she and Lettie McComber had been friends since second grade. There was no pretense with her, and Margaret knew she could be as open and honest as she wanted to be.

"Why don't you come in to the shop? Let me give you a new 'do.' " Lettie reached forward and raked her fingers lightly through Margaret's dark hair. Her actions were serious and studied, as if something were drastically wrong with what she saw.

"Why? Do I look that awful?"

"No. God, I never saw the day when you looked awful. You using a rinse?" Lettie's dark eyes surveyed Margaret's hair.

"Well yes. I'm getting gray and—"

"Looks like midnight mists." Lettie's nod was so professional that Margaret almost laughed.

"When a woman gets to be our age, she needs to go lighter, not darker. Dark hair makes you look older . . . emphasizes the lines in your face."

Margaret sighed, then chuckled. "Well, gee thanks."

"If you want to come in, I'll fix you right up. Make you sparkle. Make the men sit up and take notice."

"I don't think I'm ready for that just yet," Margaret said with an affectionate smile. "Besides, we can't talk there. Our conversation would be broadcast all over town."

"Yeah, you got that right," Lettie said thoughtfully. "Might as well just get a bullhorn and make an announcement down at city hall."

"Why don't you come out to the house? You have plans for the evening?" Margaret's eyes sparkled with mischief as she asked the question.

"Are you kidding? It's been so long since I had a real date that . . . well, never mind. I'd love to come. Shall I bring anything?"

"Hmmm, not unless you happen to have some of

those gooey graham cracker and marshmallow things lying around the house that you'd like to get rid of."

Lettie's eyes lit up. "I don't, but I can pick up the ingredients while I'm here. We'll have a 'pig party,' just the way we used to." She reached forward and hugged Margaret. "Oh, I'm so glad you're here. Well, I've got to run if I intend to buy any groceries at all. I have an appointment at noon." She glanced again at Margaret's hair. "Think about what I said about the 'midnight mists.' "

With a jaunty little wave of her manicured hands, Lettie maneuvered her cart away. Margaret smiled as she watched the sway of Lettie's hips in her snug fitting jeans.

As Margaret moved through the grocery store, she thought a lot about her friend Lettie. Margaret's mother had been horrified at the girl's behavior and her brazen way of dressing. Now, people would hardly give it a second thought. Back in that day and age, Lettie had certainly been different.

"But she makes me laugh Mother," Margaret had explained.

"Well, I guess so. The way that girl looks would make anyone laugh."

Margaret chuckled to herself even now as she thought about her mother's stubborn insistence that Lettie was not the kind of girl Margaret should associate with.

The truth was that Lettie had been a "good girl."

Yes, she did have a bold, forthright way of talking and she dressed in some of the most outlandish garb Margaret had ever seen, but that was part of her charm. She had been a good, moral girl in spite of the unsavory reputation she acquired.

Lettie was just Lettie. Nothing or no one had ever been able to change that. Lettie had been true to herself.

And she still made Margaret laugh.

Fourteen

Margaret drove home from the grocery store, excited about the prospect of having Lettie out to the house. Once home she set about cleaning the refrigerator and putting the kitchen in order.

The chores took much longer than she expected. She barely had time to grab a slice of cheese and some crackers for lunch. She placed several pieces of chicken in a pot to boil and also a pan of rice, letting it cook while she prepared a crisp green salad to store in the refrigerator. She even enjoyed chopping celery and onions, enjoyed the scents of cooking as she stirred casserole ingredients together and poured it into a favorite earthenware dish.

It was late afternoon before Margaret finally enjoyed a long, warm bath and dressed in a comfortable pair of cotton slacks and a long knit sweater. She hurried back to the kitchen and placed the casserole into the preheated oven.

She was tired when she went out onto the porch swing to rest and wait for Lettie. She eased herself down slowly onto the swing, noting the tug and ache of muscles she didn't know she had.

As she sat quietly, pushing the swing with the toe of her shoe, she began to feel the reality of being home. For so long it had been a dream, a wish that she kept in the back of her mind like a child's secret. But now it was real; she was here.

Oddly, she felt a slight fluttering of her heart and she frowned. She sat very still, hoping the uneasy feeling would go away. Moments later when it happened again, she felt slightly breathless.

She placed her hand on her chest, frowning curiously as she sat very still. Her heart seemed to be beating normally, but she felt afraid, an almost overwhelming sense of fear swept over her.

In that moment of facing her own vulnerability, Margaret had never felt so completely alone. Even with all the lonely nights she had spent, she had never felt this way.

With a sense of doom that she wished she could make go away, she wondered what would happen if she died suddenly here alone in Florida. After all, women her age did have heart attacks.

"This is silly." She rose quickly from the swing as if to assure herself she was all right.

She walked about the porch, gazing thoughtfully out at the yard and telling herself almost frantically that she was all right.

What on earth was wrong with her? Was there something physically wrong? Or worse yet, was she suffering a mental breakdown of some kind?

It was the most curious thing. She had never been the sort of woman to worry unduly about herself or about her health. Suddenly, it was all she could think about. It seemed one of life's ironies, now, when she hoped to build a new life for herself, something terrible would happen to her.

Perhaps she should find a doctor here in Ocala and have a complete physical.

Lettie would be there soon. She went back into the house to make tea. Perhaps the task would divert the gloomy thoughts she was having about herself and her own mortality.

Moments later when she heard the crunch of gravel in the driveway Margaret went to the front door with a sense of relief. She smiled as she saw Lettie step from the car with a foil covered plate and glance up toward the house.

Margaret waved, feeling the tension leaving her almost immediately. She was being ridiculous, she told herself, feeling such a rush of relief at Lettie's presence.

Soon the two of them were chattering gaily. The air was filled with the mouth watering aroma of the chicken casserole as it baked and bubbled in the oven. Margaret's heart beat normally and the feelings of anxiety had completely vanished without her even realizing it.

"What shall I do?" Lettie asked. "Want me to set the table?"

"Sure, the plates are in the cupboard there above the sink." Margaret took the salad from the refrigerator and placed the serving forks in the bowl. Then she placed the still simmering casserole on a hot pad on the table.

"Oh my," Lettie murmured with a long, delighted sniff. "This looks and smells wonderful. I'm starving."

"So am I, come to think of it," Margaret said with a quiet laugh.

It felt so good to share a meal with someone, to be able to sit and enjoy good food without the tension that she so often experienced when Charles did take the time to come home.

"You are still as good a cook as ever," Lettie said, savoring her first forkful of creamy casserole. "I remember how you used to cook in the summertime when your mom was working in the garden, or sometimes when she didn't feel well."

"I've always loved to cook," Margaret acknowledge with a nod.

"I don't mind it. Although my efforts usually run more to pre-packed stuff. You know, Betty Crocker potatoes and Pillsbury cake mixes." She laughed, her movement causing the light to gleam upon her reddish blond curls. "I'll bet you still make everything from scratch."

"Well . . . yes. But then I never worked outside

the home so I had plenty of time for such things."

"Tell me what happened with your marriage . . . other women?"

Margaret frowned and reached for her glass of iced tea. "Why do you ask that? Have you heard something about Charles or . . . ?"

Lettie frowned, then laughed. "No, I haven't heard anything. God, Margaret don't be so defensive. It's me, Lettie, remember? The woman who's been dumped and cheated on more times than Bayer has aspirins."

"I'm sorry," Margaret said with a sheepish laugh. "It's just so humiliating. I feel as if anyone can look at me and tell."

"What? That your husband ran around on you? Hell, it happens to all of us sooner or later."

Margaret frowned across the table. "You don't really believe that, do you?"

Lettie took a long sip of tea and set the glass back down slowly. There was a dreamy, distant look in her brown eyes.

"Oh, I don't know. Maybe I just tell myself that to soothe my own feelings of inadequacy." She glanced at Margaret. "But if your problem was Charles and other women, then I certainly do sympathize. I know how it hurts when the man you love and trust does that to you. You begin to doubt your own self; you begin to see all your faults, and your age suddenly seems more important than anything. You notice bulges you never gave a second thought to before and the lines in your face suddenly begin to look like gullies."

Margaret laughed, even though she knew Lettie was dead serious. She couldn't help it. That was exactly the way she had felt sometimes. But somehow, Lettie's way of expressing it made it seem shallow and not quite so important.

"I know the feeling," she said.

"Oh, I don't know," Lettie said, continuing her own thoughts. "I suppose there are men who are loyal, and stay with their wives because they truly love them and want to be with them more than anything in the world. I just haven't met any of them lately, that's all."

"Well, I don't intend to find out," Margaret said firmly. "I can't imagine ever trusting my heart to another man. Charles has hurt me so deeply. He had affairs before, but God, Lettie, this just killed me."

Margaret stood up and went to the window over the sink. She stood gazing out at the yard.

"Was she young?" Lettie asked dryly.

"Oh yes, very. She's no older than Cyndi."

"Charles is a bastard."

"He said she meant nothing to him and he still loved me."

"Sure. Did you tell him it certainly meant something to you?"

"I just couldn't take it any more. It seems like one day you're twenty years old and the next you're fifty. I don't know where the years have gone. And worse yet, I don't feel I have anything now to show for those years."

"You certainly do have; you have the girls."

"Yes, at least I do have that." Her look toward Lettie was sympathetic. "What about you, Lettie? Did you ever want kids?"

"Oh sure. I really wanted children that first time when I married Earl. You remember Earl?"

"Of course I remember him. He had curly black hair and the sexiest blue eyes." Margaret's smile was reminiscent.

"Oh, those blue eyes! That's what got me in so damned much trouble to start with . . . those eyes. I was absolutely wild about that boy. I would have died to have his children. I used to dream about having his babies . . . a girl and a boy. I wanted a little boy with black hair and blue eyes and a girl like me with sandy hair and brown eyes. God, I thought my life would be just about perfect."

Margaret stood with her hips against the kitchen cabinet. She saw the pain in Lettie's eyes and heard it in her voice. Strange that after all these years, those hurts could come back so quickly with just one thought, just one word.

"But Earl was like Charles as I recall," Margaret reminded softly. "He couldn't seem to leave the women alone."

"That's right," Lettie said a bit too brightly. "Couldn't keep his pants zipped." She sighed and made a face. "Oh, that Earl! He thought he really had it. Thought he was God's gift to women."

"Yeah, well, I seem to recall you thought he was pretty hot stuff yourself," Margaret teased.

"God, he was wonderful," Lettie said with a sigh. "No one was ever as good in bed as Earl McComber. And I ought to know! After we split up, I tried just about all the rest."

Margaret laughed at Lettie's openness. "Is that why you kept his name even after your other divorces?"

"Yeah." Lettie's smile was almost shy. "Besides, it just sounded right — Lettie McComber."

"Those other men . . . you probably were just trying to prove to yourself that you were still desirable."

"Well, I proved it to about half of Marion County while I was at it."

"But not to yourself?"

"Nope," Lettie whispered, a faraway look in her eyes. "I guess it just doesn't work that way, does it? But I was young; I thought if enough men wanted me, then that would somehow prove that Earl was wrong. What he did made me feel about as ugly and undesirable as anyone could ever feel. You know?"

"Oh, I know . . . believe me, I know. I feel as if I've spent my entire life trying to prove something to Charles Avery. Trying to keep myself young and attractive so he would love me. The perfect wife and mother, the perfect housekeeper. I was such a fool."

"No, you're not." There was a stubborn gleam in Lettie's eye. "He's the fool. Men like Charles and Earl are the losers, not us."

"I'm trying to believe that. But right now, it seems to be the hardest thing I've ever done in my life."

"It is hard. And it will continue to be hard for a while yet. But I think you did the right thing by getting away from Atlanta, and by starting a new life here among friends in a place where you feel comfortable."

"I hope so."

"And take my advice, don't go off the deep end and try to prove your attractiveness the way I did."

Margaret took a deep breath. "Actually, I think I've gone the other way. I'm afraid I can never trust a man again."

"Oh, you'll get over that when the right man comes along."

Margaret frowned when a vision of Jonathan Bradford came unbidden to mind. For a moment they were both quiet, each of them lost in their own thoughts.

Then Lettie spoke. "You know, I remember that day . . . so many years ago. I came home from work at noon because I wasn't feeling good. I never came home early and I guess Earl was counting on that. I walked right in on my husband in bed with another woman."

"I remember . . . you wrote me about it. It took you a long time to get over that, didn't it?"

"Oh Margaret, I thought I would die from the pain I felt every time I thought about it. I thought the vision of them together would never go away."

Margaret remembered how sick the pictures she'd seen of Charles and Shelley had made her feel.

"I know."

"Life is cruel, you know. Even after all these years, my mind still remembers Earl McComber in that bed, holding that woman. Oh, it hurts even now. He was so gorgeous lying there. Isn't it strange what we remember? I can see his blue eyes as if it were yesterday . . . staring at me with such shock and disbelief. I remember how tan his chest and arms looked against the white sheets, against her skin."

"Lettie . . ." Margaret soothed.

Lettie looked at Margaret and there were tears in her eyes. "Oh, its all right. I let myself cry about it now and then. If I had it all to do over, I might have kept him for awhile longer . . . just until I could bear giving him up. I don't think I ever really got over him. Not really . . ." Her voice trailed away.

Margaret stood very still looking at her friend. There was nothing she could say or do, but she certainly had not intended to remind Lettie of her own sad first marriage.

"Say, where are those gooey goodies you promised to bring?"

Lettie looked up, smiling brightly and brushing back the tears from her dark, mascara-laden eyes.

"Right here," she said, standing to go to the cabinet. She hesitated a moment, smiling at Margaret. "I'm sorry, sweetie. I came out here intending to cheer you up and instead I end up crying on your shoulder about something that happened thirty years ago."

"Don't apologize," Margaret scolded. "Not to me. Do you know that's one of the things I always liked about you? We could talk about anything. I've missed that so much."

Lettie put an arm around Margaret's shoulders and hugged her. "I've missed it, too. And we'll talk darlin'. We'll just talk each other's ears off until we have this all out of our system. Kind of like a neighborhood psychologist shop for amateurs."

"Sounds good to me," Margaret agreed, reaching for one of the chocolate and marshmallow confections Lettie had brought.

"And I'm going to give you a make-over that will turn you into the talk of the town."

Margaret frowned and shook her head doubtfully.

"Now, don't say no right away. You never know when it will pay off. There are some good-looking bachelors in this town. Some very eligible men, if I do say so myself. Why if I recall, one of the most eligible lives just down the road from you."

"Lettie, I don't want to talk about. . . ." She looked away, not even wanting to say Jonathan's name aloud.

"You don't want to talk about Jonathan Bradford? I wonder why that is?"

"Lettie . . ."

"Okay . . . Okay, I won't push it. But honey, if I had a man look at me the way he looks at you . . . whew . . ." She shook her fingers as if she'd been burned and her eyes twinkled merrily.

Margaret couldn't resist a smile. Lettie could always drag one out of her. Even sometimes when it pertained to a subject that scared her half to death.

Fifteen

Margaret tossed and turned in the bed for most of the night before finally falling to sleep sometime well past midnight. She had lain in bed and felt the fluttering of her heart again. Its soft reminder of her vulnerability had driven her wide awake.

Even now in her sleep, she seemed to feel its pounding.

It was beating, pounding with some strange, uneasy rhythm. Was it fear . . . excitement?

In her sleep she could see a man coming nearer to her. She could see the shape of his male body, the broad shoulders and narrow hips. But she couldn't make out his face. As he came closer, her heart began to beat even harder and faster in anticipation.

The man held out his arms to her and without hesitation she went to him. With a soft, quiet murmur, she fell against him and felt the length of his body against hers, felt the hard pull of his hands as he held her close.

Her head was nestled against his chest and now she could feel his lips as they brushed against the side of her neck and up to her ear.

Everything about his slow, sensual movements filled her with excitement and a sweet, familiar rush of desire. She found herself wanting to be closer, wanting to move her hands over his chest and up to his shoulders.

She gasped, feeling the nakedness of his skin, somehow his shirt had just disappeared. She was dreaming but she couldn't seem to make herself come awake.

It was Charles, her sleeping mind explained. Sometimes in the early years, he would come to bed in the middle of the night, after she was asleep. She would awaken to his hands moving over her and to the hungry bourbon-tinged taste of his mouth on hers. It had been exhilarating to have him want her so desperately. And she had responded; she had always responded.

She wanted to be kissed. She looked up into the face of the man whose arms still held her and whose body had begun to excite her.

"Charles . . . ?"

The man's head dipped toward hers. She saw the flash of blue eyes beneath dark brows and her eyes flew open wide as she tried to pull away from him.

"You." Her voice was a whisper of denial, a choked gasp that seemed to echo around the silence of her dream.

His mouth covered hers in a hungry, searching kiss that sent hot sparks rushing through her body. She arched toward him, returning the kiss, savoring the taste of his lips and the feel of his solid body against hers.

How she wanted him to make love to her.

"Now Jonathan . . . please."

She was gasping for air as she felt the heat sweep over her and rush through her body. She was aware of moving her body against his, of wanting him, and urging him silently to make love to her. But it was ending . . . too soon and even as the passion swept over her, she felt regret that it was almost over.

Even as he kissed her, she felt the responding release of her body, felt the heady, unbelievable pulsing of her own desires.

"No," she whispered, wanting more, knowing the dream would end when she gave in. "Jonathan . . ."

"Love me Maggie," the man whispered, his deep voice sending her body into another spasm of desire. As she reached for him, wanting him desperately, wanting him to finish it, she felt the pleasant, sensual tightening and releasing of her body.

She looked up into his face, seeing clearly now that it was Jonathan. She knew she should deny it, even in her dreams. She should banish his face from her thoughts and put Charles in his place.

But she couldn't. His face would not go away;

neither would his strong arms release her.

"Jonathan . . . no . . . don't go . . . don't leave . . ."

She woke suddenly, thrashing about in bed, and still experiencing the heat and pulsating desire of her dream.

Slowly she began to relax, soaking in with a quiet disbelief what she had just experienced. As the memory of the dream came back to her clearly, she became very still as she stared dumbstruck into the darkness of the room.

She could feel the warm flush on her face. What she was feeling now was no dream; her reaction had been hot and real, so real she still felt the slow, drugging effects on her body.

She was feeling the hot, physical desire for a man like she had not felt in years.

And for one particular and disturbingly sexual man.

She let her mind wander over every detail; she felt the erotic effects that lingered and bathed her body in a warm, pleasant glow. Even though the feelings were still very much there, the dream had faded. She could not recall Jonathan's voice, or even his face very clearly now. She felt strangely disappointed.

"What is wrong with me?" She pushed her pillow behind her and sat up in bed.

In the distance she thought she heard the sound of morning songbirds. She stepped out of bed and walked to the window, pushing the curtains open and wishing it was indeed daylight. It was still very dark though and she wasn't sure what sounds she had heard.

She ran her fingers through her tousled hair. She simply could not go back to bed and lie there fantasizing about a man who was not her husband.

She stopped, her hand in midair, as she realized soon she would have no husband . . . only an ex-husband, like Lettie.

She would be free to do as she pleased. Why should her attraction to Jonathan be forbidden to her then?

She closed her eyes and sighed, as a fearful trembling began in her knees and reached upward.

Why indeed? Only because she was frightened out of her wits at the thought of a relationship with another man. She felt wholly inadequate to deal with the pain and rejection he might inflict. Most overwhelmingly, she had never been with any man except her husband. That alone was intimidating enough.

The mere thought of having another man see her mature and imperfect body, in her mind, left her shaking with fear. Why, she could not even imagine making love with another man.

Swiftly she felt the heat move over her face and down to her neck. Of course, she could imagine it. Her subconscious had just proven that, hadn't it?

She had read an article that said women needed a

warm, intimate moment after lovemaking to bond with their partner. The same article also said that many men responded in just the opposite way, by pulling away.

She frowned, thinking of the times Charles had turned over and gone to sleep. That had always left her feeling abandoned.

With a wry grimace, Margaret turned from the window and back toward the bed.

She could hardly snuggle and bond with her sexual partner. He had been only a fantasy. Even in the erotic dream, she had not made real love to him. The climax had been exciting, but the dream had left her wanting more.

She crawled back into bed, determined to forget the dream. And Jonathan Bradford.

After sleeping late, Margaret felt guilty. There were so many things to be done that she knew she should have been up hours ago.

For the rest of the day she threw herself into the chore of cleaning out closets and of washing all the linens and curtains.

As busy as she kept herself, she could not completely banish the dream from her mind, nor the way her body had responded to Jonathan's imagined kisses.

"My Lord, it was only a dream," she would whisper angrily to herself. Then her cleaning and dusting would take on an even more desperate quality.

She was so tired that night that she had no trouble sleeping. Just as she drifted off, she did think she felt the odd skipping rhythm of her heart again. She was simply too tired to worry about it.

She spent the next few days setting the little house in order. At least it was clean, but something would definitely need to be done about the furniture.

She spoke to Claire and Cyndi and assured them she was well and happy. She spoke to Lettie who urged her to come into town for lunch.

"Oh Lettie," Margaret had protested. "Not just yet. To tell you the truth I only want to be alone. I can't face meeting people or seeing old friends and having to explain . . . not yet."

"Hmmm," Lettie responded. "What old friends are you avoiding? Anyone I know?"

"You know what I mean. It's no one in particular."

"Oh, no? Does Jonathan know you're home?"

"I have no idea." Margaret could not help the coolness that crept into her voice. She knew Lettie heard it, too.

"Uh huh. Is it him you're avoiding? Although for the life of me I can't imagine why any woman in her right mind would avoid a man like that."

"Lettie, don't you have work to do?"

"I am working," she said blithely. "I'm buffing Mrs. Symington's nails. Isn't that right, Mrs. Symington?"

"Lettie, for heaven's sake. Has she been listening

to everything you said? Does she know who you're talking to? I don't want everyone in Ocala to know about Jonathan. I mean . . ."

Lettie laughed aloud, giggling like a teenager.

"Lighten up, Mags. Geez, you sound like some old maid schoolteacher who never got any in her life."

"Never got any . . . ? Lettie, I can't believe you're doing this to me. Mrs. Symington is—"

"Mrs. Symington has her head in a huge, round and very noisy hair dryer. She couldn't hear World War II if it dropped right on top of her. In fact she might even be asleep." There was another giggle and a whispered voice. "Are you asleep, Mrs. Symington? Good, my friend Margaret Avery doesn't want you to know that she has the hots for Jonathan Bradford. In fact, I think she's trying her best to convince herself that she doesn't feel anything for the man. Can you imagine that? What's that? Is she dead? No, as far as I know she's still alive . . . last time I checked anyway—"

"All right Lettie," Margaret drawled with a soft laugh. "You've made your point, and had your laugh for the day in the bargain."

"You're too serious," Lettie said. "You need to loosen up a bit."

"So I've been told."

"So, what are you going to do today? Still cleaning and dusting?"

"Actually I think I've cleaned just about every

nook and cranny of this house. I'm seriously thinking about buying some new furniture, although what I get will probably be antiques. You know the kind of stuff I like."

"Oh yes. You know you can get some beautiful old things now at flea markets and yard sales. If you want to do it gradually, that is. Besides, it's something to do on weekends. I'll even go with you if you like."

"I would love it. That's exactly the kind of thing I'd like." Margaret smiled at the thought. "But that's not something that's going to occupy all my time. I've been thinking seriously about job hunting, although the thought scares me absolutely to death."

"Oh my goodness. With your looks and your intelligence, you should be able to get any job you want."

"Well, I don't know about that."

"What did you have in mind? I'll keep my ears open around the salon. We hear things here sometimes even before the Help Wanted ad is put in the paper."

"Oh, I don't know. The only job I ever had was while I was in college. I worked at a newspaper; fancied myself as quite a reporter." Margaret chuckled at the memory.

"You're kidding." Lettie gave a soft little shriek that took Margaret by surprise.

Margaret held the phone away from her ear and

looked at it curiously. "What was that?"

"Oh, nothing. I'm just excited that's all. It just so happens that I have a . . . huh . . . friend who works at the local newspaper. If you'd like I'll call him . . . see what I can do. That is, if you think that's the kind of job you want."

"Well, yes, I think it is. I'd probably take anything at this point, but I am vaguely familiar with journalism, although it's been years since I did such work." She stopped to think for a moment. "This is terrific, Lettie. If you can could speak to this friend . . ."

"I will," Lettie declared. "In fact I'll call him right now. I'll let you know tonight what the deal is."

Margaret hung up the phone and smiled to herself. Could it really be this easy? Lettie was quite a character, but she also had her practical moments. Perhaps this was one that would pay off.

Margaret sat quietly, gazing at the sparkling kitchen and making mental notes about what things she would keep and what pieces of furniture might fit into the small area. Of course there were sentimental items she could not bear to replace. But the prospect of scouring the flea markets pleased her, as did the anticipation of spring.

She leaned back in her chair with a satisfied sigh. She had been home almost a week and already her new life was beginning to take form.

The nights were not always so great; that was

when she missed the girls. From her confusing and sometimes erotic dreams, she had to admit she also missed having a husband.

But that would change. She'd make it change. She said a silent prayer that she'd get the job at the newspaper office.

Working there could make all the difference in the world to her self-esteem, not to mention her peace of mind.

Sixteen

That evening when the phone rang, Margaret went quickly to answer it. Expecting Lettie, her voice was bright and upbeat as she said hello.

"Well, Mom . . . you certainly sound cheerful."

It was Cyndi and the ring of her voice sounded sweet to Margaret.

"Cyndi, I'm so glad you called; I miss you. And Claire, too."

"How are you? How's Ocala? Is it warm there?"

"The weather has been wonderful. So far none of the cold rain that often plagues Atlanta this time of year. You wouldn't think that a few hundred miles would make that much difference. But there's a warm breeze here most of the day. It feels like spring."

"You sound good. Are you doing okay?"

"I'm fine. It'll take awhile, but I think I'm feeling better every day that passes."

"We miss you."

"I miss you, too, sweetheart. How's Steven?"

"He's terrific . . . busy. I hardly see him any more."

"What about those classes you wanted to take? Have you decided to register for this semester?"

"Oh, I don't know. Steven thinks it's a waste of time. He complains that he wants his supper ready when he gets home." There was a low sigh at the other end of the phone. "When he manages to make it home, that is."

The disappointment in her daughter's voice hurt Margaret. She had to bite her tongue to keep back the words, the advice that she knew would not be welcome.

"I'm sorry, darling. But what about morning classes? How could he object to that? You'd still be home in time to cook dinner."

"Hmmm, I don't know. I'll think about it. What are you doing with your time? Have you looked for a job?"

"As a matter of fact, I'm expecting Lettie to call tonight about a job prospect. I thought you were her."

"Oh. Well, let me know. I just wanted to call and say hello. Steven is working late and I had dinner at home with Dad."

"Oh, are you there now? At your dad's house?"

"It's your house, too, Mom." Cyndi's voice was softly scolding.

"No, darling. Not any more. And I don't want you to feel bad about that. This is the way I wanted it."

"He misses you."

"Cyndi . . ."

"He's right here. He'd like to talk to you." Cyndi's voice became a whispered plea. "Please, Mom. He misses you so much. He's just lost without you."

"No Cyndi, I . . ."

Margaret sighed as she realized that Cyndi had already handed the phone to her father.

"Hello . . . Margaret." Charles's voice sounded hesitant and deceptively humble.

"Yes . . . hello Charles. How are you?"

"Doing the best I can under the circumstances."

Ah yes, she wanted to shout. Those blasted circumstances were always screwing up someone's life.

"How's your work going? The Simmons contract—"

"Fine . . . fine. How are you, Margaret?"

"I'm fine." She didn't care that her voice sounded cold and indifferent. How dare he pretend concern for her at this point.

"We miss you. The girls and I miss you more than you know. The house is so cold and empty without you."

"Charles, please. Don't do this. I don't understand why you're saying any of this. It's what you wanted, isn't it? What you've wanted for years? Can't you just relax and enjoy your freedom? I can assure you it's what I intend to do."

"I just want to ask you one question. I want you to answer it honestly. Is there someone else? Is there a man at Ocala that you're interested in?"

"For heaven's sake. No! I can assure you, your years of infidelity were quite enough to send me here. I hardly needed another reason, or another man. Please, put Cyndi back on the phone."

"I know you're bitter and I understand that, but for whatever it's worth it's over between Shelley and me. Your leaving has finally opened my eyes; you're the only woman I've ever loved, the only one I've ever really wanted."

"Let me talk to Cyndi."

"Margaret, baby . . ."

She sighed audibly, but said nothing else. Instead she waited, tapping her foot and hoping Charles would not say anything else. Finally she heard muffled voices and the shuffling of the phone.

"Mom . . . you still there?"

"Yes, Cyndi, I'm here."

"Claire had to work late tonight or she'd be here, too. I told her I was going to call you. She said she sent you a card yesterday and you should get it soon."

"Good. Is she doing okay?"

"Oh, she didn't want me to tell you, but I think

she had a date with Brian a couple of nights ago. He's still crazy about her, you know."

"Really? That's wonderful. I'll keep my fingers crossed. Have either of you heard any more from Ginger?"

"No. You?"

"No. I'm not even sure she and Catherine Jane got the Christmas gifts I sent. I mailed her a letter before I left Atlanta, but I've heard nothing. I don't know if she's still picking mail up at general delivery or not."

"If I hear from her, I'll let you know."

"All right, darling. Be careful and tell everyone hello. Give Steven a kiss for me. I'll call and let you know if I get the job."

"You sound excited about that."

"I am." Margaret felt the surprise wash over her in a pleasant wave. She realized just how desperately she was hoping for this job at the newspaper.

"Well, I love you." Then in a whisper, "I take it you weren't encouraging to Dad."

"No. And I hope you don't expect that to change. If nothing happens, the divorce should be final in a few weeks."

Cyndi was very quiet for a moment. "Well, I'll talk to you soon. Tell Lettie I said hello. Love you."

"Love you too, darling. Goodbye."

After she hung up, Margaret stood in the kitchen for a long while, staring at the walls and wondering why she felt so dejected and blue.

Cyndi was still such a baby in so many ways. It hardly seemed likely that a twenty-eight-year-old woman would feel such loss at the separation of her parents. Cyndi was married and had a life of her own, but Charles had always been able to finagle his way into her heart. He had always been able to make her feel sorry for him somehow.

Just the thought of him making her sweet, sensitive daughter feel sad was simply infuriating to Margaret. How dare he play this poor suffering husband routine after all he had done. Margaret wanted to wring his neck.

When the phone rang again, it was Lettie.

"Hey, I tried to call earlier, but your line was busy."

"I was talking to Cyndi. And Charles." The last words were dry and cool.

"Oh, what did he say?"

"That he loves only me and that his affair with his latest sweet young thing is over for good."

Lettie hesitated for a moment.

"You don't buy that, do you?"

"Heavens, no. I told him it was no use. But it just infuriates me that he's using Cyndi to try to worm his way back. I'd be willing to bet it either has something to do with money or a prestigious client he wants to impress who favors family men instead of swinging bachelors."

"Well, you sound as if you know him pretty well."

"Oh, you bet I do. No one in Atlanta, Georgia knows Charles Avery the way I do. If they did, he'd probably be disbarred."

"You know, you sound more like your old self tonight. Got some of your old spunk back."

"Yeah? Well, I'm working on it, although some nights are mighty long and hard."

"Well, perhaps from now on, you'll be too tired at night to notice."

"Does that mean — "

"Can you come downtown tomorrow for an interview? To the *Ocala Sun?*"

"Yes! What time?"

"Around one o'clock."

"Oh, Lettie, how can I thank you? If I get this job I'll take you out for the biggest steak in Marion County."

"Hey, that sounds like plenty enough thanks for me. You got a deal. Unless I miss my guess, I'll be collecting on that promise sooner than you think."

"Oh, I hope you're right."

"Well, I've got to take a bath and get in bed. I'm really beat tonight. Remember, the *Ocala Sun* and don't be late. See ya."

"Wait, Lettie. Who is the interview with? Who shall I ask to see?"

"Oh, just ask the receptionist. I'm sure she'll direct you to the right person. 'Night."

There was a click and then the hum of a dial tone as the phone disconnected. Margaret stood for a second looking curiously at the phone and wondering at her friend's mysterious answer. Oh, well, perhaps Lettie didn't know who Margaret was supposed to see. Not that it really mattered anyway. All she had to worry about now was being on time and being prepared.

Margaret was dressed and ready an hour before time for her interview. The drive into town would take less than ten minutes.

She went to the mirror in the bedroom one last time. She knew the Nolan Miller suit was much too expensive to wear to the small newspaper office, but it was simple and understated. She doubted that anyone there would realize it was a designer suit. Besides, she thought the pale peach color was flattering to her full figure and to her complexion. She wanted to make the best impression possible, even if the interview was with a small town editor.

By the time she drove along the straight, level roads and into the city, she was still fifteen minutes early. She parked her car on the street and waited, watching people walk by and listening to the flutter of birds in the huge old magnolia trees that lined the mid town park.

Finally it was time and with a sigh of determination, she opened the car door and walked the half block to the newspaper office.

It was in one of Ocala's older buildings and Margaret was pleased to see that a great deal of restoration had been done in this part of town.

She stopped at the sign reading *Ocala Sun,* and looked with approval at the beautiful restored wood and stained glass windows. Stepping inside she was pleased to see that the interior was just as lovingly restored. Whoever owned the newspaper evidently had a love for history and tradition. Margaret liked that.

There was a young, blond-haired girl at the front desk who looked up and smiled as Margaret walked in.

"May I help you?"

"Yes, I'm Margaret Avery. I have an appointment with . . . for an interview . . . I'm not really sure who it's with." She wished again that Lettie had known who she should ask for.

"Oh yes, he's expecting you." The girl smiled brightly at Margaret. "Right this way."

Margaret followed her down a narrow corridor, past several offices where people sat hunched at computers, or watching noisy printers. At the far end of the hall, the girl stopped at an office. The door was open and she stepped aside and motioned for Margaret to enter the room.

Margaret took one step, then stopped. Across the large office with its expensive Indian rug, sat a beautiful antique walnut desk. Behind the desk, a man worked, obviously unaware of Margaret's walk down the carpeted hallway, or of her presence now.

On his desk was a gorgeous antique brass lamp with a dark green printer's shade. Its light fell upon the man's long tan fingers where he scribbled upon a yellow legal pad. The other lights in the room gleamed upon his silvery hair and fell across the shoulders of the dark, obviously expensive jacket he wore.

Margaret stared openmouthed, unable to say a word.

The girl beside her grinned, noting the man's lack of attention and Margaret's obvious chagrin. She cleared her throat loudly and rapped her knuckles on the glass portion of the oak door.

"Huh, Mr. Bradford?" the girl murmured, still smiling. "Your one o'clock appointment is here." Then with a smile at Margaret, she turned and left.

Jonathan's head came up and he stared straight into Margaret's astounded eyes. His blue gaze caught the light and reflected a twinkle of amusement as he scanned Margaret's elegantly clad figure from the top of her designer suit to the bottom.

"Well, Maggie," he murmured. "I'm not sure I can afford to pay you a salary that will keep you in a Nolan Miller suit, but come in anyway. I'll see what I can do."

Seventeen

Margaret was dumbfounded, rooted to the floor where she stood. She wanted to turn and flee down the corridor and out the door as if she had not seen him and he had not seen her.

She was going to kill Lettie McComber.

Jonathan smiled patiently, then stood up and walked toward her. She felt only the slightest bit of relief, thinking her feelings were not reflected too blatantly on her face.

Her legs were trembling and she frowned, irritated by her own body's betrayal. When he reached a hand forward to usher her into the room, she moved toward him woodenly. She was certain he must think her a complete and total fool.

"Come in Maggie. It's good to see you." He was cool, his voice steady and his eyes moved only the slightest bit to survey her from head to toe. She thought there was approval in his warm look.

Did he know how completely he reduced her limbs to jelly? She was certain it must only be her. For if he felt the same tingling sensation where their hands met, it did not show in his actions or his manner.

"I had no idea that you . . . I mean, Lettie didn't tell me you were the . . ." She hesitated, not knowing exactly what his title was at the newspaper office.

He motioned her to a dark, nail-studded, maroon leather chair near the desk and with one foot, kicked the door shut behind them. As he went around the desk he grinned boyishly and his head nodded toward the door.

Margaret turned and saw the letters upon the glass door pane and even thought they were backwards now, she could read the title clearly.

Jonathan Bradford, Owner and Publisher.

She swallowed. She had wondered about him before, but somehow she had not expected this. Perhaps if she had ever allowed Lettie to talk about him she wouldn't be feeling quite so awkward now.

"Owner and Publisher," she murmured.

She thought he seemed much too calm to be a newspaper man. Certainly no one could accuse him of flaunting his prestigious position. She had

212

thought he was a farmer, or a land speculator, but not a publisher.

He seated himself behind the desk and propped his elbows on the surface, one hand atop the other with his chin resting upon his knuckles. His expressive eyes studied her carefully.

"Lettie was afraid you wouldn't come if you knew."

She blushed, knowing exactly what Lettie thought.

"I don't know why she would think that." But of course she knew. And Lettie was right . . . if Margaret had known she probably would have run like a scared rabbit.

"Neither do I. Why don't you tell me?" He frowned and cocked his head to one side. There was the slightest hint of a grin on his lips and his eyes glittered at her. "Personally, I can't imagine why you would not come to me for a job . . . considering we are friends."

She thought he had a smile that would charm an alligator.

"We are friends . . . aren't we?" he urged in a light teasing tone.

"Well, yes," she said with a nonchalant shrug of her shoulders. "Of course. I just don't make it a habit to ask favors of friends." He could see right through her. She knew he could.

"Ah," he said, resting his chin against his hands. "Well, in this case, consider it's yourself who will be doing the favor. I'm in desperate need of help in this office. As you can see, we're small and understaffed. Debbie, the girl who brought you in, is supposed to be the receptionist, but some days she finds herself doing classifieds or church socials. She's not really fond of that."

"What would you need me to do?"

"Lettie said you were a journalism student in college."

Lettie's conversation with Jonathan must have been a considerably long one. She found herself wondering what else she had told him.

"That was a long time ago."

"Doesn't matter . . . it'll come back to you. Besides, this is a small town newspaper; I'll teach you everything you need to know."

Why did his words make her blush? She clenched her fists against her skirt, wishing she could stop the swirl of thoughts in her mind.

"I just need a junior reporter, someone to fill in for me sometimes. I have to warn you there will be days when you'll find yourself doing everything from secretarial duties to personal errands."

"That won't bother me." She nodded her agreement, hoping she didn't look as embarrassed as she felt.

There was something in his eyes, in the way he looked at her that completely unnerved her. It didn't help any that her erotic dream about him kept popping into her mind at the most unsuitable moments.

She gritted her teeth and took a long, deep breath, looking away from his eyes as she tried to compose herself. Self-consciously she brushed at the skirt of her suit, although there was absolutely no trace of lint to be seen. She glanced up at him and found him smiling.

"You may want to dress more casually when you come to work."

"I will," she murmured, looking away from his amused eyes.

"So, you'll accept the job?"

"Yes," she said immediately, turning to stare at him. "Of course I will. Thank you and I'm grateful for . . ." She swallowed hard, feeling the blood rush to her face. Why was she finding it so difficult to express her gratitude to him? Or to say anything that made the tiniest bit of sense?

"Let me get a few papers for you to sign. I'll be right back."

As he walked past her, she was struck again by his stature and the quick youthful way he walked. As he passed, the air behind him stirred with some sexually evocative fragrance.

While she waited for him to return, she stood trying to calm herself. She walked slowly about the room, touching the expensive mahogany tables and noting the imported decorative pieces. Some of them were breathtaking and she knew very well how expensive they were.

The wall behind his desk was covered with dozens of framed photos and awards. She stepped closer to stare at them.

She frowned as she recognized numerous photos of Jonathan; some with people she did not know, but many of the people who embraced him or shook his hand were well-known celebrities. She recognized several congressmen, as well as Presidents Ford and Carter . . . beautiful movie stars who pushed themselves against Jonathan or looked adoringly up into his face.

How could she not have known how successful and famous Jonathan was? The array of framed awards staggered her. She shook her head. Perhaps she had, but simply had not associated the prize-winning and world renowned journalist with the tall, skinny boy in glasses of so many summers ago.

There were prestigious journalism awards from almost every important newspaper in the world. There were at least a dozen cover photos of Jonathan on various business and literary magazines.

She did not miss the fact that one particular woman stood out in most of the pictures. A very beautiful blond woman who looked at Jonathan in a certain way.

Margaret's heart sank. Was this his wife? The woman in Jonathan's life that she had not had the nerve to ask about? Surely if he were married,

MORE PASSION AND ADVENTURE AWAIT... YOUR TRIP TO A BIG ADVENTUROUS WORLD BEGINS WHEN YOU ACCEPT YOUR FIRST 4 NOVELS ABSOLUTELY *FREE* (AN $18.00 VALUE)

Accept your Free gift and start to experience more of the passion and adventure you like in a historical romance novel. Each Zebra novel is filled with proud men, spirited women and tempestuous love that you'll remember long after you turn the last page.

Zebra Historical Romances are the finest novels of their kind. They are written by authors who really know how to weave tales of romance and adventure in the historical settings you love. You'll feel like you've actually gone back in time with the thrilling stories that each Zebra novel offers.

GET YOUR FREE GIFT WITH THE START OF YOUR HOME SUBSCRIPTION

Our readers tell us that these books sell out very fast in book stores and often they miss the newest titles. So Zebra has made arrangements for you to receive the four newest novels published each month.

You'll be guaranteed that you'll never miss a title, and home delivery is so convenient. And to show you just how easy it is to get Zebra Historical Romances, we'll send you your first 4 books absolutely FREE! Our gift to you just for trying our home subscription service.

BIG SAVINGS AND FREE HOME DELIVERY

Each month, you'll receive the four newest titles as soon as they are published. You'll probably receive them even before the bookstores do. What's more, you may preview these exciting novels free for 10 days. If you like them as much as we think you will, just pay the low preferred subscriber's price of just $3.75 each. *You'll save $3.00 each month off the publisher's price.* AND, your savings are even greater because there are never any shipping, handling or other hidden charges—FREE Home Delivery. Of course you can return any shipment within 10 days for full credit, no questions asked. There is no minimum number of books you must buy.

4 FREE BOOKS

TO GET YOUR 4 FREE BOOKS WORTH $18.00 — MAIL IN THE FREE BOOK CERTIFICATE T O D A Y

Fill in the Free Book Certificate below, and we'll send your FREE BOOKS to you as soon as we receive it.

If the certificate is missing below, write to: Zebra Home Subscription Service, Inc., P.O. Box 5214, 120 Brighton Road, Clifton, New Jersey 07015-5214.

FREE BOOK CERTIFICATE

4 FREE BOOKS

ZEBRA HOME SUBSCRIPTION SERVICE, INC.

YES! Please start my subscription to Zebra Historical Romances and send me my first 4 books absolutely FREE. I understand that each month I may preview four new Zebra Historical Romances free for 10 days. If I'm not satisfied with them, I may return the four books within 10 days and owe nothing. Otherwise, I will pay the low preferred subscriber's price of just $3.75 each; a total of $15.00, *a savings off the publisher's price of $3.00.* I may return any shipment and I may cancel this subscription at any time. There is no obligation to buy any shipment and there are no shipping, handling or other hidden charges. Regardless of what I decide, the four free books are mine to keep.

NAME

ADDRESS _____ APT

CITY _____ STATE ZIP

TELEPHONE
(   )

SIGNATURE _____ (if under 18, parent or guardian must sign)

Terms, offer and prices subject to change without notice. Subscription subject to acceptance by Zebra Books. Zebra Books reserves the right to reject any order or cancel any subscription.

would Lettie be encouraging her to show some interest in him?

She was completely engrossed when Jonathan stepped quietly back into the room.

She turned to stare at him. He had seen her looking at the display of pictures and now his smile was modest as he came to stand beside her.

"I'm impressed," she said, still studying his face. "And I'm embarrassed to admit that I had no idea who you were, or that you were so renowned a journalist."

"Don't be. The Jonathan Bradford you knew was very different, not to mention, much younger." He laughed in a way that mocked himself.

She liked a man who knew how to laugh at himself.

She turned to the photos once more.

"But you've won almost every important award there is in journalism. You must be very proud of yourself."

"Oh I suppose I was at one time. Most of those pictures were taken years ago as you can see. Now I'm only a small town publisher, and that's exactly the way I like it."

He turned as if he didn't want to talk any more about himself. He tossed several sheets of paper on the desk.

Margaret frowned, studying the back of his bent head. Then she looked again at the pictures, and the same blond woman that appeared in several of them. The woman had a possessive air about her as she stood beside Jonathan, and a haughty look of self-assurance that made Margaret wonder.

"Is this your wife?"

Her question forced him to turn back toward the wall of pictures. His face was expressionless and the teasing quality was completely gone.

Margaret pointed to the woman in the pictures.

"She was," he said, his voice very soft.

"Oh, I'm sorry. Are you divorced?"

"Sylvia is dead. She died in a car crash two years ago."

Margaret felt an immediate jolt of sympathy. As she looked at the pain in his beautiful eyes, she also felt something that took her completely by surprise.

She was jealous. She even felt resentful that this man who intrigued her, who drew her to him like a magnet, could be so hurt by the memory of his beautiful wife. Margaret knew it was a petty, infantile emotion, one not worthy of her. But it was there nonetheless and now as she stared at him, she tried to reason it away.

"I am sorry. I had no idea."

His eyelids flickered toward the pictures on the wall and he gazed at them for a long moment. Then with a frown, he turned back around to the desk.

She barely heard his muttered reply. "Thank

you."

She came back around the desk and sat in the leather chair, reaching for the papers he had brought.

"Are these the papers you wanted me to complete?" Quickly, trying to put him at ease, she took the papers in her hand just as he reached for them, too.

Their hands touched and they both stopped and stared at each other across the shining surface of his desk.

Slowly Jonathan smiled. His easy grin was still tinged with sadness. He pushed the papers forward and smiled at Margaret.

"There's no reason for you to think you have to tiptoe around the subject, Margaret. I've adjusted to my wife's death; actually I'm happier than I ever thought I'd be." He looked into her eyes with a steady look. "The sadness I feel about Sylvia's death encompasses so many other things. Years, actually, of problems between us. I'll tell you all about it some day."

"Oh. Yes, I see. I know what you mean; I understand perfectly what years like that can do."

"I know. Lettie told me about your divorce."

"Did she?" Margaret looked down at the papers as she tried to concentrate on the questions before her.

Jonathan dipped his head, looking beneath his brows and up into her face.

219

"Perhaps that's a subject we *will* have to tiptoe around."

She looked up at him and smiled. His questioning look was gentle and patient, but there was also humor present and she was glad the lightness was back in his voice. She shook her head, grateful for his kindness and that his easy manner had begun to help her relax.

"No," she said, still smiling. "I'm doing much better than I ever thought I would, too. It's something I'll tell you all about . . . one day."

"Deal," he said with a nod as he placed his hand toward her across the desk.

Smiling into his eyes she took his hand, feeling more at ease now. The tingles she felt earlier were still there; there was no denying that. But it didn't frighten her half so much. In fact, she found herself wondering what it would be like to explore those feelings. To just let herself go . . . loosen up, as Lettie said, and let herself feel things she hadn't felt in years.

How would it feel to give in to those powerful sexual urges that had begun to stir again and enjoy the attention of a very attractive and appealing man?

Eighteen

Margaret was practically walking on air when she left the office of the *Ocala Sun*. She had a job!

But that wasn't the only reason for the light spring in her step or the bemused smile on her face. She was almost afraid to admit it, even in the deepest recesses of her own heart, but she thought Jonathan was just as attracted to her.

She drove by Lettie's salon, thinking she would stop and tell her the good news. She felt so happy that she had already decided to forgive her talkative friend for pulling such an underhanded trick on her.

As she got closer to the salon, she saw the parking lot was full. Lettie was probably very busy, she told herself. Besides, the salon was not the best place to discuss personal business, although the news of her new job would be all over town soon enough.

She'd talk to Lettie some other time. Perhaps when they went flea marketing together over the weekend.

It was a beautiful day and Margaret drove slowly, taking the time to savor the brilliant clear blue sky and the touch of green that had begun to spring up in many lawns and pastures. The breeze that stirred the palmetto leaves and high tops of the pines was warm and gentle. Spring was here, something that might take several more weeks to reach Atlanta.

As she turned into the driveway, her heart lifted to see the small house. The thick forest that lay beyond the backyard looked dark and mysterious, so dense that even the bright sunlight could not chase all the shadows away. It was a house that was haunted by the memories of good and loving events.

As a girl Margaret had loved to explore those thickets, had loved pushing her way through the heavy palmetto to a clearing that contained huge pines that towered above the ground. The area beneath the trees was smooth and thick with brown pine needles, that made a warm rich carpet, just right for picnicking or napping. She and Lettie had played there often.

As she put the car in park, she smiled, recalling those glorious, carefree days of childhood.

Who'd ever have thought that she'd come full circle, back to the place she loved so dearly?

As she sat in the car she thought about the chinaberry tree that grew in the backyard. She wondered if it was still there.

The strange tree with its thick trunk and oddly furrowed bark had fascinated Margaret as a child. She'd loved the drooping purplish flowers that sweetly scented the entire backyard in spring. No matter how many times Margaret went to play beneath the tree, her mother would always warn, "Don't you eat any of those berries, Margaret. They're poisonous, you know."

"Yes, Mother." Margaret smiled as she sat in the car, repeating the words she'd always given at her mother's warnings.

And then, more than likely, she'd gone and done whatever she wanted anyway. Except for eating poisonous fruit, that is.

With a carefree laugh, Margaret walked onto the porch and let herself into the house. She took a deep breath, pleased with the clean, fragrant scent that greeted her.

Once she began to accumulate the antiques she wanted, the little house would be just about perfect.

After she changed clothes, Margaret went into the kitchen to fix tuna salad. She was humming as she chopped the celery and gazed out the back window at the birds that flitted from tree to tree.

The phone rang and Margaret turned with a grin, wiping her hands on a dish towel that hung over her shoulder.

Lettie probably.

"Hello?"

"Margaret?"

"Yes, this is Margaret." She didn't immediately recognize the woman's voice.

"Hi, this is Jane Ann Tilton."

"Oh yes, Miss Tilton. How are you?"

"Still very busy. How's the weather there in Florida?"

"It's beautiful," Margaret exclaimed. "I just drove home from town and you would not believe how perfect the weather is. Like spring."

"Ah, I envy you that."

There was a pause. Why did Margaret get the feeling that the woman almost added "at least" to her sentence?

"Is anything wrong?"

"Well, not wrong exactly. I expected something like this from your husband; it's not that unusual. Just a slight glitch, I hope. But I wanted you to be aware of what's happening."

"What?"

"Charles and his lawyer have placed a hold on all the bank accounts that bear your name. I hope it won't be a problem; you did transfer enough money with you when you left, didn't you?"

That was something Margaret and Miss Tilton had disagreed about. Margaret had refused to empty the bank accounts without telling Charles. She had taken only what she thought she would need.

Margaret's hands on the phone grew cold and clammy and she felt her stomach muscles knotting painfully.

"Actually I took less than five thousand." She realized her voice sounded apologetic. She had wanted to be fair, and she was not a greedy person.

"Well, that's not bad, considering you have no bills of any significance."

"I think it will be enough," Margaret said, frowning. "I have a job now, too." She simply could not believe Charles was doing this, not after their last conversation.

"Good, that's good."

He had said he loved her and wanted her back. Was this simply a punishment for her refusal to forgive him and take him back? What game was he playing this time?

225

"Margaret? You still there?"

"Yes . . . yes. I just can't believe Charles has done this. He was always generous at least. Why would he do such a thing? And what exactly does it mean?"

"It means you won't be able to touch any of the money in the bank accounts which bear your name, not until this is settled. Neither will Charles, but you can be sure that he's already transferred what he wants into new accounts, ones with only his name on them. In fact I think you should be prepared . . . when we do receive access to these accounts, they could very well be empty."

"No."

"I'm sorry."

"But they will be released after the divorce is final, won't they?"

"Yes, but I'm concerned now with what he's already taken." She paused for a moment. "I'm sorry, Margaret. This was not very good work on my part. I should have placed a hold on the money myself."

"It's not your fault," Margaret said, her head still reeling. "You asked about this very possibility and I assured you naively that Charles would never do such a thing."

"A sharp lawyer would not have taken your

word," she said wryly. "It happens all the time."

"It's all right," Margaret said, even though she felt shaky and scared at the thought of being completely broke. "I know you'll do the best you can to get it back. I just can't believe Charles did this." Margaret rubbed her fingers at her temples where a headache had begun to throb.

"It's not that unusual. Usually one party or the other is vindictive. And money is always a method of punishment. In your case I can't understand your husband's incentive. He's the one having an affair."

"Well, I think I can. I spoke to him last night," Margaret admitted with a sigh.

"Oh? What did he say?"

"That he loves me and wants me back. And that the affair with Shelley is over."

"I see . . . and you refused?"

"Yes, I refused. Now that I'm away from him, I can see what a prisoner I really was. I have sacrificed most of my life to a man who didn't give a hill of beans about my feelings. It was always Charles. Charles's job, Charles's possessions . . . whatever was important to Charles's happiness."

"Looks like it still is."

Margaret grunted. "Yeah, looks that way. But

227

I'm beginning to start a new life here. I feel good about that and I was beginning to feel good about myself. I just came from a job interview and I was actually feeling satisfied with the way things are going. Ironic, isn't it?"

"Listen, don't let this set you back. I'm going to do my damndest to clear this up, and soon. If we have to, we'll take him to court in a civil lawsuit. But I don't think that will be necessary. After I get proof of what he's done, I can't imagine any judge will go along with such selfish, unfair attempts."

"You're right," Margaret murmured. "If Charles thinks he can blackmail me into coming back, he's got another thing coming."

"Good," Miss Tilton said with a chuckle. "Well, look, I'll call you as soon as I know anything for sure."

"All right. Goodbye."

Margaret placed the receiver slowly back in its holder. She walked to the small kitchen table and plopped down in the wooden chair, stretching her legs out tiredly in front of her.

No matter what Margaret had said on the phone or how convincing she tried to sound, Miss Tilton's news had left her completely dejected. She sat for a long moment, gazing out the window at the same view that had given her such pleasure only minutes ago.

The birds outside in the trees were quiet now. All she heard was the far distant cry of a small falcon as it hunted its prey. Its shrill cry of *killy, killy, killy,* sounded haunting and sad.

Suddenly, she stood up, gazing at the bowl of tuna which now looked unappetizing. She dumped the celery into the bowl with the tuna and snapped the plastic lid on, then placed it in the refrigerator along with the salad dressing. Her appetite had vanished.

Slowly and without really thinking about where she was going, she moved to the back door and opened it. The breeze from the marsh ruffled her hair and fanned warmly against her skin. She glanced to the corner of the backyard to a large umbrella-shaped tree. She was glad the chinaberry was still there.

She walked slowly down the back steps and across the brown springy grass of the lawn. A small rectangular plot of ground caught her attention immediately. The rich black soil of her father's garden lay tilled and ready, waiting for spring, ready only for a handful of seeds and a sprinkle of warm Florida rain to transform it into a lush green treasure of vegetation.

Her eyes wandered to the western side of the yard and the row of pines and cedars along a fence row. Scrubby palmettos filled in every free inch of space between the trees. Here and there were small monkey apple trees with their thick magnolia-like leaves. They were Margaret's favorites and had been her mother's as well. She smiled as she remembered how many times her father had threatened to cut the pesky trees down.

Margaret loved the stunted look of the trees, the wild irregular shapes as if the wind had transformed them all into different patterns. They reminded her of bonsai trees and of mystical enchanted forests.

The land beyond the monkey apple and pine trees was Bradford land, Jonathan's farm, and his grandfather's before him.

She found herself wanting to call him, wanting to tell him what Charles had done. Run to him and throw herself in his arms, cry her protests against his chest and see his blue eyes crinkle with understanding.

But she only shook her head, silently chiding herself. She simply could not go running to a man like Jonathan for sympathy every time there was a problem. Or *any* man for that matter.

As she turned and walked toward the shelter of the chinaberry tree, she took a deep breath and straightened her shoulders.

She was on her own now. She had to learn to handle her problems alone. Jonathan was there for her; she knew it, sensed it in the way he looked at her. She was almost certain she could find comfort with him, whether it was in a quiet conversation, or in the disturbing warmth of his arms.

But that dependence on him was not something she could accept. She had been dependent on a man for far too many years, all her life it seemed. Now something deep inside, some primitive urging, told her she needed to take care of herself for awhile.

The chinaberry tree beckoned her and the clear bare earth beneath it reminded her of another time. She had been different then — wild and independent with the confidence and energy of youth.

She ran to the tree as if it could somehow restore all the treasured strength that she had lost along the way.

Nineteen

Margaret felt much better when she came back into the house. Sometimes when she came in, she forgot the house had been her parents'; it was becoming her own. She was glad of that, for there had been a time when she wondered if she could ever be happy living here with their memories, knowing she'd never see them again.

Perhaps it was the walk outside and the time spent beneath the chinaberry tree, but it had given her a quiet feeling of acceptance and peace.

Now, if only she could muster up the same feelings of acceptance with Charles. She could only think of how much she wanted to wring his neck!

She laughed at her thoughts and went to the refrigerator to retrieve the tuna salad. She had just finished eating when the phone rang.

"Hi," came Lettie's voice. There was hesitation in the tone and a soft feigned shyness that was not typical.

Margaret could not help laughing.

"Hi indeed. You know I was very upset with you today."

"Were you? Are you still?" There was a slow, almost pleading tone in her voice.

Margaret laughed again and she heard Lettie giggle. It was impossible to stay mad at her, always had been.

"No, now that the ordeal is over, I'm not mad."

"Ordeal? Since when is talking to the best-looking man in town an ordeal?"

"When it involves begging for a job! When it means having no idea that a man you thought you knew is really an award-winning journalist. Not to mention, somewhat of a celebrity."

"Begging . . . ? Geez Mags, lighten up. I'd hardly call it begging. You have too much pride is all. Both of us are getting too damned old to be taking pride as a bedfellow."

Margaret sighed and shook her head. There was no sense trying to argue with this woman.

"Well, did you get the job?" Lettie chirped.

"Of course, but you knew I would, didn't you?"

"Well . . ." Lettie laughed and she sounded

like a young girl. "What are friends for?"

"Yeah . . . right. I start work on Monday. It looks like it couldn't have come at a better time."

"What do you mean?"

Margaret explained quickly about Charles and what he had done with their accounts.

"Well, that sorry dog," Lettie exclaimed.

"But I'm not going to let it worry me. I'm certainly not going to let him force me to come back to Atlanta. I think that's what it all boils down to. Charles just wants to have control. He even told me when I left that I'd never make it without him. I suppose now he's only trying to prove a point."

"I can't believe he's being such a rat."

"I should have known I suppose. Charles is basically a very selfish man."

"I'm sorry, kiddo. Is there anything I can do?"

"You've already helped more than you can imagine. Besides finding me a job, you make me laugh. Believe me, that's quite an achievement these days."

Margaret was still smiling after she hung up. She could hardly wait until tomorrow and their trip to the flea market. She glanced around the kitchen and small living room, making mental notes about the things she would like to look for.

The next morning Margaret drove toward town to pick up Lettie. She noticed that the car was making a loud, clicking noise, a sound she'd never heard before. Now, what would she do? She knew absolutely nothing about cars.

She picked Lettie up and pulled into the nearest service station. The old man inside just shrugged his shoulders and rolled his eyes when she told him about the car.

"We ain't got no mechanic," he drawled.

"Well, what about you? Could you listen to it? Perhaps you could just tell me what's causing the noise."

The man shrugged again. "Don't know nothin' about cars."

"All right." Margaret went back out to the car and slid into the driver's seat. "He don't know nothin' about cars," she mimicked with a bemused smile.

Lettie laughed. "We can go back and get my car."

"No." Margaret glanced down at the panel of the car. "Surely one of the lights would be on if something were seriously wrong."

Lettie lifted her hands and shrugged.

"How far is the flea market?" Margaret figured if the ride was short then she'd chance it.

"Just outside town. Less than two miles."

"Oh. Well, in that case, I'll have it checked when we come back."

Margaret's ear was attuned to the car's engine all the way on the highway. She hoped it wasn't only her imagination, but the clicking sound did not seem so loud or so abrasive now.

She breathed a sigh of relief as they drove into the sandy lot that served as a parking area. People were milling about and gathered around the various colorful stalls.

"Oh, this is great," Margaret murmured as she locked the car. "Daddy used to come here I think. Especially after Mom died. He liked to visit with the old-timers and trade stories."

The morning passed quickly. Although Margaret didn't find any furniture, she made several trips to the car to unload an armful of antique accessories.

She was thrilled to have found an old copper and pewter chandelier, even though it was darkened so badly one could hardly tell what it was. Once it was cleaned and rewired, it would be perfect to hang over the kitchen table.

She also found several very good pieces of blue delft crockery and decorative plates, along with a grocery bag full of old kitchen tins which she would display on a knotty pine table.

Although she had no idea what she would do with them, she had bought an entire collection of Uncle Sam figures and rag dolls.

She had just gone back to meet Lettie when she saw a familiar figure walking toward them. Her pulse quickened as she watched Jonathan slowly walk their way. Margaret couldn't help noticing the way his soft faded jeans clung to his thighs. Or that, despite being tall and slim, his legs looked firm and muscular.

He was laughing, causing a long deep groove to appear beside his mouth. As he turned his head, the morning sunlight reflected on his silver streaked hair.

He had not seen her or Lettie yet, and suddenly Margaret saw the reason why.

He had turned slightly, as if waiting for someone. A young woman ran to catch up with him, her long blond hair swirling about her head as she ran. She slipped her hand into the crook of his arm and looked up into his face, telling him something that made him laugh softly again.

Margaret felt as if someone had punched her in the stomach.

She was not aware of making a noise until Lettie turned to look at her oddly.

"Margaret? You all right?" She turned to follow Margaret's gaze. Lettie smiled when she saw Jonathan.

"Look, it's Jonathan." She turned with a frown. "But you already know that, don't you?" She stared at Margaret, studying her face and the stunned expression in her eyes.

"Let's go," Margaret said, turning in the opposite direction.

"Go? What are you talking about? You can't just pretend you don't see him." She stared hard at Margaret. "You really surprise me, you know that? You can't run away every time you see him; you're going to be working for the man for God's sake."

Margaret could feel her face growing warm. Her skin felt stretched and tight, making it almost impossible to smile as Jonathan and the girl approached. She saw that the girl on his arm was Debbie, the young, blond receptionist from the newspaper.

"Hey, Mrs. Avery . . . Mrs. McComber. How ya'll doin'?" The girl's smile was genuinely warm and friendly.

And why shouldn't it be, Margaret said to herself. The girl has no idea what I'm feeling, or how this man affects me every time I see him.

"Well," Jonathan said with a warm smile. "What are you two doing out here?"

When Margaret did not answer, Lettie acted quickly. She glanced sideways at Margaret and nudged her discreetly with an elbow.

"Margaret is on the lookout for some antiques. She's going to do some redecorating."

"Oh, you should get Jonathan to take you antiquing," Debbie said brightly. "He's an expert on all the antiques in this part of Florida."

Debbie could hardly stand still. She seemed the kind of girl who was constantly perky and excitable and who found joy in everything. She reminded Margaret of Ginger.

Margaret smiled at the girl, seeing her now as she might her own daughter. She wondered wryly why it was that sometimes the traits she found so likeable in her daughters were not always what she liked to see in a rival.

Margaret stiffened immediately, horrified by her own thoughts. A rival? She was seeing Debbie as a rival? When in the world had she begun thinking of Jonathan Bradford as her own personal property?

She realized they were all staring at her oddly, waiting for her to say something.

"Oh, I'm sorry," she muttered. "I guess I was daydreaming. You were saying?"

"She was saying that you should get me to take you antiquing." Jonathan was studying her, the look in his eyes odd and unreadable. "Which, I might add, I'd be happy to do anytime you like."

Margaret's laugh sounded forced. She was acting like an idiot and she couldn't seem to do anything about it.

She was aware of Jonathan's eyes on her, of the little furrow that appeared between his brows, and the look of amused curiosity in his eyes.

She didn't know why that irritated her so much.

"That's very nice of you," she said. She couldn't seem to control the stiffness in her voice. "But I really don't want to trouble you or—"

"It's no trouble," he said, grinning down at her. "Really."

They were all staring at her and she felt her skin flush beneath their quiet inspection.

"Thank you. I'll let you know." She turned with a jerky movement toward Lettie. "Are you ready to go?"

"Sure." Lettie's face held a puzzled look as she stared hard at Margaret.

"You all have fun now," Debbie yelled as they walked away. "And we'll see you Monday, Mrs. Avery."

"Yes," Margaret waved a hand back toward them, not even bothering to turn around.

As soon as they were out of sight, Lettie tugged at Margaret's sleeve.

"What the bejesus is wrong with you? You acted positively snotty to them."

"Snotty?"

"Yes, snotty. You haven't forgotten what the word means, have you?"

Margaret stopped and turned to Lettie. She seemed genuinely angry and that surprised her.

"What did I do?"

"You were cold as kraut, that's what. That girl's a sweet kid. She doesn't mean a thing to Jonathan, at least not the way you think. They're friends; Jonathan is always taking somebody under his wings for one reason or another. He's just that kind of person. My Lord, if I had a man who looked at me the way Jonathan Bradford looks at you, I'd count my blessings. And I tell you what else I'd do."

"Why don't you just tell me then?" Margaret was surprised and exasperated. She could not understand why Lettie was so upset. Had her jealousy been so obvious? She had thought by being cool that she could hide whatever emotions she was feeling.

"I would stop playing coy and let that man

know I was just as attracted to him as he is to me."

"But . . ."

"Don't! Just don't you dare say you're not." Lettie's face was hard and closed. "This is me you're talking to, remember? I can read you like a book . . . still. Oh, you're more sophisticated now. You dress better and you talk better. But I know you, girl. I can see every little doubt that swirls around behind those big gray eyes of yours."

"I don't want to talk about it." Margaret turned and started toward the car.

Lettie followed, not saying anything else, but glancing toward Margaret from time to time as they drove. They were almost back into town before either of them spoke.

"Margaret," Lettie finally said. "What is it? What has happened to make you act the way you do?"

"Lettie . . ." Margaret took a long, deep breath. She felt tired, and she felt wrong. She had withdrawn at the flea market, withdrawn into a protective shell just the way she always did with Charles. She hadn't meant to do it with these people who were kind to her, and certainly not with Lettie who had been her friend for forty years.

242

She drove right past the service station, not even aware of the clicking noise in her car's engine.

"I didn't think I was being rude, or that anyone would notice. Oh, how can I explain?"

She pulled into one of the parking spaces in front of Lettie's apartment building.

"You like Jonathan a lot." Lettie stared at her, waiting for a confirmation.

Margaret didn't want to admit it. It seemed much too soon. How could she possibly be this emotional about a man she barely knew? After all, her divorce was still not final, and she felt guilty about this newfound attraction. And she felt afraid.

"Lettie, believe me, I'm not trying to be difficult or snotty. It's something that I just can't talk about right now. How can I explain how I feel about Jonathan, when I don't even know myself?"

"You're attracted to him though, right? I mean, he is one damned sexy man."

Margaret turned and gave Lettie a look that told her she did not want to discuss it.

Lettie smiled and threw her hand up in mock surrender.

"All right. All right, I'll hush. I hate to sound like a cliché, but you're not getting any younger

243

you know. Don't waste any more precious time with these self-doubts. Don't make this attraction out to be more than it really is."

"What do you mean by that?"

"I mean, you don't have to marry him for pete's sake. If he wants to take you out to dinner, if he wants to come over and help with the chores . . . whatever, let him. What's wrong with that? What's wrong with having a sexual relationship with a man you're attracted to? Both of you are single and over twenty-one."

Margaret rolled her eyes and shook her head. "What's wrong with it is, I'm afraid I can't be quite that casual about it or about him. I'm afraid I'll care more than I should . . . more than he does about me. I'm afraid I can't live up to his expectations." She turned worried eyes toward Lettie, who sat staring oddly at Margaret.

"Oh my. Sounds like my advice is just a little bit late."

"And what advice is that?"

"I was going to suggest that sometimes a purely sexual relationship is best. No strings, no ties. After all, we're not kids. I was going to tell you that you don't have to get serious or fall in love."

"Heavens, Lettie. I'm not in love." Margaret turned away as if in disgust and stared out the window.

"What is it then? What's really bothering you kid?"

"I'm not sure I know. All I know is that when I see him, I get weak-kneed like a teenager. I get little butterflies in the pit of my stomach. He makes me feel hot and cold at the same time . . . mostly hot." Margaret made an attempt at smiling. "I find myself stammering like an idiot and behaving 'snotty,' as you so aptly put it."

"Uh oh." Lettie rolled her eyes heavenward.

"I'm too old for this. Aren't I? I came back home to start life over, to have a little peace and quiet. And now—"

"Good Lord. You sound as if you're ready to be committed to the old folks home. Of course you're not too old, not if you feel the way you do. Hell, I'd say you're lucky. Do you know how hard it is to find a man who can still make you feel that way?"

"Oh, Lettie. That's another thing. You might not believe this, but Charles is the only man I've ever made love with."

Lettie's smile was sweet and her face grew soft with understanding. "Of course I believe it, knowing you. You were always the most loyal person I knew. That's admirable. If anything, it will only make Jonathan want you more."

Margaret leaned her elbows on the steering wheel and put her face in her hands, rubbing at her eyes and eyebrows.

"This is crazy," she said. "Here I am discussing Jonathan as if he and I actually have some sort of relationship. The truth is, neither one of us has ever spoken about such a thing. He's been very kind and helpful to me. He said we were friends, but that's all. I think I'm putting the cart before the horse here."

"It's all right," Lettie said, still gazing at her sympathetically. "Just relax . . . take it easy. If it's right, it'll happen. I just don't want you to scare him away before you have a chance to see what's there, that's all. Be friends. If it happens, it happens. If it doesn't, it doesn't." She rubbed a hand across the back of Margaret's shoulders. "Okay?"

Margaret turned and smiled. Then nodded.

"Okay, Dr. Ruth. I'll try to do as you say."

"Goot," Lettie said, twisting her mouth into a Dr. Ruth imitation. "Just listen to ze old Doctor. Nobutty knows sax like Dr. Ruth knows sax."

"Get out, you nut," Margaret said with a quick laugh. "I'll call you tomorrow."

She started the car, hearing the clicking noise again and realizing she had forgotten to stop at a service station.

"And don't forget to have the car checked," Lettie cautioned with a wag of her finger.

Twenty

That evening Margaret called Claire.

"What? At home on a Saturday night?" Margaret said.

"Mom! I tried to call you today but you weren't home."

"Lettie and I went to the flea market of all things."

"You did? That sounds like fun. I'm glad you have Lettie now. Did you have a good time?"

"It was fun," she said with a smile. "I have a whole trunkful of stuff, junk mostly. But you know I can't resist the old things. I'm going to re-do the house. Of course, when I get through it probably will look older than it does now."

"You sound good; you sound much happier."

"Oh, I'm doing okay. Even though I do have my 'not so good' moments, mostly when I miss you and your sisters."

"We miss you, too. But I don't want you to feel sad because you're there living your own life. You deserve it." Then as if Claire had moved her mouth away from the phone, she said softly, "Yeah, you can get the salad out of the refrigerator." Margaret thought there was a smile in her voice.

"Who are you talking to?"

"Brian." Claire practically whispered the young man's name.

"Oh . . . Brian. Is there anything you'd like to tell your old mom?"

"No, there isn't." There was a feisty, teasing note to her daughter's voice. "Except I'm re-thinking my position, thanks to you."

"Thanks to me? But I didn't say anything—"

"I know you didn't. But when you made the decision to take control of your own life, it made me stop and think. I know what a hard thing this has been for you. Well, I guess I was impressed."

"Really?" Margaret repeated to herself and a slight grin of self-satisfaction played around her lips. "Well."

"So, I decided I had not been fair to Brian. I mean, he never knew how I felt about husbands and ambitions and all the other stuff that's mixed up in my weird mind. I decided to discuss it with him."

249

"And?"

"And, he was wonderful, Mom." Her voice actually sounded breathless. "I don't think I ever realized before just what a special man he really is. He's so understanding and sweet and . . ." Claire stopped and sighed.

"I get the point." But Margaret's laugh was one of delight. She knew the things that had tortured Claire all her life, things that were mixed up with the day she found her father making love to a stranger. Margaret said a quick, silent prayer that this could be the beginning of the end of Claire's doubts and unhappiness.

"Oh, Cyndi said you were going for a job interview. How did it go?"

Margaret laughed again, at herself this time. She explained to Claire about Lettie's little deception.

"That sounds like Lettie," Claire laughed. "But you did get the job?"

"Oh yes, although I probably won't have any idea what I'm doing. But I am looking forward to it. I start Monday."

"And what about this Jonathan Bradford guy, the publisher. Isn't he the same man Cyndi mentioned before?"

Margaret hesitated for a moment. She certainly didn't want to restart the discussion about

Jonathan having something to do with her moving to Florida.

"Yes, he's the one. We're neighbors actually."

"Is he married?" Claire's question was slow and measured and deliberately filled with mischief.

"Claire. I'm not even divorced yet, and from your own father!"

"Ha! You know how I feel about that. Well, is he married or not?"

"Not."

"Great!"

"Now you're beginning to sound like Lettie. Just give me a little time, won't you?"

"Okay, I'm just teasing you a little. I'm really glad you found a job that you like and that you'll be working for someone nice."

"Thank you."

"Cyndi told me what Dad and his lawyer did with the bank accounts."

"Did she? I'm surprised he told her."

"Oh, he tried to make her think it was only routine and that it meant nothing. As if he were only trying to protect himself in case you decided to be vengeful."

"Bless her heart. I so hate that she's always in the middle between her dad and me."

"Well, she didn't believe him this time. It's just about killed her. I mean, you'd think

251

she'd lost her best friend."

"Oh no. I'm sorry to hear that. I should give her a call."

"That would be good. But don't mention it unless she does. She's really hurt about this, Mom."

Tears sprang to Margaret's eyes. For the first time since coming to Ocala, she doubted the wisdom of her actions. She longed at that very moment to be able to drive to Cyndi's house, walk through the door, and put her arms around her sensitive daughter and assure her that everything would be all right.

"Mom?"

"Yes, I'm still here. Oh Claire, I just hate this. I hate that Cyndi has to suffer this way because of me."

"Don't you dare say that! It's Dad's actions, not yours that have hurt Cyndi. Just the way it's always been. Don't you let him make you feel guilty and put you back where you were. You're past that now."

Claire paused and when she spoke again her voice was softer, more imploring. "Cyndi is a grown woman. She has to grow up and face the real world. She might never believe you and me if we tell her about Dad's faults. But believe me, when she finally sees it and realizes it for herself, she'll remember."

Margaret wondered if Claire was thinking about the past and her own lessons about Charles that she had learned the hard way.

"Well, I never thought I'd see the day when my daughters would have to give me advice," Margaret said lightly. "But you know, I think I like it. It makes me feel . . . hmmm . . ."

"Loved?"

"Yes," Margaret said with a soft laugh. "Loved."

"You are loved Mom; I hope you always know that."

"Yes, I do. Well, listen, before I start to cry into the phone . . ." Her laugh was a little unsteady as she wiped the tears from her cheeks. "You'd better get back to Brian and your dinner. I love you, sweetheart, and I'll call you soon."

Margaret sat for a long moment at the kitchen table. Finally she put her head in her hands and cried. How she hated Charles for doing this to Cyndi. She looked at the phone. She'd like to call him right this moment and tell him exactly what she thought about him.

But she knew she wouldn't. For no matter what anyone said to Charles, including herself, he would go right on doing the things he wanted to do. Claire was right. As painful as it was for her to sit by and let Cyndi suffer, she knew it was a lesson she would have to learn on her own.

She decided not to call Cyndi just now either. She was afraid that her tears or her trembling voice might betray her, or that as soon as she heard her daughter's soft voice she might burst into tears. That would only make Cyndi feel worse.

She wiped her eyes and stood up, going into the bathroom and sliding open the door to the medicine cabinet. She shook out two Tylenol tablets and washed them down with a glass of water. Then she went back into the living room and flipped on the television. She needed a little diversion tonight. She needed to feel pampered.

In her case, she guessed she would have to pamper herself.

"Looks like TV will be it," she muttered. She put on a long, soft cotton robe that was sprigged with tiny pink flowers. She looked at her hair in the mirror, noting how much longer it had grown in the past weeks. She frowned at herself and used a wide pink ribbon to hold her hair back. Perhaps it was time to see Lettie and let her do her "magic" on her.

As she went back into the living room she heard the murmur of wind in the trees outside. It was going to rain. She could hear the creaks and pops of the frame house as the wind continued to rise.

She didn't hear the car in the drive. In fact, it was not until she heard the thump of footsteps on the porch that she realized someone had driven up.

"Oh dear," she muttered, running her hands quickly over her robe and wondering if she should go to the door at all. Perhaps it was Lettie.

She went to the door and, with a curious frown, opened it.

Jonathan seemed very tall standing in the soft light of early evening. He seemed to blank out the light and cause a shadow to fall across Margaret's face as she stared at him in astonishment.

"What . . . what are you doing here?"

"Well, is that any way to greet your neighbor, or your employer?" As he studied her face he frowned, and his blue eyes darkened. He reached a hand out quickly and touched her cheek.

Margaret had to almost physically restrain herself from jumping away from him.

"What's wrong? Have you been crying?"

"Well, for heaven's sake." She turned away from him. The last thing on earth she needed was his sympathy. Or the possibility of that sympathy making her fall into his arms.

He followed her into the house and closed the door.

"Why don't you just come in?" she mumbled coldly.

"Lettie said your car was making a funny noise today. I thought I'd come by and check it out for you. I wouldn't want you to have an excuse not to come to work." His attempt at humor fell flat and he frowned again.

"Sometimes Lettie takes too much on herself." Her voice was much sharper than she intended. "I can find a mechanic. There's no reason for you to put yourself out this way."

"Margaret," he said, placing his hands at the top of his hips and breathing a heavy sigh. "What in hell is this all about? Why are you being so damned stubborn?"

Margaret only stared at him, her lips clamped tightly together.

He sighed again. "Let me go look at the car. Maybe when I come back in, you'll be in a better mood."

"I'm not—"

He held up his hand and grinned. "I'll be back." As he left he turned and glanced back at her, his eyes flicking quickly up and down her robe-clad figure. "You look cute."

Cute? Had he said she looked cute? She shook her head, trying to retain the anger she felt toward him, toward all men. She tried desperately to banish the vision of his darkening blue eyes and his look of concern. Why did he always have to be so damned sweet? As hard as she tried, even the thought of how she'd felt at the flea market when she saw him with Debbie could not help her hold on to her anger.

She had felt betrayed today and it had hurt. But now, seeing him again she felt all those doubts fading away.

She sensed that her will power would always be at this dangerously low level with Jonathan.

Quickly she ran into the bedroom, intending to change into some decent clothes before he came back in.

"Cute indeed," she muttered.

When Jonathan opened the door several minutes later, Margaret could hear the loud rush of wind in the pines and palmettos. The sky was growing dark but she couldn't be certain if it was because it was going to rain, or simply because it was evening.

She finished measuring coffee into the coffee maker and then turned to him. Jonathan was standing at the large entryway between the kitchen and living room, his shoulders against the doorframe.

"Could you tell anything about the car?" She hoped she sounded more pleasant at least.

"Needed oil. Have you had it checked since you've been here?"

Her cheeks brightened and she looked away, feeling foolish and inept.

"Well, no, I guess I haven't. I've been so busy, I guess it was foolish, but I didn't even think about that."

He smiled and walked to her. He was standing very close, and even though he made no effort to touch her, she felt her knees trembling as if he had.

"Hey, it's no big deal; you're probably not used to having to worry about a car. Don't look so glum. Just make it a point every few weeks or so to get gas at a full service station so they can check the oil. Okay?"

He was so nice, always so calm and reasonable. Was he always this way, or was it only an act until. . . .

She had to stop thinking this way. It wasn't fair to compare his actions with Charles's. She could not imagine Jonathan resorting to angry, frantic tirades like her husband did.

"I'm sorry. I don't mean to be so distracted or rude. I'm just not used to someone being so kind."

Oh God, she sounded maudlin, as if she were begging for sympathy.

"Would you like a cup of coffee, Jonathan?"

"Sure," he said with a grin. "I'll get it. You go sit."

She stared at him, then turned and went into the living room. "The sugar and creamer are in the cabinet above the sink."

"You want a cup?"

"No," she said. "I'm wound up tight enough as it is."

"So I noticed." His voice was only a low murmur from the kitchen.

When he came into the living room he sat on the other end of the old faded sofa. His long jean-clad legs were stretched out toward the middle, almost reaching Margaret's feet.

Cautiously he sipped the hot coffee as his searching eyes gazed at her above the steaming cup.

"Now," he said with a hint of purpose. "Why don't you tell me what has you so wound up?"

Twenty-one

Margaret's mouth opened slightly as she stared at him, but his eyes were steady and filled with the quiet glint of authority. She thought he must be very good with authority.

"Tell me," he demanded softly.

She could see he meant to stay until he had some sort of answer from her.

But where to start?

"Jonathan, I don't want to burden you with my problems."

"Burden me," he said with a slight grin and a furrowing of his brow. "Tell me what has your pretty eyes all red and swollen."

That finally made her smile.

"I just finished talking to one of my girls. Claire, the oldest. And Cyndi . . . well, first I should tell you that Cyndi has always been very close to her father, very protective of him." She stopped and gazed into his eyes. "Oh, this is such a long story and it's complicated."

"I have all night."

His look touched her like a caress and it caused Margaret's breathing to become troubled and shallow. She had to look away to regain her thoughts.

"Cyndi is my middle daughter. You remember her . . . she came with me when Dad died."

"Of course I remember Cyndi. She's very sweet and pretty."

Margaret nodded. "She is sweet and sensitive. I'm afraid that, like me, she's also somewhat of a people pleaser. She tries so hard to do what's right for everyone else and . . ." Her lips trembled and she had to stop.

Jonathan's gaze was encouraging and tender as he waited for her to compose herself.

"Anyway, she was just devastated by this divorce. She thought I should stay with her dad and try to work everything out. What makes me really furious is the way Charles manipulates her and uses her. He doesn't seem to care that it's Cyndi who is being hurt in the long run."

She stopped to look at Jonathan, wondering what he thought about her problems and her family.

"Go on." His face was noncommittal. If he had an opinion about Charles, he was not going to say what it was.

"I just learned that Charles has cleaned out our bank accounts. Put them into a secret account somewhere under his name. Normally I would expect Cyndi to defend her father. But tonight when I spoke to Claire, she told me that Cyndi is terribly hurt by her father's actions. I'm sure she must be torn. She loves him so much and . . ." Again, she had to stop. She could not seem to keep her emotions under control lately. She placed her fingers on her lips to try and still their trembling.

Jonathan set his coffee down, then reached forward and took her hand, pulling her fingers away from her lips. The warmth of him, the excitement of his touch, ran from her fingers all the way to her shoulders. When she looked into his eyes, her vision was blurred by the swim of tears in her own.

"Maggie," he whispered. "Come here." He pulled her into his arms and held her tightly against his chest.

She had not meant to cry; she never allowed herself to cry in front of other people, especially someone she barely knew. The feel of his shirt beneath her cheek, the comforting warm scent of cleanliness and masculine cologne . . . it was all more than she could bear.

She needed to be held; needed to be comforted. She realized it was what had been missing from her life since that terrible day when she'd overheard Charles speaking to his lover.

Jonathan's hand stroked her hair as he rocked her gently back and forth like a child. Her crying against his chest seemed normal and sane.

"I'm sorry, Maggie," he murmured. She thought once she even felt the touch of his lips on her hair.

She clung to him, unable now to make herself pull away or remember any of her vowed resolutions where he was concerned. He simply felt too good to resist.

Finally Jonathan was the one who pulled back. He looked down into her face and took a folded white handkerchief from his back pocket and dabbed at her wet cheeks.

To her surprise, she did not protest. She sat obediently, letting him administer to her, letting the warmth and the feel of him penetrate all the way into her soul.

He placed the handkerchief in her hand and folded her fingers around it. One arm was still around her and his fingers still stroked her hair.

"What exactly is the divorce all about? Do you want to tell me?"

She grimaced and looked at him from the corner of her eyes, then away.

"You mean Lettie hasn't already told you?"

If he noticed the sarcasm in her shaky voice he paid no attention. Instead he answered honestly.

"I did ask her. But she thought it was something you should tell me on your own."

She shrugged her shoulders, reluctant to admit that her husband preferred someone else to her. What would Jonathan think? Would it make him see her in a different, less appealing way?

Jonathan thought she looked like a little girl, with her dark hair tumbled around her face, and the pink ribbon in her hair. He smiled and refrained from pulling her into his arms. She needed time to recuperate from the hurt of this divorce, whatever had caused it.

"Charles was seeing someone else." Margaret practically blurted the words out as if it were a confession. "A very young, very beautiful girl who is the same age as Cyndi. If it had been the first time, I might have gone on. I might have tried to forgive him." She turned pleading eyes toward Jonathan. "But it's happened so many times." She closed her eyes and leaned her head back against the sofa. "So damned many times."

She felt the brush of his fingers against her cheek. Her eyes flew open and she turned to stare at him.

He looked straight into her eyes when he spoke, as if to make a point.

"Your husband is a damned fool."

Her face crumpled. She could not bear it; she simply could not handle his sweet, gentle sympathy.

She put her face into her hands, hunching over until her elbows rested against her thighs. Her crying was silent, but Jonathan could see the trembling of her shoulders. He put an arm around her and pulled her back so that she was lying in his arms.

"It's okay, baby," he whispered into her hair. "Cry it all out. I'm here . . . I'm here." His husky words drifted away and Jonathan found himself aching to do more than just hold her.

His bold, adventurous, little Maggie of so many summers ago had been hurt. It had changed her, and she was like a sick colt that needed to be gentled and made to trust again.

He found that the thought of her being hurt, of being treated shabbily, struck at his heart like a blow. The feel of her in his arms was so right that he wanted to forge ahead, wanted to kiss her and make love to her right here and now.

The realization of those feelings was like a ray of sunshine into his darkened soul. For so long, he had felt empty, had felt that at this stage of life, he probably would never feel such powerful feelings for any woman again.

When Margaret finally stopped crying, she lay in his arms, unmoving and unspeaking. She was drained and completely exhausted.

But for the first time in years, she felt safe.

When she twisted about to look up into his face, there was a sweet look of gratitude across her features. Although her eyes were even redder and more swollen than before, there was only a fading shadow of the sadness that had been there.

Her hand touched his thigh and then slid away to push herself up into a better position. Jonathan looked into those eyes, taking a long, slow breath.

He would be patient. He would give her plenty of time to heal before . . .

"Thank you, Jon," she whispered, lifting her lips toward him. She kissed his cheek very close to the corner of his mouth.

He couldn't help his unwitting response any more than he could have stopped himself from breathing. All his control and his vow of patience just flew out the window at the scent of her light, woodsy perfume and the sweet touch of her lips.

In that second, when her lips were so near, all it took was one movement, one turn of his head and his mouth was on hers. That was the moment he stopped trying to convince himself of anything.

He could not stop his response, nor the heat that flashed so quickly between them. He had sensed a portion of it that night in the fall when they said goodbye. But this was beyond anything he had ever imagined.

Margaret's gesture had been one of gratitude, now she too was surprised. Her quick and unexpected loss of control and Jonathan's eager response left her breathless.

Both of them were lost in the white-hot flash that rushed from one to the other and then pulled them even closer together. It left them struggling with their own senses; until they both gave up their struggle for control.

Jonathan's hands raked roughly through her hair, pulling her head closer until he was kissing her with a wild hunger that came from deep inside him.

"Maggie," he whispered, his breathing ragged.

Margaret felt the heat of his kisses and his touch. It reached every inch of her body. She wanted to laugh as a crazy thought popped indiscriminately into her head. Who needed foreplay when the chemistry was this hot? She was ready for him now.

It was this admission more than anything that

made her realize what she was about to let happen.

It had to stop.

"Jon," she whispered, straining against him as she pushed gently to free herself. "Please, I'm sorry. But I can't do this. It's too soon. . . . I just can't."

Without protest he released her, but the blue eyes that gazed into hers were tortured and filled with a heated desire that still blazed. He took a deep breath and made no further attempts to pull her back into his arms.

Jonathan wanted so much to tell her it was where she belonged.

"I'm sorry," she whispered, not wanting to hurt him. By denying him, she was also denying herself.

He took several long, slow breaths, as his hand reached to her face and caressed her skin. His eyes became clearer and less troubled and he smiled.

"It's all right," he said, his smile unsteady. "I understand. I hadn't meant to. I don't want to push you into anything you're not ready for. I know it will take some time. I can wait."

Margaret wasn't so sure she could.

She didn't know what to say to him, never had she been treated so sweetly. She could not remember the last time her feelings had been given meaning and consideration. His restraint touched her; his actions touched her as nothing or no one ever had. She found herself quickly on the verge of tears again.

Jonathan wasn't sure as he looked into her eyes what was happening inside her head. When he saw the sparkle of unshed tears, he frowned.

"Maybe I'm being presumptuous," he said slowly. "Maybe you don't want—"

"No," she said, taking the hand that caressed her face and holding it between hers. "No, you're not. It's just . . . I hardly know how to react to you, Jonathan. You're so sweet and gentle. I didn't expect patience, too."

His grin at her was almost shy. "I didn't say I was patient. Just that I understand and that I can wait."

They laughed together.

"Well, that's patience enough," she said. "This has all happened so fast that my head is reeling."

His eyelids lifted slowly and he gazed into her eyes. His head came closer and he kissed her lips lightly. She could see the spark still in his eyes, even as he pulled away and sat quietly watching her.

"I think maybe I should go." His fingers played with a strand of hair at her cheek.

She nodded, still stunned, still feeling the passion. She didn't want him to go, but she couldn't ask him to stay when his compensation would be only to hold her. As much as she wanted him and needed his closeness, she simply couldn't expect him to do that.

He stood up to go and she rose with him.

"I also came today to tell you that I have to go to Tampa tomorrow. I won't be in the office Monday, but Debbie can get you started and show you the ropes. She'll introduce you to everyone."

"Oh. All right." She felt the disappointment crash upon her like a stone.

"I'm sorry I won't be there," he said, leaning close to her again.

"I'm sorry, too," she whispered, lifting her mouth for the light touch of his lips.

He groaned and shook his head, looking at her as if she had injured him somehow. She laughed and took his arm.

"I think it's time for you to go, Mr. Bradford," she said as she led him to the door.

Jonathan stopped at the door and turned to her again. Damn, but he couldn't seem to get enough of her. He was behaving like a kid, like some silly, lovestruck schoolboy.

This time he gathered her into his arms and pulled her hard against him. He took his time as he lowered his lips to hers in a very thorough goodbye kiss.

Her body felt so good, so soft beneath his hands. He had to force himself to pull away from her.

"Good night," he whispered, opening the door. "I'll see you Tuesday."

"Yes . . . Tuesday."

Twenty-two

It had begun to rain and now the wind whipped the misty spray across the yard and onto the end of the porch.

Margaret watched from the window as Jonathan ducked his head and jogged down the steps and across the grass. He paused for a split second and glanced back toward the house.

Margaret stood at the window long after Jonathan's vehicle had backed out of the drive and moved down the highway toward his house. Her fingers moved to her lips, feeling the unfamiliar tenderness and sensitivity of her skin. It had been a long, long time since she had been kissed that way.

She shook her head and turned back to the living room. She felt bemused. She could have been in a dream for all she knew. Nothing seemed real.

She would watch television, just as she planned. She would sit and listen to the rain and enjoy a quiet, pleasant evening, snug in her house.

But thirty minutes later, she had not heard a word that had been said. She sat staring at nothing, seeing neither the television program, nor her living room walls. All she could see was Jonathan's face, his lips and his beautiful, expressive eyes.

Margaret looked at the big, empty flagstone fireplace. Almost without conscious thought she jumped up and went to the fireplace, thinking it was the perfect evening for a cozy fire. She had seen firewood in the small shed just beyond the back porch.

She bent and looked up into the dark cavernous space above the grate. She hoped it was not clogged with bird nests. She knew her father had used the chimney often in January and early spring. She jiggled the iron handle that controlled the draft, making sure it was open.

She made several trips across the soggy grass, bringing as much wood as she could carry and stacking it on the back porch out of the rain. By the time she went back inside she was completely soaked from the rain, but she didn't mind. She felt exhilarated.

Back home she rarely did anything on the spur of the moment.

Holding her breath, Margaret watched as the flames crackled to life and the smoke rose in the chimney.

"Good," she murmured, holding her wet, cold hands out to the dancing flames.

She would take a shower and change back into her robe. She'd make herself a cup of hot tea and let the flames hypnotize her tension away.

She held out her arms and twirled around several times until she felt giddy and silly. Then she fairly danced toward the bedroom.

She had not been this happy in years.

Later, with her robe wrapped cozily around her and her legs outstretched on the couch, she sipped a cup of tea and watched the firelight flicker across the walls.

She tried to recall every word Jonathan had said . . . every movement, every look.

Oddly it was not Jonathan her mind turned to, but Charles.

It happened because she tried to think of the last time she'd felt so hopeful. As always, she thought of Charles and their first years together.

Oh, she had been so in love with him. She'd almost forgotten how much.

She frowned into the dancing flames, envisioning Charles's face and hearing his voice.

She had been young when they married, probably too young. She had been a virgin. Charles was older, more experienced. He had been the master, the teacher. . . . She had practically adored him.

But had she ever felt this way? The way she felt when she was with Jonathan?

"No," she whispered aloud. There was a note of awe in her voice.

What an odd thing it was to realize at this point in her life that there could be a different kind of emotion involved in the sexual attraction between a man and a woman. She sensed that with Jonathan, he would never demand or be selfish in his needs. Yet, he was sexually aggressive and masculine, more even than Charles had been.

She shook her head, bemused by it all. Everything was different now.

"I'm going to enjoy it," she said quietly. She thought she would enjoy learning about Jonathan very much.

Setting her tea aside, she closed her eyes and leaned her head back against the arm of the sofa. Red-gold lights danced behind her eyelids and she smiled.

She thought of her shower earlier and how she had stood naked in front of the mirror. She had tried to see herself as Jonathan would, the idea of that frightened her more than anyone would believe.

Her body was still shapely, although her hips were wider and her waist not nearly so small as it had been in her youth. Her breasts were larger and heavier, but well shaped.

Margaret's hands moved to her breasts, imagining the feel of Jonathan's hands, his mouth. . . .

She sat up, eyes wide open as she told herself she should not conjure up such powerful images. Not if she wanted to sleep at all tonight.

With the remote control, she turned on the television again, hoping its images would distract her. She felt like a kid on Christmas Eve, all nervous and restless.

Soon, the low muted sound of the TV, the tea and the flickering firelight took its toll. As she drifted off to sleep, she thought she heard the drip, drip, drip of water. For a moment, she roused, but she couldn't quite make out where the sound was coming from. Probably outside on the porch.

She snuggled down into the sofa and pulled an old afghan over her legs as her eyes slowly closed.

Margaret woke several times during the night. She wasn't sure what woke her, whether it was the sound of the rain, or the loud roar of the wind.

Each time she woke the image of Jonathan and the touch of his hands quickly filled her mind and her heart.

The next morning she was tired. She could still hear the rain hammering upon the roof and blowing against the side of the house. The fire had gone out, and the house felt damp and cold.

She wished she could sleep the day away, wished she could just snuggle back down beneath the afghan and let the rainy, dreary day pass her by.

But she was too keyed up for that. Her night's sleep, such as it was, had not seemed to help at all.

She noticed that her heart was beating heavily and every now and then there would be a light fluttering of her pulse, almost as if her heart skipped a beat.

Maybe she needed a cup of coffee.

Margaret was on edge all day. She didn't know what was wrong with her. She thought often of the girls, hoping they were safe. She wasn't quite able to push the worries about Ginger to the back of her mind. She was so afraid something had happened, that Ginger had done something even more foolish than usual and gotten hurt somehow. And she worried about Jonathan driving on the rain-slick roads to Tampa.

"This is ridiculous," she muttered, wishing she didn't feel so edgy.

She called Lettie, but got her answering machine.

"Lettie, it's me. I don't want anything, just wanted to chat. This weather is driving me crazy. Call me when you get home."

She paced the floor, glancing out the window

from time to time, wishing the rain would stop. All the while she could not dismiss the continued fluttering of her heart, or the way her pulse had accelerated.

She flung the front door open and went out onto the porch, breathing in the cool, sweet scent of the rain. When the phone rang, she almost jumped out of her skin before turning and running back into the house.

"Yes . . . hello?"

"You sound breathless. What are you doing?"

Jonathan's slow, masculine drawl filled her immediately with gladness. He sounded solid and warm and she wished he was here with her now.

"I was out on the porch, watching the rain. I'm about to go stir crazy today for some reason."

"So am I," he murmured softly. "Do you suppose it's related?"

She laughed.

"I just stopped for lunch and thought I'd call. How are you?"

"I'm fine . . . great." She was smiling and for the life of her, she could not think of a single, intelligent thing to say.

"Maggie, I've been thinking about last night . . ."

"Yes," she said. "So have I."

"I want you to know it wasn't something I planned. I mean, I didn't come over to try and seduce you or anything." His words were light and teasing.

"I know that."

"We'll take it slow, Maggie. As slow as you want it to be." His voice had grown soft and husky, as if his lips were very close to the phone.

"Thank you. That means a lot . . . you don't know how much. I'm just so confused about everything, so vulnerable right now." Why had she said that? She didn't want him to think she was confused about her feelings for him. That wasn't it at all.

But she felt uncertain about his feelings for her. That was the real problem. And she could not find the words to express that to him, not even by phone.

"I understand. Or at least, I'll try," he added with a quiet chuckle. "If I get too bold for you, just kick me or something."

"I will," she whispered. She realized she was holding onto the phone as if it were some kind of lifeline. Her fingers felt cramped and stiff from holding on so tightly.

"Well . . . I just wanted to call. I suppose I should get back on the road if I'm going to make my appointment."

"Yes. And Jonathan . . ."

"What?" His reply was soft and intimate.

"Is it raining there? Please be careful driving."

He laughed. "Yes it's raining, pouring, as a

matter of fact. And I'll be careful. See you Tuesday."

"Bye." But he was already gone.

The rest of the afternoon passed slowly. The rain didn't let up, not even for a moment. She tried to call Cynthia and then Claire, but both of them were out. She tried not to worry, or wonder where they were.

"You silly fool," she said to herself. "It's probably not even raining in Atlanta. And here you are worrying that they're out in the traffic in some storm."

She couldn't eat, but drank several cups of coffee, a mistake considering how caffeine made her so nervous.

She thought she was going insane. Or even worse, that she was about to die. Her heart was beating erratically and she was beginning to feel strangely breathless and disoriented.

A terrible sense of doom fell over her; she couldn't seem to do anything about it. She was terribly afraid that she was going to die all alone. Wasn't that the way it always happened? Just when she thought her life was on track. . . .

"This is crazy," she said finally. But she knew there was something wrong and that she probably should see a doctor.

Impulsively she grabbed her purse and an umbrella.

"If I'm going to die, I'll do it at a hospital." At

least she'd have a chance of survival if something was wrong.

She glanced out at the rain and her car. She only hoped she could make it to the hospital.

Her pulse reacted even more erratically as she drove toward town. By the time she parked the car near the emergency entrance, her legs felt so weak she could hardly walk. But she also felt relieved and hopeful. At least she had made it.

When she told the nurse on duty what was happening, they took her immediately to one of the treatment rooms. It was a cold, colorless room, filled with stainless steel and white cabinets. When Margaret stripped off her clothes and put on the stiff green paper gown, she was shivering.

The nurse took her blood pressure and listened for a moment to her heart. Margaret watched her face, alert for any sign of pity, any frown of dismay. But there was none.

The woman stripped the blood pressure cuff off and hung it back on the wall, then she smiled noncommittally at Margaret.

"The doctor will be right in."

"Thank you."

By the time the doctor arrived, Margaret had calmed a bit, even though her pulse still raced and her heart continued to flutter.

"Good evening, Mrs. Avery," the doctor said, glancing down at the clipboard in his hand. Then he looked up at her and smiled.

He was a tall man with an outwardly calm appearance. Margaret guessed he was about her age, although she thought he looked young for his age. His skin had a golden tan and although his hair was thinning, it was still dark and devoid of any gray streaks.

"So, you've been experiencing rapid heartbeat?" he said, taking his stethoscope and placing it at the side of her breast.

"Yes, and I feel as if my heart stops sometimes, then starts again." She gazed up at him. But like the nurse, his face was calm and expressionless.

"Well, let's see exactly what it's doing, Mrs. Avery. I'm going to have the nurse bring in the EKG cart. We'll just hook you up and have a look." He patted her arm, even though he was not looking at her. "Have you ever had an EKG before?"

"No."

"It's completely painless, so don't be nervous. There's nothing to it. When you're finished, I'll come back in to talk to you. All right?"

Margaret nodded as the doctor marched quickly from the room.

When the nurse came back she placed small wired pads on different parts of Margaret's body and explained the procedure.

Margaret lay quietly as the machine whirred quietly beside the table and then made pleasant clicking noises as it slowly spit out a long roll of paper. The nurse watched the paper and the jagged streaks of black ink that were being etched on it.

Margaret felt her heart flutter and she glanced at the nurse.

"Was that it?" the nurse asked, watching the machine.

"Yes."

"Good. We got it on paper."

In only minutes, the nurse began to remove the cold pads. She ripped the long strip of paper from the machine and turned to leave the room.

"The doctor will be right in."

When the doctor came in, he was studying the strip of paper that he had stuck into the clipboard. He sat on a metal stool and looked up at Margaret where she was sitting up on the table.

"Well, Mrs. Avery. It looks just as I suspected it would." He hesitated and then smiled reassuringly at her. "You're not having a heart attack. In fact there seems to be nothing seriously wrong with you at all."

"But . . . what is it? The skipping and—"

"Oh, I know it can be a frightening feeling. I've even had it happen to me a few times, especially when I was in medical school and staying up night and day." He scooted the stool closer to the table and held up the clipboard, pointing at several peaks on the chart. "It happened several times during the EKG. It's called Extrasystoles,

283

which means an extra beat in the rhythm of your heart. Now, to you, it feels as if your heart has stopped, but actually it's thrown an extra beat in. But it's nothing to worry about. In fact it's very common and quite normal for a lot of people. Has this never happened to you before?"

"No, not that I can recall."

He rolled the stool back a bit and flipped a sheet of paper upward on the board. "Let me ask you a few questions. I think it would probably be a good idea for you to have a complete physical later. But as I said, I'm certain there's absolutely nothing wrong with your heart. In fact, your reading looks very healthy and normal."

She felt an almost immediate release of tension in her body.

"Are you married?"

"No. I . . . I'm just getting a divorce."

He looked up and nodded. "Were you married long?"

"Yes, actually. Thirty-three years."

He frowned and looked at her with sympathy. "You're getting a divorce after thirty-three years of marriage?"

"Yes." Her answer was only a whisper. "I grew up in Ocala, but moved away when I got married. My husband and daughters are still in Atlanta. My father lived here; he died recently and—"

"Your father just died?" The doctor began to scribble again.

"Yes. He died in the fall. After I filed for divorce I decided to come back to Florida. I'm fixing up my father's house in the country."

"I see," he said, still writing. "And you live alone . . . probably for the first time in your life?" He glanced up at her questioningly.

"Yes."

The doctor looked back up at her and she thought his smile was very kind. "Well, you know, Mrs. Avery, all these things . . . your divorce, your father's death, even living alone in a place no longer familiar to you could explain why this has happened to you. Anxiety and stress often cause this problem. As well as losing sleep. Actually, any number of things can trigger it. But you do seem to be experiencing more than your share of stress right now. Your blood pressure is a bit above normal; that could also be stress, although it could be from being frightened. Some people are scared to death when they see a doctor." Again he smiled. "Do you smoke?"

"No."

"Good. Drink coffee?"

"Yes and tea. In fact I drank several cups of coffee today. I was so tense and nervous all day."

He nodded wisely. "Coffee will do it, too. I want you to get some decaffeinated coffee and decaffeinated tea as well. I could give you a mild tranquilizer if you'd like, to help you sleep."

"No," she said with a shake of her head.

"I'd really prefer not to take anything."

"That's probably a good decision. Exercise will help relieve most of your tension. But I'm afraid it will take time, what with your divorce and everything else that's happened. Just try walking a couple of miles every day if you can. I think you'll find it helps a great deal. All right?" He stood up and smiled at her.

"That's all?"

"That's all," he said with a grin.

Margaret thought she had never felt such relief in her life. She was not having a heart attack; and she was not going to die. Not at this moment anyway. Best of all, he had not even prescribed medication.

"Go home and try to relax, Mrs. Avery. Stop and get yourself some decaf coffee and tea. When you have time, you might arrange for a complete physical." He patted her arm and smiled again. "But I think you're just fine."

Twenty-three

As Margaret drove away from the hospital, she thought she had never experienced such a feeling of euphoria. She made a mental note to remember the feeling the next time she was afraid or anxious about her life.

She stopped at the grocery store, feeling absolutely energized as she strolled down the long clean aisles. She felt light and carefree, as if a huge burden had just been lifted from her shoulders. Even the occasional flutter of her heart did not bother her, now that she knew what it was.

It occurred to her that with Jonathan's attention and her eagerness to begin a new life, she had become fearful. She had always been an anxious sort of person, strangely enough when things were going well. She was always afraid that something would happen sooner or later to end the happiness, that something usually involved Charles.

She was beginning to see and to understand. Away from Charles she might actually one day be able to feel happiness and not be afraid it would vanish right before her eyes.

She smiled and quickened her step, picking up decaffeinated tea and coffee. With a quiet laugh, she tossed a bag of soft chocolate chip cookies into the shopping cart.

"Why not?" she muttered. "I deserve it."

She also treated herself to a couple of new magazines, something to pass the evening. Later, as she drove home through the fog left by the earlier rains, she hummed along with the radio.

She was going to be happy. Everything was going to be all right.

When Margaret stepped through the front door, she noticed a damp musty smell. She thought her cleaning had fixed that. She hesitated a moment and took the groceries into the kitchen.

After putting everything away, she wandered back through the house, turning on lights and looking about. There was something she should remember; the musty smell had made her think of it. But what?

She went to the extra bedroom at the back of

the house. The light that flooded the room reflected in shining streaks down the back wall. The room actually felt cold from the rain that had seeped in.

"Oh no," she murmured, closing her eyes for a moment as if she could make this new problem disappear.

The dripping noise she had heard last night as she dozed off to sleep was what she had been trying to remember. Besides the streaks that marked the rain's path down the back wall, there was also a huge puddle in the middle of the floor.

She felt the now familiar flutter of her heart and took a long, slow breath.

"No, I can handle this," she said, calming herself and squaring her shoulders. "It's only a leak, nothing that can't be fixed. Everything is going to be all right."

With that resolution firmly in mind she marched to the bathroom and grabbed some old towels. Once the water was cleaned up and the towels put in the laundry room, she turned toward the phone, wondering who she could call.

She would call Lettie, who knew practically everyone in town.

As she waited for Lettie to answer, she wondered how much the repairs would cost. She hoped the modest amount she had in the bank would cover it.

"Lettie, I'm so glad you're home."

"What is it? You sound positively breathless."

"Oh, it's nothing tragic or anything. Just that the rain has leaked very badly into my back bedroom. I'm afraid the old roof is completely worn out. Would you happen to know anyone who does that kind of work?"

"Sure. Let me look up his number for you."

Margaret could hear the shuffling of papers and Lettie's mutterings.

"Here it is. His name is Sam Carter. He's an older gentleman who's been doing roofing all his life. He's honest and he won't hold you up." She gave Margaret the number.

"Do you think he'd mind if I call him now, on a Sunday evening?"

"No, of course, he won't mind. He's a very nice man."

"All right. I'll call him. Talk to you soon. And thanks."

Margaret felt much relief after Mr. Carter agreed to come out the next day and look at the roof. She had forgotten what it was like in a small town where everyone knew everyone else. Mr. Carter had known her father well, he said. Of course he'd be happy to help her any way he could.

They made arrangements for Mr. Carter to

come by the newspaper office and pick up the key to the house.

Finally Margaret built another fire in the big fireplace. The weather had turned cool after the storm.

She showered and changed into something warm, noting each time her heart fluttered and reminding herself to calm down. Later she sat in front of the fire, drinking her first cup of decaf coffee and indulging in several chocolate chip cookies. There was something about the taste and texture of cookies that soothed and comforted like nothing else could. She didn't care what psychologists said about such ideas.

Each time she thought of the trip to the hospital she felt a thrilling little tingle of joy in her chest. How grateful and relieved she had been when the doctor said nothing was wrong.

She was going to be all right. She could do anything she wanted, see whomever she pleased . . . live life finally the way she wanted.

She smiled and thought of Jonathan. She could hardly wait until he got home.

Margaret slept better that night than she had since coming to her father's little cottage in Ocala.

Her first day at work went better than she expected. Debbie was very gracious and friendly and seemed to know everyone in town, along with their life history. There was only a handful of employees in the front offices, an older woman who worked part-time in classifieds and a young man named Sandy who didn't seem old enough to be out of high school.

"I'm the local sportswriter," he said with a grin.

There were more employees working in the press room where the big printing press was. The smell of ink and paper filled the air and Margaret breathed it in, savoring the odd scent. She smiled as some of the men waved or nodded as she was taken through that part of the building.

The day passed quickly. Margaret did a little work, mostly editing and proofreading. The majority of the day had been spent getting acquainted and learning about different jobs and machines.

As she drove home she wondered what Mr. Carter had found out about the roof. He had come by the office and picked up her key just as he said he would, and he'd known everyone there.

Margaret smiled, this friendly home town atmosphere was something she had missed very much.

Later at home she couldn't tell anyone had been inside except that her key was on the kitchen table. Quickly she picked up the phone and dialed Mr. Carter's number.

"The old roof is in pretty bad shape ma'am. It needs to be replaced, that's for sure."

"Oh, I was afraid of that. How much? Were you able to make an estimate?"

"Sure did. Hold on here a minute. Let me see what I did with that. Ah, here it is. Hmmm, looks like with roofing materials and labor it's gonna run you somewhere in the neighborhood of fifteen hundred, two thousand dollars."

Margaret groaned silently. She had already spent several hundred dollars out of her cache, counting the stuff she'd bought at the flea market. This was really going to make a dent in her checking account.

"That much? Well I guess it has to be done." She was talking more to herself, trying to decide what she should do, but there was nothing to do.

She couldn't let the house rot around her. In Florida, the dampness combined with the hot summer sun would soon reduce the place to rubble if she didn't keep it repaired. That was something her father had always preached to her.

"Well, we could probably patch it, get you through the summer. But sooner or later, the whole thing's gotta go."

"No, I don't want to wait; I should go ahead with it now. Can you do it for me, Mr. Carter?"

"Sure can. Might be sometime next week though, before I get to it."

"That will be fine. I appreciate it."

"I'll call you a couple of days before we come out."

That night Margaret went to bed early. She wanted to be fresh and alert tomorrow when Jonathan returned to the office. She felt her face growing warm just thinking of seeing him again.

She couldn't sleep. Every noise on the highway seemed to drift into her bedroom. Even the house seemed to make strange creaking noises that night. And she wondered about Jonathan. Why hadn't he called? Surely he was back by now.

She was almost asleep when the phone rang. Jumping up so quickly made her heart pound and she felt disoriented for a moment.

She was going to have a phone put into the bedroom, that was all there was to it.

She made her way through the darkness, not stopping to turn on lights, lest whoever was calling would grow impatient and hang up. There was only the faint glow of coals in the fireplace to light her way.

"Hello?"

"Mom?"

"Ginger! Oh, Ginger, honey, is it really you? Where have you been? I've been worried sick about you."

"Mom, calm down," Ginger said with a giggle. "I'm fine. I have a new job. Everything is going great." Her voice sounded loud and slurred.

Margaret's shoulders slumped as she recognized the presence of alcohol in Ginger's voice and the typical resulting bravado.

A new job. How many more jobs was she going to have? Why couldn't she settle down like Claire and Cyndi?

"How's Catherine Jane? Is she there with you?"

"She's fine. She really likes her new school."

The same thing she had said about the last school. Poor Catherine Jane . . . how she must hate it.

Margaret's first reaction was to scold, but she bit the words back. She rarely had the chance to talk to Ginger and she didn't want to alienate her every time they did talk.

"That's good," she said, trying to remain calm. "Where is your new job?"

"A place called Pedro's. You know, a casino and bar, like the other jobs I've had. This place is new . . . it's really a classy joint, Mom. You'd like it, with all the crystal chandeliers and beautiful furniture."

"Hmmm. Crystal chandeliers and the word 'Pedro' just don't seem to go together."

Ginger laughed loudly. "No, I guess not. I hadn't thought about it. How are you doing, Mom? I couldn't believe it when Claire finally got in touch with me."

"I tried to find you. I even sent letters to you at General Delivery. When you never called, I was worried sick that something had happened."

"Oh geez, Mom. I've been on my own for years now. Besides, if anything happened, I'm sure the authorities would contact you."

How could she be so callous? How could she make it sound like nothing?

"Ginger," Margaret said in a scolding voice.

"Mom, please don't lecture. I just called to say hi, and to see how you're doing on your own. I don't need another lecture. You should know by now that I'm never going to be as responsible as Claire or as sweet and perfect as Cyndi. Why don't you just give up already?"

"Because I love you, that's why. I want what's best for you and Catherine."

"Yeah, yeah. Well, I'm living the kind of life I like. I'm having a blast. You should congratulate me for not sponging off the old man."

"Sponging . . . ? Ginger, where do you get

such ideas?"

"Oh, I don't know. Possibly from the time he kicked me out. And you stood by and let him."

Margaret could hear the repressed anger in her daughter's voice. And the bitterness.

"Sweetheart . . . I was wrong. I've told you that a hundred times. I should not have let Charles do that; I can see that now. But at the time I was—"

"Embarrassed?"

"No! You always say that, Ginger. But it wasn't embarrassment. I was shocked and hurt and worried. But mostly I was concerned about you, and afraid about your having a child at so young an age. I—"

"Yeah, well, it's worked out all right." Ginger's voice was stiff and defensive.

"Sweetheart, how can you say that? You don't have a home; you live like a gypsy. Catherine Jane needs a real home. She needs to go to the same school and have friends that she will see again next year. She—"

"Oh . . . a real home? Like we had? Huh, Mom? With everything sugary and nice on the outside and dark and rotten on the inside? Face it, Mom. We were a dysfunctional family. And you know what I wish? I wish you'd had the guts to get out years and years ago when we were kids." Ginger was breathing heavily as the anger spilled out of her.

Margaret's mouth flew open. Her lips worked, but no words came out. She felt a deep gnawing pain that went to the very deepest part of her soul.

"Well, I've done it now, haven't I?" Ginger said in her slurred, sarcastic voice. "I've finally said it and now I guess you'll never speak to me again."

"No . . . Ginger. I'm just stunned I guess. Dysfunctional? You think our family is dysfunctional? Is that word something else you've picked up out there?"

"Oh, for God's sake! I'm going to go. If I could ever talk to you without getting that holier than thou, prissy attitude, Mom. I just wanted to talk, you know? I thought maybe something had changed, that maybe you had changed. But I guess I was wrong. You're just as cold and sanctimonious as ever. You never cried, Mom, you know that? I never saw you cry. Not even when I told you I was pregnant. You were such a rock, so unemotional and solid." These were no compliments Ginger was throwing at her Mother, but angry, hateful accusations, spat out with rage. "But you know what I wanted more than anything? I wanted you to scream at me, yell and scream and tell me how wrong I was. I wanted you to hold me, Mom, and cry with me." Her voice had gone very soft. "Oh, hell, what does it matter now?"

Margaret heard the click of the phone and her heart sank.

"Ginger!? Ginger, please don't . . ."

Margaret hung up the phone and walked slowly, unseeing through the kitchen and to the fireplace in the living room. She tossed another log on the fire and watched it blaze and light the room with a soft glow.

With a deep wrenching sob she sank to her knees in front of the fire. She cried as she had never cried in her life.

In the dancing flames she seemed to see Ginger as a little girl, her dark curls and flashing dark eyes filled with fun and mischief. She had been such a funny child. She had always made everyone laugh.

"Oh Ginger," Margaret groaned. She thought the ache in her heart was so intense it might never go away. "My little Gincy."

If she could turn back time, she would. If she could just go back and do everything over again, she would cry with Ginger and hold her. And she would never allow Charles to throw her out of the house or send her to a home for unwed mothers.

But she had been weak and she had been trying to protect herself, her own aching heart and sense of betrayal. As a consequence she had locked away all her feelings, never letting the world see how much pain she felt.

But Ginger had seen her as the stoic, the one who kept a stiff upper lip, no matter the consequences. In the process of putting on that brave face, Margaret had hurt her daughter more than she ever dreamed possible.

Twenty-four

Margaret hardly slept that night. Every time she closed her eyes she seemed to see Ginger as she had been at sixteen. The tears of shame in her dark eyes, the trembling lips and uncharacteristic bowing of her head in humiliation. That day was one of the most painful of Margaret's life and one she would never forget. Only the birth six months later of her beautiful granddaughter, Catherine Jane, helped ease the pain.

Margaret sighed and pounded the pillow. She wished now she had allowed the doctor at the hospital to give her a mild tranquilizer. At least she could sleep and would not have to arrive at the newspaper tomorrow with dark circles under her eyes.

She had wanted to look her best for Jonathan's first day back. It had been so long since she felt this intense, jittery need to look just right for a man.

The next morning, staring with dismay at herself in the mirror, she felt tempted to call in sick, even if it was only her second day at work. Her eyes were swollen and bloodshot, and she had dark circles beneath them. Even her freshly shampooed hair looked limp and sad.

With a grunt of weary dismissal, Margaret turned to the clothes she had laid across a chair. She had wanted to wear something smart and flattering. But, thinking of the designer suit she'd worn before, she wanted to make sure what she wore was not pretentious.

"Oh, the devil," she finally muttered to herself. "Does it really matter? The rest of me looks like heck anyway."

Jonathan was in the computer room when Margaret walked into the office. He had been scanning the Associated Press copy when he caught the movement of someone walking past the door.

Margaret had not seen him; she seemed to be lost in thought about something. Jonathan could see into the office across the hall. He frowned as he noticed the wrinkle on her brow and the look of exhaustion on her face. The pale pink sweater and gray tailored slacks looked good on her.

But Jonathan was more interested in the fact

that her eyes seemed swollen beneath the expertly applied makeup. Was it her ex-husband again? He felt his chest tighten in anger at the thought.

He stood holding a sheet of paper in his hand, lost in thought as he stared across the hall. He tossed the paper aside and had taken two steps in her direction when the phone rang. Before he could get back to the desk, Debbie was at the doorway, her eyes wide with excitement.

"Boss, it's Jeeter Clinton on the phone. He says there's a big fire in one of the warehouses down by the railroad tracks."

Jeeter was usually the first one to call in a local news story. Knowing everybody's business seemed to be his life's work.

Jonathan's quick frown reflected his irritation. He glanced again toward Margaret, then went to answer the phone.

"It's a big fire, Mr. Bradford," the man shouted over the phone. "Better send somebody with a camera down here right away."

"I'll be right there," Jonathan said. He turned to Debbie, who stood waiting in the doorway. When he glanced across the hall, Margaret had looked up during the commotion and was staring straight into his eyes.

He smiled at her, wishing with all his heart he had time for coffee, wishing he could go in her office and close the door, and tell her how much he had missed her. But with a newspaper, he had learned to follow the story. It was one of the first things he ever learned and now that training was a force of habit.

"Debbie, you and Margaret will have to handle everything today. Send Sandy out to the fire as soon as he gets his sports column squared away. Leave me room—about half a page, four columns and the headline plus a picture. If it turns out to be nothing, I'll call and free it up. But if you don't hear from me, we'll go with it that way. Okay?"

"You got it, boss. The big camera is on my desk. You can pick it up on your way out."

Jonathan headed through the doorway into the hall. He glanced at Margaret and gave her a quick wave, wishing he could ignore the questions in her beautiful, smoky eyes.

As soon as Jonathan grabbed the camera and headed out the door, he could feel the adrenaline kick in. This was what he had missed, the excitement of a story, the feeling of total involvement when you ran out the door, never knowing what would be waiting out there to greet you.

Margaret sat very still after Jonathan left, wondering what was going on and waiting hopefully for someone to tell her. Should she ask? A well-bred Southern lady learned to quell her curiosity at an early age, at least until she could ask discreetly. But this was simply driving her crazy.

She stood up to find someone when Debbie came into the office. In her hand was a large sheet of blank newspaper along with strips of newsprint.

"Looks like it's just you and me today, Mrs. Avery," Debbie said. There was a feigned look of disgust around the girl's mouth, but Margaret sensed right away that Debbie loved being in the center of the storm and relished the authority. She could see it in the tense way she held her body and in the quick high-pitched tone of her voice as she began to speak.

"There's a big fire down along the tracks. The boss will probably be there most of the day. You and I . . ." Her voice trailed off as she frowned and began to sort through the numerous strips of paper. ". . . will have to mock up the front page and do the rest of the stories." She glanced at Margaret out of the corner of her eye as she bent over the desk. "You remember how to do this?"

"Yes," Margaret said with a nod. "I think so."

"Good, 'cause I've got to get back out front. I'm doing the classifieds today, too." Briskly she walked out of the room, pausing at the door and turning back to Margaret. "If you have any questions, just come out front and yell. It's going to be one of those days."

Margaret nodded and stared mutely at the jumbled pile of papers on her desk. Things hadn't changed that much since her college days. Working in a newspaper office had always been hectic and messy.

All morning as she worked, she tried to fight her feeling of disappointment. As much as she tried to dismiss such thoughts, she wondered if Jonathan had changed his mind about her. Perhaps she had simply put too much meaning into what happened between them the other night.

"I don't know," she said. She ran her fingers through her hair and groaned, then turned her attention to the front page before her.

It was growing late, well past noon. Margaret's neck was stiff from bending over the desk all morning. She was relieved when Debbie came in and suggested that she take a few moments out for lunch.

"It'll do you good to get outside for awhile. And soon as you get back, I'll go."

After lunch and a quick walk around the park, Margaret did feel much better. Later as she sat at the front desk, waiting for Debbie to return, she began to grow sleepy and lethargic. She was thankful when the door opened and a woman stepped across the threshold.

Margaret's eyes scanned the woman quickly from head to toe. She was one of the most stunning creatures Margaret had ever seen. Her straight, shoulder-length blond hair was tied back at the nape of her neck with a wide black ribbon that matched the lapel of her tweed riding jacket. The sleek tan riding pants she wore encased amazingly slim hips and thighs, especially for a woman who looked to be past forty-five. She had a pleasant if somewhat haughty look on her lovely face as she glanced toward Margaret.

"Where's Debbie?" she asked.

"She just stepped out for lunch. She should be back soon."

"No matter," the woman said with a polite, forced smile. "Actually I came to see Johnny. We have a luncheon appointment."

Margaret's mind seemed blank.

"Johnny?"

The woman closed her eyes, an effect aimed to show her impatience. "Jon Bradford . . . the publisher here . . . and your employer, I presume."

"Oh yes, I've just never heard anyone call him Johnny, not in a while at least."

"Yes, well, just give him a call. Tell him Ashley is here." Her voice had a tendency to rise at the end of the sentence, as if everything she said was a question. "I'll be waiting in the car." She turned to go.

"Wait. Jon, I mean, Mr. Bradford is not in the office. He's on a story, although he'll probably be back soon if he intends to make the deadline."

"Oh damn." Then with a tight smile, the woman said, "Well, I guess I know where that puts me on his priority list." With a shrug she walked back to the desk. "Please give him a message. Tell him . . ." She stopped and stared at Margaret. "Shouldn't you write this down? Tell him that Ashley came by for our luncheon date and that she was very disappointed. Tell him that I did buy the Arabian . . . the one he recommended. He'll know what I'm talking about. And tell him I expect him to drop by this afternoon to see the animal. Will you do that please?"

"Yes, of course." Margaret was still writing. "I'll give it to him as soon as he arrives."

"Who are you?" the woman asked, as if it were only an unimportant second thought.

"My name is Margaret Avery. This is my first week here and—"

"Really? That's nice. Well, gotta run."

Margaret stared at the door long after the woman had dismissed her as unimportant and left. Realizing the implication of this "Ashley's" visit, she felt like a fool.

Had she actually thought that a man like Jonathan Bradford would not already be involved with a woman? Had she really thought that there was something special in the way he treated her?

The truth was, she had not thought at all. She had only felt and responded.

"Like a kid," she hissed. "Like a silly, twittering schoolgirl." She felt her cheeks burning with humiliation.

She was back in her own office when Jonathan finally rushed in later. She could see by the sparkle in his eyes and the flush of color on his cheeks just how much he enjoyed his work. She tried not to let her heart flutter when he stopped briefly at her door on his mad rush down the hallway.

"Hi. Sorry I haven't had time to talk. It's just been one of those days."

"Yes," she said with a smile. "Just what Debbie said." She pulled her eyes away from his and shuffled through the papers on her desk. "Oh, I have a message for you here somewhere."

He had already turned as if to go down the hallway.

"Bring it to my office, would you? I've gotta get these pictures to the guys in the back."

She was waiting for him when he came hurrying into his office, although she had been tempted simply to leave Ashley's message on his desk and leave. But she could not resist seeing his face and the expression in his blue eyes when he read the note.

"Now." He was rummaging through his desk and glanced up as he took the note from her hand.

Jonathan thought Margaret's eyes seemed a little cool. Even as busy and distracted as he was, he had already wondered at her gaze. As he read the message from Ashley, he felt a pleasant warmth surge through him. He glanced up quickly from the paper and gazed directly into Margaret's questioning eyes.

She was jealous! Irrationally, that thought pleased him very much.

He smiled at her.

Margaret stared at Jonathan, noting the smile

that moved across his lips and unable to dismiss the twinkle that rose in his distracting eyes. It caused her to turn on her heel to leave his office.

"Wait. Hey . . ." He ran to catch her arm, pulling her back. With his free hand he closed the door.

"What is this? Are you upset about the message? About Ashley? Did she say something to make you feel . . . ?"

Margaret conjured up her coldest look, that stone face she had learned to perfect over the years.

"I'm sorry?" she said, deliberately misunderstanding him. "I'm not upset. I just have a lot of work to do, that's all." She stared at him with a tight little smile.

His eyes narrowed and he stepped back, staring at her with a look of open curiosity.

"Wait a minute now. What the hell is this all about? After the other night I thought . . ."

Margaret's brows lifted and she gave a shrug of dismissal. "Oh, that. I hope you don't think I become that friendly with everyone. And I do appreciate your being there as a friend, of course. And listening to my problems. But really Jonathan, that's all there was to it, wasn't it? You don't need to feel obligated—"

311

"Obligated?" He frowned as he took her arm and pulled her toward the desk. Then he lowered his voice, "Damn it, Maggie. What I felt the other night had absolutely nothing to do with obligation. And you know it. Now, do you want to tell me what this really is all about?"

"I don't know what you're talking about. The last thing I want right now is a relationship with a man. If I gave you that impression, then I'm sorry."

His hand released her arm and he stood for a moment staring at her, his hands resting on his slender hips. As he studied her cool, expressionless face and the blank gray eyes, he pursed his lips, then nodded.

"Well," he said. "I suppose I'm the one who should apologize. Are you telling me there was nothing between us that night? That what I felt was totally of my own imagination?" He had moved closer as if to challenge her.

Margaret swallowed hard and stepped backward. The nearness of him made her knees feel like jelly, made the pit of her stomach begin to crawl with butterflies. The heady exotic scent he wore reminded her of his mouth and the taste of him that she actually felt faint with desire.

She could not deny it, not when she was certain he could read it so well in her eyes. But damn it, neither could she let herself be pulled into another relationship where she was the one to be hurt.

"No," she whispered. "Of course it wasn't. I did feel something, too, I'm not denying that."

He moved closer even still, threatening to touch her, threatening to make her lose all sense of perspective.

"What? Tell me what it was you felt, Maggie." His voice was a low sexy growl that made shivers run down her neck.

"Jon," she said, trying desperately to break the spell. "I have to go. This is just not something I'm willing to talk about right now. Not here anyway."

Jonathan gritted his teeth and his blue eyes glinted with intense frustration.

"Then when, damn it? And where? I'm not going to give up on you, Maggie. You might as well know that from the beginning. Don't push me away if you don't mean it."

Margaret's hand went shakily to her hair and she could hardly force her eyes to meet his. His intensity and persistence frightened her and confused her even more. She simply could not bear to make another mistake and be humiliated again. She was afraid that this time, with this man, it would destroy her.

"I . . . I don't know. I have to go."

Jonathan watched her leave, shaking his head with frustration. She had been hurt badly; he knew that. He meant to be patient and now he reminded himself again of that vow. But she was driving him crazy.

Somehow he had fooled himself into thinking she trusted him. He thought her reaction the other night had proven that.

"Just shows how much you know, Bradford," he muttered as he walked back around to his desk. "Have to take it slow, man. . . . Have to take it real slow."

Twenty-five

That first week at work was torture for Margaret, but it had nothing to do with the job. That, she enjoyed.

She wasn't sure about anything where Jonathan Bradford was concerned. Was she being ridiculous, drawing away from him the way she had? Was it only petty jealousy that made her behave that way?

It was something she wanted to discuss with Lettie. They spent several evenings together that week talking about men and relationships and how women seemed always to want something entirely different than a man.

"You know, I tease you a lot about Jonathan," Lettie said. "He is sexy and he is probably the most eligible bachelor in town. But you know I do understand what you're going through right now. And if you don't feel the time is right, that's something only you should decide."

Margaret nodded, but said nothing.

"Although I will say, I think you have holes in your head." Lettie grinned at her.

They were sitting at Margaret's small kitchen table.

"Well, there are some days, not to mention nights, when I would certainly agree with you. I mean, besides his looks, Jonathan has so much to offer. He's intelligent and professional. He's very personable and funny when he wants to be. I can't remember ever having met a man who is more considerate and easygoing. He hasn't pushed me at all since I told him I wasn't ready for a relationship."

"You sound a bit disappointed," Lettie said with a funny lift of her eyebrows.

Margaret's grin was wistful. "Maybe."

"Jonathan is a mature man, Margaret. He's giving you a little room, that's all. Waiting for you to say the word. That's what I like about older men . . . that wonderful patience."

"Yes, I suppose you're right. You know from what I've heard, there were problems between Jon and his wife long before she died. And that surprises me." Margaret looked at Lettie. She didn't actually want to ask about it and she hoped Lettie would take the hint.

316

"She was an alcoholic," Lettie said. "They lived all over the world during their marriage. He only came back here after she died, so I really don't know that much about her. She was different though. I never could understand what they had in common."

Margaret's face turned thoughtful and she smiled. "Oh, I think that's something we all have said every now and then."

"Yeah, with me it was every husband I had."

After Lettie had gone home, Margaret cleared away the dishes. She was distracted; sometimes she would stop and stand for a few moments, lost in thought, before she could rouse herself and begin again.

She had expected her new life to be lonely . . . hard even. What she hadn't expected were these other complications with Jonathan. Or her own confusing thoughts where he was concerned.

Even so she was beginning to feel better about herself and her ability to handle her own life. She'd made arrangements to have the roof repaired, and she had set aside enough money to cover the expense. Her checkbook was balanced and she'd just had her car serviced, had even started a small notebook that would help her remember such crucial items as oil change and new tires.

All this was entirely new to her. Charles had always handled their personal business. She was surprised to find that the daily, menial routines she had given over so easily to him gave her a sense of satisfaction and self-confidence.

She thought of a night recently when she called Cyndi. She had been unusually quiet and withdrawn. Margaret had had to pull every response from her. When her father's name was mentioned, Margaret thought she detected a coolness in Cyndi's voice. Had he said something to hurt her? Done something that Cyndi didn't want to mention to her mother?

But she couldn't worry about every far, distant possibility, she told herself again. She had enough to concern her, right here at home.

Home. She realized she had truly begun to think of Ocala as her home again.

Just as she put away the last dish, the phone rang.

"Hi, it's Jane Ann Tilton. Sorry to call you this late. I have been so busy that I'm making calls at night from home."

"That's fine," Margaret said. "Is everything going all right?"

"Well, if you mean, will the divorce go through on time, the answer is yes. On the other hand, if you're wondering about the order to divide the money from those accounts, the answer is no."

"Oh."

"I just wanted to tell you that your divorce will be final tomorrow. Charles has not filed an appeal, so it won't be necessary to have a hearing."

"So, I'll be divorced and I won't even have to appear?"

"That's right. And believe me, this is best."

"I agree. I have no wish to come back to Atlanta just now."

"Good. Charles has managed to throw a monkey wrench into the works regarding these accounts. They got the judge to agree to a separate hearing. I don't want to get your hopes up, because you never know about the court system. But I'm very optimistic that things will go our way, especially since you're not insisting on anything unreasonable. That should sit very well with the judge. Personally I feel he will be able to see this for exactly what it is—harassment and an attempt by Charles to hold onto his money as long as he can. That, and pure meanness."

Margaret laughed. Jane Ann knew Charles very well.

"So . . . any questions?"

"No, I guess not. You seem to have everything well in hand. And after tomorrow I'll be a divorced woman?"

"That's right. Congratulations."

"Thanks. Thanks for everything."

"Call if you need me, Margaret. Bye bye."

Margaret made herself a cup of tea. Her face was blank and expressionless as she worked. She walked slowly to the sofa in the living room. She glanced around, pleased with the new rug she'd bought. After the floors were cleaned and waxed, the rich wood had shone through, and not wishing to hide their beauty, Margaret had chosen only a small braided area rug.

She'd also found a place for her collection of Uncle Sam figures upon the wide cypress mantel above the fireplace.

She did love the little house. And she liked her new job, too. But the call from Jane Ann Tilton made her feel melancholy and lifeless.

She sat on the sofa, remembering the times when the girls were small. How Cyndi would run to greet her daddy when he came home from work, her little arms clasping around his knees.

"Daddy, Daddy, Daddy," she would shout.

Those were the good times. Those were the days when Charles still actually came home from work.

When had it all gone wrong? She guessed it had happened gradually. She had tried, but it was impossible to make a marriage work when only one worked at it.

She felt tears sting her eyes, and she felt a surprising ache in her heart when she thought of Charles. They had shared so much, and they still shared three beautiful daughters. She didn't really want it to end bitterly.

Perhaps Charles didn't either.

Impulsively she picked up the phone and dialed Charles's number. She glanced at the clock. Surely he would be home by now since it was past ten o'clock.

"Hello?" Margaret frowned when she heard the woman's voice. It wasn't Cyndi or Claire. Had she dialed the wrong number?

Then she heard the rumble of a male voice near to the phone. "Who is it?" Margaret recognized Charles's voice even though it was muffled and distant.

"I don't know. They won't say anything." The girl's voice was a soft drawl of complaint.

"Just hang up the damned phone, Shelley," Charles muttered.

Oh, how Margaret recognized the authority and impatience in that voice. She had heard it so often.

She placed the phone softly back onto its cradle and leaned against the kitchen cabinet.

So Charles had lied again. He was still seeing Shelley. He'd even moved the girl into Margaret's home and her bed. She wondered if that was what had caused Cyndi's odd behavior last time they talked.

Margaret was trembling as she hugged her

arms tightly about her body and closed her eyes. She hadn't meant to cry and she didn't even know why she was.

Later as she lay in bed she thought about what had happened. She hadn't cried because of pain or jealousy. There was no love left in her for Charles Avery. She realized there had not been love there for a long, long time. And hearing Shelley's voice tonight had only made it final.

What she had felt was sadness for a lifetime spent with the wrong person, for all the wrong reasons. She had cried for the end of something that had once been precious. She knew part of her sadness had to do with guilt.

She felt guilty that she had subjected her daughters to a loveless marriage all these years. She had been afraid of what a divorce might do to them when they were young, and she had wanted to protect them. But in pretending at happiness, she had not protected them at all.

After a long night of remembrances and tears, Margaret felt surprisingly good the next morning.

So good that she did something quite impulsive. She walked jauntily into the office, feeling pretty in her jade green spring suit and cream colored silk blouse.

She looked toward Jonathan's office and saw him sitting at his desk. His head was bent as he wrote on the pad before him. As usual when he worked, he seemed oblivious to anyone around him.

She opened the door, tapping on the glass pane as she went in.

The way his eyes lit when he saw her made her feel even better. With one quick glance he let his gaze move from her knees and the bottom of her skirt, up to her face.

"Wow. You look terrific. Did I give you a raise that I don't know about?" His smile was intoxicating and she stood for a moment reveling in the way he made her feel. She liked the way he let the past go, how he refused to pout over their differences.

"Hardly," she said with a quick laugh. "I suppose you could say I'm celebrating today."

"Oh?" his brows lifted and his eyes questioned.

"My divorce is final today." Her smile wavered only the slightest bit as she stared across the desk at him.

He nodded, his eyes never leaving her face. "You okay?"

"Yes, actually I am." Her returning smile revealed her own surprise. "I'm feeling pretty good."

"Good enough to let the boss take you out for dinner?" Jonathan leaned back in his chair. The blue shirt he wore emphasized the brilliance of his eyes and the golden tan color of his skin. He was teasing her and his smile reflected that emotion. But the blue eyes that studied her so carefully were quiet and serious.

"Yes," she answered softly.

His lips quirked to one side and a brief frown flickered between his eyes. Slowly he let his chair back down and leaned forward as if he had not heard her reply.

"Yes? You, Margaret Avery, are agreeing to go out to dinner with me?"

She glanced away, trying to will herself not to blush beneath his teasing look. He was not going to let her off the hook so easily.

"Actually I thought . . . if you like . . . I would cook dinner for you, at my house."

"Tonight?"

"Yes, tonight," she said with mock exasperation.

"Oh." He made a big thing of rummaging through his desk drawers. "Let me see. Where did I put my appointment book? I think tonight will be all right, but gee . . ." He stopped rummaging and grinned up at her like a little boy. "Oh heck, since I know you so well and we are neighbors, why not?"

Margaret pursed her lips and smiled at him, her gray eyes alive with amusement. "You really don't deserve my having to humble myself this way you know."

"I know."

"Well, I'll see you about seven then?"

"I'll be there." He smiled and watched her turn and walk out the door, letting his eyes linger on her hips and the way she moved beneath the green material of her skirt.

Jonathan sat back in his chair. For some reason he couldn't seem to stop smiling. Was he going to have to have another talk with himself? One of a hundred little pep talks he'd had over the past few days?

"Just remember not to push it, Bradford," he mumbled. "Take it slow." He wanted to be patient and he would be.

For he had a feeling this woman was worth all the patience he had to give and then some.

Twenty-six

Margaret couldn't remember ever being more excited or nervous. Not even a first teenage prom date could rival the way she felt.

After work she went quickly through the grocery store and bought all the ingredients for her special dinner. In her excitement, she forgot she was celebrating a divorce; the evening was becoming so much more than that.

Promptly at seven she heard Jonathan drive up to the house. She gave one quick glance at herself in the hallway mirror, noting the soft blush of color on her cheeks. From the heat of the kitchen, she told herself with a wry smile. She brushed her hair back, pleased with the shine of it. And she thought the pale blue sweater she wore made her eyes look blue instead of gray.

Going to the door, she looked about the house with pleasure. A fire crackled pleasantly, sending

326

the sweet aroma of apple wood into the air. And the rest of the house fairly sparkled.

She was smiling when she opened the door.

"Well," Jonathan said as he stood on the porch. He made no effort to come in, any more than he made an effort to hide the way his approving gaze moved over her.

Margaret stared at him, at the straight cut of his tan pants, and the way his dark wine-colored sweater emphasized his eyes and hair. And she stared at the bouquet of fresh flowers in his hand.

"It's good to see you smile," he said, still not moving.

"Come in," she managed. "It's cool out there."

"Our last cold spell before summer," he said.

He stepped past her into the house and behind his back she closed her eyes, enjoying the heady and sexy masculine fragrance he wore.

She came around in front of him and with a smile nodded toward the flowers in his hand.

"Oh," he said with a boyish grin. "These are for you." His eyes darted around the house and rested on the fire in the fireplace. "You really have done wonders with this place, Margaret." He turned to look at her, nodding his head with approval. "I like it."

"Do you? But then, I remember Debbie saying you were somewhat of an antiques expert. So you must like old houses."

"Debbie thinks anyone over the age of thirty must be an expert at something."

Margaret took the flowers and held them briefly to her nose. "I love spring flowers," she said as she gazed at him over the colorful array. She turned to find a container and placed them on the table, noting their fragile colors of pink and yellow.

Why did everything seem so delicate and new in springtime?

"Something smells good," he said.

"It's almost ready." She glanced at him as he moved from the living room into the kitchen. He leaned his hip against the cabinets and stood watching her. He reached toward where she worked at the sink, and plucked a carrot stick from a dish.

She smiled, happy that he felt comfortable in her home. But then, why wouldn't he? He had been here many times to visit her father. Had she ever thanked him for that?

She liked his patience, the way he seemed in no hurry. Charles sometimes became impatient when she took too long in the kitchen. She shook her head, not wanting Charles to intrude on this evening.

She glanced at Jonathan, who stood watching her work as he munched on the carrot stick. She realized what a pleasure his presence was in the house. His being here did not intrude or interfere; it warmed and enhanced the small house, making it even more cozy and pleasant.

She set the bowl of fresh vegetables on the table and turned to the stove. She was more distracted than she realized, and she grabbed the hot lid with her bare fingers.

"Ouch." She jerked her hand away and shook her fingers as the pain stabbed through her skin.

In one step Jonathan was beside her. He took her hand in his and turned it over, examining the smooth red area on the tip of her fingers. Then, pulling her with him, he stepped to the refrigerator and opened the freezer compartment. He reached in with one hand, as he held her fingers with the other. He took an ice cube and rubbed it on the end of her finger.

Neither one of them spoke and suddenly Margaret felt warm and slightly breathless watching his face and his concentration as he applied the ice to the burn.

He looked up then, catching her eyes and staring directly into them. She could see the reflection of the lights in his eyes, the way his pupils slowly darkened.

He tossed the ice cube into the sink and slowly, very slowly, pulled her hand toward his lips. She held her breath as his mouth touched the tip of her fingers and kissed it.

When his lips moved around her finger, sucking it gently, she felt the rasp of his tongue on her burned skin. Her eyes closed and she felt herself begin to tremble.

She wasn't sure how it happened, but she was in his arms, an almost automatic response as natural as breathing.

His hand still held hers between them. His other hand was at the back of her neck and head, pulling her closer as their lips touched. She felt his quiet groan as he released her hand and freed his arms to gather her closer to him.

She loved the way he held her, tightly as if she were a precious something he couldn't let go. She thought nothing had ever felt so good as the feel of his body against hers.

Her breasts tingled where they were pressed against his chest. She couldn't recall the last time she had felt such an overwhelming need for a man. Had anyone ever kissed her this way . . . made her feel so completely lost and out of control?

She could feel his own response, could feel the hardness of him against her belly.

It was only the sound and smell of food boiling over on the stove that finally yanked her back to reality, and out of his arms.

"Oh," she said, reaching for a pot holder and snatching the lid from the boiling pan.

She turned back to Jonathan. Attempting to check his emotions, he stepped apart from her. His chest rose and fell slowly as he took a long, deep breath of air. His blue eyes looked very dark and shadowy.

"I . . . I suppose we should eat dinner, or . . ."

His smile at her was sweet and gentle and so understanding.

"Yeah, I suppose we should. Is there anything I can do to help?"

"No, nothing. All I have to do is put it on the table. You sit here." Did she sound as breathless as she felt?

Before she sat down, she turned the kitchen radio on, hoping the quiet, relaxing music would banish any awkwardness.

As she served the chicken breasts with their rich lemon caper sauce, she knew there was no need. Jonathan was fine. He was talkative and interesting and there was no need to worry that they would become bogged down in some silly, embarrassing silence.

He even teased her about the heat that had surged between them, the fire still sparked in his eyes.

"How's your finger?" he asked, giving her a mischievous smile.

"It's fine. I think you cured it." She returned his smile just as playfully.

He chuckled and took another bite of the chicken. "You are a wonderful cook, Maggie. I can't remember when I've had a better meal."

"I'm glad. I love to cook, especially something

new and different."

"Yeah? Well, anytime you have the urge to cook something new and different, feel free to invite me over."

"I will."

"You haven't seen my place yet. I have some old furniture you'd probably like. One night I'll cook supper for you."

"Oh? Can you cook?"

His look was wide and innocent. "Of course I can cook. I'm a modern man, a man of the nineties."

"Oh, well, in that case, I accept. It would be a real treat to have someone cook for me for a change."

They laughed and joked as they did the dishes together. The coffee gurgled and filled the house with its pungent aroma. Then Margaret turned to glance about the kitchen, pleased with the order and neatness of it.

"If you'll get a couple of logs from the back porch, I'll take our coffee into the living room where we can enjoy the fire."

Jonathan put the logs on the fire and came to sit on the opposite end of the sofa from Margaret. She sat in the corner with her legs tucked beneath her. He made no effort to move close to her.

"This is nice," he said, leaning back against the sofa and holding his coffee cup against his thigh.

"Yes," she said, gazing around the cozy room. "Not very elegant, but nice."

"Do you prefer elegant?" he murmured. "Do you miss your home in Atlanta? As your dad used to say, 'Margaret's got a real fancy house up there in Georgia.' "

She laughed, thinking she could almost hear her dad's voice. "It was pretty fancy," she said with a lift of her brows. "But it's not a fancy house that makes a woman happy."

"Or a man." He was looking down into his coffee, studying it thoughtfully.

"Where did you live before coming back to Ocala, Jon?"

He shrugged and smiled. "Everywhere. New York, Chicago, Los Angeles." He turned to look at her as he sipped his coffee. "Paris, London. It's more like where didn't we live."

The "we" captured Margaret's attention and she studied his face for a moment. He had grown quiet and more introverted than he usually was.

"You miss your wife?"

He smiled a sad, rather weary smile. "I guess I miss what could have been."

That was it. What could have been. Jonathan had said it perfectly. Margaret thought it described exactly the sadness and regret she felt about Charles and the end of her own marriage.

She stared at him with a look of wonder and he turned to see it.

"You know what I mean?" he asked.

"Yes, I know exactly how you feel."

"And, how are you feeling, Maggie?" he asked. "This was the big day, wasn't it?"

"Yes, as far as I know. My lawyer said there would be no hitches, no reason why the divorce wouldn't be legal today. Charles didn't fight it or . . . anything."

He bent his head so he could look up into her face.

"Did you want him to?"

She turned quickly. "Oh no, I'm glad it's over." She shrugged. "But, it's like you said, there's a sadness there for what might have been."

"It wasn't your fault, Maggie." He set his empty cup down and reached for her hand, forcing her to turn and look at him. "You gave it thirty-three years of good, hard effort and you raised three beautiful daughters in the process. From what your dad said, three pretty terrific ones at that. That says a lot for you."

"Does it?"

Jonathan looked into her gray eyes. They sparkled with moisture, and they pleaded for understanding and comfort.

He moved closer to her and put his arm around her shoulder, pulling her head down against his chest.

"What is it?" he asked. "What's bothering you?"

Softly, in a muffled voice, she began to tell him. She lifted her head from time to time and looked into his eyes as she told him about Ginger. She spilled everything, from the beginning ten years ago, to the last phone call she'd received from her troubled daughter. When she would look up into his eyes, he'd nod, his face thoughtful and concerned, as he urged her to continue.

"I'm afraid she drinks too much. Oh God, Jonathan, what if she's becoming an alcoholic? How can she take care of her child and—"

"Maggie . . . shhh." He pulled her close, his hand moving to cup her face as he soothed and caressed her.

"I just don't know what to do, or how to help her."

"There's nothing you can do to help an alcoholic, Maggie. Not until they're ready to help themselves." His voice now was flat and emotionless.

She lifted her head from his chest and gazed into his stricken blue eyes.

"Oh Jon, I'm sorry. Lettie told me about Sylvia."

"It was alcohol that killed her; she was drunk the night she wrecked." He looked at her and shrugged.

"Jonathan," she whispered, wishing she knew how to comfort him.

Her hand reached up to his face. She let her

335

fingers feel the warmth of his skin, the intriguing groove beside his mouth. Beneath the skin, she could feel the angular bones of his cheeks and jaw. Then, curiously, her fingers moved shakily to his mouth.

He drew in his breath.

"Maggie . . ." His eyes warned her of what might happen if she continued.

When Margaret reached up to kiss him, she told herself it was meant only to comfort. But she knew it wasn't true as soon as their mouths melded together.

All the hunger, all the passion they'd felt earlier was still there, smoldering and waiting for that one spark to ignite it again.

He was against her, leaning her back against the sofa as his mouth and hands explored and excited her. She moaned and strained toward him, surprising herself with her response.

Finally, his hands pushed at her sweater and she felt the heat of his skin against hers. She felt fear then, pure and genuine fear that rushed over her like the heated winds of summer.

What would he think of her? Would he find her attractive or would he only wish for a younger, tauter body? How could she bear it if she saw disappointment in his eyes?

"Jonathan . . . please. I can't . . . I'm sorry, but I just can't."

As she struggled from beneath him and stood

up, she looked into his face. She winced at the surprise and disappointment in his eyes.

He raked his fingers through his rumpled hair and sat back on the sofa, letting his arms rest along the back of the cushions as he tried to compose himself.

"It's all right Maggie. Sit down . . ." He reached for her hand but she moved away, wary not of him but of her own inadequacies.

"No . . . Jonathan. I owe you an apology. What must you think of me? A woman my age, teasing you . . . inviting you over before a cozy fire." She flung her hand ineffectively toward the fireplace. "Kissing you, letting you . . ." She sank into a chair across the room. She put her elbows on her knees and rested her hands against the sides of her face, looking at him balefully across the coffee table.

"How can I explain to you, Jon? It's not that I mean to lead you on. God, you must think I'm awful."

His smile was as gentle and understanding as ever, even though she knew he must be aching with frustration.

"Maggie, sweetheart. I don't think you're awful. I understand what you're going through. How many times do I have to tell you that?"

She shook her head and her eyes were troubled. "But I need to explain to you, Jon; I want to explain. I can't keep doing this and I can't expect

337

you to put up with it. But I'm just so afraid." She looked at him as if for understanding. "I've only been to bed with one man in my entire life, do you realize that? My God, I feel like the oldest virgin in the world."

He laughed then and shook his head as he looked at her with affection. "Maggie—"

"No, let me finish," she said, exasperated by his smile. "I just want you to know that I understand if you never want to have anything else to do with me. And I understand if you want to see other women. But I just can't . . . I'm so afraid . . . I've been fighting insecurities for the past thirty years and that's something I need to take care of before I jump into a relationship with anyone. Especially one like ours . . ." Her voice trailed away as her eyes fastened on his. "So intense . . . so . . ."

"Hot?"

His look and his smile told her he knew exactly what she meant, and that her acknowledgement of it pleased him.

He stood up and walked to her, taking her hand and pulling her up from the chair. He saw the question in her eyes, saw her real fear, and he smiled.

"Walk me to the door."

When she looked at him the tension on her face relaxed into one of relief and sympathy.

"Oh Jon . . ."

"It's all right, Maggie. A man doesn't die from sexual frustration, you know." His hand moved upward to flick her teasingly on the chin. "If so I'd have been dead years ago."

She was in a daze as she walked with him to the door. He bent his head and brushed his lips lightly against hers.

"Good night, Maggie. I'll see you Monday."

" 'Night."

That evening was only the beginning of many sleepless, thought-filled nights for Margaret. Her thoughts would tumble, first clear and avowing, then reverse and become doubtful and questioning.

She spent the entire weekend in a bewildered daze, not aware of what she was doing or what she ate.

Through it all, Jonathan's face was before her, his blue eyes gentle and understanding. Had there ever been a man like him? Was she a total fool for taking a chance on losing him this way?

His kisses and his response to her were real, she knew it. But could anything possibly change that? Would their going to bed together change it or make him lose interest in her?

She thought she couldn't stand for him to think of her in only a casual way.

God, she just didn't know any more what to think. Or what to do.

Part Three

Tomorrow

Above the cloud with its shadow
is the star with its light.

— *Victor Hugo*

Twenty-seven

On Sunday evening Margaret drove into town to have supper with Lettie. Although she mentioned Jonathan several times, she did not tell Lettie about this latest development or her confusion about becoming intimate for the first time with someone other than her husband.

It was not that she didn't want to tell Lettie, or that she wouldn't tell her later, but Lettie had problems of her own. She was terribly concerned about her mother who was in a nursing home in a neighboring community.

"She doesn't know me any more, Margaret," Lettie said with tears in her eyes. "She thought I was Wanda."

"Who is Wanda?"

"That's Mama's sister. She's been dead for twenty years." Lettie's hands shook and she finally laid her fork down beside her plate.

Margaret reached to cover her hand. "I'm sorry, Lettie. I know how hard it must be for you, seeing your mother this way."

The anguish in Lettie's eyes only affirmed Margaret's words.

"I hope you won't take this the wrong way. But you know I think you were lucky with your parents. Your mother was sick for awhile, but she was still alert and she knew everyone. And your dad . . . dying the way he did is really best for everyone."

Margaret's smile was gentle. "It's all right. I understand what you mean. I think I agree, although I'm still too selfish to let him go completely."

Margaret drove back home through the darkness. She let the windows of the car down, enjoying the warmth of the breeze and the croaking sound of frogs in the wet areas along the roadside. The sky was exceptionally clear, the stars so bright they almost gave out their own glow.

She loved it here, loved the rich, pungent smells of the earth and vegetation. She loved the peacefulness and the quiet, and she realized every day just how much she cherished the independence she'd found here. That was quite a revelation.

She didn't know what to expect at work on Monday, but knowing Jonathan, she didn't fear any awkwardness or brooding.

344

He was the same sweet, wonderful man she had grown to admire so much.

It was a busy week, with Jonathan being in and out of the office a great deal. That should have given Margaret a sense of relief, but in fact it did just the opposite. She found herself missing him, looking up anxiously every time someone walked down the hallway past her office. She listened for his deep familiar laughter or the sound of his booming orders above the noises of the press in the back.

Yet, when he was in the office, his presence was disconcerting to say the least.

There were times when she couldn't seem to tear her eyes away from his easy smile. They would exchange quiet looks above everyone else's head, or laugh together at funny little things that meant nothing to anyone else. Both of them were aware of the quizzical looks they received from Debbie and Sandy.

There were moments when Margaret would look up to find Jonathan watching her, his blue eyes dark and serious. He would smile and her heart would turn over; she'd feel her muscles weaken and her bones melt a little.

Nights were the worst for her, they were long, thought-filled, and restless. Nights when she would have to get out of bed and pace the floor, her eyes glancing toward the windows to the west where Jonathan lived. A couple of nights she even made it as far as the kitchen and stood staring at the phone, her fingers itching to dial his number.

There were others nights when she would talk to Claire or Lettie and not remember what was said. She was almost grateful that Cyndi had not called, for she wanted to be able to give her complete attention. Right now she knew she could not do that.

By the end of the week, she still had not resolved anything in her head. The closest she came was making affirming statements to herself as she lay in bed at night.

"I can do anything I please. I am a grown woman, an independent woman. Nothing is holding me back except myself."

If only Jonathan would wait that long.

The weather had turned very warm. When the purple flowers hung from the chinaberry tree in the backyard, Margaret was certain that spring had arrived. Or what could be considered spring in this part of Florida. Some years it seemed there was only summer and a couple of months of fall.

On Saturday morning she pulled on a pair of faded jeans and a long cotton shirt that came below her hips. After checking the supplies in her father's shed out back, she made a list and drove into town. Within an hour she was back with her trunk full of annuals for the flower beds. She also had fertilizer and mulch that she would have to drag out of the car the best way she could.

She slipped on a pair of gardening gloves and started with the beds around the front porch, first digging and softening the rich black earth. She hummed as she worked, stopping periodically to look up at the sky or at a songbird that serenaded her from the surrounding trees.

Usually when she was outside she managed to block out the noises of the highway. And she had today, except when one particular vehicle went by.

She knew the sound of Jonathan's Bronco and today she heard it coming from half a mile away. She glanced toward the highway as he drove by and her heart skittered wildly when she saw the flash of brakelights. Then there was the whine of the transmission as he backed up and wheeled into her drive.

She stood up and watched as he stopped, then stretched his long legs out the door. Margaret's arm was above her forehead as she shielded her eyes from the sun. For a moment, Jonathan's face was in darkness as he walked between her and the brilliant light.

He walked very close to her and she dropped her arm, staring up into his eyes and waiting for him to speak.

He took the trowel from her hand and tossed it on the ground. As she stood frowning up at him, he slowly stripped the gloves she wore from her hands.

With no preliminaries, no word of greeting, he pulled her into his arms. His kiss was slow and deliberate and there was a hunger in him that caused her lips to open voluntarily beneath his. His arms encircled her so tightly she could hardly breathe.

When he finally pulled away she gasped and stared up at him.

"Jon . . . the neighbors . . . the—"

"To hell with the neighbors, Maggie."

She thought she'd never seen him look so serious as when he pulled her into his arms again. His kiss was so long and thorough that afterward she had to lean against him for support.

When he stepped back, he lifted his hand and wiped away a smudge of dirt from her cheek. His look was warm and so intense that she thought she could not bear one more moment without turning away.

"You look beautiful," he said. "Irresistible."

"Beautiful?" She laughed and shook her head with bewilderment. "Have you had your eyes checked recently?"

He ignored her, his face still serious and quiet.

"Maggie . . ." There was a look in his eyes, a determination this morning that made her wonder why he had come.

She realized she was glad he had. If he had

come to force her hand, she didn't care. It was as if some dream she had been waiting and hoping for had just come true. She had made the decision without even realizing it; she felt gladness rising within her chest.

"I know I said I'd be patient," he said. "And I will be. But there's something I need to say to you, something that's been eating at me all week. If I don't say it now, I think I'll go crazy."

"What?" She was worried about what he had come to tell her.

He took her arm and pulled her toward the front porch. Willingly she moved up the steps and into the shade with him, feeling empty when he removed his hands from her and stood without touching her.

"I know that you're afraid of this relationship, and I understand that. You think it's too soon after your marriage has ended and I know you're afraid of being hurt again. But Maggie, sometimes you're stubborn and close minded and downright prissy in your attitudes."

She blinked, then smiled sheepishly. She'd been told that more than once in her lifetime.

"I know what you've been through, Maggie, I do. But can't you see . . . ?" He took her hand and placed it on his chest above his heart. "I know I'm not perfect. I don't always say what I intend to say, or behave the way I really want to with you. But God, I'd cut off my arm before I'd do anything to hurt you or bring disappointment to those big gray eyes."

Her heart was melting. Couldn't he see that?

She started to speak, but he wouldn't let her. He had to finish.

"I admire you and what you've done, more than any other woman I've ever known. Coming here alone and starting a new life wasn't easy. It's one of the things I like about you—that strength and stubborn independence. I'm not going to take that away from you, Maggie."

Strength? Independence? Was he talking about her?

She was staring at him now, amazed by his words and the look on his face. He was so serious.

"I was drawn to you the first time I saw you at the airport, looking so alone and scared. I know you felt the same thing, Maggie. What we share when we're together is hard to deny."

She nodded her agreement mutely, feeling the heat even now as she acknowledged its presence.

"I want you Maggie more than I've ever wanted anyone or anything. God, I feel like a schoolboy when I look at you. One look and I'm ready to throw you down and drag you into a cave somewhere." He laughed shakily.

She smiled up at him, completely charmed and entranced.

"But I'd never do that, you know that, don't you?"

She nodded, staring into his eyes.

"But damn it, we're not kids any more. I want to seize every moment I can get with you. Sometimes waiting is more than I can bear because I know it will be so good, so right. Do you understand? Am I making any sense at all?"

"Yes," she said, mesmerized by the intensity of his eyes. "You don't want to wait any longer, and I—"

"No, that's not what I'm saying. Well, it is but . . ." He raked his hand through her hair and turned around sharply, leaving her to walk to the swing, then turning to come back again. His gestures were quietly controlled but she sensed how hard he was trying to be patient.

"God . . . what I'm trying to say is, Maggie . . . I love you. *I love you.*" He took her arms and shook her as if for emphasis. "And I don't care about anything else. I can wait. As much as I want you and need you, I can wait forever if it's what you want. Just don't shut me out, thinking that it's my way or nothing, thinking that you will displease me."

Her chin trembled as she heard his words.

"Oh, Jon—"

He held up his hand and she could see he was fighting back emotions as well. "One more short speech. Whatever it takes to make you happy, I'll do. Years ago I'd have said that Jonathan Bradford doesn't compromise for anyone, but that was before I met you. I always thought I could resist anything, any temptation, but I can't resist you." His voice had grown husky, his eyes almost hypnotizing as he refused to let her look away from him. "I can't just walk away and leave this, leave us and what we have. Don't you know that?"

She was speechless at his eloquence. And she felt her heart doing the most unusual things as she stared up into his eyes. Those waiting, questioning eyes.

She smiled and took his hand. He looked doubtful as she pulled him toward the front door.

"Maggie?"

"Jon . . . shut up," she said with a smile as she lifted her mouth toward his.

When he pulled away there were still questions in his eyes and she smiled. Could she blame him for being skeptical after all her hesitation and doubts?

Silently, she pulled him into the house and toward the bedroom. And this time she was more certain than she'd ever been about anything in her life.

Margaret didn't know why or how. All she knew was that her fears had vanished . . . practically. Jonathan's love had given her the confidence to overcome what remained of her insecurities.

She pulled him into the cool, shadowy bedroom and turned to him. She watched his eyes darken as he reached to close his fingers about the buttons of her shirt.

"Are you sure?" he asked, his voice husky, his breathing unsteady.

"Yes," she whispered. "More sure than I've ever been about anything."

Margaret could feel her skin tingle where his fingers brushed against her. When he pushed her shirt back, he groaned softly and kissed her bare shoulder.

She felt her breasts tighten as his eyes moved hungrily down over her.

"Oh," she said weakly. "When you look at me that way I . . ."

"What?" he murmured, lowering his head to trail faint, delicate kisses across the top of her breasts. "How do you feel when I look at you?"

"Warm," she whispered, arching her body against his mouth. "Very warm."

Jonathan groaned. He could feel his body throbbing, feel the heat of his skin through his clothing. As her fingers moved to unbutton his shirt, he held his breath, waiting . . . trying to control the fire for a few moments longer.

"Ah, Maggie . . ."

His mouth trailed hot, hungry kisses from the

corner of her lips to her ear, finally ending where he buried his face against her neck. He pulled her hard into his arms, relishing the feel of her full breasts against his bare chest.

Margaret turned her head, searching again for his lips. She was panting with her need for him, and her skin felt alive with each touch of his hands.

They both felt the fire and the longing. Quickly they finished undressing each other and he stepped back, admiring her with a hint of wonder in his eyes. He touched her full breasts, his hands warm and massaging. The erotic movements caused her to close her eyes, made her weak with yearning.

She wanted him now, there was no need for anything else. His hands, his kisses were quickly melting away all her years of holding back, her years of uncertainty about her femininity and sexuality. Jonathan made her feel beautiful and wanted.

They tumbled onto the bed. Jonathan felt an almost uncontrollable surge of lust rush through him as their bodies met, as they lay entangled together in the softness of her sweet smelling bed. He wanted to wait; he meant to be as patient as she needed him to be. But God, he felt himself quickly losing control, losing himself in the luscious feel of her body.

Hungrily Margaret took his face in her hands,

kissing him in a long, soul stirring kiss. She pulled away to take small panting breaths and looked into his eyes, her hands still touching his face.

"Please . . ." she said, closing her eyes and arching against him. "Oh Jon, I can't stand it . . ."

Jonathan could hardly think straight any more. For all his vows of patience and wanting to please her, her sweet entreaties moved him to a point of desperation. His entire mind was filled with her, with the way she felt, the way she moved beneath him.

When he joined his body with hers, he thought he could gladly die from the pleasure.

Maggie moaned her satisfaction and threw her head back against the pillow. Her hands moved to his shoulders and back, then downward, feeling his movements and relishing the power and rhythm of his body.

He laughed softly, carried beyond any pleasure he'd ever known. As they moved together he kissed her open mouth until both of them were wild with passion.

Margaret was trembling, already on the brink of some wild, secret delight. She could feel it moving over her, downward . . . spreading through her body. She saw in Jonathan's eyes that he felt it, too.

Her soft moan of surrender was all he could

bear. With a hoarse cry that was both joy and agony, he let himself go, moving hard and fast against her, pulling her upward against him and kissing her lips as they ended it together.

"Jon . . . oh . . ." Her lips were against his neck as she clung desperately to him. She was smiling and gasping for breath, unable to believe what had just happened between them.

She felt as if she never wanted to let him go.

Twenty-eight

They lay wrapped in each other's arms, letting the fire between them die down to a soft warmth. Jonathan's breathing was still unsteady and rough. Margaret could hear the steady beat of his heart beneath her ear.

She felt his lips in her hair, then his hand pushed the dampened tendrils back from her face as he kissed her forehead.

"Oh Maggie," he said with a soft explosive rush of air from his lungs.

She laughed softly, delighted with the pleasure in his voice and wondering with awe why she had waited so long to experience this with him.

She moved her head back so she could look up into his face. She reached up and kissed his mouth, feeling grateful . . . feeling so much more than gratitude.

She felt free. She felt safe and unfettered. She felt loved.

Thoroughly.

As their breathing slowed, she felt the cool air brush against her naked skin and she reached to pull the comforter up over both of them.

Jonathan propped himself up on one elbow and looked down into her face. He was smiling.

"Well," he said in a light, teasing voice. There was pleasure and satisfaction in that one word.

Margaret thought she also detected a hint of "I told you so."

"Why did you let me wait so long?" she asked, nuzzling against his neck.

"Why did I . . . ? Hmmm. You'd better stop doing that or . . ."

"Or?"

"Or I won't be responsible for my actions." His hand reached beneath the covers to caress her breasts, moving to her ribcage and down to the curve of her hips. With a slow, easy grin, he pulled her against him, so she would have no doubt of his meaning.

"Jonathan, you devil."

They both laughed, then sighed. Margaret rolled her head back and forth on the pillow.

"Oh, Jon, I've never felt this way in my entire life." She turned to look at him. Her face was serious now, her eyes shining with wonder. "At my age, after being married more than thirty years, I can't believe what I just experienced."

"Kind of like the oldest virgin in the world?" he teased.

"Yeah," she said, hiding her face against his chest. "Kind of like that, I guess. I mean, I do feel as if all this is new; as if I'm new. And you're the first man who's ever loved me so completely, or made me feel this good about myself."

"You should feel good about yourself," he said. His fingers moved enticingly around the tips of her breasts. "With or without me, or anyone else to help you feel that way." He pushed the comforter back to look at her. "You're wonderful, Maggie. I can't remember when I've been so happy." He laughed and bent to kiss her shoulder. "I'm glad I stopped to see you today."

"So am I." She turned in his arms, stretching her legs out so the lengths of their bodies were touching. "Do you know what a miserable week this has been? How much I've missed you and wanted you? There were times in the office when you would look at me and I just wanted to run into your arms and kiss you, beg you to take me home and make wild, passionate love to me."

"Oh Maggie," he said with a delighted laugh. "Tell me more."

She moved closer into his arms, accepting his light kisses and moving her hands over his chest and shoulders until both of them were warm and breathless again.

359

She heard his soft groan and saw his long dark lashes close, then open again. His blue eyes were so expressive.

Margaret looked at him questioningly and then shook her head; there was a satisfied glint of mischief in her gray eyes as she read his look.

"No," she said, her eyes wide with pleasurable surprise.

"Oh yes," Jonathan laughed as he pulled her against him again and wrapped one long leg across her lower body.

This time their lovemaking was slow and deliberate. There was time for exploring with the hands and eyes. Margaret gasped with disbelief as he expertly carried her from one peak of delight to another. Finally they were both weak and sated with pleasure.

They fell asleep in each other's arms, like exhausted children after a summer romp. It was mid-afternoon before they woke.

"Jon," Margaret whispered, watching his sleeping face.

She could not resist touching his rumpled hair, or letting her fingers move slowly down the groove beside his mouth. She was amazed that it took only that light touch to bring back a pleasurable little tingle to her heart.

Dear God, she was completely entranced with the man.

Jonathan lay watching her, his sleepy eyes

warm and filled with affection.

"Hmmm?"

"I think we'd better get up."

"Why, is the house on fire?"

She laughed. "No, but Mr. Carter—"

"Mr. Carter? Are you trying to tell me something?"

"No, silly. I just remembered that Mr. Carter is supposed to be out this afternoon about the roof. I'm getting a new roof put on the house."

Jonathan kissed her quickly, then threw back the covers and swung his long legs over the side of the bed.

"Good. Your dad meant to do that last summer."

There was absolutely no false modesty in him as he moved to his discarded clothes. He turned once to find her watching him and he smiled.

Margaret thought she could actually feel her heart turn over when he looked at her that way.

"If you like, you can shower here before—"

"No, that's okay," he said. "I need to go home and change; I was on my way to the office to do some research." He held up his rumpled shirt with a grin. "But this shirt looks as if I slept in it now and I'd hate to have to explain why to everyone on Main Street. It might ruin *your* reputation."

"Yes, or enhance it," she said with a twinkle in her eyes.

Had she ever been so happy? Had she ever felt so good as she did at this very moment?

She remained in bed, smiling at him and enjoying looking at him. She still felt a bit modest about her own body.

After he had dressed, he walked back to the bed. "Are you going to work outside with your flowers again?" he asked.

"Well, yes, I suppose I will. Why?"

"I thought if you did you might be tired later. Maybe you'd like to drive over to the house for that supper I promised to cook for you."

Her eyes sparkled up at him. "Oh Jonathan, I'd love it."

"Good. I'll see you about seven o'clock."

He bent to kiss her lightly and she threw her arms around his neck, reluctant to let him go. Following their newly formed pattern, one light kiss always seemed to turn into something else.

When they both pulled away, he stood up and looked down at her. Then he chuckled softly.

"You're going to kill me, lady."

He smiled at her from the door and then left.

Margaret lay quietly until she heard his car start and pull away, she stretched her arms above her head and closed her eyes. She remembered every touch, every sensation, the taste of his mouth on hers and every heated word of love he had whispered in her ear as he made love to her.

Was this love? Could this really be happening

so soon after the end of her marriage? She didn't want to go to Jonathan on the rebound. That wouldn't be fair to him.

But what she was feeling seemed wonderfully real to her. She was sure that what was between them would only grow better and better.

The afternoon was glorious. Margaret's work with the flowers, the scent of the rich earth and the warm Florida breeze was simply heavenly.

She would work awhile, then sit back on her heels to survey what she had done. She reveled in the soft wind that ruffled her hair and cooled the moisture on the back of her neck. She seemed more aware of everything; her senses had bloomed.

And she knew it was all because of Jonathan.

The sky above was a perfect, clear blue, outlining the palms and pine trees that swayed and whispered in the wind. Margaret even noticed with glee a couple of creamy blossoms on a tall evergreen Loblolly Bay tree at the edge of the yard. Like a young girl she jogged across to the tree, plucked one of the blossoms from a lower branch and tucked it into her hair.

She had almost finished working when Mr. Carter arrived. She walked with him around the house, nodding as he talked about how many squares of roofing he'd need and other details she knew nothing about.

He paused, nodding his head with approval, as

he looked at the house. "This is a good solid house, Mrs. Avery. They don't build houses like this any more. Good and sturdy. Your daddy didn't scrimp on material when he built this house."

"No, knowing Dad, I'm sure he didn't. I remember hearing that he cut most of the timber from this tract of land."

"Probably did. Well, we'll have a new roof on 'er by this time next week. If it don't rain and the creeks don't rise." He sauntered away, not bothering to say goodbye, but merely giving her a wave of his hand before stepping up into his truck.

Margaret stood looking at the house after Mr. Carter had gone. It was a good house and she felt secure living here, knowing it was hers, that it was paid for and that so far she had been able to keep it in good repair.

She was excited about going to Jonathan's. She remembered the old Bradford place from years ago. But now, one could hardly see it from the highway. Most of all she was excited about seeing Jonathan again.

She showered and shampooed her hair, thinking there was no better feeling in the world than working hard and enjoying an exhilarating shower afterward.

In fact, she could not remember when she'd felt better or happier. Today reminded her of those glorious days of summer when the girls had been small. When they were all happy and satisfied and had no problems except the simple ones of childhood.

She had just stepped out of the bathroom and wrapped a towel around her when she heard the phone ringing in the kitchen.

She ran lightly through the house to the kitchen and picked up the phone.

"Mom? Were you outside?"

"Oh, Cyndi." Margaret laughed and tried to catch her breath. "I was just getting out of the shower. I'm so glad you called. Where have you been? I've tried to call you a couple of times this week."

"Mom, the most wonderful thing has happened. I think . . . I hope. Steven and I have been out of town for a couple of days. We were in Americus, you know where it is?"

"Well, yes. It's a small town in southwest Georgia, isn't it? Hardly a vacation kind of place."

"Oh, it wasn't a vacation. Well, actually it was, just because it's been so long since we've been anywhere together." She paused and took a short breath. "Mom, Steven was interviewed for a job at a law firm there. Oh, and I love the town. It's wonderful with lovely old restored antebellum homes down Main Street and huge oaks. You know how I always loved live oaks. And—"

"Cyndi," Margaret interrupted. "What in the world are you talking about?" But she couldn't help smiling. It had been a long time since she'd heard such enthusiasm and happiness in her daughter's voice.

"Oh," Cyndi laughed and the sound rang lyrically through the phone. "Steven and I have had some long, serious talks lately. He knew I wasn't happy, living the way we were. Oh Mom, he's been so sweet and understanding. He said he had no idea how I felt about his going into the firm with Dad or joining the club and trying to keep up with all the other up-and-coming lawyers in Atlanta. And the best part is, he said it was not what he wanted either. He thought, because of the way I grew up, it was what I expected. Isn't that amazing?"

Margaret laughed. She felt as if an old, wearisome burden had been lifted from her shoulders.

"Yes it's amazing," she agreed. "And wonderful. I'm really happy for you. Do you think this might become a reality? Is Americus the town you really want to spend your life in and —"

"Yes, it's perfect. We both love it. And we've already met so many nice people there. People our age. And it's not far from Atlanta, even a little bit closer to you, too, Mom."

"I don't think I've heard such happiness in your voice in ages, darling."

"I *am* happy. And I can't wait till we find out if Steven has the job or not. I would love to be there for summer."

"What does your father say?" How disappointed and angry Charles must be. He was not the kind of man who liked to invest his time in something only to lose it. And that included people.

"We haven't told him yet."

"Oh."

"We will. We wanted to wait until we know for sure. Well, what about you? Dad said the divorce is final, and this is Saturday night." Her voice was softly teasing and affectionate.

Margaret wasn't sure if she should mention Jonathan just yet. Their relationship was so new and what she was feeling seemed so fragile.

"Actually, Jonathan has offered to cook supper for me tonight at his house. I haven't seen his home . . ." She hesitated, wondering why Cyndi was so quiet. Was she upset? "But I'm looking forward to it . . ."

"Oh Mom, I'm happy for you. He's a very nice man. I'm sorry about those remarks I made before, you know . . . about . . ."

"It's all right. We were all upset then. But I'm taking it slow, so you don't have to worry."

"That's good. It's more than I can say for Dad."

Margaret frowned, wondering at the unfamiliar bitterness in Cyndi's voice.

"Are you talking about Shelley moving into the house?"

"How did you know?"

"I called there one night. I guess I was feeling a little melancholy. You know, wishing things could have been different, missing those days when we were together and happy."

"Let me guess," Cyndi said, her voice dry with sarcasm. "Shelley answered the phone. She is just thrilled out of her little empty skull, Mom, to be living in that house. And it burns me up."

"Don't let it. Don't you let anything your dad does upset you. I don't want that. You and Steven have a wonderful chance now to get out on your own and I think it will be a revelation to you both. Don't let your dad or Shelley spoil that for you."

"I won't. And Mom—"

"Yes?"

"I love you, and I'm really happy for you."

"Thanks, baby." Margaret's chin trembled and her eyes filled with tears. "I love you, too."

"Well, gotta go. I'll call you soon. Have fun tonight."

Margaret sat in one of the kitchen chairs, losing herself in the luxury of tears. This time they were tears of joy and relief, tears of happiness for her daughter.

Twenty-nine

The sun was just dropping behind the line of trees to the west when Margaret drove toward Jonathan's house. She noted the impressive new fence that outlined his acreage and the glimpse of green pastures that glimmered and moved in the distance through the trees.

She came to what she remembered as the old Bradford place, or the driveway to it at least. But now, instead of a sandy, rutted road, there was a wide paved strip winding toward the house through the overhanging limbs of the huge trees.

Margaret turned into the drive, wondering if she was at the right place. Everything was so different. Large brick sentinels flanked the drive and held the elegant wrought iron gate that stood open. She saw a large brass nameplate at the top of the gate.

"Bradford Farms," she read. Her eyes opened wide and she smiled as she surveyed Jonathan's farm. "Very nice," she murmured. She dipped her head and looked through the top of the windshield at the line of trees that curved around the drive toward the house.

She could see the house moving in and out of her vision as she drove along the beautifully landscaped drive. As she drew nearer she saw the changes Jonathan had made in it as well.

It had always been a beautiful house, although it was a bit shabby and run-down. But it certainly was no longer that.

With an indrawn breath, she stared at the house. The old Spanish style hacienda had been completely restored. Its fresh coat of creamy paint illuminated the house in the late glow of day and made the red tiled roof look new and bright.

She parked the car in the curve of the oval drive just in front of the house. Stepping out onto the pavement, she glanced at the orderliness of the farm, at the neat sideroads and the sparkling white horse barn in the distance.

Jonathan had done wonders with the place, just as he had the newspaper office. Walking toward the house, she could hardly wait to see the interior.

The walkway led through small walled courtyards on either side and straight to a dark mahogany double door.

Margaret rang the bell and waited.

The small woman who opened the door smiled up at Margaret. Her black hair was combed back into an old-fashioned knot and the black eyes that twinkled at Margaret reflected the older woman's Spanish ancestry.

"You must be Mrs. Avery. Come in. Mr. Bradford is expecting you." Margaret smiled at the woman's soft accent.

"Oh, this is lovely," Margaret said as she stepped into the wide foyer. She looked down at the polished rust-colored tile floor and beyond the entryway to steps leading down into a living room.

"Mr. Bradford is in the kitchen. Right this way."

Margaret glanced toward the living room as they walked past. She loved the creamy white carpet and sofas, and the accents of red and black. She also caught a glimpse of dark, burnished furniture and the gleam of brass and copper accents. Everything had the look of old Spain about it.

Debbie had been right. If Jonathan was responsible for the remodeling and refurnishing, then he certainly knew his antiques and his styles.

Margaret was smiling as she followed the Spanish woman down a hallway and into a very large and brightly lit kitchen.

Jonathan turned from the stove, his look warm and welcoming.

Margaret's breath caught in her throat at the sight of him. He was simply too handsome for his own good. Their morning of lovemaking came back to her in a flash and she thought it was a good thing the old woman stood nearby, or else she might not have been responsible for her actions.

Jonathan dropped a dishtowel onto the counter and came to take her hands and pull her into the kitchen.

"Well, how do you like it?"

"Oh Jonathan, I'm overwhelmed. It's simply lovely."

"He did it himself, you know." The Spanish woman who stood nearby smiled proudly. "Some of the furniture was his grandfather's and he had it restored. The rest he bought or had made especially for this hacienda."

"Margaret, this is Anya, my housekeeper and cook, and my right-hand . . . person." Jonathan stepped toward the small dark-haired woman and put an arm around her shoulders. Anya looked up at him, her black eyes sparkling with delight at his compliments. "She runs this place and I couldn't do without her."

372

"Ah," Margaret said, smiling at Jonathan knowingly. "Your cook, did you say?"

He knew exactly what she meant and he laughed. "I can cook and I did cook your meal tonight."

"This is true, Mrs. Avery," Anya said with a nod of her head. "He has done it all himself. I did take the grocery list and do the shopping. But the rest of the afternoon, he would not let me come near the kitchen."

Jonathan's eyebrows lifted smugly and his blue eyes challenged Margaret.

"All right," she laughed. "I believe you."

"Well, if there is nothing else Mr. Bradford, I think I will go now."

"Thanks Anya, there's nothing else. I promise that your kitchen will be spotless, or almost, when you arrive for breakfast tomorrow morning."

"Oh you," she said with a wave of her hand. She glanced toward Margaret. "He is so nice; sometimes he acts as if he works for me. You must not worry about the kitchen," she said to Jon.

As the woman hurried toward the hallway, Jonathan came to take Margaret in his arms.

"She seems very nice," Margaret said.

Jonathan kissed her, ignoring her words. He buried his face against her neck. "God, you smell good." He stepped back, holding her at arm's length. "Look good, too."

Margaret hardly knew what to say or what to do. She was still unused to such compliments. As much as she loved hearing him say such things, she had to fight back her own thoughts of self-doubt.

He pulled her back into his arms, his hand moving down her back and to her hips. He held her against him, enjoying the feel of her in his arms, and the fragrance of her hair where it brushed against his chin.

"I'm so glad you're here," he whispered. "It seems like a year since I was at your house." He kissed her ear, "A year since I was in your bed."

"I can't believe how much I missed you today, Jon. You see? I knew this would happen," she teased. "One time with you and I'm a total fool."

"Hmmm, that's good. That makes two of us. Now, do you want to see the rest of the house before I feed you?"

"Yes, but what are we having?" She turned her head toward the stove, sniffing the air with exaggeration. "I don't smell anything burning."

"You'll pay for that." He took her arm and led her back into the hallway, pointing out various objects and pieces of art.

"I love the living room and the fireplace."

"Yes, I know how you love a fireplace." He

brushed his lips against her cheek. "I'll build a fire later, just for you."

"Don't you think it's too warm for a fire?"

"I'm afraid I'm no judge. I'm always too warm when I'm with you."

She shook her head and smiled, pulling him by the hand toward the curving stairway that led upstairs. "And, what's upstairs?"

"The bedroom, my dear." He deepened his voice into a mocking tone of danger.

"You're in an awfully good mood tonight."

"It's because you're here and because today was one of the happiest of my life." Suddenly he was serious. He wrapped his arms around her waist, looking down into her face. "You make my home seem warm and complete . . . and my life."

She couldn't believe he felt that way; it was exactly the way she had felt when he came to her home, how she felt in his arms.

They ate supper in the large kitchen. Margaret loved the Spanish painted tiles on the counter tops and the warm glow of copper pans that hung from a baker's rack above the rustic butcher block island. The entire back wall of the kitchen was filled with windows, letting in the lush green vision of a Spanish courtyard.

She had seen the very formal and elegant dining room. It was gorgeous, like a picture in a magazine.

But she preferred the small breakfast nook before the sparkling windows that looked out onto the pool and courtyard.

"You are a wonderful cook." She closed her eyes, savoring the taste of the rice and shrimp dish that tasted faintly of marjoram.

"Why, thank you. I knew I would win you over with my cooking skills." He smiled at her warmly over his glass of wine.

Margaret turned to stare out at the pool and the lush green grass that outlined the landscaped flower gardens.

"You have turned this into a magnificent home, Jonathan. A wonderful, warm house with just the right touch of elegance."

Later, he built a small fire as he had promised, and they settled on the soft white couch with their glasses of wine. Margaret snuggled against him, already feeling safe with him. Feeling warm and secure.

"Sylvia loved this place; I'm sorry she never got to see it this way," he said, looking into the fire. He held his glass up, letting the flames sparkle through the wine. "It was the one thing we seemed to always agree about."

"She didn't help you decorate the house?"

"No, but coming back here was something we had talked about and planned for years. And she knew what she wanted — many of the ideas were hers." He looked around, nodding his head. "She would have liked it."

"I think any woman would be happy here."

That evening they talked for hours. They held each other and kissed, savoring all the things they felt when they were together. There was a special pleasure in holding each other unhurriedly and knowing their love awaited them whenever they wished.

For Margaret it was a wonderful feeling . . . a completeness she'd never experienced before. She thought this warm, fulfilling glow was something she had longed for all her life . . . hoped for and had always missed.

That night she found herself telling Jon everything. She admitted how Charles had used her to entice his clients, or to impress his staid, family-oriented cronies. How he had used the children.

There was pain in her gray eyes as she spoke about Claire and her unconcealed bitterness toward her dad. And she confessed the reason for it.

Jonathan kissed her then, murmuring words of comfort against her ear, telling her all the things she needed most to hear.

She brightened as she spoke of Cyndi and Steven's plans for the future.

"Sounds as if it will be the best thing for them both," Jonathan agreed. "And Americus is a very nice town."

"Oh yes, I'm so relieved about that at least."

"What about Ginger?" His voice was comforting.

She laid her head against his shoulder, breathing a helpless sigh. "I don't know. I really don't know what's going to happen to her, Jon. Or to Catherine Jane. And it just makes me heartsick."

She talked about Ginger for a long while, about her dreams for her youngest daughter and about how she feared she had let her down that summer so long ago.

"You can't blame yourself for that forever, baby," he murmured. "The problems Ginger has now are certainly her own. As much as you want to help her, you have to wait. One day when she comes to you, you'll be able to help her."

"*If* she comes to me."

"*When*," he said firmly, his arms tightening about her shoulders for emphasis.

"You are so good to me. I feel so good when I'm with you." She reached up to nuzzle his ear, and trailed soft kisses down his jaw to his mouth. "Not only are you a wonderful, exciting, unbelievable lover, but you're also a very good friend."

"Hmmm, and you, my little Maggie, are driving me crazy." He pulled away, withholding his lips from her searching ones and looking into her eyes. "I suppose that after your exhausting day you wouldn't be interested in seeing the upstairs of the house."

His eyes were warm and tantalizing.

"The bedrooms, you mean?" Her words were a whisper against his mouth.

"Yeah . . . the bedrooms."

"I thought you'd never ask."

Thirty

Margaret thought it was the most glorious spring of her life. Every day spent with Jonathan was a revelation, every moment a joy. He cheered with her when Cyndi and Steven moved to Americus, and they celebrated together when the young couple reported how much they loved their new home. Jon even answered the phone one day when Cyndi called.

Margaret was never certain exactly what that conversation was about, but she could see the pleased smile on Jonathan's face.

There were long, quiet moments in each other's arms, when they talked about their past, and about their problems.

Jonathan revealed for the first time how much he missed having children, although he insisted that it was as much his fault as Sylvia's that they had chosen not to be parents.

"I was ambitious," he said, his tone almost wistful. "I often think that it was my burning ambition that caused Sylvia to turn to alcohol."

"You know better than that," Margaret said in a quiet voice. "How many times have you told me that we can't be responsible for someone else's behavior?"

"I know," he said, pulling her back into his arms. "It's just that sometimes when I look back I see what a selfish bastard I really was." He looked down into her face. "Not unlike your Charles."

"Don't ever say that," she scolded. "You could never be like him, even if you tried. I think you are the kindest, most decent man I've ever met. Everyone in Ocala looks up to you and respects you."

He brushed his lips against her hair. "You sure you aren't prejudiced?"

"Well, I could be," she said, smiling.

Margaret had told Claire about Jonathan. She thought her oldest daughter seemed much happier now and she wondered if Brian had anything to do with that. But knowing Claire, she didn't ask. It would be best if she waited and let Claire tell her on her own.

Margaret could see, since she'd moved to Ocala, just how obsessed she had been sometimes about her daughters. Even though she only wanted what was best for them, she could see how they might have resented her constant worrying and interference.

She loved the work at the newspaper. Everyone knew about her relationship with Jonathan, and they even seemed to approve.

She felt a special glow when Jonathan included Lettie in their plans as they usually did when they went antiquing or to the flea market. Jonathan teased Lettie good-naturedly about everything, from finding her a male companion to spending too much money.

"You just let me take care of the money, Johnny boy," she'd say with her loud, spontaneous laughter. "You concentrate on finding me a man."

Margaret finally had a phone installed next to her bed. Mostly because it was a rare evening that she and Jonathan did not talk to each other before going to sleep.

She had wondered if Jonathan would suggest their moving in together. She didn't want that; it was too soon. Besides, she was just beginning to enjoy her newfound independence. When Jonathan understood and agreed with the way she felt about that, she felt even closer to him. She had to pinch herself sometimes to see if she were dreaming.

She could hardly believe such a man as Jonathan existed, much less that he could be in love with her. He listened to her with empathy, was always there for her as a friend and lover. Yet Jon was also a man who let her go her own way and make her own decisions. She thought she had the best of all possibilities.

Margaret had received only one strange phone call from Ginger since that night they argued. The jangling of the phone woke Margaret and she reached groggily to the nightstand beside her bed.

Ginger was the most ebullient of her daughters, the one most likely to do something on the spur of the moment, something fun and off the wall. But this night her voice was soft and plaintive. It sounded as if it were coming from somewhere way down deep in her soul.

That haunted sound in her voice alarmed Margaret more than anything had in months.

"Ginger, what is it? What's wrong?"

She realized then that Ginger was crying.

"Nothing, Mom. I miss you, that's all."

Margaret felt her heart breaking, even as she felt the edge of irritation. She realized that Ginger was drunk.

"I miss you too, honey. Where are you? Is Catherine Jane there with you?"

"No, she's with one of the neighbors. She's all right. She's a good kid, Mom . . . a real good kid."

"I know she is, Ginger." Margaret glanced at the clock, seeing it was not that late in Las Vegas. Still, there was a sad urgency in Ginger's voice.

"Are you at work?"

"Work?" Ginger laughed and there was a bitter, cynical edge to it. "I got fired today, Mom. Ain't that a kick? The damned boss fired me because I took one teenie weenie drink on the job. Can you imagine that? In a place that sells liquor, and from a man who makes his living selling alcohol to anybody and everybody." Ginger began to laugh and Margaret thought the sound of it was almost hysterical.

"What will you do? Do you have enough money to get by? I can send you—"

"No," Ginger interrupted. Her refusal sounded harsh and abrupt. "I don't need your help . . . told you that before."

"Ginger, honey, are you drinking now?"

"Drinking?" She laughed loudly again. "I'm afraid that's the understatement of the year."

"Don't you think you should be holding onto your money now instead of—"

"Don't want a lecture," the girl slurred. "Don't need a lecture. If I did I'd call dear old Dad again."

"Again? Have you spoken to him lately?"

"Oh yeah. He was in a real lousy mood. Must be 'cause his sweetie has moved out. He doesn't have time for me anyway . . . never did."

It was the first Margaret knew of Shelley moving out of the house.

Now Margaret could hear Ginger's quiet sobs and it surprised her.

"Ginger? Honey?"

"Mom, I'm messed up . . . so messed up. I've done some things in my life . . . so ashamed. What am I good for? My baby . . . C.J., she's got a lousy rap out of this life. You know?"

Margaret had never heard such anguish in her youngest daughter's voice, and it frightened her to death. She sat up in bed, gripping the phone tightly and willing herself not to burst into tears of hysteria. What was happening? Was Ginger about to do something crazy?

"Baby, listen to me. It's all right. We've all done things that we're not happy about." Margaret tried to keep her voice calm. All the while she wanted to cry, and plead with Ginger, she wanted to command her to get some help.

"Not you Mom. Not Mrs. perfect Mom . . . Mrs. perfect wife. You're just about perfect, Mom, you know that? You're just about the most damned perfect person I know."

Ginger's slurred sarcasm would have hurt Margaret a few months ago, even a few weeks

385

ago. But not tonight. For some reason, Margaret could feel where the words came from and she put her personal reactions aside.

"I'm certainly not perfect, darling. Not by a long shot. If I were I would be able to help you."

"Help me? I don't need any help." Ginger laughed again as if for emphasis.

"I love you, Ginger, do you know that? I've made so many mistakes with you, with all three of my daughters. But I love you and I want you to be well and happy."

Ginger had begun to cry, the sound soft and touching.

"I love you, too, Mom. You'll never know how much. I just want to be good for you, to be the kind of daughter you'll be proud of."

Margaret could not keep the tears back any longer.

"I am proud of you, Ginger. You're a sweet, wonderful, funny person. I love you, baby. And no matter what you do, that will never change. And I'm here if . . ." she thought of Jonathan's firm assertion about Ginger. *Not if . . . when.* "When you need me, Ginger, I'll be here. Whatever you want, whatever you need, I'll help you. Do you hear me?" The girl sniffed and Margaret thought she actually heard the hint of a smile in her voice when she spoke.

"Yeah, Mom. I hear you. I hear you. Thanks."

There was a soft click in Margaret's ear. The sound of the dial tone troubled her so that she dropped the phone on the bed and doubled over with grief.

What was going to happen to Ginger? Margaret was afraid her daughter would not be able to make it safely through the night. That fear kept her awake the rest of the night. She could hardly wait until dawn to call Jonathan and tell him what had happened.

"I know you're afraid, Maggie. But this could be encouraging."

"Encouraging? How can you say that? She's desperate, Jonathan; I could hear it in her voice. She's reached rock bottom and I'm so afraid of what she might do."

"Baby, listen to me. Whatever her problem is, alcohol, drugs, whatever, she has to help herself. In order to do that, some people have to reach absolute rock bottom before they will begin to pull themselves up. At least she's beginning to admit her doubts about herself. I think her declaration of love is just her way of moving back toward you . . . of moving back into your life."

Margaret took a long, shuddering breath. "Do you really think so? You're not just saying that to make me feel better?"

"I wouldn't lie to you," he said softly. "Baby, I know how this hurts. But just try to hang on. I have a feeling she'll call back soon. Wait and see what she has to say. If you're still worried, then you and I will take a few days off and fly out to Vegas to see her."

Margaret was stunned; she was speechless. No one, not even her own husband, her daughters' father, had ever offered to do such a thing just to soothe her motherly fears. She started to cry softly.

"Jon, I love you."

There was a long silence on the line.

"I've waited a long time to hear that, angel. A long time."

"I mean it. I think for the first time in my life I know what it really means to love a man. And better than that, to have him love me back so sweetly and unselfishly."

"You deserve to be loved, Maggie. You deserve that and so much more. One of these days, whenever you're ready, I'm going to prove it to you."

Margaret felt much better after talking to Jonathan. In the next few days he did everything he could to keep her hopes up about Ginger. When the phone rang on Sunday morning, Margaret had a feeling it was Ginger. She glanced toward Jonathan who had just come by to pick her up for a day on the river.

"Mom?"

"Ginger." Margaret breathed a sigh of relief and looked toward Jonathan. He smiled at her as if to say "I told you so."

"How are you darling? I was worried about you the other night."

"I know you were Mom, and I'm sorry." Ginger's voice sounded sober and rational. "You know you said the other night that you would help me." Her words were tentative, almost shy.

"Yes, of course. And I will. Whatever you need."

"I do . . . need . . . your help." Ginger sounded as if she had to force the words from her throat.

"Anything. Just name it." Margaret held her breath in anticipation.

"I'm going to send C.J. to you."

At Margaret's quick indrawn breath, Ginger continued. "Just hear me out, okay? I'm sick, Mom. I know I have a lot of problems that I'm not able to handle myself. But I'm going to get some professional help; I'm checking myself into a clinic here. And I need someone to take care of C.J., someone who will make sure she's all right. Someone who loves her, Mom." Ginger's voice cracked.

"I understand, darling. Don't cry."

"I've messed her up so bad, Mom. I sure didn't have any right to criticize you or Dad after the mess I've made with my own daughter."

In those few seconds, Margaret's mind ran through a tingling gamut of emotions. She felt relieved at hearing Ginger finally admit to her problems, but she also felt agonizing pain for what she must be going through at this moment.

The idea of taking care of a ten-year-old granddaughter that she barely knew absolutely scared her to death. Especially now that she was just beginning to get her own life in order.

"It's all right." Margaret's response was automatic. "Don't worry about that now. You do whatever you have to do to get yourself better." Margaret glanced at Jonathan who was watching and listening carefully. Oh, how she appreciated his being there at this moment.

"I'll take very good care of Catherine Jane, baby. And when you're able, you can come to Ocala to get her, even spend the rest of the summer here if you like."

"That sounds good; you can't imagine how good at this point."

"Just tell me what you want me to do."

"I . . . I'll need a plane ticket for C.J. — "

"I'll take care of that. Tell me the time and

day."

"Tomorrow." Ginger's voice was flat and emotionless. Margaret could just imagine how humbling this was for her. "If that's not too soon . . ."

"No, of course not. We need to do this as quickly as possible I suppose, before—"

"I'm not going to change my mind this time, Mom."

Margaret smiled, encouraged by the determination in Ginger's voice.

"Good, darling. That's good."

"I already have the flight number and time. All you have to do is call and make the reservation. I can pick up the ticket when I take her to the airport."

"It's going to be all right, Ginger. For whatever it's worth, I think you've made the best decision for C.J. And I promise I'll take such good care of her. It will be a wonderful summer. She's never been to Florida, has she?"

"No." Ginger's voice was softer and she took a deep breath that Margaret could hear over the phone. "I . . . I hope she won't interfere too much with your own life, Mom. I realize you're just beginning to adjust, to enjoy yourself and I'm sorry—"

"Don't you worry about that. It will be fun having her here." Margaret rolled her eyes at

Jonathan as she spoke and he smiled, getting the gist of the conversation. He gave her an encouraging nod.

Only later after Margaret made the flight reservation, did she let herself think about what all this really meant.

"Jon, what am I going to do? I hardly know my own granddaughter."

He came and took her in his arms, holding her tight against his long, lean body as he caressed her back. "You'll do fine. How could anyone not love you, hmm?"

She smiled skeptically into his face. "But what about us, Jon? I can't expect you to take on my family problems. And I don't want my granddaughter to cramp your style."

He shook her gently and laughed. "Will you give me a break? Do I look like some overaged lothario? She won't cramp my style and neither will you. This won't change anything between us . . . unless you want it to." His look was thoughtful and questioning.

"No," she whispered. "I don't want it to. I just want you to be happy."

"I will be, as long as I'm with you. Besides," he said, jostling her ever so slightly. "I think it will be fun. It will give us a good excuse to go down to Disney World one weekend. And she'll love the farm and the new spring colts."

"Yes," Margaret said. "I think she will."

"Then it's settled. I'll go with you tomorrow to pick her up at the airport. I can get to know her right along with you. It's going to be fine, so I don't want to hear another word about inconveniencing me."

"All right," she agreed. "Although I might have to take a leave of absence from work until—"

"As much time as you need."

"You are so good to me," she said, nuzzling her face against his neck. "Why are you always so good to me?"

"That one's easy. Because I love you . . . with all my heart."

Thirty-one

Margaret paced nervously as she watched the plane land and taxi down the runway toward the small airport. What if something had happened? What if Ginger changed her mind? Even worse, what if she had taken the ticket and cashed it in, took the money and . . . ?

She turned to Jonathan and smiled weakly, wishing her mind would not conjure up such ridiculous thoughts. Borrowing trouble as Lettie would say.

Jonathan could almost read Margaret's mind. He saw the doubt in her smoky eyes he had learned to love so dearly and could read very well.

"It's all right," he said. "She'll be here."

"I know . . . I know." Margaret broke away

and walked to the expanse of windows that looked out toward the loading areas. The big silver plane was coming closer even though it seemed incredibly slow.

She looked down at the roses in her hand. She'd bought them impulsively at one of the counters. Pink roses, wrapped in green tissue paper. Were they too grown-up for such a little girl?

She looked toward Jonathan, her thoughts wavering. Then she walked to a nearby trash container, staring at it and wondering if she should just forget the roses.

She felt the warmth of Jonathan's hand on her shoulder as he turned her to face him. She moved into his arms as naturally as she would take a step.

"I feel like a kid on my first day at school," she said, trying to laugh at herself.

"Come on," he whispered, pulling her back toward the entryway. "She'll be getting off the plane soon."

With the roses still in her hand, she stood watching each passenger that emerged down the narrow corridor.

Finally they saw her. Margaret broke away from Jonathan.

"There she is. Oh Jon, there she is."

The child looked so small and defenseless; the bag she half carried and half dragged was much bigger than she was.

Jonathan stepped forward quickly and took the bag. The girl looked up from him to Margaret, her face unsmiling, her eyes dark and troubled.

"Who are you?"

Margaret's eyes opened wide at her granddaughter's belligerent tone.

"This is Mr. Bradford," she said, making sure Catherine Jane understood the slight reprimand. Then with a smile, as if to soften the scolding, she handed the pink roses to her granddaughter.

Catherine Jane's mouth clamped together stubbornly and her dark eyes flicked upward to her grandmother's face.

"I hate flowers."

Margaret turned to Jonathan and there was a stunned look in her eyes, but he didn't miss the anger and frustration either. He smiled, then bit his lip as he shrugged his broad shoulders.

Margaret's hand dropped to her side. She should have thrown roses in the trash after all. She looked down at the little girl, who was practically a stranger, wondering what in heaven's name she would do with her for the next few weeks.

This was not the sweet, easygoing child she remembered from a few years ago.

Jonathan stepped very close, whispering so only Margaret could hear. "Patience is a virtue, they say."

She frowned at him, noting the innocent look on his face and the twinkle in his eyes. She gritted her teeth and reached down to take her granddaughter's hand. It felt very warm and slightly grubby.

"Are you hungry?"

"No."

"Well then, I suppose we can go home. Do you need to go to the restroom or anything before we go?"

"No." Catherine Jane's look was challenging and blatantly self-satisfied.

Margaret sighed. This simply was not going to work.

Catherine Jane said nothing as Jonathan helped her climb into the backseat of his Bronco. She sat back in the seat, arms crossed, staring straight ahead with a look of smug defiance.

Margaret had to fight the despair she felt. The child was only tired after the flight, she told herself. It was perfectly normal to be wary of new places and new people.

As they began to move toward the main highway and into traffic, Margaret turned with a smile to Catherine Jane.

"Did you enjoy the flight, sweetheart?"

"I hated it."

"You did? Why?"

"It was boring."

"Oh, boring." Margaret turned back around. She glanced at Jonathan who only smiled his encouragement at her.

"I have to go to the bathroom," Catherine Jane said, whining.

"But . . . but I just asked you at the airport. You said—"

Jonathan's hand reached across to cover Margaret's. "It's all right. There's a service station just at the next exit."

But Margaret found herself growing angrier and more frustrated with every word that her granddaughter spoke.

What on earth was going to happen? How was she ever going to be able to put up with this rude, belligerent little girl for another minute, not to mention several weeks?

When they got back in the vehicle, Margaret decided to try again.

"Mr. Bradford has a farm just next door to my place. And he has horses. You'll love the new colts he has, darling."

This time Catherine Jane said nothing. But she turned her head to look curiously at Jonathan.

"Is he your shack-up?"

Margaret gasped and turned to the child with a disbelieving frown.

"Excuse me?"

"Your shack-up . . . you know . . . your boyfriend."

Jonathan chuckled and shook his head. He said nothing to help Margaret even though she threw him a pleading look.

"Catherine Jane, we're going to have to do something about your language."

The child only stared at her blankly.

Margaret sighed and rolled her eyes. "Mr. Bradford and I are friends. But we do not live together. He has a house and I have a house. But we are very good friends and for lack of a better word, I suppose boyfriend describes it well enough."

The crooked smile Jonathan turned her way made her knees weak and she could not suppress the smile that came automatically to her lips. At that moment she was so glad she had him for support, or at least to help her keep her sense of humor.

This was going to be much more difficult than she ever dreamed. It was not only the way her granddaughter spoke. It was the way she dressed, the way she looked.

Her dark, unruly hair was cut short around her face and stood in stiff spikes about her head. At the back of her neck, the hair was longer and thinner. Margaret thought it did not suit the child at all. It was much too sophisticated for a ten year old.

And the clothes she wore . . . black tights and a long black sweater with huge geometric blocks of bright colors were unsuitable as far as Margaret was concerned. They looked cheap and much too mature for a little girl.

Margaret glanced over her shoulder at Catherine Jane's bored face as she stared out the windows. The huge gold hoops she wore in her ears would have to go.

"This is going to be a challenge," she whispered to Jonathan.

He laughed softly, never taking his eyes off the road.

As they grew nearer home, Margaret began to tell Catherine Jane about the house, wanting to prepare her for the small, rural setting.

"I don't like to be called Catherine Jane," the girl interrupted. "My name is C.J."

"No," Margaret said slowly. "Your name is Catherine Jane. You were named for your great-grandmother. And it's a very special name to me because she was my mother." She kept her voice deliberately soft and patient. "It's her house you'll be staying in while you're here in Ocala." Margaret paused and smiled at the girl. "But if you prefer being called C.J., then I'll call you C.J."

The little girl's face looked disbelieving and Margaret knew with a glimmer of satisfaction that she had expected an argument.

They drove past Jonathan's place.

"This is Mr. Bradford's farm. See the pasture back there. That's where he keeps the horses. And the barn . . . see the barn just through those trees?"

"There's also a swimming pool and a pond." Jonathan looked at C.J. In the rearview mirror. "We'll all go fishing one day if you'd like."

"Yeah, I guess that'd be all right."

Jonathan pulled slowly into Margaret's driveway. Margaret opened the door, anxious to see C.J.'s face when she saw the house. Although by now she expected a negative reaction to everything.

C.J. looked around, her eyes critically assessing the yard and the masses of flowers that bloomed about the porch. Margaret thought her dark eyes were hard and much too cynical for her ten years.

"I hope you'll like it here, sweetheart. And as soon as your mother is better she can—"

"She ain't sick, you know. She's an alcoholic."

Margaret felt a stab of pity for the small girl. She was trying so hard to be tough and unforgiving. Did she think she might be hurt if she enjoyed herself? That it might all suddenly be taken away? How well Margaret could relate to those emotions.

"Yes, I know. But she's going to be well when she comes home. And perhaps your life and hers will be better."

"There's nothin' wrong with my life. Ginger's either. I like it in Las Vegas. It's a happenin' town. Nothing like this burg." She looked about at the rural countryside with a sneer.

Margaret gritted her teeth. It was hard to sustain any pity for such a rude, obnoxious child.

With a grin, Jonathan took the bags and they went into the house.

Margaret was proud of her house. She had everything arranged just the way she wanted. The walls, with their fresh coat of white paint, looked clean and cool. The white also emphasized the gleaming wood floors and the stark grays of the flagstone fireplace.

She'd found a honey-colored pine hutch, just what she'd been searching for. It now contained her delft ironstone collectibles and a hand carved white swan.

Margaret glanced proudly at the restored antique copper and pewter chandelier that hung over the kitchen table. It had turned out better than she'd ever expected. On the kitchen table was a red and white homespun tablecloth and a fresh arrangement of flowers. Lacy curtains and a border of country blue and red at the top of the walls made the little kitchen look new and very fashionable.

"What do you think?" Margaret asked, knowing she probably shouldn't.

C.J. flopped down on the couch. "It's all right I guess."

Margaret followed Jonathan as he carried C.J.'s bags into the extra bedroom. There had not been time to redecorate the room, but Margaret had put one of the colorful, newly cleaned quilts on the bed. She frowned now,

403

thinking that was probably a mistake. C.J. would surely disapprove. She doubted the child would like anything she chose anyway.

"I'm getting nowhere fast with her, Jon," she muttered as she came up behind him.

He put the bag on the floor and turned to take her in his arms.

"You're doing fine. The child's a little rebel, that's for sure. But I think it's only a defense mechanism. From what you've told me, she hasn't had the most stable childhood."

"No, she hasn't."

"It'll be all right. Perhaps it might go easier if there's just the two of you here tonight."

"No, Jonathan! You don't have to do that."

He saw the fear in her eyes and knew what she was thinking.

"It's only for tonight, angel." He kissed her, his lips warm and reassuring. "Don't think she's going to run me away from you so easily. It would take more than a ten-year-old child to do that, believe me."

He was teasing, but it made her feel warm and loved just the same.

"Call me later tonight, after C.J.'s in bed. We'll decide what to do about your job. And we'll make some plans for her. All right?"

"All right," she agreed reluctantly. She

reached up to kiss him. "But if I haven't called by ten o'clock, you might consider sending the rescue squad."

He laughed and kissed her again. He was still smiling when he told C.J. goodbye and waved to Margaret from the door.

Thirty-two

Margaret was certain it was the longest week of her life. By Friday she was completely exhausted. Each day had been a constant battle, a contest of wills between herself and C.J.

At the moment she thought the child was winning.

Ginger had called once. She had sounded so sick and so depressed that Margaret didn't have the heart to tell her what was going on with C.J. This was something she'd have to handle on her own until Ginger was feeling better. She gritted her teeth and pretended everything was fine.

But she felt like crying when she heard C.J.'s terse conversation with her mother.

"Yeah," she said blankly. "Yeah . . . okay. Yeah. Okay. Here's Margaret."

Margaret took the phone and stood staring at her granddaughter.

"Mom," Ginger said. "I gotta go. My group therapy session starts in five minutes. I'm doing okay. It's tough but I'm going to make it and I don't want you to worry. Give C.J. a hug for me. And say an extra prayer for me, too. Bye."

"Goodbye darling." Margaret stood numbly, wishing she could have had another minute of conversation with Ginger. Wishing she could be there to help her through this. Finally she turned to C.J.

"C.J., sweetheart. I know you call your mother by her name, but I really don't like your calling me Margaret."

"Why?"

"Well, because it sounds . . . disrespectful."

C.J. shrugged. "Okay. What do you want me to call you?"

"Well, I called my grandmother, Grandmother." She watched C.J. for any sign of surrender.

"Sure. Whatever."

Margaret sighed and rubbed the back of her neck. God, but it was going to be a long summer . . . and an equally long weekend.

She had seen Jon only a couple of times

during the week and she felt guilty because they were rarely alone. She thought she would give almost anything to be able to spend the evening with him. To lie in his arms and have no worries, no commitments, nothing to come back to if she chose to stay at his house until morning.

The phone interrupted her thoughts.

"Well, how's grandma holding up?" Lettie's voice was bright and full of fun.

"Not all that great, actually." Margaret kept her voice low. C.J. seemed to have ears that captured every word and every sound.

"Have I ever told you what a terrific person I think you are, Margaret Avery?"

Margaret's lips twisted and she smiled.

"What's this leading up to?"

"I *am* leading up to something . . . it's true. Play along, please."

Margaret laughed. "No, you've never told me what a terrific person you think I am."

"Well, I do. And you know that I love Jonathan Bradford dearly. And because I think so highly of the both of you I'm willing to do you both a tremendous favor."

"And what's that?" Margaret was listening more carefully now.

"I'm going to come over to your house tonight and entertain dear little C.J. . . . . might even make a batch of brownies. And you, my dear friend, are going to spend the evening with Jonathan at his house."

"No," Margaret sighed, feeling a tingle of pleasure that began at her toes.

"Yes," Lettie said with a giggle. "Unless of course you'd like me to go entertain Mr. Bradford while you — "

"No thanks. No way." Margaret's headache had already begun to subside. "What brought this on anyway?"

"Actually it was bribery."

"Jonathan?"

"You got it."

"Oh dear. And exactly what did he offer you?"

"I'll tell you later," she said with another giggle. "You just be ready when I get there. And oh, yeah, you might want to explain to the little br . . . huh, I mean angel, that her Aunt Lettie is in charge tonight."

"I will. Are you sure you're up to this after working all day?"

"Me? Heck, I can handle a ten-year-old kid with my eyes closed. Besides, she's not so bad. Kind of reminds me of *me* when I was a girl. Remember how your mama hated me?"

"She didn't hate you."

"Well, she thought I wasn't exactly the kind of girl her daughter should hang out with."

"She didn't know you the way I did."

"Yeah, I guess that's water under the bridge, huh? Anyway I do kind of relate to C.J. in that way. So don't worry, we'll get along great."

"Oh, Lettie?"

"Yeah?"

"Do I have a curfew?"

"Why, Margaret Avery, you little fox. I suppose you can stay out as late as you wish. As long as I get to work by ten tomorrow." With a laugh, Lettie hung up.

Margaret was smiling when she hung up the phone. She suddenly felt exuberant and full of energy. Her mind was racing with thoughts of enjoying a long bath and dressing in something besides shorts and a T-shirt.

C.J., not one to miss a thing, looked up from the sofa where she lay sprawled watching television.

"You going somewhere tonight?"

"Yes, as a matter of fact, I am. Jonathan and I are having dinner, and Lettie is coming over to stay with you. I hope you don't mind."

C.J. shrugged, not moving her eyes from the television. "I like Lettie; she's nice."

Margaret's eyebrows lifted with surprise as she watched the girl. It was the closest thing to a compliment she'd heard from her since they picked her up at the airport. Maybe Lettie was right; maybe the two of them were alike.

Later as Margaret dressed, she felt a strange weakness move over her; the same weakness she felt every time she thought of Jonathan, of kissing him and making love. She smiled at herself in the mirror, noting the blush of color beneath her newly acquired tan. As her eyes studied her image, taking in the lightweight white slacks and silky rose-colored blouse, she thought with satisfaction that she looked better than she had in years.

Despite her hectic week with C.J., there was still a spark of happiness in her eyes. That blank, defeated stare that had looked back at her for so many years was gone.

She felt like dancing . . . like singing!

She stood in the doorway to the living room, silently watching her granddaughter for a few moments. She felt such pity for C.J. . . . when she wasn't feeling annoyed. The girl rarely did anything except sit in front of the television. She didn't like to read and she had shown no interest in any outdoor activities. Perhaps this weekend would be a good time to take her to Jonathan's farm, see what she thought about the mares and their frisky new colts.

She walked to the sofa and sat beside the girl. Without thinking she ran her fingers through C.J.'s dark, spiky hair. Despite the look of it, it felt soft beneath Margaret's fingers.

C.J. turned to stare at her and for a fraction of a second, Margaret thought she saw a flicker of pain in her dark brown eyes.

"Maybe Lettie could give you a new 'do,' as she calls it."

"What's a 'do'?"

"You know, a new hairdo."

Characteristically, C.J. only shrugged, feigning disinterest.

"Shall I mention it to her when she gets here?" Margaret questioned in a chirpy voice. She didn't want to sound domineering.

"I don't care."

"Then I think I will. The weather's getting so hot now . . . perhaps a shorter haircut would be nice."

C.J.'s eyes scanned Margaret, from her

freshly pressed slacks to the new rose-colored lipstick she'd bought just to match the blouse.

"You forgot your earrings," C.J. said.

Margaret's hand went to her ears and she smiled. "You're right, I did. I'll be right back."

She came out of the bedroom, putting the pearl earrings on her ears.

"You look pretty." C.J.'s words were so muffled that Margaret wasn't sure for a moment what she said.

"What, darling?"

"I said you look real pretty."

"Why, thank you, C.J." Margaret smiled at her, but the girl had already turned back to the television as if she had already said more than she intended.

One step at a time, Margaret thought.

Finally Lettie came rushing in, her reddish gold curls bouncing as she closed the door and juggled a grocery bag in her arms. Bracelets jangled gaily on both arms and large gold earrings swung riotously from her ears.

"Hi," she said breathlessly. "Sorry I'm late, but I had to stop at the grocery store and get some goodies for me and my pal here." She nodded toward C.J. as she walked into the kitchen and deposited the bag on the cabinet.

413

"She and I are going to have a slumber party, aren't we, kid?"

Margaret noticed that C.J. had perked up considerably. At least her attention was no longer riveted on the television screen.

"I told C.J. a moment ago that you might like to experiment with a new haircut for her. What do you think?"

"Hey, I think that sounds like a good idea. What about you, C.J.?"

This time when the child shrugged her thin shoulders, there was the faint glimmer of a smile in her dark eyes.

Lettie and Margaret exchanged quick, hopeful looks.

"Well, I'm off," Margaret said. Her heart was racing with anticipation and she could hardly make herself stand and chat politely for one more moment. She wanted to see Jonathan so badly, she thought she could run the entire distance to his house.

She kissed C.J. and waved to Lettie, receiving a wink and a nod that spoke volumes.

As Margaret pulled out onto the highway and headed toward the farm, she smiled to herself. She didn't think she'd ever felt so excited and anxious about seeing anyone as she was about seeing Jonathan tonight.

And if having C.J. for the summer had accomplished nothing else, Margaret knew it had given her a better appreciation of Jon. She still had to pinch herself sometimes to make sure he was real and that he loved her. She could see that he did every time he looked at her, in the gentle look that washed over his face when she said something funny. Sometimes he would interrupt her words with a kiss for no reason except that he could not seem to contain himself one moment longer. She thought she would melt.

When Margaret drove up to the house, Jonathan opened the front door. He stood waiting, a smile of appreciation on his handsome face as he watched her approach. Without speaking she placed her hand in his and lifted her lips for his kiss.

Savoring the moment, she breathed deeply of the sexy masculine scent of him. Her eyes quickly moved with approval over his white shirt, noting how it flattered his dark skin and blue eyes.

"I'm so happy to see you," she whispered. "You've no idea how happy."

"Oh, I think I do," he said, pulling her into the house with him.

"Where's Anya?" she asked, looking around

at the now familiar, welcoming house.

"She's already gone home for the evening."

"Good," Margaret purred.

"Good?" He smiled down into her face, his blue eyes clear and warm.

"I want you all to myself for awhile."

"Baby, I'm all yours."

They laughed and he took her hand, pulling her with him toward the kitchen. "Are you hungry?"

She was, but seeing Jonathan had banished all thought of food from her mind. In her entire life she had rarely initiated sex, but now she found it so natural and easy. Jonathan's acceptance of her and his delighted reactions gave her confidence and power, something she'd never had before. And she loved it.

He turned to find her staring longingly at him.

"I like that look," he said, pulling her around until her back was against the wall. His hands moved slowly down her sides to her hips.

"What look?" Margaret's voice was languid. Rubbery, she thought, just like her knees.

Between words, he nibbled at her lips and trailed soft kisses up her cheek to her eyes. "The look that says you want me." His hands cupped her hips, pulling her against him and making her gasp as she felt his maleness.

She had to grip his shoulders to keep from falling. His mouth was at her ear and as she closed her eyes she found herself dizzy with excitement. "Oh yes . . . I do."

When he pulled away, he took her hand, leading her back toward the hallway.

"Dinner can wait; this can't."

The stairs took awhile. Jonathan stopped, leaning back against the wall and pulling her body against him as he kissed her.

By the time they reached the bedroom, both of them were trembling. Jonathan thought the desire he felt for Maggie was the most powerful force he had ever experienced in his life. His need for her was so strong, so addictive that he found himself holding back sometimes. The last thing he wanted was to frighten her by letting her see how much he wanted her. But tonight, for the first time, he saw the same thing in her, that same heady sensual need that could not be denied, could not be ignored.

And that thrilled and excited him beyond words.

"Oh Maggie," he whispered, as her hungry lips reached for his.

He watched as she undressed. His eyes never left her even as he unbuttoned his own shirt and removed the rest of his clothes. They were comfortable together now and he was pleased that Maggie no longer felt shy and insecure with him.

But being comfortable did not detract from the sexiness or the spark that still flashed between them every time they were together. He had never met a woman who could make him so ready with only a glance.

Impatiently they moved together onto the bed. Jonathan lowered his head, trailing kisses from her throat down to her breasts, making her arch upward to be closer to him. Her rosy nipples were hard, waiting for him. Softly he drew one into his mouth, teasing her skin with his tongue and making her groan and move restlessly beneath him.

Margaret's head moved down, searching almost frantically for his lips, as if she could not endure another moment without feeling his mouth on hers.

"Oh Jon . . ." she whispered. "Please . . . please."

Her whispered words and her hungry kisses only exaggerated Jonathan's own need. The one he'd been trying to control since she walked through the front door. But he was pleased and surprised that she was eager and ready so soon. There would be time for playing later, more time for long, slow kisses that left both of them trembling and hot.

He moved his hand beneath her thighs, feeling the heat and hearing her soft panting moans as he caressed her. With each rhythmic movement she grew more frantic, pleading softly with him to make love to her. He smiled and murmured soft love words to her, waiting until he felt her desire rising to an explosive level that made her close her eyes and push her head back into the pillow.

Only as her body began to pulse did he enter her quickly, feeling the heat, feeling the clenching of her body around his. It took every bit of willpower and control he possessed to make himself stop then and wait, feeling her relax, hearing her sigh of satisfaction.

"Oh . . . Jon," she whispered, staring up at him with wonder and love.

He smiled and kissed her as he began to move again. They stared into each other's eyes as he took control, putting his hands beneath her and lifting her toward him. But this time when she began to respond again, he knew he could not control the fantasy much longer, could not control his own heated response to her.

The intense pleasure he felt was intoxicating, something he wished could last forever. But even as he wished it, her small whispered cries of fulfillment fueled his own heightened senses until he trembled and shuddered against her.

They lay in each other's arms, gasping for air and waiting for their breathing to return to normal. Jonathan held her in the crook of his arm, kissing her hair and whispering soft words of love.

Margaret was aware of the cool air against her heated skin as she stared into the dimly lit bedroom and felt reality returning. She was aware of every inch of Jonathan's body against hers. It felt so perfect that an ache swelled in her throat for all the years she had missed with him, all the splendid years she might have had with someone like Jonathan.

"I have never felt anything like this in my life," she whispered truthfully.

"I feel very selfish when I hear you say that."

"Why?" She turned her head on the pillow to look at him.

"Because as much as I wish your life had been better, that you'd been happier, I can't help feeling good when you say you've never experienced this before. I guess I want to be special to you." He brushed his lips against the corner of her mouth.

"You are special, Jon. I never thought this could happen to me. I didn't think I could feel anything like this with a man."

"Not just any man . . ." he teased.

"No . . . you're certainly not just any man. What I'm feeling with you, at this time of my life, is just beyond comprehension. These unbelievable feelings, these . . ." She stopped and stared into his eyes. "I suppose I sound foolish, saying such things. I suppose it's hard for you to believe that I—"

"Shhh." His lips stopped her doubtful words. "No, love. It isn't hard for me to believe at all. I'm not so insensitive that I can't see, can't feel your reactions. And I love it." He kissed her again.

She hid her face against his chest and Jonathan laughed. He found her response charming and very lovable.

"You're something else, you know that, Maggie Avery? And I love you. I adore you. Does it still make you uncomfortable to

421

hear me say that?"

"No," she whispered, realizing it was true, realizing she relished the words and treasured his love beyond anything. "I love you, too, Jonathan. More than I ever thought it was possible to love anyone."

Thirty-three

It was much later when Maggie went into Jonathan's bathroom to shower. He brought her a terry robe to wear.

"There's no need for clothes," he said, kissing her bare shoulder. "The night is ours to enjoy. After you've finished bathing, we'll throw a steak on the grill, toss a salad and sit around with no underwear for the rest of the evening."

She laughed at his nonsense and the way he wiggled his brows *à la* Groucho Marx. But she knew that beneath his light bantering he had planned this evening just for her, as a break from the stress she'd experienced this week with C.J.

Jonathan went down the hall to shower in the guest bedroom. Not that Margaret wouldn't have been perfectly content for them to shower together. But Jonathan always gave her her privacy. It was something she didn't have to ask for. He was simply aware of her needs and he responded accordingly. She loved that about him.

She smiled and shook her head in bemused happiness as she let the warm jets of water spray over her body.

It was a wonderful evening, more perfect than Margaret could have envisioned. They ate outside on the tiled patio that overlooked the pool and the lush courtyard. The warm scent of flowers surrounded them and the wind murmured softly.

The steaks were succulent and tender, the salad fresh and crisp. As they toasted one another over tall, sparkling glasses of iced tea, there was something different. Something had changed between them, something deep and wonderful. Margaret could feel it in each touch and each kiss.

She thought how much she enjoyed talking to Jonathan. He was easy and relaxed, yet he didn't mind expressing his opinion or arguing with her about one of hers. There was always laughter bubbling between them.

Jonathan reached across the small table and took her hand. "How is C.J.? Have you heard any more from Gincy?" Margaret smiled, pleased that he called her youngest daughter by her nickname. Even though he had never met her, he had already taken an interest in Gincy as well as her daughter C.J.

"Yes, she called. She sounded very quiet and depressed."

"Try not to worry; it's still early. After the first two weeks, she'll probably be much better."

"Did Sylvia ever go to . . . ?" She let her voice trail away, uncertain if she should ask him about his wife's drinking problem.

"To a rehab center? No. Sylvia never reached the point where she thought her drinking was a problem, although I'm certain she knew it in her own mind. But no, it wasn't something she ever admitted to me or to the rest of the world."

"That's very sad."

"It was a waste, Maggie. A damned waste. Sylvia was intelligent, educated, beautiful. She had everything." He looked up, his eyes troubled. "And she threw it all away as if it were nothing."

"And you resented her for that?"

"Hell yes, I resented it. I resented her. There were times when I actually thought I hated her. But then . . ."

He shrugged his shoulders in a gesture of helplessness.

"I know," she said, squeezing his hand. "I know how frustrating it must have been."

"But that's over now," he said, looking into her eyes. "I'm trying to put it behind me. Actually, I have begun to make a good life for myself here where my roots are." He glanced at the house and the beautifully landscaped gardens around them.

"I think you've done very well," she said gently. "It's not easy to start over."

"We're a pair, aren't we?" he said. There was a wistful smile that played around his lips. "But I think you're beginning to feel better about your own life, too."

"Yes," she said. "Yes, I am. Actually I suppose as long as one has children, there will always be problems and worries. But I must admit, things are not going so badly for me." She smiled. "It's been much easier because of you, Jon. When I'm with you I'm happier than I ever dreamed I could be."

He smiled and shook his head in a sweet, denying gesture that made her heart ache with tenderness. How she loved him!

"Yes," she said. "You, Jonathan Bradford. You have captured my heart so completely that I'm not sure I can ever live without you."

His eyelashes flicked upward and he stared at her, his eyes dark and serious. "Be careful, angel. I might take you up on that."

She looked away, not knowing what to say.

She did love him, and she was sure it was right between them. But she simply was not ready to make a commitment, not this soon after the end of a long marriage.

She felt him move toward her. He took her hand and pulled her up from the chair, holding her easily in his arms and lifting her chin so that she had to look up into his face.

"Don't worry," he said, his words teasing and bittersweet. "I won't make you commit to something you're not ready for. I love you too much for that. When you come to me, Maggie, I want it to be for good, and because you want it, because you want me, and not because you think you will lose me and what we have if you don't."

"Oh, Jon." She felt the tears burning her eyes as she looked up at him. "How on earth have I gotten so lucky to have found a man like you?"

"We're both lucky," he whispered before he kissed her. "Just remember that."

That night Margaret fell asleep in Jonathan's arms. It felt so right. Now she had the extra benefit of having no pressure to conform, or to do anything because the man she loved expected it. She felt she was truly free for the first time in her life to enjoy and to think about what she wanted before merely stumbling headlong into it.

She woke early, wanting to get home before C.J. was up. She tiptoed downstairs to make coffee. She had intended to take a cup to Jonathan, but when she turned around he was there. Standing in the doorway of the kitchen, he watched her with the most wonderful expression.

"What?" she said, ducking her head shyly away from his intense gaze.

"You look very pretty standing there, even at this hour of the morning."

"Your eyes are dulled by sleep."

"No. I don't think so. Love maybe." He came to her and took the cup of coffee, bending to place a light kiss on her lips.

"You didn't have to get up so early. It's Saturday; you should sleep in," she said.

"And let you leave without a goodbye kiss? Never."

When he kissed her, Margaret thought of last night and of how amazed she had been by his lovemaking. Nothing had ever taken her to such heights. It was as if an entirely new world was opening up for her. She pulled away and looked up into his eyes.

"I love you, Jon."

"And I love you." He had a momentary look of surprise, then pleasure. "I'll come over late this afternoon. Perhaps we can take C.J. to a movie tonight."

"That sounds wonderful. And Jon, thank you."

He grinned and his blue eyes twinkled. "I've never been thanked before for—"

"No," she whispered, giving him a playful shove. "I meant thank you for being so good to C.J. It means a lot to me."

"Oh, that." Again he grinned crookedly at her.

When they said goodbye the sun was just coming up over the flat line of trees to the east. The early morning breeze stirred all the earthy summer scents to life. As they stood enjoying the sound of birdsong that filled the trees, Margaret thought that she had never felt such contentment.

At home, she tiptoed quietly into the house and smiled when she saw the lights on and Lettie sitting at the kitchen table having a cup of coffee.

"How was it?" Margaret whispered.

"Actually, it was really nice. C.J. even laughed out loud a couple of times."

Margaret lifted her eyebrows in a gesture of congratulations.

"Well, I'm impressed. She does like you, Lettie. She told me so last night before I left."

"I like her, too. I cut her hair."

"How does it look?"

"I think it looks terrific, if I do say so myself. It's short, but no punk stuff. She looks more like a little girl now."

"I can't wait to see it."

"She has such a pretty little face. But from some of the things she told me, she doesn't think so. Doesn't trust anyone either. She's had a pretty unhappy life, Margaret."

Margaret sank into a chair. She felt a deep ache of guilt every time she thought of C.J.'s and Ginger's life. As always she felt she should have been able to do more for them.

Lettie saw Margaret's expression. "She's going to get better, Mags. She needs a lot of love, maybe even some therapy later. But she's a tough one; she's going to be all right."

"I hope so."

Lettie took a sip of coffee and there was an odd expression on her face. "Charles called last night."

Margaret's head came up and she stared across the table.

"Charles? Called here?"

"Yep. Sure did. He didn't seem too crazy about the idea of you being out."

"What did he say?"

"He wanted to know where you were. Demanded would actually be a better word."

"What did you tell him?"

"I told him you were out with a friend. Although personally, I don't think the bastard deserved to know even that."

Margaret smiled across at Lettie, amused by her tigerish, protective manner.

"I wonder what he wanted."

"If he has any sense, he wants you back."

That thought hadn't occurred to Margaret. If anything, the thoughts that came to mind were negative ones. Charles either wanted to harass her or tell her what was wrong with her life, or maybe repeat his opinion that she would never be able to make it without him.

He had tried his best to prove that by withholding her money. But even that had not worked. She was managing very well on her own and when the money was finally released, it would only be a bonus, something to fall back on if she ever needed it.

Suddenly Margaret smiled. Her face brightened as if she'd had a quick flash of positive memory.

"I *can* make it without him," she declared, her tone one of amazement. "And I like my life now more than I have in years, since the girls were little." She looked up at Lettie, her eyes shining.

"Yeah," Lettie said aggressively. "You've

come a long way, baby."

Margaret laughed and stood up, feeling suddenly young and buoyant.

"Lettie, do you have time to fix my hair today?"

"Well, sure. Saturday's usually very busy, but I could probably work you in around noon. What did you have in mind?"

"Oh, I don't know. Something light and cool, something that makes me feel beautiful."

"Well, personally, I think you've already found that secret." Lettie winked at her. "But hey, I'll do what I can."

"Great. I thought I'd take C.J. shopping. And tonight Jonathan and I are taking her to a movie."

Lettie's smile was warm and filled with genuine pleasure for her friend's happiness. "I'm so happy for you, Mags. You deserve a good life. And I can't think of a nicer man than Jonathan. But tell me, is he as terrific as he seems?" Her dark eyes were alive with mischief and curiosity.

"Every bit," Margaret said, her voice soft and whispery. "Every bit and then some."

That afternoon when Margaret emerged from the beauty salon, hand in hand with C.J., the girl looked up at her in an odd, sweet way. There was a bond growing between them; mor than their hands were linked. Margaret silently thanked Lettie for kindling this spark.

"Lettie's a good hairdresser, isn't she?"

Margaret laughed, feeling lighthearted. Her new short haircut was back to its natural brown color and the streaks of gray now appeared as pale gold highlights.

"Yes, she is, baby. She's made me feel like a new woman."

"Me, too." C.J. straightened her shoulders and stood straight and tall in a mature, womanly fashion. It reminded Margaret of some of Ginger's childhood antics.

Margaret laughed and squeezed her hand. Just as Lettie said, C.J. really did look more like a little girl now. C.J.'s haircut emphasized the natural curl in her dark hair and allowed it to fall about her face in soft wisps.

"Just wait till we get to that shopping mall, C.J. When we get through, you're going to be the prettiest, best dressed, little girl in Ocala."

It pleased Margaret to see the soft, expectant look in C.J.'s eyes. She still rarely smiled, but Margaret had a feeling that would come soon, too.

Margaret saw that day as a new beginning for C.J. Little by little she became more animated, more talkative. She could still be rude, but Margaret thought that was only a lack of training.

The child simply didn't know any better.

Sometimes Margaret would grow angry with Ginger, thinking of how she had brought C.J. up. And then she would be angry with herself and Charles. Ginger had only been a baby herself when she had C.J. What did she know of raising a child? Margaret blamed herself for not being there to help. But she was here now, she would remind herself firmly.

C.J. fell in love with Jonathan's farm. And she adored Jonathan. Margaret would often catch the girl looking at them when they were together. There would be a soft, wistful look in her eyes, a look of longing that Margaret understood all too well.

"We're probably the closest thing to a family she's ever known," Margaret said to Jonathan.

Jonathan would nod and unveil that warm smile of his. Sometimes he would put his arms around her and hold her. He seemed to sense how torn Margaret was. She looked forward to the day Ginger was well and back home with her daughter. But he could also see how attached she had grown to C.J. and how she dreaded losing her.

Margaret thought the thing that helped C.J. most was Jonathan's colt, the one named Wildflower. The name was perfect; the little filly was a pale, delicate creature that had been sickly from birth.

"The trainer says she'll never be worth anything," Jonathan said one day when they were in the barn.

Margaret saw C.J.'s eyes flash toward him, the curiosity alive in those dark eyes.

"He's just a big dummy," she said in her old defiant manner.

"C.J.," Margaret scolded.

"Well, he is. Wildflower is the sweetest, most beautiful horse I've ever seen. When she looks at me with those big eyes, I just know how smart she is, Gran. I just know it." She turned to Jonathan and there was a panic stricken look in her eyes. "You won't let him shoot her, will you, Jonathan? Please, you can't let him do that."

Jonathan frowned and knelt down before the girl. His hands reached for her and she went into his arms as if she desperately needed shelter and comfort.

Jonathan looked up, catching Margaret's worried look and warned her away with a frown. The compassionate smile that followed was reassuring and Margaret stepped back.

"Of course I won't, C.J. Where did you ever get such an idea?"

He leaned back and looked into her face.

Margaret was stunned to see tears on C.J.'s

pretty face. She never cried about anything. Now when her chin quivered, Margaret found tears filling her own eyes as well. She pressed her fingers against her lips and watched as Jonathan tried to reassure the child.

C.J. shook her head, unable to reply.

"Wildflower probably won't ever be show-worthy, sweetheart. That's all he meant. But I would never destroy her, C.J . . . never. You do believe that, don't you?"

"Promise?" C.J. looked up into his face and her lips trembled.

Margaret thought she knew Jonathan so well, but she had never seen such a look as the one that transformed his face. There was a slight frown between his brows and the whisper of a smile on his lips. She could see his heart melting and she smiled tearfully.

"I promise." His voice was husky and filled with some emotion Margaret had never heard there before.

Jonathan took C.J.'s chin and lifted her head.

"Would it make you feel any better if Wildflower belonged to you? If you were responsible for seeing that she's fed and warm and safe?"

"Do you mean it?" Bright glistening eyes stared so hopefully into Jonathan's blue eyes that it made one's heart ache to watch.

"Yes," he said with a soft chuckle. "I mean it.

But only if you promise to take very good care of her."

C.J.'s indrawn breath of delight could be heard all through the big barn. Then she threw her arms around Jonathan's neck, almost propelling the both of them backwards into the hay.

"Oh, thank you, Jonathan. Thank you! Thank you!"

When C.J. pulled away and ran back toward the stall where the little colt was, Margaret went to Jonathan and reached her hand down to him.

"Has anyone ever told you what a wonderful man you are?"

"Not recently," he said. He came to his feet and pulled her into his arms. "I think I could stand hearing it again."

Thirty-four

The weeks passed quickly and Margaret was pleased to see C.J. blossom into a high-spirited child with a quick laugh and a perpetual bounce in her step. Margaret often thought she must wake up in the morning with a smile etched on her face. The eager question, "When can we go to the farm?" always springing from her lips.

At first it seemed easier for C.J. to loosen up with Lettie and Jonathan; she still remained shy and hesitantly affectionate toward Margaret. But Margaret remained patient, pleased at the smallest signs of progress and willing to wait her turn.

When it finally happened, she thought it was well worth the wait. . . .

It was a sweltering afternoon and Margaret had been working outside. She'd just stepped into the house for a drink of water when the phone rang. C.J. ran to answer it, then handed it to Margaret with a shrug.

It was Charles.

"Margaret? Was that Catherine who answered the phone? My God, what has Ginger gotten herself into this time? Cyndi told me several weeks ago that she was in some rehab program somewhere and that Catherine Jane is with you."

How typical of him, Margaret thought. Not one word of concern for the struggle that Ginger was going through.

Her head was beginning to ache from being in the sun too long. She was sweaty and needed a shower. Impatiently, she wiped the back of her hand across her forehead.

"How nice to talk to you, too, Charles," she said.

He hesitated a moment. "I'm sorry. I didn't mean to start out this way after all these months. How are you, Margaret?"

The deliberate lowering of his voice and the little note of pity there infuriated Margaret. What on earth did he think? That she had spent the spring and summer pining away somewhere . . . that her life was dark and gloomy and filled with misery because she was no longer married to him?

"Actually, I'm doing quite well, Charles. How about you?"

"Oh, as well as could be expected . . ." he said, his voice wallowing in self-pity.

Margaret waited for the rest of the phrase and

almost laughed aloud when it came.

". . . . under the circumstances."

"Yeah, those darned circumstances are rough sometimes, aren't they, Charles?" She felt a sense of exhilaration at being able to express her sarcasm so easily.

Charles cleared his throat, ignoring the fact that she was making fun of him. "I suppose Cyndi told you about Shelley?"

"That she moved out? Yes, I knew about it."

"Yeah, she left me, Margaret. I'm all alone in this big house. It seems awfully empty without you and the girls running in and out."

"Oh? Well, I'm sure you'll find someone else soon, Charles."

"I don't want anyone else, Margaret. I want you. I want us to be a family again, the way you always wanted."

"Charles . . ." she began. She did not want to feel sorry for him.

Knowing Charles, most of what he said was manipulation. Still, she could not help the pity that coursed through her. She hated thinking of him alone, of his growing old with no one to care about him, even if it was his own fault.

"Please, baby, just hear me out, won't you? I'm not asking you to make a decision right now. Just think about it. I'll do anything you want, give you anything you ask for."

She shook her head impatiently, aware of C.J.'s

watchful eyes upon her.

"I don't want anything—"

"Let me come down for the weekend. We can talk—"

"No, Charles. Listen to me. This is no good; you're only feeling alone and sad right now. But nothing has changed between us except that I am farther away. And I don't just mean that you're in Atlanta and I'm in Ocala. I could never go back to the life we had . . . never. I'm happy here; I have a wonderful life with friends who care about me and like me for just being me. I have a job that I love and a better relationship with my daughters than I ever dreamed I would have." She paused and listened for his protest. But he said nothing.

"I'm sorry, Charles, really. I wish you could be happy, I really do. But I'm not responsible for your happiness, I'm not the one who can give you that."

She heard his sigh and it actually made her heart ache. Why did life have to be so complicated?

"Well, you certainly sound sure, as if you've made up your mind."

"Oh, I have."

"You know . . . I almost wish you had done this years ago, Margaret. I never realized how much I loved you, or how much you meant in my life until you were gone. And the girls . . ."

Margaret closed her eyes and rubbed the back of her neck. Then she smiled. She recognized the accusation, his attempt to blame everything on her and make her shoulder the responsibility for what had happened. But it didn't work any more. It simply didn't.

"Wait a minute, Charles. Don't put this responsibility on me, too, you hear? I won't have it. Don't make it sound as if I could have done something to prevent this by my actions. You caused our divorce and nothing else. It's you who's built a wall between yourself and the girls. I had nothing to do with that."

"You've changed," he said, still accusing. "You used to be so sweet and—"

"Gullible? Yes, I was. But I can assure you, I am no longer that. Look, Charles, I have to go—"

"Please, Margaret."

Margaret opened her eyes wide at the uncharacteristic pleading in Charles's voice.

"The girls have turned against me. Even Cyndi . . ." His voice cracked, then trailed weakly away.

He was crying. Margaret could not believe it, but Charles was crying.

"I need you, baby; I don't know what I'll do without you, without my girls."

"I'm sorry, Charles. Really I am. But I don't know what else to say to you. I have to go."

She hung up the phone, pushing it away from

her as if it were on fire. When she turned around and saw C.J.'s questioning eyes, saw the fear there, she could not hide her emotions any longer.

She sank into one of the kitchen chairs and laid her head against the tablecloth. Her shoulders shook as the tears came.

She felt C.J. beside her, but she couldn't speak, didn't know what to say or how to explain what she was feeling to a ten-year-old child.

C.J.'s small hand caressed her shoulders and touched her hair. "I love you, Gran. Please don't cry. Everything will be okay. I love you, and Jonathan and Lettie love you, too."

Margaret looked up, her face streaked with tears. She took C.J. into her arms and they held each other, the grandchild consoling the grandmother. It was wonderful and it was touching. Margaret thought it was the destruction of the last stumbling block in their way, the last bastion of defense that C.J. had erected between herself and the cruel world that hurt her.

"I love you, too, baby. More than you can imagine. I suppose there are a lot of things I should tell you about the phone call and your grandfather."

C.J. nodded, and her dark eyes reflected her need to know.

"And about me and Ginger? I mean my mom."

Margaret smiled and touched C.J.'s face.

"Yes sweetheart, about you and your mom. Tell you what. Why don't you fix us something cool to drink and make us a plate of cookies? Let me take a quick shower, then we'll go out on the porch in the swing and I'll tell you everything. All right?"

That day was the real turning point in Margaret and C.J.'s relationship. They became family, and C.J. seemed to feel safe showing affection to her grandmother.

C.J. blossomed beneath the Florida sun and fresh air. Her long thin legs grew tanned and muscular as she ran and frolicked with Wildflower. Some hot afternoons Margaret and Jonathan would sit by the side of his pool, talking and laughing as C.J. swam and splashed. She looked and acted like a normal ten year old, and she seemed genuinely happy. Margaret tried not to think what would happen when Ginger came and C.J. would have to leave.

The week before Ginger was to be released from the clinic, Margaret received a call from Cyndi.

"How would you like to have guests for the weekend, Mom?" she asked.

Margaret gave a low squeal of excitement, bouncing and smiling at C.J. who stood nearby, listening.

"Do you mean it? Can you really come? Oh Cyndi, don't tell me this if you might not come. I want to see you so badly."

"And Steven, too, I hope."

"Of course, Steven, too. Well?" Cyndi teasingly confronted.

"We're really coming, Mom. It has to be this weekend. I need to get back if I'm going to register for school."

"You're going for sure? Oh, Cyndi."

"Yes, for sure," she laughed. "Georgia Southwestern is here; it's a very good school. If I'm lucky, I'll be able to enroll in the fall semester."

"Oh darling, I'm so happy about that. What does Steven think?"

"He's been wonderful. But I'll tell you all about it when I get there. We'll leave Friday as soon as Steven can get away from work. It's not far from Americus to Ocala, so it shouldn't be too late when we arrive."

"It doesn't matter how late. I'll be up waiting. Just drive carefully."

"We will. How's C.J.? I can't wait to see her; I probably won't even know her."

"She's terrific. I'm so pleased that she will get to know her Aunt Cyndi." Margaret winked at C.J.

"Have you heard from Ginger?"

"Yes, she's doing great. It's been tough, she says, and I know she's worked really hard at this. I'm so proud of her."

"I know, Mom. It's great."

"She should be released next week. She's coming to Florida for a couple of weeks to rest, and until she can decide what she wants to do."

Margaret frowned as she saw C.J. turn away. Her shoulders were slumped and Margaret knew she didn't like to talk about her mother coming for her.

"That's terrific. Well, I'll let you go. We'll see you for sure Friday night. Bye, Mom."

Margaret hung up the phone and went straight to C.J. putting her arms around her.

"Your Aunt Cyndi is coming for a visit this weekend. I don't suppose you remember much about her, do you?"

C.J. shook her head.

"Well, you're going to love her. And Steven. He's very nice and very handsome." She nudged C.J. good-naturedly, but the child didn't respond.

"What's wrong?"

C.J. shrugged her shoulders and her dark head bent forward as she stared at the floor.

"Tell me now. You know you can tell your Gran anything."

C.J. leaned against her grandmother, letting her head fall dejectedly against Margaret's shoulder.

"I don't want to go back to Las Vegas, Gran. want to stay here with you and Jonathan . . . and with Wildflower." She looked up pleadingly and there were tears in her eyes.

"Oh, sweetheart. I don't know what to say. You have to live with your mother, you know that." She hugged C.J. against her. "But you can always come to Ocala for the summer. We'll have such wonderful summers together."

But it was small consolation for a ten year old who was feeling loved and secure for the first time in her life and now saw it all slipping away.

C.J. couldn't stop crying. Her small body shook with the grief of her tears and she could not seem to stop.

Finally Margaret just held her and rocked her, trying to soothe away her fears. Margaret was at a loss how she could make her feel better about her future, when she herself had no idea what it would be.

Thirty-five

Margaret cleaned house and baked all week. She knew it was probably ridiculous, but it felt good and it reminded her of all those holidays and birthdays when the girls were still at home.

Besides, it seemed to make C.J. so happy and excited, how could she resist?

Finally on Thursday, Margaret declared she had done all she was going to do. The house was spotless, the yard perfectly manicured, and she had enough food in the refrigerator to feed a small army. Besides, Jonathan had already begun to plan a party at his house for Saturday night.

Debbie called that afternoon. She had grown fond of C.J. during Margaret's visit to the newspaper office, and she had introduced her to several of her nieces. Slowly C.J. had made friends. This afternoon she asked Margaret if C.J. could spend the night with the girls.

"Please, Gran," C.J. pleaded. "I've never slept over with a friend."

"You haven't? Well, then, indeed, you must. There's nothing like an overnight stay when a girl is ten years old and the summer breeze is warm enough to keep you up all night laughing and talking."

Jonathan came over and they drove C.J. to her friend's house. Then he insisted on taking Margaret to a very quiet, out of the way restaurant for dinner.

"Oh, this feels so good," she declared as they settled into one of the padded booths. "I forgot how much work there is to hosting a family for the weekend."

"But you enjoy it." He reached across the table to take her hand.

"Yes, I confess I do. This will be the first time in years that I can look forward to having the children home without a big scene, or without having to soothe over some disagreement between one of them and their father."

"It will be good for C.J., too."

She looked at him, her eyes filled with love.

"You love her too, don't you?"

He smiled crookedly in that special way that made her heart turn over. "Yeah, I do. She's a very special little girl. And she has a natural way with horses."

"She loves you, too, Jon. I'm afraid it's going

to break her heart when she has to leave."

"I wish she didn't have to." His eyes were questioning.

"I know, but she needs to be with Ginger. And as much as I — "

"Maybe Ginger would like to move to Ocala."

"I wish that were true. It would be perfect, wouldn't it? But no . . . knowing Ginger and how she loves excitement and the bright lights, I just can't imagine she'd want to stay here."

"It might be worth mentioning."

Margaret thought he kept his words especially light, although she could see how much it meant to him.

"Yeah," she said with a smile. "It's certainly worth mentioning."

They went back to her house alone, reveling in the peace and quiet and in the night that lay before them.

They undressed in a slow, leisurely manner, enjoying the touching, enjoying just being able to fill their eyes with each other. There was no hurry, no urgency in their lovemaking that night. Jonathan took a very long, deliciously pleasurable time proving to her how much he enjoyed her body and having her in his arms.

He watched as her gray eyes turned dark and stormy. Sometimes he thought he could lose himself completely in those eyes, in her soft arms.

"Love me," she whispered.

"I do Maggie . . . I do."

As her soft eyes urged him on, he made slow, earth shattering love to her. The kind of love that made her head spin, that made her feel faint with the overwhelming pleasure he gave.

Later she lay quietly in the crook of his arm, letting her fingers trail over the soft mat of hair on his chest, wondering how she had ever lived without him.

"Do you know what I remember most about you, Maggie? About that summer when I fell head over heels in love with a girl who wouldn't even give me the time of day?" His voice was a quiet rumble beneath her cheek.

"If that's true, then I must have been out of my mind."

"It was true," he said, taking her fingers and kissing the tips of them before letting them return to their exploring.

"I remember those enormous gray eyes." He turned to look at her. "And long slender legs that were golden from the sun." He brushed her hair back from her eyes. "Hair that tumbled and fell over your eyes, making them even more mysterious and defiant than before."

"Defiant? I wasn't defiant."

"Sure you were. And fierce and independent. You were different, not the usual kind of girl who ran after the boys. And that was an aphrodisiac to me."

"This is embarrassing," she murmured, rubbing her cheek against his chest. "I had no idea—"

"No, I know you didn't. And that was probably even more of a turn-on for a fourteen-year-old boy. I thought if you didn't notice me soon, if I couldn't have you, I might just possibly die."

"Oh Jon," she said, chuckling now. "I can hardly believe this. You're making this up."

"I am not," he said, shaking her gently. "Show a little respect."

They tumbled on the bed, laughing and giggling like school kids. Later when Margaret fell asleep in his arms, she was still smiling.

Jon had dinner with her and C.J. on Friday night. But he insisted on going home afterward, telling Margaret that she needed to greet her family alone.

"You don't need me here to interfere or to make things awkward. It's the first time you've seen them since you left Atlanta."

"No, Jon . . ."

He kissed her and smiled. "I'll see you tomorrow afternoon at the house. Tell everyone to bring a swimsuit. Anya is cooking all the things you and C.J. like."

Reluctantly she kissed him goodbye and stood

at the door watching as he got into his Bronco and drove away.

Margaret was jittery and restless. It seemed that every car on the road slowed at the driveway, then sped on through the night. When one finally did turn in, she could hardly believe it.

"They're here," she said to C.J.

She and C.J. went out onto the porch. The heat of the night air was very warm, stifling almost and she hoped it would not rain and spoil Jonathan's Saturday pool party.

Cyndi ran to the porch and up the steps, throwing herself into her mother's arms. Steven walked behind her, carrying a suitcase and grinning broadly at his wife's enthusiasm.

"Mom, oh Mom, it's so good to see you." Cyndi stood back to study her mother. "You look wonderful." She could not hide the surprise in her voice. "You look really wonderful. What have you been doing to yourself?" Her hand went to her mother's hair. "I love your hair."

Before Margaret had a chance to answer, Cyndi had turned her exuberance toward C.J.

"Oh, C.J.," she whispered. "I can't believe this is little C.J. Come here honey . . . give your aunt a big hug."

C.J.'s smile was slow and shy as she moved into Cyndi's outstretched arms. By now Steven was on the porch. He set the bag down and put an arm around Margaret.

That night they talked and laughed until C.J. finally fell asleep against Margaret on the sofa.

Steven carried the little girl to bed before sticking his head back around the door. "I think I'll turn in, too, and give you girls a chance to gossip privately."

"Certainly, Steven," Margaret said. "You and Cyndi can sleep in my bedroom. I'll take the sofa."

"Are you sure?" he said with a frown.

"I'm sure. I've slept on this old sofa more times than I can count. You go ahead."

Margaret and Cyndi talked until early morning, stopping only when both of them were quiet and sated with conversation.

"Did I tell you that Claire and Brian are coming to visit us in Americus?"

"No, you didn't." Margaret didn't voice her optimism, but her wide gray eyes and her expression told everything.

"Steven and I plan to be on our best marital behavior, you know, set an example for them." Her laughter was soft and teasing.

Margaret nodded. "Oh, I wish . . ."

"Claire and I have talked a lot, Mom, especially since you left. I guess your not being there has made us even closer. She loves Brian, I'm sure of that. But I don't think we should get our hopes up too much about this."

"Why not?"

"I don't know really. Claire still has some hang-ups about marriage. It's not something I can put my finger on. I'm just not sure she will ever get married."

"Well . . ." Margaret stared at the wall, thinking of Claire and all the things that bothered her. Her daughter was a very independent young woman.

"Steven oftens reminds me that marriage is not for everyone," Cyndi said.

"That's true. As much as I'd love to see your sister married and settled, if it's not what she wants, then . . ." Margaret shrugged and turned again to Cyndi. "I just want her to be happy. I want all of you to be happy and content with yourself and your choices."

"We know, Mom. We've always known that."

They were silent for a moment before Cyndi spoke.

"What do you think Gincy will do when she's released? I noticed C.J. doesn't like to talk about it much."

"I don't know. Cyndi, you should have seen C.J. when she first came. She looked and acted like a little rebel. She had a punk haircut and the black clothes . . . oh." Margaret's hands went to her cheeks as she remembered. "She's come so far since then. I think this is the first really stable home she's ever had and she is thriving on it. She adores Jonathan."

"She talks about him all the time, and about the horses."

"Yes. It's been really good for her . . . the farm and the horses. And no one could have been a better father figure than Jonathan . . ."

Cyndi looked at her mother, noting the faraway look in her eyes, the smile on her lips as she talked about Jonathan Bradford.

"Looks as if the handsome Mr. Bradford has put a glow on someone else's cheeks, too."

"I love him, Cyndi. I know you might think it's too soon. But it's not as if we plan on rushing into anything. He's been very patient about that, more patient than I ever expected. And he's so good to me."

"I can see that." Cyndi reached across and placed her hand on her mother's arm. "I'm happy for you, Mom. I don't think it's too soon at all. I might have once, but I've grown up a lot since then. The first moment I saw you tonight I knew how happy you were. And I was really pleased. Whatever you want with Jonathan is fine with me."

Margaret hugged Cyndi and watched as her petite daughter got up and went into the bedroom.

It was a wonderful weekend. Perfect, Margaret thought later. Anya and Jonathan went out o their way to make everything special for Cyndi and Steven. And the young couple was impressed with Jonathan's house and farm.

"This is what I'd love to have," Steven said, standing against one of the fences and surveying the lush green fields. "I've always wanted a farm."

Cyndi stared at him as if she couldn't believe what she was hearing. "You . . . a farmer?" Her smile was indulgent and tender.

"Well, I'd still be a lawyer. But yeah, man, I'd love for us to have a place like this some day. Be a great place to raise kids."

Margaret and Jonathan smiled at one another as Cyndi put an arm around Steven's waist. They left them there at the fence, staring quietly at the grazing horses and the verdant countryside.

After the weekend was over and Cyndi and Steven had gone home, Jonathan and Margaret sat on the porch swing talking. C.J. was inside watching television.

"I think the visit was a success, don't you?" he asked.

"Yes," she nodded. "Definitely a success. I feel so much better about Cyndi and Steven now that they've left Atlanta. I think it was the right move for them."

"Now, the next big hurdle," he said, putting an arm around her shoulders.

"What's that?"

"Gincy . . . and C.J."

She knew he was right. She did regard it as a hurdle, even though she had not voiced that sentiment out loud.

As the week went by and the time grew nearer for Ginger's arrival, C.J. grew restless and irritable. She even reverted to her rude way of talking once or twice. But Margaret didn't scold; she understood perfectly what her granddaughter was going through.

The weather had grown very hot and the air held the smell and taste of salt. It was as if the ocean were very near instead of an hour's drive away. On the day they were to pick up Ginger at the airport, the clouds rolled low and heavy across the horizon. They were black and ugly, and the sight of them filled Margaret with some dread she could not name.

"I'm afraid," she told Jonathan quietly as they drove out of town toward the airport.

"Of what?" His voice was soft and sympathetic as he leaned toward her.

"I don't really know. It's just a feeling." She kept her voice low, not wanting to alarm C.J. But looking back at the girl, she need not have worried. C.J. seemed lost in her own thoughts. Her face was serious and unsmiling as she stared blankly out the windows.

"It's the weather," he said, reaching across to put his hand on her thigh. "And nerves. Ginger will be all right. I think the storm will hold off until afternoon. She'll be safely on the ground by then."

"I hope you're right. I hope so."

Jonathan had been right. The plane landed safely and Margaret could hardly believe it when Ginger stepped across the threshold and stood staring toward them.

She dropped her bags and began to run, falling to her knees and taking C.J. in her arms. Margaret looked down at the two of them with tears in her eyes. They were so much alike, from the dark, expressive eyes to the softly curling dark hair about their faces.

When Ginger stood up, Margaret studied her face, before wrapping her arms around her youngest daughter. She had changed and matured. Her life-style had robbed her of many years and she looked older than her age. Still she looked healthier than she ever had.

"You look wonderful, Ginger. How do you feel?"

"I feel great, Mom. Better than I ever thought I could. Of course, seeing you and my baby helps a bunch."

Her dark, questioning eyes turned toward Jonathan, then flashed briefly to her mother. There was a hint of approval and surprise as she looked at Margaret.

"Ginger, this is Jonathan Bradford."

"I guessed," she said, placing her hand in Jonathan's. "I don't know which one talks more about you Mr. Bradford, my mother or my daughter." Ginger had not lost any of her flirtatious mannerisms.

They all laughed and Margaret put her arm around Jonathan's waist.

She noticed how quiet C.J. was. But she didn't want to say anything to spoil Ginger's homecoming. She would mention it to her later at the house. Besides, the weather had grown much worse and, as Jonathan had predicted, the storm would be there by afternoon. Margaret wanted to get everyone home safely before bringing up Ginger's plans for the future.

And despite Ginger's safe arrival, Margaret still had this niggling feeling that something was wrong. That something terrible was about to happen.

Thirty-six

By the time they turned into the driveway, the storm was raging around them. There was no time for Ginger to see the outside of the house or the yard. They all simply made a quick dash through the heavy curtain of rain toward the porch.

Margaret had prepared a cool summer meal and left it in the refrigerator. As she took the covered dishes out and placed them on the table, her eyes moved to Ginger and C.J. She was pleased that C.J. had not tried to pull away from her mother. She had been afraid she might reject her and she was relieved about that, at least.

C.J. was quiet and withdrawn, answering her mother's questions through the meal with one word when possible. Margaret caught Ginger's worried look once and smiled encouragingly.

They could hear the rain pounding on the roof as they cleared the table. Margaret turned to C.J. and hugged her. "Darling, would you like to take one of your books to your bedroom and read? Your mother and I have a lot of things to talk about."

C.J.'s eyes were dark as she stared at her grandmother. There was a flicker of the old anger deep down inside.

"It's all right," Margaret soothed. "You go ahead."

But C.J. ran to Jonathan and her actions took them all by surprise as she threw herself into his arms. Jonathan held her tightly, glancing up over C.J.'s dark curls toward Margaret and Ginger. He seemed as surprised as they were.

"You won't go home now, will you, Jonathan?" C.J. asked. "You'll stay for awhile, won't you?"

Margaret nodded her encouragement; she wanted him to stay, too. She was not about to let him run out on her, not when C.J.'s future was at stake.

"Sure I'll stay," he said, pulling back and smiling at C.J. "But I'm going to see you tomorrow, too. You'll be over at the farm, won't you?"

"Yeah, I guess." Her voice was muffled and low.

After C.J. left the room, Ginger turned toward her mother.

"What's this all about?"

"Darling, sit down. We need to talk about C.J."

"What about her? Is something wrong? Has she gotten into trouble or —"

"No," Margaret said. "She's a wonderful little girl. You must remember how troubled she was when she first came here."

Ginger took a long, slow breath and sank into a chair across from the sofa. "Yeah. I'm afraid I messed her life up pretty good." Her eyes gazed across the room to where Jonathan and Margaret sat side by side.

"She's been happy here, Ginger. You can't see the changes in her right now . . . she's a little upset tonight but —"

"But why is she upset? I thought she'd be happy to see me."

It was the first time Ginger had voiced her concern, but they could see it had been on her mind since her arrival.

Thunder rumbled now, shaking the small house and causing them to talk loud above the sound of it and the rain.

"She is happy to see you," Margaret said, sitting forward on the sofa. "She loves you and she's glad you're here. But all this has confused her. I have a feeling that being here is the first security she's ever known." She kept her voice soft and sympathetic, not wanting to sound accusing.

Ginger's eyes moved away from her mother. "Yeah, you're right about that. That's my fault, too."

"Your mother is not trying to attach blame, Ginger. She loves you and C.J. and she—"

"Excuse me, Mr. Bradford, but I don't think I need you to tell me anything about my mother or my daughter."

"Ginger." Margaret frowned, disturbed by the old defiance in her daughter. After all she had been through, surely she wasn't going to revert back to her old ways.

Margaret and Jonathan exchanged glances and she put her hand lightly on his arm.

"Jonathan has been wonderful with C.J., and she cares about him very much. If you knew him better, you'd know he was not trying to interfere. He cares about her, that's all."

Ginger frowned and looked sheepishly at Jonathan. "I know. I know how much C.J. loves you and all the things you've done for her. I'm grateful; I don't mean to sound as if I'm not."

"We only want to help you and C.J., Ginger." Margaret was not willing to let the conversation slide into accusations and denials. "Whatever you need."

"I do appreciate that. I know I've never accepted your help, but at the clinic, I learned that stubborn pride won't get me anywhere. So many people there didn't have anyone they could depend on, Mom. They didn't have anyone to help them. And here I was, turning away from the most giving person in the world . . ." Her words trailed away and she looked at Margaret with dark, shining eyes.

"C.J. loves it here so much," Margaret continued. "She's made friends and she has the colt she told you about on the phone. Stay here in Ocala, Ginger. Let C.J. start school here in the fall and—"

"No!" Ginger rose quickly from the chair. "Oh, no. I could never live way out here in the middle of nowhere."

"You wouldn't have to live here. You could get your own place in the city and—"

"City? You call this a city? No, I'm going back to Vegas, Mom. Now, don't give me that look. That doesn't mean I'm going to start drinking again or that I'll go back to my old way of living. But I need the excitement, the hustle and bustle. No, I could never live here, not in a million years." She paced restlessly, glancing nervously from Jonathan to her mother.

"Ginger, can't you see you'll only be putting yourself in jeopardy. By going back to what's familiar, there's a good chance you will—"

"Oh, I see. So nothing's really changed after all, has it? You still don't trust me. You think I'm so weak that I'll go right back to drinking again without you to watch me, don't you?

"Ginger, no . . . I—"

"I'm not going to let that happen. I intend to get my life straightened out this time. I'm going to find a decent job and a house . . . put C.J. in a proper school, one that she can stay in. And you can help me with that if you like, you can loan me enough money to get started on. But that's all."

"Ginger—"

"I'm tired, Mom. I'm going to bed." Her lips were clamped tightly together, her faced closed and inaccessible.

Margaret sighed and her shoulders slumped as she leaned back into the sofa. "All right." She pointed toward her bedroom door. "You can take my—"

"I'll sleep with C.J. There's no need to inconvenience you." Her eyes flickered from Margaret to Jonathan. There was an unspoken accusation in them.

"Oh, Jon," Margaret whispered as Ginger walked away. "I'm sorry to subject you to this. I didn't expect her to still be so angry, so resentful—"

Her words were broken by Ginger's shriek from C.J.'s bedroom.

"C.J.! Mom . . . C.J.'s not here. She's gone!"

Jonathan and Margaret ran to the bedroom door and stood looking dumbly at the empty bed. Through the open window, rain splattered against the windowsill and onto the floor. Lightning bolts lit up the yard, revealing the swaying trees in the heavy winds.

"My God," Jonathan whispered. "She's gone out the window, out into this storm."

"We have to find her," Ginger said, her voice trembling with near hysteria. "Mom, if anything happens to her . . ."

"It won't, sweetheart; we'll find her." But Margaret's words were much more confident than she felt. She turned to Jonathan, not knowing what to do or where to start.

"Could she have gone to Lettie's?"

Slowly a look of hope crossed Jonathan's face and he smiled. He pointed toward the window. "Just think for a moment. What lies beyond that fence?"

Margaret's eyes widened with hope as his meaning sank in.

"What?" Ginger asked. "What are you talking about?"

"The farm," Margaret said as she ran toward her bedroom. "Jonathan's farm lies to the west, past the fence and across the pasture. C.J. might have gone to the farm." She pulled two rain jackets from the closet and ran back to Ginger. "Here, put this on. She's probably gone to Wildflower, her colt. When she first came and Jonathan gave the colt to her, it was always where we'd find her when she was angry or troubled."

Ginger seemed stunned, as if she didn't know what to do. Margaret took her arm and pulled her with them out the door and through the pouring rain to Jonathan's Bronco.

In the reflection from the headlights, Margaret could see Ginger's stunned, worried look. As they drove, her eyes moved frantically to the roadway and toward the dense brush that grew alongside the rain swollen ditches.

"I can't believe she's out in this. She could fall; she could be snakebit. Oh God, Jonathan," Ginger said, turning to him. "Is there a creek or canal between Mom's place and yours? She might stumble into it—"

"No," Jonathan said, his voice firm and certain. "It's a flat stretch of land, Ginger. Even in this storm she'll have no trouble finding the barn. Don't worry, we'll be there in a few minutes."

Jonathan wheeled the vehicle into the paved road leading to the house. He took one of the roads to the right, slowing down as he maneuvered from pavement onto a sandy road and past trees that rained down debris and spanish moss as they passed.

A security light burned outside the barn, but they couldn't tell if there was anyone inside.

All of them jumped from the car and ran toward the wide doors. They swung open in Jonathan's hands, freeing the pleasant scent of hay and leather into the rainy night air.

"C.J.?" Jonathan called, moving quickly toward the back of the barn.

It was a huge barn with many stalls. Horses whinnied as they approached, and stood staring at them with great, soft eyes.

Jonathan stopped at a stall and Margaret held her breath, not knowing if C.J. was there and afraid she might not be. What if she wasn't?

"Come and look, Ginger," Jonathan said. There was quiet relief in his deep voice.

Seeing the look in his eye, Margaret breathed a sigh of relief before she stepped behind

Ginger and looked into the stall.

C.J. lay snuggled against the small colt in a mound of soft golden hay. An old blanket covered them both and C.J.'s small hand lay upon the animal's neck. The little girl's hair was still wet from the storm.

Ginger stepped forward, then stopped. She turned to look at Jonathan with questioning eyes.

"It's all right," he said. "Let her sleep. She'll be all right here. Why don't we go to the house and make some coffee?"

As they turned away from the stall, Ginger glanced back once at her daughter as if to make sure what she saw was real. Then she crumpled against her mother and the tears flowed.

Margaret held her close as she moved with her down the long corridor between the other stalls.

"Oh, Mom, I'm so selfish. She ran away because of me." She glanced up into Margaret's face and there was fear in her eyes. "Didn't she? She heard us talking and she knew I was going to take her away from here, away from you and Jonathan. And her little colt . . ." Ginger's voice cracked. "Oh, God, I can't believe I do such thoughtless things sometimes."

Margaret didn't answer. What could she say? It was probably all true.

They sat for a long while in the kitchen. Ginger sipped her coffee silently and gazed out the windows at the wind-lashed trees and shrubbery that surrounded the pool.

Margaret and Jonathan watched her, but left her in peace. She didn't seem to want to talk about anything.

Jonathan led Margaret into the living room and they sank down onto the sofa. She curled up against him, finally feeling warm and dry. Feeling secure, the way she always did when she was with him.

"I feel so sorry for her, Jon. She seems lost and uncertain. And I don't have any idea how to help her get through this."

"You can't right now," he said, his lips moving against her cheek. "I think this is something she's going to have to work out for herself. But whatever she decides, I guess we're just going to have to accept it."

She moved her head, looking up at him. "I like the sound of that," she said.

"What?"

"You said 'we.' I like the way it sounds. Makes me feel as if I'm not quite so alone."

"You're not alone, baby," he said, kissing the corner of her mouth. "I'm here; I'll always be here."

Both of them fell asleep on the sofa. Margaret thought it was the silence that finally woke her. The violent storm had lashed across them and moved on, leaving the morning quiet and the fresh clean air smelling of crushed flower petals.

She and Jonathan walked into the kitchen. Ginger was no longer there. They looked at one another, knowing she'd gone back to the barn, then they turned to move toward the door.

They tiptoed toward Wildflower's stall where they could hear the quiet murmur of voices as they grew nearer. Jonathan smiled down at Margaret and pulled her close as if to reassure her that everything would be all right.

They stopped outside the stall, not wanting to disturb Ginger's talk with C.J.; not wanting to influence anything that was said.

"I'm sorry, baby," Ginger was saying. "I didn't see how much you were hurting, I guess. I was too caught up in my own problems, as usual. You know, sometimes I wonder who's the kid here and who's the mother."

"I'm the kid; you're the mom."

Margaret smiled, hearing the light tone in C.J.'s voice.

"Yeah, well, you're going to have to help me remember that I guess. You really like it here, huh?"

"Yeah. Jonathan's so nice, Mom, and I never

knew a grandmother could be as neat as Gran. And Lettie, she's the one who fixed my hair."

"So I see," Ginger said. "It looks really pretty, too. So, you were upset when you heard me say I was going back to Vegas, huh? And you ran away to see your little colt?"

"Yeah."

"You know, I always wanted a pony. I was quite the little tomboy when I was young."

Margaret smiled. She had forgotten that.

"You wanted a pony?"

"Yeah, I did. I used to read all those books about horses and about little girls who tamed them with their love and gentle ways. I guess I could always relate to that."

"Like *Black Beauty?*" C.J. asked.

"Yeah, like *Black Beauty*. Baby, listen to me now. I'm not sure how I'll do, if I stay here. But I love you; I want you to know that finally and for sure. I haven't always let you know it, but you're the most precious thing in my life. And I want to do what's best for you."

"Are you going to leave me here with Jonathan and Grandma?"

"No." Ginger's voice was surprised and hurt. "I would never leave you. No, we're going to be together, just the two of us. But we'll stay here in Ocala if that's what you want. You can be near your colt and your friends. Near Gran and Jonathan."

"Oh, Mom, do you mean it?"

"I mean it."

Margaret and Jonathan stepped to the door of the stall then. C.J.'s eyes lit when she saw them and she jumped up and ran to Margaret.

"Gran, Mom says we can stay. We're going to live here in Ocala."

Margaret hugged C.J. and looked across at Ginger. Her dark eyes were wistful and full of uncertainty.

"That's wonderful C.J., just wonderful. And we'll help you, won't we, Jonathan?" She looked straight into Ginger's eyes, wanting her to know they would be there for her. "We'll help your mom find a job that's exciting if possible." She smiled at Ginger's skeptical look. "So she won't be bored the way you were when you moved to this burg."

Ginger looked at her daughter and laughed at the sheepish look on her face. "Why C.J.! Did you actually say that? You didn't like it here at first? Maybe there's hope for me after all."

They all laughed as C.J. went to her mother and hugged her.

"But that's good, Mom. You see, you might think it's boring at first, but that's just because you don't know anybody. There's Lettie and Debbie and Anya. And maybe Jonathan could even give you your own horse . . ." She paused, looking up at Jonathan with eyes that were filled with mischief and hope.

Jonathan laughed and shook his head.

"How could I refuse those eyes?" he said with a smile. "Your daughter is quite a little charmer, Ginger. I think she's going to be a politician when she grows up."

"Right now, I think I'll take the little charmer in for a bath and a bit of breakfast, if you don't mind."

"Of course I don't mind. Anya probably has breakfast started by now." Jonathan said. He made a little bow and stood aside for them to pass. "My home is yours."

Ginger nudged her mother as she went by. "Speaking of charmers," she said, rolling her eyes toward Jonathan.

Margaret and Jonathan stood for awhile, watching C.J.'s skipping run, watching the way she would turn and wait for her mother with that exuberant, happy look on her face.

Margaret sighed and moved to put her arm around Jonathan's waist.

"Oh, Jon, I think this might work out after all."

"I think you're right."

He turned and pulled her around, putting his arms around her and letting his hands move slowly down her back to her waist. There was a sparkle in his blue eyes as he kissed her lightly on the lips.

"What are you looking so smug about, Mr. Bradford?"

"Ummm, just wondering about something."

"What?" She nuzzled her lips against his neck, breathing in the warm masculine scent of him.

"Oh . . . wondering if the scent of rain appeals to you . . . the scent of hay . . ." His lips moved across her face to her ear making her squeal softly with delight. "Wondering if you've ever made wild, passionate love on an early, stormy morning in a barn." He moved her slowly toward one of the dark, empty stalls, flicking off the light switch as he went. "In the hay."

"Oh," she whispered, her voice husky with emotion and wonder. "Tell me more. What else were you wondering?"

"Oh, just wondering about our future together. There will be a future together, won't there?" His lips were tantalizing and sweet.

"Yes," she sighed. "Oh yes."

"And sweet tomorrows . . . as sweet as this one?"

"I think you already know the answer to that," she said. She snuggled against him and

476

sighed with pleasure as his kisses continued to make her pulse do the strangest things. Her lips moved quickly to his as she gave him his answer. "As long as I'm with you, I know tomorrow will be so good, Jon. So warm and good and . . . much, much more."

They were inside the stall and he slowly lowered her onto the sweet-smelling hay.

She smiled up at him. "But back to your other questions. Would you repeat the one about a stormy morning . . . and love? Something about a barn . . . and hay?"

CATCH A RISING STAR!

ROBIN ST. THOMAS

FORTUNE'S SISTERS   (2616, $3.95)

It was Pia's destiny to be a Hollywood star. She had complete self-confidence, breathtaking beauty, and the help of her domineering mother. But her younger sister Jeanne began to steal the spotlight meant for Pia, diverting attention away from the ruthlessly ambitious star. When her mother Mathilde started to return the advances of dashing director Wes Guest, Pia's jealousy surfaced. Her passion for Guest and desire to be the brightest star in Hollywood pitted Pia against her own family—sister against sister, mother against daughter. Pia was determined to be the only survivor in the arenas of love and fame. But neither Mathilde nor Jeanne would surrender without a fight. . . .

LOVER'S MASQUERADE   (2886, $4.50)

New Orleans. A city of secrets, shrouded in mystery and magic. A city where dreams become obsessions and memories once again become reality. A city where even one trip, like a stop on Claudia Gage's book promotion tour, can lead to a perilous fall. For New Orleans is also the home of Armand Dantine, who knows the secrets that Claudia would conceal and the past she cannot remember. And he will stop at nothing to make her love him, and will not let her go again . . .

SENSATION   (3228, $4.95)

They'd dreamed of stardom, and their dreams came true. Now they had fame and the power that comes with it. In Hollywood, in New York, and around the world, the names of Aurora Styles, Rachel Allenby, and Pia Decameron commanded immediate attention—and lust and envy as well. They were stars, idols on pedestals. And there was always someone waiting in the wings to bring them crashing down . . .

DISCOVER DEANA JAMES!

CAPTIVE ANGEL (2524, $4.50/$5.50)

Abandoned, penniless, and suddenly responsible for the biggest tobacco plantation in Colleton County, distraught Caroline Gillard had no time to dissolve into tears. By day the willowy redhead labored to exhaustion beside her slaves . . . but each night left her restless with longing for her wayward husband. She'd make the sea captain regret his betrayal until he begged her to take him back!

MASQUE OF SAPPHIRE (2885, $4.50/$5.50)

Judith Talbot-Harrow left England with a heavy heart. She was going to America to join a father she despised and a sister she distrusted. She was certainly in no mood to put up with the insulting actions of the arrogant Yankee privateer who boarded her ship, ransacked her things, then "apologized" with an indecent, brazen kiss! She vowed that someday he'd pay dearly for the liberties he had taken and the desires he had awakened.

SPEAK ONLY LOVE (3439, $4.95/$5.95)

Long ago, the shock of her mother's death had robbed Vivian Marleigh of the power of speech. Now she was being forced to marry a bitter man with brandy on his breath. But she could not say what was in her heart. It was up to the viscount to spark the fires that would melt her icy reserve.

WILD TEXAS HEART (3205, $4.95/$5.95)

Fan Breckenridge was terrified when the stranger found her near-naked and shivering beneath the Texas stars. Unable to remember who she was or what had happened, all she had in the world was the deed to a patch of land that might yield oil . . . and the fierce loving of this wildcatter who called himself Irons.